S0-AXR-419

"A tremendous science-fiction romance that affirms what many fans thought after reading the prequel (*HeartMate*): that Robin D. Owens is one of the subgenre's giant stars. The story line is faster than the speed of light, but more important is this world's society seems so real that psychic powers feel genuine . . . [a] richly textured, other-planetary romance."   —*BookBrowser*

Praise for

HeartMate

Winner of the 2002 RITA Award
for Best Paranormal Romance
by the Romance Writers of America

"Engaging characters, effortless world-building, and a sizzling romance make this a novel that's almost impossible to put down."   —*The Romance Reader*

"Fantasy romance with a touch of mystery . . . Readers from the different genres will want Ms. Owens to return to Celta for more tales of HeartMates."   —*Midwest Book Review*

"*HeartMate* is a dazzling debut novel. Robin D. Owens paints a world filled with characters who sweep readers into an unforgettable adventure with every delicious word, every breath, every beat of their hearts. Brava!"
             —Deb Stover, award-winning author of *A Moment in Time*

"A gem of a story . . . sure to tickle your fancy."
                              —Anne Avery, author of *All's Fair*

"It shines, and fans will soon clamor for more . . . A definite keeper!"   —*The Bookdragon Review*

"This story is magical . . . doubly delicious as it will appeal to both lovers of fantasy and futuristic romance. Much room has been left for sequels."   —*ParaNormal Romance Reviews*

Heart Dance

Robin D. Owens

BERKLEY SENSATION, NEW YORK

F pbktan
OWENS
T

THE BERKLEY PUBLISHING GROUP
Published by the Penguin Group
Penguin Group (USA) Inc.
375 Hudson Street, New York, New York 10014, USA
Penguin Group (Canada), 90 Eglinton Avenue East, Suite 700, Toronto, Ontario M4P 2Y3, Canada
(a division of Pearson Penguin Canada Inc.)
Penguin Books Ltd., 80 Strand, London WC2R 0RL, England
Penguin Group Ireland, 25 St. Stephen's Green, Dublin 2, Ireland (a division of Penguin Books Ltd.)
Penguin Group (Australia), 250 Camberwell Road, Camberwell, Victoria 3124, Australia
(a division of Pearson Australia Group Pty. Ltd.)
Penguin Books India Pvt. Ltd., 11 Community Centre, Panchsheel Park, New Delhi—110 017, India
Penguin Group (NZ), 67 Apollo Drive, Rosedale, North Shore 0632, New Zealand
(a division of Pearson New Zealand Ltd.)
Penguin Books (South Africa) (Pty.) Ltd., 24 Sturdee Avenue, Rosebank, Johannesburg 2196,
South Africa

Penguin Books Ltd., Registered Offices: 80 Strand, London WC2R 0RL, England

HEART DANCE

A Berkley Sensation Book / published by arrangement with the author

PRINTING HISTORY
Berkley Sensation trade edition / July 2007
Berkley Sensation mass-market edition / May 2008

ISBN: 978-0-425-22221-8

BERKLEY® SENSATION
Berkley Sensation Books are published by The Berkley Publishing Group,
a division of Penguin Group (USA) Inc.,
375 Hudson Street, New York, New York 10014.
BERKLEY SENSATION and the "B" design are trademarks belonging to Penguin Group (USA) Inc.

PRINTED IN THE UNITED STATES OF AMERICA

10 9 8 7 6 5 4 3 2 1

To readers

Characters

Dufleur Thyme: Heroine of *Heart Dance*, Embroiderer and Experimenter with Time (Fam Fairyfoot).
Dringal D'Thyme: WinterberryHeir, mother of Dufleur, cuz to D'Winterberry.

Saille T'Willow: Hero of *Heart Dance*, FirstFamilies GreatLord and premier Matchmaker (Fam Myx).
Arbusca Willow: Willow housekeeper, mother of Saille.
D'Willow (Saille also): Saille T'Willow's MotherDam (Grandmother on Mother's side), former GreatLady and Matchmaker, now in a cryonics tube in *Nuada's Sword*, awaiting the cure of her disease.

Ilex Winterberry: Hero of *Heart Quest*, a Guardsman, cuz to Dufleur Thyme, distant cuz to the Hollys (Fam Vertic).
Trif Winterberry: Heroine of *Heart Quest*, Journeywoman musician, protégée of Passiflora D'Holly (Fam Greyku).

D'Winterberry: Mother of Ilex and Meyar, cuz to Dringal Thyme.
Meyar Winterberry: Brother to Ilex, cuz to Dufleur Thyme.

Ruis Elder: Hero of *Heart Thief*, a Null who suppresses Flair, Captain of the Starship *Nuada's Sword* (Fam Samba).

Ailim Elder: Heroine of *Heart Thief*, SupremeJudge of Druida, telempath (Fam Primrose).

Rand T' Ash: Hero of *HeartMate*, Jeweler, armorer (Fam Zanth).

Danith D'Ash: Heroine of *HeartMate*, Animal Healer, Verifier of Fams (Cat princess).

Holm Holly (Jr.): Hero of *Heart Duel*, HollyHeir, warrior (Fam Meserv).

Lark Holly: Heroine of *Heart Duel*, FirstLevel Healer (Fam Phyl).

Passiflora Holly: Mother of Holm Jr., Composer.

Holm Holly (Sr.): GreatLord, HeartMate of Passiflora, working to be Captain of the Councils.

Tinne Holly: Second son of Passiflora and Holm Sr., will inherit the Green Knight Fencing and Fighting Salon.

Genista Holly: Wife of Tinne Holly.

Quert Apple (Sr.): GrandLord and painter, father of Passiflora Holly.

Quert Apple (Jr.): Proprietor of Enlli Gallery, brother of Passiflora Holly.

Note: Straif T'Blackthorn and Mitchella (Clover) D'Blackthorn, hero and heroine of *Heart Choice*, are only mentioned. Their adopted son, Antenn Blackthorn, is a dance partner of Dufleur Thyme.

Huathe Hawthorn: GreatLord and current Captain of the Councils, father of Lark Holly.

Holly/Blackthorn Family Tree

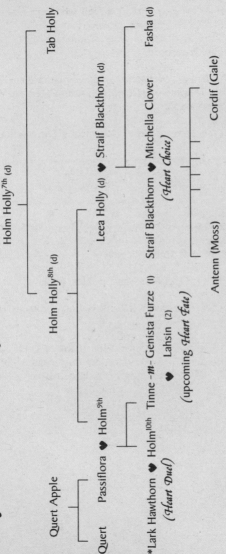

❤ HeartMate marriage

* Lark's full name: *Mayblossom Larkspur Bella Hawthorn Collinson*

(d) Deceased

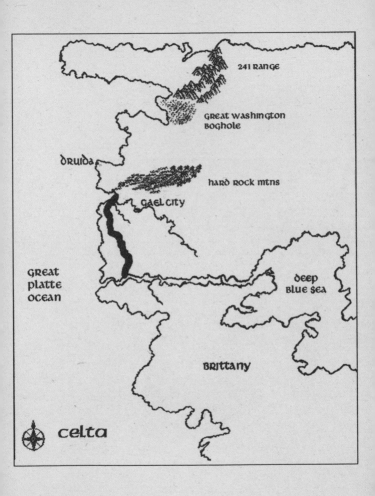

One

*D*ufleur Thyme watched the fresh pinecone wither before her eyes and fall into dust. This experiment with time was not going at all well.

Not good, her FamCat, Fairyfoot, said telepathically. Fairyfoot had insisted on a cat tree the level of the table next to Dufleur's chair. Her chair was scuffed wood. Fairyfoot's perch was quilted velvet with gold-thread embroidered mice.

"No, not good." She wished she had her father's notes.

You want to reverse time.

She knew what she wanted to do and didn't need a cat to point it out, but managed to keep her comment between her teeth.

With a Word she dismissed the clear forcefield around the tube holding the pinecone. The cylinder exploded, sparks flying. Dufleur flung her arms in front of her face, shoved back her chair. What had happened? And why now and never before?

A yowl came from her left along with a nasty singeing odor. Fairyfoot was hopping around, the ends of her whiskers glowing red. Dufleur snapped her fingers, and the fire went out. Flakes of black fell away. "That was interesting," she said.

Noooo, moaned Fairyfoot, racing through the only door of the secret room into Dufleur's bedroom. *My whiskers are ugly! Horrible, horrible, horrible! How am I to judge distances with damage to my whiskers?* She jumped up and down and spat at her reflection in the spotted mirror on Dufleur's bedroom closet door.

"I'm sorry," Dufleur said. Her stomach clenched. Is this what had happened to her father's lab that fatal night? She shoved the thought aside; that would lead to emotion, and emotion had no place in touchy scientific experiments. "Want me to—"

You have done enough. Fairyfoot plopped down and began meticulously stroking each whisker with a licked paw.

Dufleur gulped and braced herself on the battered table set in the middle of the large stone room on the lowest level of D'Winterberry Residence. Now she became aware of muscles cramped from her work, eyes burning from her concentration. She wished she had the funds to leave this place and set up a proper lab, but the Family fortune was as ruined as her childhood home.

With a writestick, she noted down the failed results. She hadn't slowed time but had done the complete opposite, sped it up to such a rapid rate that the fresh spruce pinecone had disintegrated. There might be a use for this spell someday, if she could standardize it and incorporate it into an object people could use, but right now it was an incremental addition to her knowledge base and a failure of what she really wanted to do.

A knock came at the door of her bedroom, beyond this hidden room she used for her illegal, secret experiments.

Damn, her cuz, *Guardsman* Ilex Winterberry was here a little early to collect the gift she'd made for him and his wife.

Using a voice-projection spell she called, "One moment!" Shrugging from her lab coat at a run, she flung it onto the chair, shot into her bedroom. Then she muttered a couplet to slide the stone door of the concealed room shut and grabbed her outdoor cloak.

She opened the hall door to her cuz. "Greetyou," she said, only a little out of breath.

"Greetyou, cuz," Ilex said, smiling. He was always smiling now, his serious nature lightened by his HeartBonding to the vivacious and optimistic Trif Winterberry and with a baby on the way. "Trif sent me for the baby robe. Still six months before the child comes, and she's wild to have the gown. And when she's anxious, she gives me no peace." He sniffed, and a puzzled look crossed his face.

Oh, no! Dufleur'd forgotten he was sensitive to smells. With less care than she should have, she picked up the small gown she'd finished the night before and handed it to him.

He held the robe by both tiny shoulders, studying the dark green, intricately embroidered pattern. "Exquisite. Simply exquisite." He met her eyes. "This will be a treasured Family heirloom."

The kindness in his eyes, the affection emanating from him for her, closed her throat. "Thank you." She'd wanted it to be perfect, so she'd used her Time Flair to add another dimension to her stitches, catching a little of the Time Wind in the garment.

"You're ready for work? Why don't I walk you to the public

carrier plinth?" He set the gown back in the box and sealed the lid with a tap of his finger.

Was she acting suspicious? Guilty? He'd notice that, too.

Fairyfoot hissed. He glanced down. "My apologies for rudeness, Fairyfoot. Greetyou."

Dufleur looked down at her Fam. Her whiskers looked fine. *One word about the experiments, and you find yourself a new FamWoman,* she sent privately to the cat.

Fairyfoot sniffed, then offered an ingratiating smile to Ilex. *Doing anything interesting today, cuz Guardsman?*

Ilex looked at Dufleur with raised brows.

She sighed. "Fairyfoot cannot resist the temptation of very costly thread. She has been banned from the work area of the embroidery shop."

I am an adventurous Cat. I could help you, Fairyfoot said, whiskers twitching. Tail high, she left the bedroom for the basement hallway. Dufleur exited the chamber and let Ilex shut the door behind her. He sent a glance around the bedroom, but she sensed he saw nothing out of place. Still, this was his childhood home. He might very well know of the secret room. She hurried to the stairs up to the main level entryway.

"Dufleur?"

Tensing, she turned back with a strained smile that froze on her face when she saw his fingers curve over the door latch. "Yes?"

He said a short spell. "You forgot to spellshield your rooms." Now his gaze was blank. "You might want to keep your personal things . . . personal."

Her heart thumped hard. Did he have any idea she was carrying on her father's work? She wished she could do it openly, but that bitch D'Willow had made a mockery of her father's name and experiments. If anyone knew she was as fascinated with time as he, she'd lose all credibility of being a sensible person, perhaps even her job. Perhaps this place where she lived and worked. Hot rage sizzled deep inside.

Ilex cleared his throat. "Our mothers can . . . pry."

She forced herself to present a calm front, to pull her mind to this lesser concern and answer him. "They're snoops, you mean."

His lips curved. "Yes." The smile didn't reach his eyes. Neither of them had good relationships with their mothers, both of whom lived upstairs. Of course that was because neither of their

mothers was a reasonable person. She spared him the knowledge that his mother, D'Winterberry, was too deep into the yar-
duan liquor addiction to leave her rooms anymore.

"Your mother has paid little attention to me. As for mine . . ."
Dufleur shrugged. "Fairyfoot has been a blessing in many ways,
not the least because my mother is allergic to cats. If she pries,
she pays." Her smile was just as bleak as his.

He nodded.

Me! Can I go with you to the guardhouse, cuz Ilex? Another
perky smile from Fairyfoot.

They were out the front door and into the winter cold before
Ilex answered. He looked down at Fairyfoot. "Not today, Fam-
Cat." Then he whistled. A few seconds later his animal companion, a fox, slid out of the shadow of a nearby building and
trotted up to them. "Fairyfoot, it's been a long time since you
accompanied Vertic on his travels, perhaps that would appeal to
you?"

Fairyfoot snorted but touched noses with Vertic. Then she
opened her mouth a little and curled her tongue, using that sixth
sense cats have. *He smells like interesting places,* she admitted
grudgingly.

Vertic lifted his muzzle. *Cat may come with me today.*

"Gracious of you," Dufleur murmured.

Vertic inclined his head. *Yes.*

Ilex coughed.

The fox tilted his head. *Cat's whiskers on the right side of
her face are shorter than the left.*

Fairyfoot hissed, sent a nasty look at Dufleur.

Cat, come now. With a fluff of his full tail, Vertic turned and
ran in the opposite direction. Fairyfoot followed. She was a
small cat, and foxes were notoriously speedy.

The FamCat would be exhausted by the time Dufleur returned
to D'Winterberry Residence after work. Not a bad thing. Dufleur
wouldn't miss her cat's comments on her time experiments, and
before she let Fairyfoot back into the room she needed to do
some serious shielding of the cat tree. The room, too.

She and Ilex had reached the corner and turned left. The public carrier plinth had several people standing by it. Four carrier
lines stopped here, in the once noble neighborhood, which was
slowly disintegrating. Dufleur rode straight into CityCenter.

"Sure you don't want to teleport?" Ilex asked.

It would take too much of her psi energy, her Flair, which she would need for her daily work as well as more experiments this evening. "I prefer not to."

He held out his hand, and she put her fingers in his. Bowing over them, he brushed a kiss on her knuckles. "Thank you again for the lovely gift."

"You're welcome."

"Dufleur . . ."

"Yes?"

"Be careful." He dropped her hand and he disappeared from view, teleporting back to his beloved wife and her large optimistic family. He lived in Clover Compound now, surrounded by cheerful people.

Dufleur had never felt so lonely.

That afternoon Saille T'Willow, GreatLord T'Willow, stood with hands clasped behind him as he stared at the cryogenics tube, holding his not-quite-late MotherDam, the Mother of his Mother. He struggled to keep his bitterness from showing.

Ruis Elder, Captain of the ancient colonist ship, *Nuada's Sword,* stood beside him. "As you can see, her life indicators are still doing well. When the Healers find a cure for her debilitating disease, we will be able to awaken her for treatment."

"I thank you for all you have done," Saille said evenly. He hadn't made any of the arrangements. *She* had, the former GreatLady D'Willow, also named Saille, who had despised him. Unlike most Celtans she hadn't accepted death like a reasonable person, but had fought its coming . . . because she loathed him, hated the fact that he was her Heir and would take the title.

For generations the strongest Flaired person in the Willow Family had been female. Until him. His MotherDam took it as a personal insult that he, a man, would be the foremost matchmaker on Celta.

Now she lay in the cryogenics tube, and deep in the fissures of her brain where a neuron still sparked with life she believed she would be revived. When she was, she'd reclaim everything he had . . . or struggle for power with a descendent of his. It was lowering to understand that he'd prefer that. Let someone else deal with her.

"You aren't the only one who had a relative who looked at you with disgust," Ruis said.

That was true. Saille's MotherDam hadn't tortured him, at least not physically, like Ruis's uncle had. She hadn't sought to kill him, merely banished him to a Willow estate far outside Druida City. But both Ruis's uncle and GreatLady D'Willow had wanted power; the land, title, riches that came with being of the highest status.

"Want to pull the plug?" Ruis whispered.

The phrase meant nothing to Saille. "What?"

Ruis bent down and opened a panel in the stand on which the tube rested, pointed at a thin, sparkling filament. "This is her life support." Leaving the door open he stood and looked at the large woman. "I can't think this will ever work. I know it doesn't seem right to me."

Saille stared at the filament. Temptation beckoned. Yes, he *yearned* to "pull the plug." But he couldn't. "She contracted with you." Paid the Captain an extortionate amount of gilt to refurbish the tube and be placed in it, kept alive before the last, fatal stage of her disease began.

Ruis tapped a forefinger on the clear material of the tube. "Sometimes rules—and contracts—must be bent to ensure justice. She'd die in, what? Two weeks, if she wasn't inside here?"

"That's the amount of time the Healers gave her." Saille found the laugh coming from himself sounding far too harsh. "I wouldn't be surprised if she proved them wrong." She was ever contrary.

"Arrogant," Ruis said. "I've never cared for arrogant people. She didn't negotiate with me, you know." His mouth twisted. "She knew better than that. She was one of the people who voted for my execution. Instead she caught my wife in a soft moment." He shrugged. "Or my wife's telempathy assured her that D'Willow should be spared." He looked around the gleaming metal walls of the ship. "Still, it's a drain upon Ship's power and systems, even though Ship considers this an interesting experiment."

"Spare me interesting experiments," Saille said.

"My feelings exactly." Ruis scratched his chin. "I was an outcast in our culture, but even I believe in accepting death, in the soul's circling the wheel of stars into reincarnation." He waved at the tube. "This is unnatural. Our ancestors used these cylinders while they traveled from one planet to a new one, not simply for life extension. Unnatural."

Saille could only agree. But he couldn't say so. "This is what she wants, and I will obey her instructions."

Ruis slanted a look at him, lifted and dropped a shoulder. "I hear your Family has welcomed you as the new head."

Now Saille could smile with real feeling. "Yes, the ladies are an affectionate bunch." He spared one last look at the mound of his MotherDam. "She was a difficult woman to live with as the disease took its toll." And for about a hundred years before that, too.

"Well, then, you have some blessings in your life."

"Many." That was the truth.

A high, giggling shriek echoed down the hallway outside the room, and Ruis laughed as the metal door slid open and his daughter toddled into the chamber.

Saille's smile faded. The little girl only reminded him that he had no beloved HeartMate. Yet.

Once more he glanced at his predecessor. She'd deliberately hidden his HeartMate from him. That had been his greatest shock when he'd ascended to head of the Family.

It had taken extraordinary measures—sending his barely spellshielded HeartGift out into the world—to find his Heart-Mate.

Now he knew who she was, and it was time to plan another casual meeting. For tomorrow.

He turned away from the woman who had ruled his life in the past and toward his own future and the woman he hoped to share it with, Dufleur Thyme.

Yet still he wondered what other traps his MotherDam had set for him.

Two

Weary from the workday, Dufleur leaned against the thick doorway opening to her laboratory, looking at the windowless blocks of light gray stone, measuring the room.

Coming home from work on the public carrier, she'd fallen into a doze and had nearly slipped into a nightmare. This one wasn't of the lab explosion and her father's death a year and a half ago. Thankfully, it wasn't of her kidnapping and attempted murder two months and a day ago. This dream that had begun to suck her down into terror was of her own negligence and the destruction of Winterberry Residence.

More often she'd been moving in the Time Wind and finding herself on that flat, gray plain. Using the Time Wind as if it were an extension of her personal Flair rather than a scientific phenomena. Her father hadn't done that. She didn't know if he *could* move through time.

In any case, huge doubts had arisen in her mind, and in good conscience, she couldn't continue to work in this place if she endangered people or the Residence. She had a small place outside city limits, but it was only four canvas walls and a roof. Not somewhere she could work in the winter.

She had several options. She could quit experimenting. That thought knotted her stomach. She wanted to clear her father's reputation! The Thymes had been studying time for generations. Why, everyone on Celta had a no-time storage, where food placed inside a properly tuned cube remained exactly at the same temperature and freshness until it was withdrawn. That had been a Thyme invention.

The new laws against time experimentation had been generated by one source, the late D'Willow, who'd convinced the FirstFamilies Council that "messing with time" was too dangerous. Dufleur's temper went to slow burn. There were certainly other scientific Families that had an explosion or two in their laboratories. Dufleur had surveyed the ruins of their house and land and sensed no temporal discrepancies. Not that anyone would believe her if she told them. The land had gotten a reputation for being haunted and perilous and thus would not sell.

She slid a portion of the wall back into place to stop temptation. She'd want to try one simple experiment, despite the fear. Then she might get engrossed and continue through the night. She went and laid down on her narrow bed and stared at the ceiling. Dark had already fallen, and the ceiling with the well-known cracks was lost in shades of gloom. Every few weeks the cracks became boring and she moved her bed to where she could map new landscapes.

Thinking mode.

Deciding mode. Her lips quivered. She didn't *want* to give up her experiments. They were the only things that gave her life purpose. How could anyone deny her the right to use and train and expand her Flair? As long as she harmed none.

Her father had only killed himself.

She had singed Fairyfoot's whiskers.

Her eyes stung in fear and failure.

With a clatter, Fairyfoot entered the cat door set into one of the high windows and hopped down to land on an old-fashioned chest of drawers.

"I'm sorry I hurt you," Dufleur said.

Fairyfoot sniffed.

"Since the experiments aren't safe, I'm giving them up."

"Rrrow!" *What? You can't stop. I want to be the Time Cat.*

Dufleur stared. "What do you mean?"

Other Cats have titles. Ship's Cat Samba. Flying Cat Meserv. Healer Cat Phyl. I want to be Time Cat.

Even in the dim light, Dufleur could see Fairyfoot's thrashing tail.

Clearing her throat, Dufleur said, "I do have a couple of other options."

Another sniff.

"I could find some way to shield the room—make a room within a room with shields, then if anything goes wrong only I would die."

And Me. I watch. But I am an adventurous Cat and have many lives.

"Huh." She didn't want to go into that. Not her specialty. "But such shields would be unusual and expensive. I don't have the gilt for them."

"Grrrr."

"I could find an abandoned warehouse. Maybe down by the docks, work there."

Nasty place.

"Probably."

We will think on shields.

Dufleur sighed. "Perhaps I could cut a deal with someone who has shield Flair." She massaged her fingers. She was an excellent embroiderer and could usually trade for those skills, but embroidering outside her work for Dandelion Silk cramped her hands.

She'd have to make a special piece, use Time in her stitches, as she was doing more often, experimenting that way.

Perhaps a shield, Fairyfoot said dubiously.

With a Word, Dufleur opened the door to the secret room. "Will you go get my notes, please?"

I am not a dog. I do not fetch.

Rising, Dufleur went into the chamber. "Lights on," she ordered. Then she closed the door behind her. She would compare the explosive experiment with every other one she'd conducted, step-by-step, and find out where she went wrong.

Furious scratching came at the stone outside. *Let Me in.*

"No. I don't want you hurt." She glanced at the equipment, and the threatening nightmare came back. She couldn't let fear trigger a flashback to her kidnapping.

A piercing yowl came from outside the room. Dufleur considered. No, her mother would *not* come down to investigate. She blocked the continuing feline hissy fit from her mind and began going over the documentation of the last two experiments item by item.

After a couple of minutes, she heard, *I will get you.*

*T*hat evening after a quiet dinner, Saille lay on his thick bedsponge, aching. What had possessed him to send his Heart-Gift out into the world? It had seemed like such a good idea at the time.

The notion *had* been good. His MotherDam, the Mother of

his Mother, had hidden his HeartMate from him, had set a spell upon him that he couldn't find his love. He ground his teeth, realized what he was doing, and stopped. The only way he'd thought of finding his HeartMate was by placing his HeartGift into a tiny box, then in a rough furrabeast leather pouch, and having it circulate.

He'd known a few things about the woman he'd connected with during his last Passage a year ago—and her last Passage four months ago. She was near him in age, he slightly older. She was in Druida City. She had a substantial amount of unique Flair, which he couldn't pinpoint. She was of the lower-noble or upper-middle class.

All those things applied to a multitude of women. He hadn't known who she was.

The plan had worked, too. She'd been drawn to the Heart-Gift. Had found it, then had immediately been kidnapped.

His HeartGift had unbalanced her Flair and led her into mortal danger. She'd nearly died. His fists clenched. He would not forgive himself for that.

He'd learned who she was, Dufleur Thyme.

But, at the start of the whole business he'd made a vow to proceed along a completely ethical course with his wooing. Let his HeartGift be found, then he would go to his Lady, ensure she accepted his gift as was demanded by law. If she did, he could reveal himself as her HeartMate. He could even claim her; erotic images flooded his mind at the thought, and he banished them. The plan had worked. Much better than Trif Winterberry's quest of going door-to-door with a charmkey to find her HeartMate.

But it had taken a toll.

He was intimately connected to his HeartGift. He suffered when it was touched by those with incompatible Flair.

The pouch had been handled roughly. By virile men whose Flair clashed violently with his. By mad women. By murderers.

Only he and his HeartMate could see it clearly, to everyone—everything—else it was a blur to all senses. He could not spell-shield it and have it call to her.

So he suffered as other fingers touched it briefly, sliding over him and engendering nausea, or absently kicked it, he feeling the blow. He thought by now, after two and a half months traveling the wintry streets of Druida, the pouch was coated with dirt . . . and worse. If he stretched his senses, he might find it. But he'd promised himself to let fate take its course.

It was somewhere dark and cold, sitting in a puddle of a disgusting liquid that was freezing around it, coating it.

Then it was found. Snagged.

Worse. It became a cat toy.

*D*ufleur studied for a couple of hours, then quit. She stood, stretched, and walked back into her bedroom, lit by two small glowing spell lights that Fairyfoot had ignited. Taking her papyrus with her, she smiled and closed the door behind her.

Then Fairyfoot, sitting in the middle of the carpet, lifted her paws.

Disorienting lust speared through Dufleur. She doubled over, dropping her papyrus, scuttled to the far corner of the room, and folded in on herself.

She'd felt this before, wave after wave of crashing sensuality coming from an object, tightening her breasts and sensitizing her nipples, so that any clothes over them caressed her to madness. Her core melted. She yearned, she wanted, she *ached*.

A golden glow throbbed in the middle of the floor, pulsing. She thought if she just watched the light, her hips would move in seductive rhythm, and she'd climax. She dared not touch the object. She knew what it was. A HeartGift, and if she accepted it, whoever he was, the man could claim her. She had no room in her life for a man.

She hadn't been able to stop herself, and had picked it up once, fallen into murderous hands.

Take. It. Away, she sent to Fairyfoot.

Fairyfoot licked her paw. *I decided we needed a FamMan to help Us.*

"No," Dufleur ground out.

The cat batted the filthy pouch with her paw, spun it.

An odor of dead things wafted to Dufleur. "Take it away. I don't accept it." She wouldn't have it near her, stimulating her senses, overwhelming rational thought, making her a creature that lived to be touched by her lover.

She struggled to find a threat, a promise, a grovel that would impress her Fam. "I'm sorry I didn't let you into the lab." Her voice was hoarse.

A Cat must go where She pleases.

"I see the error of my ways." Was the light strengthening, being mixed with red streaks? She could almost feel the man there, in her bedroom, moving toward her, ready to strip her bare. She pulled her knees up, dropped her head on her legs, turned her head away, closed her eyes.

Warm waves of darkness enveloped her. A man's hand caressed her, her cheek, her arm, lingered against the pounding of her pulse.

Take it away, please. I'll get you furrabeast for meals.

Furrabeast would be good, Fairyfoot purred.

This was blackmail. She couldn't give in to her cat.

She couldn't give in to a lover.

She couldn't give in to her own sensuality.

She sprang to her feet, leapt for the pouch, fumbled for the encrusted strings. Stench of rotting sewer rat rose, helping her keep her fingers from the pouch. Her need built.

Lunging for the door, she yanked it open, hurled through it, up the stairs. Her legs trembled with the need to raise them around a body pressing against hers, a man's tall, strong form, sex hard.

"Open, open, *open!*" She panted the spellword at the locked, shielded, secured door. Dampness dewed between her legs. The door swung outward, she fell into the cold. Big snowflakes drifted down, mesmerized her with their soft beauty. Fell against her skin sizzling with passion. Vanished. The barest touch of cold on raging heat had her shuddering with release.

She flung the HeartGift as far as she could, staggered back inside, spellshielded the door, and curled up on the landing. It had been the most intense orgasm of her life.

*S*aille arched in bed, as release thundered through him. For a few moments he'd sensed her, been with her, his HeartMate.

His breathing came rough and ragged. Sweat sheened his body. Uttering a quiet curse, he stumbled to the bathroom and the waterfall, stood under warm scented water, arms braced against the stone wall.

For a while, his gift had been with his HeartMate. A cat had taken her the gift. Dufleur had rejected it—but not before their

Flair had mingled, had spiraled them both to orgasm. Was this a good development, or bad?

He scrubbed his scalp with soap, as if he could stimulate his brain.

He'd known his HeartMate had a Fam animal, but hadn't considered that the companion could be an asset. Now he sensed it could.

Just as he sensed that his HeartMate wanted nothing to do with him for a turmoil of reasons he didn't know.

After consideration, he decided it was an indication that he had to be more persistent, more open, in the wooing of Dufleur Thyme.

*D*ufleur *didn't sleep well. She and* Fairyfoot *were not on* good terms, and the cat would creep up on her and tickle her awake with her whiskers, then yowl at Dufleur's out-flung arm. Something would have to be done. Talking would probably do no good. Threats, maybe.

She didn't even open the lab door this morning. No use. The abandoned lab would just depress her. She could read her papyrus in the bedroom, had a little table she used as a desk. Automatically she dressed in heavy woolen trous and tunic, the color drab, the fashion bland.

But when she opened the door, her mother was descending the stairs, beaming. "Dufleur, darling."

All her suspicions were alerted.

"Mother, I need to run to catch the carrier to work."

Irritation flashed in Dringal D'Thyme's eyes. She didn't like that Dufleur rode the public carrier, but the household, *D'Winterberry's* household, which Dringal ruled, couldn't afford the top-notch spells to keep the old, heavy Family glider operating. Then her smile stretched until Dufleur could see yellowed teeth. Dringal chuckled, and it was creaky. "I scried D'Dandelion at Dandelion Silk. She will not be expecting you this morning."

Shock rolled through Dufleur. "Mother, I need that job!" To finance her experiments.

Scowling, Dringal said, "You hardly contribute to the household."

Dufleur's shoulders stiffened. "I pay rent." Not as much as

she would elsewhere for two rooms, but more than enough for one, and her mother didn't know about the hidden room.

Affability faded from Dringal's face. "Come along, girl. I have our distant relative, GreatLady D'Holly, upstairs in D'Winterberry's sitting room. We *don't* want to keep such a personage waiting." She pivoted on the steps and ascended.

Stomach knotting, Dufleur knew what this meant. Her mother and D'Winterberry wanted her to go into society, snag a rich and noble husband, restore the Family fortunes that way. She couldn't see a rich nobleman agreeing to let her experiment with time. This whole endeavor was doomed.

If she didn't try, she would be tortured with nagging reproaches for the rest of her life. Or never speak to her mother again. Despite everything, she loved her mother. Dufleur just didn't like her much. D'Thyme's priorities were not her own. Then, again, with father's inventing, gilt had always been short in their household.

Dufleur opened her bedroom door and stuck her head in. Her small round-faced cat was nowhere to be seen. Right. Dufleur straightened her shoulders, closed and shielded the door again, and marched up the stairs to the second floor. As soon as she reached the landing, the scent of yar-duan lingered in the air, despite the additional odor of an herbal cleaning spell.

When Dufleur walked into the MistrysSuite, D'Holly rose with the grace of a woman who'd been of the highest rank all her life, and held out her hands. "Merry meet, Dufleur."

Three

*S*tartled at the affectionate gesture from a woman she'd only met twice in her life, Dufleur nonetheless grasped the Great-Lady's hands with her own. They were thin but strong. Scrutinizing her, Dufleur saw she looked much better now that she no longer lived under the curse of a broken Vow of Honor. She was regaining her health and beauty and Flair. A taut thread inside Dufleur eased. She leaned forward and kissed D'Holly's cheek. A light floral scent, expensive perfume, rose from the lady and was a welcome respite from the musky yar-duan.

"Merry meet, D'Holly."

"Call me Passiflora."

Dufleur's mother and aunt exchanged pleased glances. Dufleur cleared her throat. "I'm pleased to see you again, Passiflora."

"And I, you." She stepped back, still holding Dufleur's hands and looked her up and down. "And very pleased that you will be living with us."

Not in her wildest dreams could she imagine establishing a secret laboratory in T'Holly Residence. Not surrounded by all the overwhelming warrior men. Not with a strong Residence who might think she could harm it. Not as a guest. She coughed. "I would prefer to stay here."

D'Holly's face showed disappointment, and Dufleur felt a stab of guilt.

"I assure you, the Residence and estate are continuing to Heal from the . . . the previous unfortunate events." Passiflora sighed and let go of Dufleur's hands, then smiled, and it was charming. "But I can understand."

Dringal opened her mouth, to say something cutting Dufleur was sure, but then shut it, lips flattening into a thin line. Saving it for later, of course.

"Nevertheless, I'm happy to sponsor you for a social season." A dimple flashed in D'Holly's cheek. "It will be fun." Her eyes went soft. "The music, the dancing."

Dufleur nearly shuddered, but dragged up a true compliment. "Much of the music will be your wonderful compositions."

The GreatLady's cheeks pinkened, her eyelids swept downward. Why, she was pleased at the awkward praise! She straightened and lifted her chin. "I've been working, I have new music for this season." She smiled again. "Including a whole suite for my son Holm and his wife, Lark." Shaking her head, she said, "Lark cares more for her duties as a Healer than the social season. And my Journeywoman, Trif Winterberry, will be playing at many of the parties. I'll love to have a young woman as a companion with me during all the social activities. I'm sure we'll enjoy ourselves."

Despite the lightness of D'Holly's tone, Dufleur sensed the depth of her emotions and knew this was true. She couldn't protest further. "I'm sure we will."

D'Holly's eyes brightened. "I promised my HeartMate I'd return to work slowly. This season is important to show everyone I'm ready to accept commissions again." She lifted her chin. "To let everyone know that GreatHouse T'Holly is whole!"

That the Family was no longer suffering under the broken Vows of Honor of the Lord and Lady. How could Dufleur fault D'Holly's motives when they were exactly what she wanted to do herself? Finish her father's experiments. Prove he wasn't a feckless, crazy, dangerous failure, that time experiments, Thymes, could still contribute to Celta. Maybe, as much as she dreaded it, going through the social season would help. If she didn't end up with a husband at the end.

*S*aille *finished a late breakfast and entered his* Residence-Den, ready to face another few hours attempting to decode his MotherDam's encrypted pages of the Family journal on the matchmaking business. The room was large and rectangular, with a massive desk and one wall of glass that was shared with the conservatory. Plants pressed against the glass, lush and thriving, and more untidy since he'd taken over as head of the Family.

The other walls were paneled in golden-toned wood, fashioned of large, nearly three-dimensional squares. The carpet, too, was gold with a large rug atop it of faded red and gold in ancient patterns.

The furniture was dark glossy wood with plush dull golden velvet cushions. He'd changed the colors from striped scarlet and gold silkeen to the plain gold. A faint odor of the sage incense he preferred to use when doing his consultations lingered in the room. He let out a sigh. This was his domain, now.

Before he could sit in the cranny of the U-shaped desk, his mother, the Family housekeeper, knocked on the door and opened it, entering from the outer sitting room.

Plump and pretty, she appeared happy, and he smiled at her. It was good to be in Druida where she was, where he could look out for her, than on the country estate where he'd been banished all his life. Of course, the main person who'd hurt his mother was now lying in a cryogenics cube in the Ship.

The absence of the previous Saille, a female "D" Willow, had lightened the mostly female household considerably. He thought he'd injected a little more hope, and a lot more energy into the Family. "How can I help you, mother?"

Her flustered air, a mask he thought she'd hidden behind for her own mother, subsided, and she blinked at him with damp eyes. "It's good just seeing you every day."

He went and hugged her.

She held on to him tightly, sniffled, and stepped away, wiping her eyes on a softleaf and smiling. Clearing her voice, she said, "There's a creature outside the front door asking for you."

"A creature?" He lifted his brow. His MotherDam might have called people from the lower or middle class that, but he never would.

With a chuckle, his mother tucked her softleaf away in the large sleeve pocket of her red tunic. He hadn't wanted her to wear the livery, but she said she liked it. The style and fabric of the house uniforms had improved, though.

"It really is a creature, Saille." She made a moue. "Though the animal itself is simply unpreposing, the thing it carries is . . . well, foul."

A ripple of awareness tingled down his spine. No strain at all to extend his senses. Yes. Outside the door was a FamCat . . . and his HeartGift. He swallowed, kept his voice even. None of the Family knew he'd sent his HeartGift out into the world. They all had enough matchmaking Flair to be horrified. Clearing his throat, he said, "Show the Fam in."

Her brow creased. "Fam?"

"I sense it's a Fam."

"Oh, of course." She reddened and hurried to the door.

"Mother."

She stopped, tensed.

"I love you."

Her head lowered. She fumbled for her softleaf, blew her nose, then turned and gave him a watery smile. "I love you, too."

As soon as she was gone with the door shut behind her, Saille hurried to a cabinet under a bookcase and pulled out a spellshield box to hold his HeartGift and keep the incredible lust it engendered from clouding his mind.

Another slight knock.

"Come," he said.

His mother opened the door with a curtsy. After fifty years, there was no hope of curing her of that habit.

"Thank you, Mother."

She blinked, smiled. "You're welcome."

A small cat swaggered in, increasing the heat of desire he'd felt as soon as the front door opened. His skin prickled with lust, his body hardened in readiness.

The door closed with a snick.

The cat spit out his HeartGift and with a swift paw, sent it tumbling over the rich rug to him. He scooped it up, grimacing at the coat of filth and the smell of it, then slid it into the box and closed the lid, put the box on his desk.

His heart was pounding, his palms sweaty. Most of him was sweaty, but he'd been fast enough to keep from embarrassing himself. He took a softleaf from his trous pocket and wiped his face and hands.

Sitting with stiff dignity, the little cat stuck out her tongue at him. *Nasty, nasty, nasty*, she said telepathically. *I need cocoa mousse to clear the taste*.

He stared at her. He could hear her clearly, a sign that she was his HeartMate's Fam. "I don't have cocoa mousse."

She lifted her muzzle. *This is a FirstFamily GreatHouse ResidenceDen. You have food*.

A chuckle broke from him. He went to the bar built into the far wall. Eyeing the bottles, he murmured, "What about brithe brandy? No, bad idea. She'd kill me for addicting her Fam to liquor. No wonder I didn't get a Fam of my own." He opened the no-time food storage. "I have ice cream. Several flavors and several sauces."

I will have cocoa with hollandaise sauce.

He shuddered. "I meant sweet toppings."

She sniffed. *I will have cocoa with dark cocoa sauce. I suppose you don't have fresh dead mouse to go with?*

"No, thank the Lady and Lord. I don't believe we are infested with rodents." He made her a bowl of the treat.

She sniffed again.

He took the bowl to her, his mouth quirking that she had the strategic knowledge to keep her place and let him serve her. At least she hadn't gotten everything her own way. He had a feeling that this cat was all too clever in manipulating people. He wondered about his HeartMate.

"You're Dufleur Thyme's cat?"

Looking up from her dish, her eyes narrowed. *You know who she is?*

Aha! One of the cat's bargaining chips gone. Good.

He decided that he liked the idea of ice cream himself and made a bowl of dark caff with whitemousse topping and nuts. He didn't think the cat could eat nuts. After a couple of spoonfuls, he used his most haughty tone to ask, "And you are?"

The cat slurped, licked her whiskers. Was one side slightly shorter than the other? Odd. He didn't know cats came with lopsided whiskers.

I am Fairyfoot.

"Strange name."

She growled, stuck her head back into her bowl and slurped more.

He looked at the shielded box. Only he and his HeartMate were supposed to see his HeartGift easily. "You can see my HeartGift?"

I can see it a little. I am her Fam. Do you have a Fam? I thought you were supposed to have Greyku's brother.

He shrugged. "Danith D'Ash said it wasn't a good match." And he'd ground his teeth at that, felt rejected, knew what his clients felt after a futile consultation.

The cat snorted. *I will tell all the ferals that you need a Fam.*

"Thank you so much," he said politely. Though her fur was glossy, he figured she'd known the streets for a while. "Tell me what you're doing with my HeartGift."

Found it yesterday. Took it to FamWoman. Her tail lashed. *She did not like. Threw it out.*

Ouch! That hurt. Saille rubbed his chest.

Fairyfoot lifted large, round, green eyes to him. *You must make it clean again and I will take it back.*

That was a good idea.

"So, you want me to HeartBond with Dufleur?" He savored a bite of cold ice cream, thought of the warm woman.

Fairyfoot gave one last lick of the bowl, lifted her muzzle, burped politely, then glanced around the richly furnished den. *I deserve to live here.*

Saille choked. But he knew what she meant. Hadn't he just been enjoying the bounty of his Residence, finally? "I can fashion a new covering for the HeartGift—" His head came up. "Wait. Why don't you bring me a pouch that she embroidered?"

The cat sat back, grooming her whiskers. *None in Our rooms.* She scanned the den again. *Our bo-ring rooms.*

Nowhere Dufleur lived would be boring to him. He glanced at an antique timer on the fireplace mantle. "I'll check Dandelion Silk, then." He always recognized Dufleur's work. He liked her pieces. Liked buying them for his Family members. Liked staring at the depth and complexity of her expensive projects. Liked stroking the silk thread and feeling her essence.

He'd been planning on going there today anyway. He'd bought some cloth from an importer, a special raw silkeen that was new to Druida, just so he could commission Dufleur to embroider something on it.

Good idea. She sniffed. *I am here instead of at Dandelion Silk.* She slid a glance toward him. *Perhaps I should look around this Residence. Then We can go to Dandelion Silk.*

"Why don't I give you a tour and introduce you to my Family members as a friend, so they know you get the run of the Residence."

That is acceptable.

*P*assiflora *D'Holly* swept *Dufleur away,* leaving *her* mother and D'Winterberry openmouthed.

Dufleur opened the door for D'Holly and caught her breath at the cold. Three weeks after Yule and winter had set in, ice crisped the dead grass of the neighbors' foreyards and rimed the trees. Beautiful, but frigid. The sky was shades of gray, except for a faint blueness of rays coming from the pinprick of the sun.

Her cloak was too threadbare for this winter, but she'd spent gilt on laboratory equipment instead of outerwear. When she pulled the door handle behind her, the cold seared her fingers in her thin knit gloves. She turned, and her breath stopped again.

Before her a man uniformed in the Holly livery held up the door of a sleek, black glider. A brand-new model, obviously personally crafted by the Alder Family. The windows had the gleam of multi-spellshielded armourglass. The man himself was as watchful as her cuz Ilex, sword and blazer sheathed on his hips. Dufleur had no doubt that he was ready to guard, defend, kill in the service of his Lady.

Their eyes met and Dufleur felt the faintest brush of mind against mind—distant kinship, him evaluating her for danger. She nodded, forced her cold lips into a smile, and hurried into the welcome warmth of the glider, sliding in next to D'Holly.

The older woman murmured her thanks to the footman as he lowered the door, then touched the dark green leather seat between herself and Dufleur, her smile much more genuine than Dufleur's had been. "The glider is a Yule present from my husband."

Distant cuzes or not, they moved in different worlds. Always would.

"Gorgeous," Dufleur said.

D'Holly's eyes sparkled like a girl's. "He's always very generous."

He could afford to be. And that was an unworthy thought. From what Dufleur saw, D'Holly deserved all the lavish attention her household of men showered upon her. And she and T'Holly *were* HeartMates, after all, still deeply in love after many years of marriage.

Passiflora told the driver to go to CityCenter and the exclusive dress shops.

"Passiflora, I'm deeply grateful . . ." Dufleur lied, "but I don't want to take charity from you." Favors from the FirstFamilies, the greatest ranked nobles, *always* came with strings.

Lifting one beautiful shoulder, Passiflora said, "I've only promised to pay for your gowns. I assure you, my HeartMate will hardly notice the expense."

But Dufleur knew exactly how much those gowns would

cost. If she worked three years, she wouldn't be able to pay for them, let alone buy any of the basic equipment necessities to continue with her experiments. If she ever figured out how to conduct them again in a populated area. If fear didn't continue to gnaw at her.

"There, there," D'Holly patted Dufleur's knee, garbed in worn commoncloth wool. "T'Holly would do anything to please me, and that includes dressing a distant relative of his. And I would do anything for him." This time her smile had an edge. "He's always wanted to become Captain of the FirstFamilies Council, and has never achieved that title."

She waved a hand. "First because of that long-standing duel with the Hawthorns. Decades." She sighed. "Then because of . . . the problem we had with Holm Junior." The curse on them because T'Holly and D'Holly had broken Vows of Honor to accept their son's HeartMate.

"I haven't participated in a full social season of three months since I was first introduced to society as a girl." Passiflora's eyes went dreamy. "Not even then, because Holm and I loved at first sight."

Only destiny could do that. HeartMates were rare. Dufleur shifted in her seat.

Fierceness heated Passiflora's gaze. "I've been a busy composer and musician, more behind the scenes than a participant, but this year everything is different. We have mended our bonds with our children." She swallowed, sniffed delicately, then met Dufleur's gaze with an intent one of her own. "Power and politics are negotiated in the ballrooms, too, you know. By the time I am done, Holm will have the Captaincy."

Four

I see," Dufleur said.

Passiflora nodded. "I'm sure you do. I need a good reason to attend parties and soirees and balls, and you are that . . . the introduction of a young relative to society."

"I'm not that young, twenty-eight."

"Pah! A baby." She smiled with simple charm, reached out and clasped Dufleur's hands. Genuine anticipatory pleasure moved from Passiflora to her. "Just because I'd like you with me for other purposes during the social season, doesn't mean that I won't enjoy your company. I sense you're as passionate about your work as I am about my music. Like-minded, there. I truly want someone with me in this endeavor."

That was nice of her to say, and to mean, but Dufleur thought Passiflora Apple Holly had forgotten more charming social skills than Dufleur would ever know. "I'm glad I can help."

"Thank you." Passiflora squeezed her hands. "Now about those gowns."

Dufleur stiffened. "You're not paying for them."

Passiflora lifted her brows. "On the contrary, I *will* pay for them. Half of the amount because you've agreed to be my companion. The other half because . . . well, it will be easier to show you than tell you." She dropped Dufleur's hands as the glider stopped, then looked out the wide windows at the closed CityCenter shops.

She frowned. "I didn't realize it was so early."

"Any store would open for your business."

"Yes, they would, but one must not impose," she said absently. Her face cleared and she nodded. "Then we'll finalize the negotiations for payment of your gowns." She raised her voice for the driver. "Dear Myrt, please take us to the GreatCircle Temple."

Dufleur stared. She couldn't imagine what GreatCircle Temple had to do with gowns.

A few minutes later, Passiflora and Dufleur were entering

one of the outer rooms that surrounded the Temple itself, and Dufleur had her answer. Stretched upon a huge frame was a massive square of canlinin cloth, with a pattern traced upon it. Her breath hitched at the beauty of the piece. Partially done, the scene consisted of many mediums—oil painting, applique, tarpunto, sewn sequined beads—fabulous in texture, rich in color, exquisite in execution.

The scene showed a background of the nine sacred trees, the foreground was a tracing of the center of a labyrinth, and the figures were that of a nude Lady and Lord.

"I've seen your embroidery," Passiflora said. "I think you will be perfect to render the Lord's and Lady's faces."

Dufleur caught her breath. "I . . . it would be an honor." To have her embroidery on the tapestry with so many other artists. Surely the painting was done by Passiflora's father, T'Apple, a genius. Dufleur cleared her throat. "It would be an honor to contribute *without* payment. An expression of my faith."

Passiflora's laugh rippled. "Yes, it shows our spirituality, but the Lady and Lord do not demand that even primarily spiritual things not serve other purposes." She ran a light finger over part of the bottom hem, and a lovely melody poured out, delivered by a full orchestra. Stopped abruptly. Passiflora shook her head. "That's as far as I've gotten with my own contribution."

"Even with Flair, this must have taken years. Will take years to complete."

"Just so. And I want you for the faces." Passiflora glanced at her, and Dufleur already recognized the look. Passiflora would be stubborn and determined about this, and whoever was opposing her charming manner would lose.

Dufleur bowed her head. "Thank you."

"Nevertheless, working on this hanging will take time from your day, from your employment."

"I need that job." The words spurted from her lips a little too harshly.

Stroking the cloth, Passiflora sent her a mild glance. "You don't seem to understand how much of your energy the social season will deplete."

"I . . ." Words stuck in her throat. She had no idea.

Passiflora crossed to sit on one of the carved wooden cabinet benches set against the creamy tinted walls of the room. Dufleur blinked. She'd been so dazzled by the artwork that she hadn't noticed anything else. The outer curved wall wasn't very tall, about twelve feet, and the angled ceiling above them was of spellshielded glass. Fabulous light for the work.

"The room is due north." A dimple fluttered in Passiflora's smile. "My father has a great deal of influence when it comes to art."

A FirstFamily GrandLord, a Flaired genius of a painter. Of course he did.

The inner curved wall of the Temple itself was much higher, rose above the room for at least another half-story. Dufleur hadn't attended many rituals in the Temple and now felt a little ashamed. She licked her lips. "I could do more than just the faces." She turned back to the work of art. It was too riveting to ignore. She scanned the pattern, looking for another portion that might need a delicate touch. In the lower right corner were a few animals. Fams. A cat, a dog, a fox . . . Her lips quirked. "I can do the FamCat, at least."

"As I said, I've seen your Flaired work, your embroidery."

"Embroidery is my creative gift, not my Family Flair," Dufleur said absently, studying a lower corner of the huge linen rectangle with faint lines of the scene.

"Oh. You make your living with embroidery, I thought it was your primary Flair."

Dufleur stiffened, straightened. She'd already said too much. Keeping her face impassive, she said, "No."

"What is your greatest Flair?" D'Holly tilted her head. Then she stilled. No doubt she was remembering Dufleur's father. Not difficult to connect Thyme with time. D'Holly gave a little cough. "We won't talk about that. And I suggest you, ah, present your primary psi power as skill in needlework." She smiled warmly. "Your talent for embroidery is certainly lovely enough to be recognized as a primary Flair gift. I have a couple of pieces of yours. The stitches *glow.* In fact, the scenes depicted become three dimensional." She frowned, tapped her lips with her finger. "Haven't you considered making your pieces *art* instead of working on pillows and robes and suchlike? Design your own patterns and execute them?"

A lump formed in Dufleur's throat. She hadn't. When she'd been a child, embroidery had been a joy, then her skill had rescued herself and her mother from poverty. "I would love to do that," she whispered.

D'Holly nodded decisively. "My father is T'Apple, the well-known painter. My brother Quert runs the Enlli Art Gallery. I think I can promise a corner of his gallery to show some of your pieces. They should sell well. I'll let Quert determine the price, but they should at least be five figures. Do you have additional projects you can give me? Perhaps some pillow covers? Especially anything you designed yourself."

What equipment she could buy with the gilt! Dufleur's mind spun. This is what happened when you spent time with powerful Nobles, one word in the right place, one wave of the hand, and your life changed. Connections indeed! No wonder D'Holly wanted to reclaim whatever influence she'd lost while her house had been under a curse.

When she could speak, she answered, "I have a few." Not enough for a good showing, but . . . "I have a tapestry I made after my father's death. It is . . . disturbing." Shades of gray and black, rust and touches of fire red.

"All the better for contrast." Passiflora looked at the elegant gold timer encircling her wrist and smiled in satisfaction. "The shops should be open now, and we'll go to Dandelion Silk first. You must have some items there, too. Slippers, perhaps, or a flat hat?"

"Flat hats went out of style two years ago, but Lady D'Dandelion, the proprietor, might still have the sample I did." A slow smile crossed her face. "We *do* have a looserobe that the late D'Willow ordered and never paid for." Another strike against that lady. Dufleur had labored on the large pattern for days, and even GrandLady D'Dandelion could ill afford to take the loss of the expensive fabric and Dufleur's wages. But D'Willow had called it too small and caused such a fuss that they'd boxed it away.

Chuckling, Passiflora crossed to the door and opened it, glanced back at the tapestry. "Ah, I imagine that might be intricate."

"Yes. But not as gorgeous as this piece."

Passiflora said, "You truly think this tapestry is wonderful and are eager to work on it, aren't you?"

"Yes. To be a part of the community contributing their skills to such a masterpiece . . ." She shook her head. "I have no words."

"It's a pleasure to see your enthusiasm."

For the first time this morning she thought she'd be able to be a good companion to Passiflora. In truth, D'Holly seemed easy to be around; Dufleur thought she herself would be the difficult one in this pairing.

As she would be in any pairing. She took after her father, obsessed more with her time experiments than interested in any other aspect of her life—even a spouse. Just like her father had been, more interested in his work than his wife and child—until that child showed a Flair and curiosity for experiments in time.

After another long look at the wondrous work in progress, Dufleur trailed after Passiflora and into the cold, gray day. When they were in the toasty glider, the GreatLady leaned forward and tapped an icon of a clef on the burled wood panel before them. A quiet, sweet melody filled the interior of the vehicle.

"Thank you, my Lady," said the driver.

D'Holly's lips trembled, and her hand fell to her lap. She leaned back against the richly cushioned seat. She sniffed. "My first composition in two years."

"It's wonderful," Dufleur said. She didn't pay much attention to music, but a notion tickled her brain that a tune like this might stimulate her Flair. She tilted her head. "I know this music. D'Dandelion bought the flexistrip for the shop."

Now D'Holly's eyes gleamed. "It's selling very well."

A realization dazed Dufleur. She wouldn't be working at Dandelion Silk. Her days would be free. Even if she whiled her nights and early morning septhours away following her mother's and D'Holly's plans, she could work on her experiments during the day. She never needed more than five septhours of sleep.

Still disbelieving of her luck, Dufleur asked, "You really think your brother would hang a robe in his gallery? Who would buy something embroidered with Willow symbols?"

"Quert often displays textile art. Again, a contrast to my father's painting and my niece's sculpture." Passiflora smoothed the "fur" of her heavy cloak of the highest quality of mock-fox. Fox-everything had become the rage of the new year. "The looserobe will showcase your talent, not necessarily be for sale." She frowned. "I have heard that the late D'Willow did not treat her Heir as she should have done. Banishing him to the countryside his whole life—" She stopped abruptly, eyes filling with tears, flushing, and turned her gaze to the window. No doubt recalling how her own firstborn son had been disinherited and essentially banished.

Dufleur touched Passiflora's shoulder. "That's all in the past."

Clearing her throat, Passiflora said, "Yes it is. I hear T'Willow is a fine GreatLord and an exceptional matchmaker." Though her tears had been fought back—or vanquished by a silent spell—Passiflora's smile trembled on her lips. "It's odd to think of a male matchmaker after so many generations of females."

Dufleur didn't want to think about Saille T'Willow. There was something about the GreatLord that sent tingles of alarmed awareness through her when she saw him. In the last two months he'd purchased many gifts for his Family members from Dandelion Silk. More than once Dufleur had been called from the back of the shop where she embroidered to consult with them. His bright blue-eyed gaze had fixed on her, watching her the entire time.

And, of course, since she'd determined not to think of him, he was in the shop when she and Passiflora walked in.

*His HeartMate, Dufleur Thyme, was beautiful. Oh, per*haps not in others' eyes, but to him. Tall, carrying her body slightly awkwardly as if she wasn't comfortable in it—and that roused his interest with fantasies of *teaching* her how to move—under him, with him in bed. Yes.

"*Yessss*," hissed Fairyfoot as she jumped down from a chair in the corner where she'd awaited Dufleur. He and the small cat had arrived separately so they wouldn't warn Dufleur that they'd become allies. The secrecy had been to no avail, since she hadn't been at the shop. GrandLady Dandelion kept the cat within her view at all times—he'd watched their interaction from outside the large window until the store opened.

When it had, Saille had immediately asked for a pouch embroidered by Dufleur and was examining six, trying to decide on the one *she* might favor the most, when GreatLady Passiflora D'Holly and Dufleur swept into the shop.

He straightened and made his courtliest bow to the Great-Lady, sorting and discarding ideas as to why Dufleur was in the

Noblewoman's company. He came to no conclusion. With his hesitation, he'd missed the first exchanges between the women.

"—Dufleur will be attending the social season with me," D'Holly said.

The social season! He stared at Dufleur. Why? He was certain it wasn't Dufleur's choice.

Dufleur didn't seem to notice him, seemed turned inward to her own thoughts.

Fairyfoot had been vocal about Dufleur's *mean* mother. Something D'Thyme and D'Holly wished, then?

Damn. He wanted no other to polish her, would go mad if any other man won her. That couldn't be allowed.

GrandLady D'Dandelion made a distressed noise and fluttered her hands.

Passiflora's glance was full of sympathy. "I know you will be sorry to lose her, but I promise I will make it up to you. Surely you didn't expect someone with Dufleur's artistry to work for you for long?" Tilting her head Passiflora appeared genuinely baffled. "My brother will be showing her art in Enlli Gallery." Her gaze went to the pouches spread out on the glass counter.

Saille moved quicker. He scooped them all up and sent GrandLady D'Dandelion a brilliant smile, reminding her that he'd been an excellent customer. "I'll take them all."

Eyes narrowing, Passiflora said, "I'd like to see anything you have of Dufleur's."

Dufleur sank into the chair corner, eyes wide with shock, not paying attention. Saille got the idea that she'd had several major shocks this morning. He wanted to take her away. Wanted to pull her into his arms so she could rest against him. Instead, he put the pouches near the sale processor along with twice the amount of gilt, then went over to her and bowed as deeply as he had to D'Holly.

Dufleur blinked then straightened against the chair, lifted her chin. "T'Willow." Her voice was husky. With tears? He tensed, narrowed his eyes, stepped closer until he could bend and whisper in her ear, and forgot what he was going to say.

The scent of her distracted him, a cool fragrance that made him think of pristine snow on a mountaintop, but there was a slight difference in her natural scent than usual, an added note of brief mountain wildflowers.

"Yes?" she whispered.

Fairyfoot came over and swatted his calf, jarring memory back into his head. Locking gazes with Dufleur, he murmured, "Do not let anyone bully you into doing what you do not wish to do. I hope you know that you have a friend in me."

She cast him a wary look. "I have not found the Willows helpful to my Family in the past." Her mouth set, and anger flashed in her eyes. "Your MotherDam ruined my father, our entire House."

Shock snapped him upright. What was she talking about? "I didn't know," he said.

Her nostrils pinched. "How could you not know?"

"I've been in Druida less than three months." He could well believe that his MotherDam had arranged matters so that his HeartMate would hate him. Another unpleasant surprise. Another emotional ambush.

He took her hand and kissed her chilly fingers, looked steadily into her eyes, which had darkened to deep sapphire. "I don't know what my MotherDam did to your Family, but I am not she. I promise you, I'll remedy the situation."

"You can't," she said flatly. "You won't." She jerked her hand from his. "No one believes in my father's intelligence and honor except me."

Saille slanted her a look. That was an odd combination, intelligence and honor.

A little hiss issued from Fairyfoot. Saille didn't know to whom it was directed.

Dufleur looked down her nose at her Fam. "You're a traitor. I'm not speaking to you until you apologize for your behavior."

Saille didn't know much about cats, but he figured they apologized about as often as a star went nova. Both woman and cat emanated anger. So he tried to lighten the moment. "A traitorous FamCat. I've never heard of such. Interesting."

Fairyfoot arched her back, hissed again, and stalked off to jump onto the counter.

"No you don't!" D'Dandelion swept the bag containing Saille's purchases close with one protective arm, swiped at Fairyfoot with the other. The cat was forced to jump onto the floor. Now she growled and stalked to sit and turn her back to the shop and look out the glass of the door, lashing her tail.

Dufleur sighed, and the sound made Saille's heart twinge. He could see her morning had been stressful. "Whatever you thought of my MotherDam, I am not she. I will always stand your friend."

She sniffed, sounding like her cat. Her mouth twisted in disbelief.

The more he looked at her, the more he wanted her, wanted her to like him, believe him, *want him.* He'd been told by a lady or two that he had a good smile. He used it now, slow and easy, and appreciative.

Anger faded from her expression, she shifted in her seat, her head tilted slightly, and she gave him a sidelong glance.

He made her nervous, which meant she was aware of him as a man, and he liked that.

A moment spun between them, their gazes locked, hers searching, evaluating. His determined, unflinching.

Five

We'd also like to see the flat hat and the looserobe you made for D'Willow," Passiflora D'Holly said loudly to D'Dandelion.

That snapped Saille from his reverie. "D'Willow? Anything that you made for D'Willow I will purchase."

D'Dandelion looked dazed. "I'd forgotten the looserobe."

"Why haven't I seen it before?" Saille said.

"I'd forgotten it!" D'Dandelion drew a softleaf from her tunic pocket and dabbed at her face. Her gaze flickered across them all, then she bustled into the back room.

D'Holly turned to him with a steely smile. "I can't see you in a looserobe made for your MotherDam, T'Willow."

Again he made a half-bow, polite but implacable. "No more than I can see you in such a garment, GreatLady." He always enjoyed looking at Dufleur's pieces, one more would be a pleasure. "So why do you wish this?"

The noblewoman graced him with a smile as charming and polite—and with as much underlying wariness—as his bow had had. She said, "For the Enlli Gallery. I'm sure the looserobe will be an excellent showpiece of dear Dufleur's talent. Can you tell me that anyone in your household would love it and wear it?"

She was right there. He couldn't imagine any of the Willow women wanting the thing, no matter how beautifully embroidered.

"Better that it be seen by many instead of only a few," Passiflora pressed.

"My MotherDam would hate that," he murmured without thinking.

D'Dandelion thumped the box on the counter. She was smiling. So was Dufleur. Even Passiflora's lips curved. Obviously none of the women cared about his not-quite-late MotherDam's feelings. She'd cheated D'Dandelion, ruined Dufleur's father—how? He'd have to find out as soon as possible—and Saille sensed D'Holly had a personal animosity, too.

Attending the functions of the social season—and he had to do that if Dufleur was—would probably be very revealing as to nobles his MotherDam had alienated or allied with. He had a feeling that the people she'd considered acceptable wouldn't be those he'd want at his back in any FirstFamilies noble maneuvers.

Dufleur cleared her throat, glanced at him with a faint flush in her cheeks. She gestured to the box that D'Dandelion was opening, pulling back layers of softleaves that protected the looserobe. "Some of that embroidery is my best work." Her lips thinned. He wondered if she'd done the robe before or after his MotherDam had ruined her father.

Lifting her stare from the panel D'Dandelion was unwrapping, Dufleur said, "I'd like it to hang in the Enlli Gallery."

"You had but to ask," he said, then he glanced at the looserobe and caught his breath. It was magnificent—a shimmering pale green silkeen the color of new Willow leaves, with varying shades of darker green embroidery. The scene of a weeping willow shading a deep green rushing river seemed three-dimensional.

"Quite, quite fabulous," Passiflora said. "The robe certainly belongs in Enlli."

"Of course," Saille said, staring at the exquisite stitches that must have taken septhours and Flair to be so striking. Septhours and Flair of Dufleur's talented hands. What other precise talents had Dufleur's hands mastered? Desire shivered through him. He cleared his throat, met D'Dandelion's eyes. "Send T'Willow GreatHouse another bill for the looserobe. It will be paid before WorkEnd Bell."

D'Dandelion smiled. "A pleasure conducting business with *you, T'Willow.*"

A calendar sphere popped into existence, flashing red. "T'Willow, your first appointment of the day is in ten minutes."

Dufleur saw T'Willow's hand, stretched out to touch her embroidery on the robe his MotherDam had rejected, fall. He frowned at the calendar sphere, bowed to Passiflora, then to D'Dandelion. To Dufleur's surprise, he took one of her hands and pressed a kiss on the back. "Later," he said.

She nodded.

He scooped up his bag and nudged Fairyfoot away from the door before opening it and striding with masculine grace into the cold, gray day. Her hand tingled, but she didn't want to consider the attraction she had to the nobleman. So she turned her thoughts to the afterimage of the calendar sphere that floated before her eyes.

It was another small object a long-ago Thyme had invented. Perhaps, perhaps, if she could invent something small and very useful, she could persuade the FirstFamilies to lift their ban on time experimentation. She'd have to cudgel her brain.

Passiflora scooped up the box holding the rewrapped looserobe and indicated the counter where much of Dufleur's work lay.

But not all of her embroidery. Canny D'Dandelion had kept some pieces that she would mount on the wall, anticipating sales that might come her way from those who visited the art gallery. After all, Dufleur only provided the embroidery on exquisite garments. D'Dandelion and others made the expensive clothing. She'd also negotiated with Passiflora that the discreet label next to Dufleur's artwork—if this gallery showing materialized—would say "from the shop, Dandelion Silk." She might be losing Dufleur's services, but she'd definitely get something from Dufleur's change of circumstances.

Then Passiflora turned to Dufleur and examined her top to toe. "Stand straight."

Dufleur rose, snapped her spine flat, tucked in her hips, pushed her shoulders back.

Tapping a finger on her lips, D'Holly said, "You move . . ." she stopped before the discourtesy, but Dufleur knew what she meant. Outside the lab she tended to be clumsy. D'Holly nodded once. "You need dancing lessons."

Dufleur closed her eyes in horror.

D'Holly's laugh tinkled. She reached out and squeezed Dufleur's limp fingers. "I promise the lessons will not hurt at all." A considering look came to her eyes. "In fact, it will serve another purpose. I'll have my Journeywoman play for your instructions. It will do her good to understand how one must play for lessons."

"*You* can't have played for lessons."

D'Holly patted her cheek. "Of course I did. Dancing lessons for my boys."

Oh, of course.

"We must make an appointment with my hairdresser." She

glanced at D'Dandelion who was boxing Dufleur's work. "May I use your scrybowl?"

"Of course, my Lady," D'Dandelion said. The shop owner wasn't that far below D'Holly's status. Just a rung or two. The Dandelion Family was a title taken within the first generation of colonists and had thrived.

D'Holly went to the discreet china scrybowl and tapped one gloved finger against the rim. "T'Chervil."

"Here," answered a man. His smiling image formed over the bowl. "It's *wonderful* to see you, GreatLady!" His eyes narrowed. "Definitely time for a trim."

D'Holly chuckled. "Very well, but I'd like to make an appointment for my protégée, my distant cuz, GrandMistrys Dufleur Thyme." She gestured Dufleur over to the bowl.

Dufleur turned her grimace at the empty title into a polite smile. "Greetyou, GrandLord." She didn't recognize him, but knew enough about the FirstFamilies to understand they would only patronize those who were at the top of the pyramid in Flair, so the man had to be a GrandLord.

He eyed her, and a glitter came to his eyes. Dufleur had seen that own glitter, the slightly flushed cheeks in the mirror when she'd contemplated a challenging project. Oh. Dear.

"Come at once," the hairdresser said. "I have time right now." He didn't even look at his calendar sphere.

Oh. No. No. Dufleur touched her hair.

"Cutting and shaping, of course. *Must* have a tinting rinse, reddish would be most striking. I'll be waiting." The snicking of scissors came as he ended the call.

"Look at those wide eyes," Passiflora said. She shook her head. "You truly have beautiful eyes. And your smile, I think, is quite lovely, though I haven't seen it often."

"I don't know if I can afford—" Dufleur protested.

"My treat." Passiflora waved at the footman in her glider, and he left the vehicle, entered the shop, and took the boxes away.

"Too kind," Dufleur murmured weakly. She really didn't want this.

"When we're done with you, no man, especially T'Willow, will be able to resist you."

Just what she didn't want most in the world. She didn't want a husband. "T'Willow!"

"Why, Dufleur, it was obvious he lingered to see you."

Dufleur closed her eyes. Definitely didn't want a *GreatLord*, a FirstFamily husband, a man who would believe he could run her life. That would be the end of her experiments.

"I don't want a husband," Dufleur said.

D'Holly stilled, turned a shocked face to her. "Not want a mate?" She narrowed her eyes. "You've passed your Second Passage, didn't you connect with a HeartMate?"

"No," Dufleur lied. She wanted nothing that would distract her from her experiments, more, that would keep her from clearing her father's name. She was sure no man would appreciate his wife regularly breaking the law by working with time.

"And not T'Willow." She tossed her head, felt the heavy weight of her soon-to-be-cut hair, figured she wouldn't have the pleasure of flinging it around anymore, and tossed her head again.

"He's nothing at all like his MotherDam," D'Dandelion soothed—as she'd been saying to Dufleur every time she'd accepted a commission from the man over the last two months. Even now, the woman was sending the bill to the T'Willow Residence.

"No, nothing like," Passiflora agreed. "Saille T'Willow's aura resonates honor," Passiflora said. She tapped her finger against her lips.

Dufleur scrambled to think in political terms, something she'd better learn to do quickly. "He's still relatively new in his title?"

"About five months," D'Dandelion said absently, then beamed as she received payment confirmation for the looserobe from T'Willow Residence.

"Ah, uh, he probably hasn't made all the alliances he wants. My father's reputation . . . T'Willow might need to be circumspect—"

Passiflora said, "He's allied with Straif Blackthorn, that I know. If he's with Straif, he will probably be siding with all the younger lords of the same bent—T'Ash, whom we need to consult regarding your jewelry—"

Another calendar globe appeared, this one pulsing Holly green. "Overdue at T'Chervil's," it stated.

"Oh!" Passiflora frowned. "We must go, transnow. Perhaps we should teleport and let the glider catch up."

Dufleur didn't know whether to feel relieved at the end of

the topic of conversation or nervous at *more* changes that would be occurring in her life.

"Let's 'port." She held out her hand.

Me, too. Me, too! Fairyfoot abandoned her sulk to hurry and sit near Dufleur.

Passiflora glanced at the waiting glider, a guilty look came over her face. "I'm not supposed to. Security." Then she grinned. "Yes." She took Dufleur's hand, sent Dufleur a mental image of T'Chervil's shop, waved at the men in the glider. "Let us go. Dufleur and me. The cat makes *three*."

Dufleur's Flair meshed surprisingly easily with Passiflora's, then they were gone from Dandelion Silk and arriving at T'Chervil's business, Pluches de Cerfeuille, and being greeted by a bright-eyed, white-haired man, holding scissors and beaming.

Dufleur shuddered.

*S*aille refrained from the common gesture of rubbing his hands at a job well done until his mother ushered the couple out of the house. He grinned with satisfaction, too. His first high Noble match! D'Hazel's oldest, a son of seventeen, and D'Heather's sixteen-year-old Daughter'sDaughter. They'd been accompanied by D'Heather, a FirstFamily GrandLady, since they were so young, usually far too young to wed.

The girl was underage, which meant she could repudiate the marriage when she turned seventeen. But they'd been convinced they were HeartMates, had connected during his Second Passage, the fugue state when psi power, Flair, was freed.

The young couple had been right. The fact that they were HeartMates blazed in their mingled auras that had already combined in colors. They'd already HeartBonded as anyone except determinedly blind relatives should have seen. Probably the night before. Teenagers.

In the privacy of the extremely short consultation, they'd admitted as much to him, bubbling over with their happiness, with the ease of their joining. She'd come to him during his Passage, shared it with him, which had triggered her own a year early. But they were HeartMates, and they rode out the psi Flair storms together, delighted to be strong in Flair, survive their Second Passage, and be HeartBonded.

As they should be.

All they'd wanted from him was an official seal of approval from the premiere matchmaker of Celta to ease their relatives' minds.

It was easy to sit behind his desk, set his hand upon papyrus and create a proper document for them. The girl had snatched it from him and danced around the room, promising an invitation to their wedding. He'd accepted a kiss on the cheek from her and an arm-to-arm elbow clasp from the boy . . . and later, a minimal fee from D'Heather, who'd observed him from inscrutable eyes and commented that he was much different from his MotherDam.

Since there had been no real consultation and the appointment was over so quickly, he mentally reached for his own HeartMate, found her tensely awaiting the next snip of scissors as her hair was cut. He thrummed his fingers on his desk. She'd slipped out of his clutches for the day. He didn't think she'd even noticed he'd bought more of her work.

He stared at the bookcases that held the professional records of his Family. He was able to unlock and access every single volume except those of his MotherDam for the last twelve years.

She'd bespelled it against him, another indication that she'd created as much trouble in his life as she could before he sat behind her desk. More traps for him to overcome, no doubt. Somewhere in there should be information about how she'd ruined the Thymes.

Clearing his throat, he said, "Residence?"

"Here," responded the masculine tones.

"Do you know what occurred between the former D'Willow and the late GrandLord T'Thyme?"

The Residence made a humming noise, as if pleased to be consulted. "I can extrapolate."

"Please do so."

"The former D'Willow consulted T'Thyme regarding his experimentation with time itself, and slowing time that might also slow the progress of her disease."

Saille swallowed. "Of course she would."

"Both scholars of time, GrandLord T'Thyme and Grace-Lord Agave were working on such a matter."

"It would be a great boon to society," Saille agreed neutrally, even though a cure for his MotherDam's disease would be detrimental to him personally.

"We do not know of the consultation, only the results. D'Willow was outraged at T'Thyme's lack of courtesy. She called him rude, unprofessional." A heavy silence. "Then she told all who would listen that he was a fraud and a cheat. Had no true talent for time." Now the Residence made a little sound the equal of a person clearing his throat. "Since GreatLord Thyme's Residence was destroyed two days later, D'Willow felt triumphant that she'd been right about the man's character all along. She gave interviews to the newssheets for weeks and led a vote banning time experimentation through the AllClass Council."

Saille winced. "I need to know more of this. Please contact as many other Residences . . . and the Ship, *Nuada's Sword,* to collect any and all facts regarding this matter."

"Immediately." The Residence sounded cheerful.

Saille leaned back in his comfortchair, closed his eyes. Another trap.

The next minute his mother was knocking on his door.

"Enter," he called.

Face aglow, she hurried in. "GrandLord Horehound is here with his Heir's son. He wondered if you have time for a top-level consultation."

Saille stared at her.

"And Amy, who is taking appointments for us, has added two more scrybowls, manned by your cuzes." She rolled her eyes. "You don't understand."

"No."

"D'Heather has already spread word that you aren't like MotherDam."

"I'm a man."

His mother snorted. "You aren't formal, forbidding, or excessively expensive."

Unease sifted through him. "That's not bad?"

"*No!* Better, D'Heather told Horehound that your Flair was strong, your mastery of your craft excellent."

Saille cleared his throat. "Give me five minutes to prepare for a full consultation and send them in, if you think the Lord will not interfere. If you believe Horehound will be a problem, let him wait or send him on his way."

She nodded.

"Is this a request for a HeartMate Finding?"

She shook her head. "No, the GrandSir Horehound states he doesn't believe he has a HeartMate. He wants a character sensing, so you will know if you meet a woman who will suit him, and a preliminary interview for a Wife Finding." She rubbed her hands. "Oh, we will be busier than we have been in years." She met his gaze. "Saille, you do the house honor."

"It is my duty and pleasure."

With another nod, she swept from the room, closing the door behind her.

For a few seconds he just sat thinking. Though his Mother-Dam was a FirstFamily GreatLady, it sounded as if the others in her class, and those below their rank, hadn't respected her. As he'd suspected earlier that morning in D'Dandelion's shop. That was interesting and a little disturbing.

Then he straightened, put away the residual papyrus and items from the previous consultation, swept an arm across the desk in a Renewing Sacred Space spell, lit several incense sticks to purify the room, and placed a thin, smooth pad on his desk—also ritually sanctified. He withdrew his favorite divination tool from his safe, tilted a small basket. Multicolored glazed pottery disks with inset jewels and runes incised on them rolled onto the blotter. He'd made the disks himself and was proud of their beauty and their functionality. He scooped them into his hands, sat, feeling the cool smoothness of them. He prayed for a blessing of the disks and the consultation. Then he infused the runes with Flair that would reveal the character of the young man to him and signal how easily it would be to find a good match for him.

He looked up and placed the pottery disks on the blotter, as his mother opened the door to his new clients. Walking around the desk, he offered his forearm to them for a greeting and T'Horehound, a very thin, gray-haired man, took it. A small surge of Flair zipped between them. Saille sensed his psi was stronger. "A pleasure to meet you, T'Horehound."

The older man studied him with an experienced gaze. "I think you mean that."

"I do."

Inclining his head, T'Horehound released his arm, introduced his Heir's son who looked to be in his early twenties, then took a chair in the corner of the room.

Two septhours later, both Horehounds, very pleased, were

leaving. T'Horehound stopped at the threshold. "I thank you for your consultation." He'd already transferred a stiff fee to the Willow Family account.

Saille bowed. "You're quite welcome."

"I am an expert in horticulture," T'Horehound said.

"I know."

"Ah, then I will only say that you are an unsurpassed specimen, with strong roots and good staying power." A smile hovered on his lips. "And potent Flair. I'll set up an appointment for myself on my way out." He closed the door behind him.

Saille stood staring at the door, pride breaking open the last, tattered husk of the former self who'd lived a purposeless life on the Family estate, only doing a few secret consultations for country folk. For the first time since he'd stood in this den as T'Willow he felt he wasn't a fraud. He *was* T'Willow, a Great-Lord with strong Flair for matchmaking. Valued for his services.

Smiling, he decided to stroll in the conservatory and renew his drained Flair with scents of green before his afternoon appointment. He'd study the place and see what changes he'd like there, too. And he'd daydream of Dufleur.

Six

$\mathcal{D}$ringal Thyme met Dufleur and Fairyfoot as they straggled to the door that evening, no doubt watching for the sleek dark green glider.

Her mother stared, blinked, the door wide open in her loose grasp. "Dufleur, you look . . . wonderful!"

Dufleur walked in and shut the door, watching her mother. The woman hadn't complimented her since . . . she couldn't remember when. Since she was a girl.

"Thank you."

Her mother's steel-colored eyes looked a little dazed, a little envious.

"We should have taken you shopping with us," Dufleur realized. Dringal was the one who wanted this social prominence, would have enjoyed this.

"No, no." Dringal plucked at her long, full tunic that showed no trous at all. The outfit appeared fine in the dimness but would show definite shabbiness in the light. Her mouth soured again. "This is five years out of date. Not the right cut or color or fabric. I'd hate to be seen in it."

Dufleur nerved herself. "I'm a fair seamstress. I could make or alter—"

"No." Dringal jutted her chin. "I've seen those new styles. The hems of the tunics are halfway to the knee!" They'd been halfway to the knee since Dufleur could remember. Other things had changed, the style of the slits up the sides, necklines, but not the hem.

"You don't have any packages. What of *your* evening wear?"

"My gowns are being made." Daring long dresses with full skirts and *no* trous were now in fashion. Dufleur's legs felt cold as she thought of them, or because her trous legs *were* cold.

"Come up to dinner in cuz D'Winterberry's rooms and tell us all about the day."

Fairyfoot meowed.

Dringal's lips tightened. Then she sneezed, pivoted, and

started up the stairs. "Feed the animal and come to dinner. We have furrabeast roast, your favorite."

Dufleur's mouth began to water. "All right." Fairyfoot trotted down the stairs to their rooms. "Mother, you should participate in the social season, too."

"No!"

Even in the shadowy light, Dufleur could see a flush mottle her mother's face.

"I left those circles long ago. When I married. And when your father blew up himself and our house, all my other so-called friends deserted me. Only our cuz took us in."

Shouldn't have chosen friends of such poor character, but Dufleur didn't say it aloud, and how could she speak? She'd been too busy and grieving too much to contact the few friends she had, and now didn't have any at all. Entirely her fault.

White knuckles showing her grip on the banister, Dringal gazed at Dufleur. "D'Willow spread her poison about your father all too well with the Nobles. I'll not go just to be gossiped about and sneered at."

But she'd let Dufleur face the Nobles, the FirstFamilies that D'Willow belonged to. Several circles higher than the Thymes.

Silence hung as deep as the shadows.

"Come up for dinner, or not, I don't care," Dringal said.

Oddly enough, Dufleur thought that for the first time in a long time, Dringal was actually thinking about her daughter's welfare. Or just wanted to live through her. A mean thought, so Dufleur shoved it aside.

"I'll be up." Weariness made her mind like heavy wet wool, her body leaden, but if something she could do could finally scrape away a layer of her mother's bitterness, Dufleur would do it.

After a cheerful dinner with his Family, everyone sitting around the large table after the food was set on sideboards, Saille closed himself in his Den.

Behind his desk, he unwrapped the small package of the pouches on his desk. Each pouch was individually wrapped, too. Finally all the small bags lay before him. Each was a different color of silkeen with a contrasting, Flaired cord to pull it closed. Tilting his head, he wondered at their purpose. Evening bags?

Inner bags for the large sleeves on ladies' gowns or inside a pursenal? Coin pouches? Or were ladies' belts and waist pouches coming back into fashion? He didn't know.

Each one had a different design worked in perfect embroidery, too. Some had embroidery around the top and sides. A delicate tracery of cream floss on shining white. Gold thread worked in leaf patterns on emerald. A FamCat's white and brown face and blue eyes on copper-colored fabric. A spray of summer flowers on pale yellow. A bold, multicolored design that harkened back to old Earth patterns on deep red. Fanciful waves and clouds in light blue and white floating across dark sapphire fabric.

He couldn't choose. He liked them all. They were all large enough to hold his HeartGift. One side of his mouth lifted as he decided that he could spellshield the pouch much more than the original leather one, keep it cleaner, nicer. It would be a shame to ruin one of the lovely pieces before him. This pouch would not circulate through all of Celta. He knew who his Heart-Mate was, even if she didn't allow herself to recognize him.

Which one should he choose? He sank back into his floating, finely grained leather chair that shifted around him. For a moment he closed his eyes, luxuriating, grateful that he now owned such wonderful possessions. Then he opened his lashes and gazed at the bounty before him. These he'd keep, wouldn't give them to any Family members. But one would be the new outer case for the small box that housed his HeartGift.

Which one did *she* like the best? He smiled. Surely, as her HeartMate, as a man who could pick up emanations from others, he should be able to discover that small fact.

Pulling his chair forward, he sat up straight, closed his eyes and *felt* the fabric, sorting out impressions. This one she thought was too cute. He set it aside. This one was a standard piece of work, though she liked the pattern. That was culled.

He sank deeper into his Flair, sensed even more evanescent emotions. This one was commissioned and, like his Mother-Dam's looserobe, was refused. She hadn't liked that. He didn't either, and felt a spurt of pride that he'd managed to purchase it, wipe that lingering anger from her, from the pouch. Even deeper into his trance, he reached and found the one she'd enjoyed laboring over, had put more Flair, positioned her stitches just so, varied the length, breadth, and color of the stitches. This one.

Opening his eyes, he found he was holding the red one with ancient patterns. Bold, beautiful, passionate. Like the emotions she hid.

*D*ufleur *went to bed early. Her mind and body were too* weary to review her notes, let alone work with time, and fear lingered about her experiments.

She lay in the heavy darkness, thinking the day had been like one of D'Holly's own compositions where the music started slow and sped and sped until you whirled in place. Or like her own observations about time. It was completely subjective. If you were inactive and bored, time seemed to crawl. If you were swept up into a whirlwind of activity, time passed in a flash, and all you had were still, crystalline moments and the rest blurred.

She touched her hair, as she had in one of those still moments. So different from the past—this morning. A lot of it had been cut off, to make her face seem less long, she'd been told. She had had enough wits about her as she faced T'Chervil and his wicked scissors to demand a cut that would stay out of her face and be easy to manage. She'd said she couldn't have it hanging in her eyes, blocking her gaze from her embroidery.

And Fairyfoot was up to something. The small cat lay curled at the end of Dufleur's bed, purring. Dufleur was quite sure the Fam hadn't forgiven her. Though everywhere they'd gone today—the hairdressers, the evening dressmakers, the spun shawl makers; oh, how Dufleur prized that item!—the Ladies and Lords had fussed over Fairyfoot, stroked her. Inflated her ego.

Dufleur, Passiflora, and Fairyfoot were going to T'Ash Residence tomorrow. Not his shop, T'Ash's Phoenix, his *Residence.* Where the scary GreatLord would personally show them the jewelry he crafted. Disaster loomed. Dufleur was sure that she didn't have the gilt to buy even one piece, as if she'd spend gilt on jewelry instead of equipment anyway. Even she knew that a person in society was not considered formally dressed unless they had a piece of T'Ash's work hanging around them somewhere.

And adult FamCats demanded jeweled collars as indications of their rank. Dufleur had heard Fairyfoot's recital of each and

every Fam's jewels: earthsuns, ancient Earth trinkets, blue diamonds. Heard Fairyfoot's relish as she spoke of choosing her
collar from T'Ash himself. Dufleur bit her lip. Fairyfoot was
going to be furious in the extreme when she learned Dufleur
couldn't afford a collar. Would Fairyfoot leave her? Dufleur
didn't know. Despite everything, she loved the little cat.

*W*ith the utmost care, shielding himself as much as possible
from the effect the HeartGift would have on him, Saille opened
his safe and withdrew the filthy leather bag. His gorge rose. The
thing left slime on his hand, from the streets and the layers of
clashing Flair upon it, and, one of the first layers, the evil vibrations of murderers.

Gritting his teeth, he dropped it on a disposable sheet of
thinleaf on his desk. His fingers trembled as he scrabbled for a
knife to open it. He only had to set a point on the bag and whis-
tle a sharp two-noted spell, and the leather fell apart around the
small wooden and brass box holding his HeartGift.

Waves of heated sexuality enveloped him. He remembered
his Third Passage, no more than a year ago, when he'd made the
gift. How, deep in a fever, shuddering with wild Flair, he'd
reached with his mind/body/soul/*self* and connected with another, his woman. His HeartMate.

They'd joined then, in frantic sex that seemed not of the
mind, but all too real. Her long, strong, soft-skinned body sliding against his as he heard her cry of need moan through his
mind—

He shook his head, hard, casting the feelings, thoughts, sen-
sations away, biting his lip until blood came so he could fumble
for the box, shove it awkwardly at the new pouch crafted by
Dufleur. He missed. The box shot off the desk, hit the marble
top of a table. Opened. The red silkeen wrapped around his
HeartGift unfurled as it fell to the floor.

The china thimble he'd encased in a semisolid perfume ball
rolled on the thick rug. The perfume was long gone.

He was lost.

Again his entire self *reached*. Again he *found*. Her self.

His mouth touched the heated skin of the curve where her
neck met her shoulder and he inhaled her scent. This was right.
Completely and ultimately right.

They lay facing each other, but he couldn't see her. The dark was midnight velvet wrapped around them, thick and soft and encompassing them in passion.

His fingers went to her breasts, soft and fitting into his hands. Her tight nipples pebbled in the center of his palms, drawing a moan from him, a whimper of need from her.

Soft. Her skin was so soft, her long legs sliding against him, the slight curve of her stomach arching against his hard erection. Maddened by her touch, he rolled, sweeping her under him. He gasped with aching pleasure as the movement caressed his shaft. Slipping his hands over the fullness of her bottom, he found the damp heat of her, ready for him.

He plunged inside her, and all that mattered was the demands of his body.

She arched, wrapped strong legs around him, cried out her yearning. Her fingernails bit into his shoulders.

He thrust, and thrust again. Hard, penetrating, needing the feel of her warm core sheathing him, pulsing around him.

Her gasps filled his ears along with the humming of his blood, and he smiled in fierce triumph. They matched each other.

She screamed and convulsed around him. He shouted. Perfection.

Despair. He didn't want this to end. To ever end.

He hurled through a storm of black, torn from her by their very release. He *reached* and did not find.

A while later sharp pricks of pain along his back roused him to the here and now. Reality.

With a grunt, he turned his head. A light weight moved from atop him and a matted cat of browns and blacks appeared in his vision. Slit-pupiled yellow eyes stared down at him. A feral cat. In his Residence. He should care, but didn't.

Get up. I put toy into box.

The cat could speak to him telepathically. A feral Fam in his Residence. Did that make a difference?

Angling his head, he saw a tiny swatch of red silkeen protruding from the box, sensed his HeartGift was back in the small case. He could still feel the waves of lust radiating from it. He closed his eyes, too limp from the powerful climax to move.

Thwap. Thwap. Thwap.

He opened one eye. The cat, a male, was smacking his HeartGift around the floor, then pouncing on it.

He definitely should care about that.

The cat picked it delicately up in his mouth and trotted toward a place where an icy draft issued. A small square portion of the wooden panel was flipped up, and Saille could see the hole through the wall to the frigid night.

"Don' . . ." he mumbled. It didn't come out as the sharp order he'd wanted. With energy he didn't know he had, he rocked to his hands and knees, wrinkled his nose at the dampness of his trous and the rug.

He growled a cleansing spell, and a brisk breeze, with the added cold of the winter air, rippled the carpet, giving him an added boost to his feet, then whisked around him with a force that chilled him. Cleaned everything. Slapped him awake. "The night is too cold for you. Don't go out. Stay in."

Have not decided if you good FamMan.

Gaze fixed on the box in the cat's mouth, Saille bowed. "I am Saille Willow. Please stay as my guest."

The yellow eyes, pupils large since the cat was near the previously unknown Fam door and the night, narrowed. *I would accept a heated pad under the couch.*

"Done!"

Cat door never to be spell locked.

"Of course not."

Yes, Saille definitely cared that he got his HeartGift back. The cat could demand its skinny weight in gold, and Saille would pay. He tried a casual question. "Only myself and my HeartMate should be able to see my HeartGift."

You not Cats who fight to live.

"Very true." Now that he was regaining strength, Saille visualized a heat pad kept in one of his bedroom closets. His Mother-Dam had been susceptible to the winter cold. He activated it and 'ported it down from the closet shelf to under the couch, near the wall. It was too large and stuck out. He shrugged, too bad.

Warily, the cat glided over and sniffed. Wrinkled his nose, dropped the HeartGift to stick out and curl his tongue. *Smells bad.*

Bracing himself on the corner of his desk, Saille gestured and muttered another deep cleansing spell for the pad. It rolled and unrolled, flipped over and did the same.

Saille said, *"Come to me."* His HeartGift smacked into his open hand with enough force to leave an outline. Clenching his jaw, he drained his Flair for one last shielding spell. Then he leaned against the desk and fumbled the box with the swatch of red fabric sticking out into the embroidered red silkeen pouch. He dared not open the box to tuck the bit of fabric inside.

The cat had disappeared under the couch, and a low purr rolled from there. Slowly walking to the small door, Saille set one hand against the wall, bent down and flipped the panel closed. When he looked to the couch, he could only see glowing yellow eyes.

"Welcome to T'Willow Residence."

The eyes dipped as if the cat had inclined its head.

"What should I call you?"

After a few seconds of silence, the cat said, *For now, you may call Me "Cat."*

"Until you decide whether you want to be my Fam."

"Yesssss."

"Fine." He cleared his throat. "I will be sleeping on that sofa tonight."

Cat growled. Saille couldn't even shrug. Gauging the distance between the wall that held him up and the couch, he figured he could make it before he collapsed.

He did and closed his eyes, and once again darkness swirled him around and around as if he was on his own potter's wheel. Before he spun into sleep, he thought that it had been a very eventful day.

*D*ufleur *awoke as the climax shuddered through her.* She lay gasping. She hadn't felt so well pleasured since she'd suffered through her Third Passage a few months ago. When she'd *reached* for her HeartMate and he'd come eagerly to her arms. As he had tonight.

The icy gleam of twinmoons' light from frost-rimed windows set high in the room patterned on her threadbare rug. But she was hot, hot, gilded with the sweat of passion. She glanced down at Fairyfoot, who snored gently at the end of her bed. Still asleep, good.

Throwing the covers back, she shuddered as cool air met her overheated skin. She hurried to the small bathroom, murmured a spell light, and stripped off her long nightgown, putting it in the cleanser. With a wave of her hand, she started the waterfall flowing over the rock ledge and stepped under it only to find her skin so sensitized by his hands that another climax rippled through her. She propped herself up in the corner of the stall and directed the spray at herself, cooling the water, too.

He was coming closer.

She'd had his HeartGift in her possession twice.

Fairyfoot was on his side.

Dufleur's mouth flattened. She had no talent for relationships. Hadn't she and her mother argued as usual after dinner?

She *didn't* want a man in her life. She'd had no time for him when she'd been working at Dandelion Silk and experimenting in the mornings and evenings. Now with this new life pressed upon her, changing her routine, demanding efforts from her that she didn't know she could provide, she still didn't want a man. He would only complicate her life further.

She felt his determination to have her.

Trouble loomed.

Seven

As soon as *Dufleur* woke the next morning, a fine excitement fizzed in her veins, and clutched her stomach, as if she'd been successful in experiments the night before. When she realized that she was still at a standstill with an edge of fear associated with her work, her mood dimmed. Yet, she recalled what had pleased and jittered her so. She was going to show her embroidery to AppleHeir, who owned Enlli Gallery, this morning. The Apples were the premier artists of Celta.

Hopping from bed, she went to the small niche that held the minimal kitchen, a hot-square and no-time food storage. She pulled out crunch biscuits in warm milk for herself. When Fairyfoot padded in, Dufleur set down a meal specially prepared for her according to a recipe of Danith D'Ash's. And the thought of D'Ash led to T'Ash, whom she'd also see today. Fairyfoot would expect an expensive collar. Dufleur's spirits dampened even more. "Good morning," she said stiltedly to Fairyfoot, still irritated about the HeartGift and the suspicion she hadn't seen the last of it.

Good morning! Fairyfoot replied cheerily, even adding a trilling purr. *We go get My collar today.*

"I know."

Dufleur ate, then smoothed her bedsponge linens and dress. She glanced at a table stacked with her pieces. She had plenty to show Apple for the Enlli Gallery, about twenty items. Her nerves shivered. Could they possibly be good enough to sell as art?

Last night when she'd told Dringal about Enlli Gallery, her mother had been wide-eyed. She'd filled Dufleur's arms with the gifts Dufleur had made for her with such haste that Dufleur knew they meant little to her . . . or Dringal preferred the gilt they'd bring, more.

You will make much gilt this day from Quert Apple, then I will have My collar.

She wasn't about to spend a great deal of gilt, should she

ever get it, on a Fam collar. She looked at Fairyfoot, who, despite everything, was a beloved but not very pretty cat. A simple collar would suit her best. Dufleur had the idea that Fairyfoot didn't believe so.

I will take My toy to show Apple, too, Fairyfoot said. *But he cannot have to sell because it is Mine, Mine, Mine, Mine, Mine, Mine.*

Six "mines" was as good as a vow from a cat.

Dufleur blinked at the stuffed oblong bit of gray cloth that had originally been a mousekin for Fairyfoot. The ears and tail were all gone. The fabric was nubby and snagged, with a couple of bits gone, showing the padding.

She'd just finished carefully bundling the pieces in various bags and tubes when the door knocker rapped loudly. Hurrying from her rooms, she closed the door, her glance lingering on the wall to the secret room. She hadn't even spent a septhour there in the last day, for the first time in months.

The Holly footman-bodyguard waited just inside the main door. He took a couple of her light bags then opened the door for her.

Sucking her breath against the slamming cold, Dufleur walked carefully out onto the stoop. To her surprise, it and the stairs were perfectly clear and dry of the soft snow that draped the bushes around her. Either her mother or D'Winterberry had used precious household energy to ensure the safety of the steps.

The footman lifted the glider door, where an elegant Passiflora Holly sat, again in her faux fox fur. She said, "Merry meet." Her eyes gleamed.

Fairyfoot shot into the car and onto her lap, smiled up at her with a kitty grin. *Merry meet.*

Passiflora laughed, stroked the cat.

"Merry meet," said Dufleur, sliding onto the warm dark green leather seats piped in red, gratefully breathing air that didn't freeze in her nose. She kept an eye on the footman stowing her embroidery in the back cache of the glider.

"My brother awaits us at the gallery." With easy charm, Passiflora kept the conversation light during the trip. When they reached the place, Dufleur saw that it wasn't open for business, but lights were on. As they left the glider, the last of the pearly gray clouds parted from the sun, turning the day bright. The gallery's roof was bespelled glass, so there would be plenty of natural light to view her work. Good. She hoped.

She studied the building. It was so new that Dufleur blinked. The winds of time eddied around it more than usual—accustomed to sweeping over bare land. She received no impression from the building, let alone any hint of sentience. Though there was a faint sense that the Apples had made a HouseHeart in the place, unusual for a business, but these were the artistic Apples.

Passiflora swept into the gallery, with a smile and thanks to the footman and a comment that he and the driver should visit the staff lounge for pastries and caff. Dufleur's mouth watered as if she hadn't had any breakfast at all. But when Quert Holly walked toward them and her abdomen tightened, she was glad she hadn't just eaten.

He was a large and handsome man with features just beginning to soften with age. He had hair several shades blonder than his sister's bronze and the same turquoise eyes. His smile was warm, but his serious gaze told Dufleur he was reserving judgment until he saw her work. Fair enough. But it didn't make her any less jittery.

Passiflora introduced them and GreatSir Apple bent over Dufleur's hand. She managed to remain gracious as though they both didn't notice the much-mended cuffs of her coat. She should definitely have spent gilt on a new winter coat instead of another couple of scientific gauges.

Fairyfoot mewed politely.

"Greetyou, Fam," Apple said, then led them to a large, white, empty room with interesting angles. "This space should be excellent for soft art. Let's see what you have." He gestured to a long, narrow table, also white. With a Word he cleansed his hands. Dufleur and Passiflora did the same, then they began unwrapping and placing the pieces—everything from slippers to the flat hat to framed panels Dufleur had given her mother—onto the table. The last item was the Dandelion Silk box holding D'Willow's pale green, shot-silk robe, embroidered with twenty other shades of green.

When they were done, Apple stepped back, set his hand on his hip. Dufleur gripped her hands together, watching him scan the work. She frowned at the line of pieces her mother had given her. There was every Nameday and New Year's present she'd given her mother for the last few years. They'd been in storage and escaped the fire.

Except the panel of a winterberry bush, bright red berries showing against a snowy hill. Dringal had kept that. Dufleur swallowed.

But Apple was walking down the line, hands clasped behind his back. Before he was halfway down he turned on his heel and said, "Yes."

"Yes?" squeaked Dufleur.

"Yesssss!" hissed Fairyfoot, gamboling about the room.

"Yes. I'll take them all. I'll buy them outright, or you can sell them through the gallery, and I'll charge a twenty-eight percent commission."

"Outrageous! No more than fifteen percent," huffed Passiflora, now free of her thick coat. She wore a patterned cream-colored damask tunic and trous accented with black and turquoise frogs and stood toe-to-toe with her brother.

Apple grunted. "Twenty-six percent."

"Eighteen." Passiflora slanted a look at Dufleur. "You need an agent, dear. A shark."

"You're doing fine, Passiflora," Dufleur said, her voice still high. She hated bargaining.

Showing her teeth, Passiflora narrowed her eyes as she looked up at him. While Dufleur found a bench and wilted onto it, there was a flurry of offers and counteroffers. They finally settled at a twenty percent commission, with Apple buying twenty-five percent of the pieces up front—and transferring more gilt than Dufleur had made in the past five years into her bank account.

Apple kissed Passiflora's hand, then Dufleur's. He nodded to Fairyfoot who sat proudly next to Dufleur's feet. With a wave of his hand, Willow's robe lifted to a wall, spread and centered itself. Apple went over to make adjustments, and Passiflora joined Dufleur.

"So much," Dufleur whispered.

"I told you so," Passiflora gloated. "Quert Junior, Dufleur needs caff."

"No drinks in the gallery rooms."

"Oh."

"Particularly near this wonderful art." He studied Dufleur, frowning. "Why haven't we heard of you before? You've, what, gone through your Third Passage?"

She sat straight. "Yes. Embroidery is my creative Flair, not my inherent Family Flair," Dufleur said, though she set the Time Wind in some of her stitches.

He glanced at her, then back at the robe. "Necessity can refine any Flair." He swept his hand a centimeter above her work. "Exquisite. I've never seen such a pattern, such combination of three-dimensional stitches and color, yet with a vibrancy that makes this true art." He turned to her, his expression fierce. "Your art now belongs to me." He poked a finger at her. "You do not make slippers, or flat hats, or, Lord and Lady forbid, *cat toys*." He looked down at Fairyfoot's scruffy mouse, then back up at Dufleur. "I want *tapestries*. You go home and block out several in different sizes." Jerking his head at the wide space where the robe was centered, he said, "I want a large piece to fill the width of that wall."

Her mouth dropped, she searched for words. "But that will take me years!" And more Flair than she wanted to spend on her embroidery, Flair that should be used for her time experiments.

He frowned. "Don't you get a yearly NobleGilt? Surely you're an Heir?" He waved, "and you're definitely talented."

"I receive the minimum NobleGilt as ThymeHeir," she said.

Snorting, he said, "Then I'll tell them to raise it to FirstFamily GrandHouse levels." He raised a hand at her strangled gasp. "That's what you're worth."

She swallowed, then brought out a carefully protected tube. It had lived in her closet for some time.

For months after her father's accident she couldn't face a laboratory, and she siphoned all her rage and grief into her creative Flair . . . mundane objects for Dandelion Silk and this piece. A visual journal of her grief.

She carefully unrolled the tapestry of the time landscape she'd visited after her father's death. The grayness shading to distant hills under a darker gray sky that shifted to silver at the top. The two bonfires shooting red flames and smoke. Her chest tightened, and she looked away from it, left it in Apple's grasp.

He stared. "Magnificent," he whispered. "I've never seen anything like this, the varying textures to create the tiniest shadows," he lifted his hands as if to touch, fisted his fingers, "the shades of gray." He grinned. "It's like the finest painting. You'll challenge T'Apple, and that will be good for him. He hasn't had such an artist to duel with in decades. Wait til I bring him down to the gallery this afternoon." With a huge wave of his arm, all her pieces were hung.

She blinked, staggered back a step or two, swiveled her head. Every placement was *perfect*, the robe a statement of greens on green on the white wall, her most colorful work displayed in fabulous light. Curtseying low to GrandSir Apple, she said, "Thank you."

A big grin spread across his face, lit his eyes. "Your pieces will sell very, very well. My pleasure." Once again he rubbed his hands. "We'll have a special opening for this show itself. Introduce the new gallery and a new artist at the same time." He frowned. "I want it soon. Next week. Passiflora, my assistant will contact you to consult on the best date and time. There will be food and liquor of course, in the reception area." He took Dufleur's hand and bowed low over it, kissing it with great charm, and all the while Dufleur thought he did it absently, his mind already on business.

Her work art! And her on display as an artist. Scary. But wonderful. But so bittersweet. She wanted to be known for her true Flair, her Thyme Flair. Her Time Flair.

*A*s she stepped back into the glider with Passiflora and Fairyfoot, Dufleur was still shaken at the amount of gilt she now had in her account. Her mind spun with calculations. If her art sold well, she might manage to build a laboratory on the bit of land she'd inherited in the country come spring. So she was equally quiet on the ride to T'Ash's Residence as she had been to the gallery.

Fairyfoot made up for her silence, talking all the way, projecting loud thoughts that Passiflora could also hear, or making excited cat noises. Then there was the whisker twitching, tail flicking, pacing along their laps and the backseat of the glider, hopping down to the wide space of the glider floor and prancing. All her comments revolved around what sort of jewels she wanted on her FamCat collar.

Finally Passiflora said, "It's always been my understanding that a FamCat gets what she or he deserves."

Fairyfoot froze in mid-step, paw lifted. Slowly she turned her head to Dufleur and widened her big, round, green eyes. An ingratiating smile formed on her muzzle. *I have been a very Good Cat*, she said.

"Not lately," Dufleur muttered and stared at Fairyfoot's shortened whiskers. She leaned back against the soft leather, sighing, prepared to enjoy the show.

Passiflora snickered.

"Your New Year's gift was expensive—that padded cat perch of blue velvet embroidered with gold mice," Dufleur said.

But this is My COLLAR. Again the wide smile, the big eyes holding infinite appeal. *This shows how much you Love Me*.

Dufleur fingered the large gold coin Apple had given her to seal the bargain. She held it up. Fairyfoot's gaze immediately focused on the gilt. Her pink tongue came out as she swiped her muzzle.

"Despite what you think," Dufleur said, "we don't have a lot of this. We have expenses for our social season—"

Need a **GOOD** collar for that.

"I'm going to order three more Flaired gowns." Four would transform into a full wardrobe if she bespelled them correctly. She'd originally ordered only one and had bought material to make her own. "We have other bills to pay, since I won't be working at Dandelion Silk, and some gilt must go to support D'Winterberry and my mother."

Fairyfoot sniffed. *Mean to Us. We should not pay*.

Dufleur looked at Passiflora from the corner of her eyes, but the GreatLady seemed amused. "They just don't understand us." Her mother had *never* understood her father and his obsession with time. "D'Winterberry Residence is an excellent place to live and work." At least cheaper than anything she'd find on her own. *Not to mention your traitorous ways*, she sent to her Fam. Fairyfoot ignored her.

"We're here," said Passiflora.

Jumping up, Fairyfoot put her paws on the glider window and watched as one half of the great greeniron gates swung silently open. Dufleur sat up straight. She'd heard a lot about the modern design of T'Ash's Residence and now saw it— smooth armourcrete and glisten-glazed hardglass windows in angles and curves that rose three stories. She heard that it had once been white but when T'Ash wed his HeartMate, Danith D'Ash had it tinted a pale yellow.

Though the sweeping bulge of the front was quite different

than the castles of other FirstFamilies Residences, Dufleur had no doubt it was a fortress.

The glider drove up to the wide alcove of the front entrance, and the Holly footman lifted the vehicle door just as T'Ash's butler opened the Residence door. Dufleur was unsurprised to find dried flagstones under her feet. Fairyfoot hopped out first and adopted a dignified swagger, tail in the air.

The butler bowed as she entered, "Greetyou, Madam Fam-Cat." Since Danith D'Ash was *the* person who certified Fams—as she'd done with Fairyfoot a couple of months ago—the man must be used to all sorts of telepathic animals. A few animal hairs dusted his sharply pressed dark brown livery trous.

Fairyfoot nodded to him as she went by.

T'Ash waited in the entryway. He and the butler took Passiflora's and Dufleur's coats. There was an enraged child's cry from the depths of the house. Fairyfoot hopped behind Dufleur. A faint smile crossed T'Ash's face. "My son, Nuin. He's determined to get his way."

Like every other great Nobleman Dufleur knew.

"We have hired a nanny. Our fourth. Nuin is just testing him."

Dufleur suppressed a shudder.

D'Holly frowned. "I hope you don't have more problems."

"Won't happen." T'Ash grinned. "This one's a Clover. They have staying power."

"Oh, yes! An excellent idea," Passiflora said.

"Thought we'd better get a Clover while they're still middle class and inexpensive. That Family is rising fast." He winked at Dufleur, and her tension eased. Everything she'd heard of T'Ash had told her he was a formidable man. "Let's go to my work suite, shall we?" With one cool glance, he looked her up and down and led them to the back of the house. "Baubles for the social season, I've heard."

And a collar for Me! Fairyfoot trilled. She hesitated at the door to T'Ash's worksuite, nose sniffing. *Zanth is not in here?*

"No. My FamCat is watching the nanny mind Nuin. Zanth likes to torment them both."

Baubles. A flush crawled up Dufleur's neck and tinted her cheeks. "I might just be able to afford baubles."

"We'll see what we can do," he said, ushering her into a fancy workroom. She half-smiled. If she knew workmen, and she did, he had another room besides this one where he did all his rough work. This was a place where Nobles would feel comfortable and believe T'Ash worked . . . though since T'Ash was also a smith, he must have a forge somewhere, too. Probably an outbuilding.

Fairyfoot immediately leapt onto a table displaying wares—far too expensive items for Dufleur. The cat looked at T'Ash with a winsome smile and wide, round eyes. *I need a Good collar.* She hesitated, licked a forepaw delicately, glanced at him again, making her eyes even bigger. Dufleur wondered how she did that. *Zanth has an emerald collar. And earrings.*

T'Ash seemed immune to big eyes. "That's right." He folded his arms and leaned against the table. "Zanth was with me for many years Downwind. When it was a real slum."

Dufleur blinked. Seemed as if someone else was negotiating for her today. Fine with her.

Waving a hand at another polished "worktable," T'Ash said, "I brought out jewelry appropriate for a woman attending her first social season."

"I'm not a young girl," Dufleur said. "I've suffered Third Passage."

T'Ash shrugged. "There are traditions."

Honestly curious, Dufleur said, "I didn't think you attended the social season?"

"I can't think of anything Danith and I would enjoy less," he said, then, "Those emeralds don't truly match your eyes, Fairyfoot. Too dark and don't glow enough. I think cabochons—uncut round stones—would suit you better."

Unfaceted stones. The man was definitely steering Fairyfoot to his less-expensive stock. "You know Fairyfoot?" Dufleur asked. Passiflora had drifted toward some jewelry that gleamed gold and redgold and glisten, appearing "casually arranged" on another table.

T'Ash smiled, but kept an eye on the cat. Dufleur wondered if he'd ever experienced cat theft. Probably. Zanth was legendary in his arrogance. "Danith remembered examining and certifying her." His smile widened. "She had fleas."

Fairyfoot hissed.

T'Ash continued, meeting Dufleur's gaze. "And I've had plenty of experience in selling jewelry to Noblewomen for themselves and their daughters just before the social season. In my early days, those sales supported me until Discovery Day in the summer."

She nodded.

He pushed away from the table, went to an elegant desk that appeared unused, and drew a pouch from a drawer. "Fairyfoot, you should examine these. Didn't know til I saw you, but I believe they'll suit." He jiggled the pouch, and musical clicks came from it. Fairyfoot watched his every motion. "Unique. Just discovered in a new mine." Going to the end of the table, he drew out a thick felt pad and poured the stones onto it.

Eight

Dufleur caught her breath at the beauty of the green stones. They were *right* for Fairyfoot—highly polished, almost spherical jewels, glowing green with occasional darker depths. The stones were a mixture of sizes. The largest were as big as the cat's eyes, but seemed a little duller than the smaller stones. Which were the more expensive?

"I had the honor of naming them. Green moonstones," T'Ash said.

Fairyfoot strolled to the pad, but from the way the tip of her tail twitched, Dufleur knew she wanted to pounce. The cat walked all around the mat, angling her head to study the stones, sniffing or licking one or two. Then she tumbled them with her paw. Finally she sat her butt down, wriggled a little, and stared at the stones, as if she checked them out with her senses— including her Flair.

With flicks of her paw too fast to see, she separated twelve, graduated in size. *I will have these.*

Gruffly, T'Ash looked at the stones she'd chosen and then at her neck. "These won't make a full necklace. I'll embed them in Flaired furrabeast leather, and with a small spell, the leather will disappear, and it will look as if the stones float."

Like that idea. Fairyfoot beamed. She slanted a look at Dufleur. *And when We are together more and make more gilt, I will get more stones.*

Dufleur didn't think she should promise that. "We'll see," she said. She let out her breath, inhaled, and looked at T'Ash. "How much?"

He looked at her from under heavy brows. "I have not tested the Flair vibrations of this kind of stone. I don't know what effects the collar might have on Fam or person." He named a low figure.

Passiflora and Dufleur stared at them. Fairyfoot chortled and gathered her stones close to her belly.

He lied. Dufleur knew it even as she met the startling blue

eyes in his dark complexioned face. He could no sooner keep himself from experimenting with stones, knowing each and every type, than she could stop working with time.

Still, something about the fact that he made an effort to lie about it to save her gilt gave rise to a lump in her throat. But she looked at him, and his past wavered before her for a few seconds—a large boy living in the old Downwind slums, stealing. He'd known poverty.

Clearing her voice, Dufleur said, "T'Ash Residence?"

Here, said the house voice. Dufleur stiffened. It was male and sounded a little like the lost Thyme Residence. She swallowed tears. Perhaps she should go look for the HouseHeart again, see if it had Healed, but after a year and a half . . . It had broken her heart that she hadn't been able to sense it. Definitely time to do that again. If even a kernel of it had survived, she wanted it.

GrandMistrys Thyme? prompted the Residence.

"Please connect me with Cascara Bank and Financial Services."

Done, said the Residence.

Dufleur completed the transfer of funds from her account to T'Ash's. Fairyfoot amused herself by floating her stones up under her neck, one after the other. *Pretty. Mine.*

Now it was Dufleur's turn. She looked at the necklaces and earrings as if they were colored embroidery. Wonderful. Understated. Simple and beautiful. A little lust for the gems lodged inside her. "What's the minimum I need?" she asked.

Passiflora drifted over to stand next to her and T'Ash. "With the gowns you are having made," she tapped multicolored polished cabochon gemstone beads separated by gold and silver, redgold, and glisten drops. "These would be the best value."

Dufleur stared at them. They seemed quietly polished, and she hadn't much noticed them, but the more she looked at them, the more she liked them. The more she wanted them. She had a feeling that was often the case with T'Ash's work. Certainly Passiflora hadn't let the white diamond and ruby necklace go since she'd picked it up, and still held it in her fingers.

"Perfect," Dufleur said, nerving herself to meet T'Ash's blue gaze. "How much?"

He smiled, and she stiffened.

"Let's discuss this," he said with a smooth lilt in his voice.

He took her to another room across the hall. Passiflora followed, Fairyfoot stayed behind. Lined up in a row were eighteen large, old no-times. "These don't work anymore," he said.

She stilled, slowly turned to him. His face was impassive. Awareness prickled over her.

This man obviously believed she carried the Family Flair for time and that her Flair was strong. He was a powerful member of the FirstFamilies Council. People would cross the Captain, T'Hawthorn, or even T'Holly, before they'd go against T'Ash.

Was this a test?

What would happen if she refurbished the old machines? Would T'Ash report her skills to the Noble Councils? She wasn't allowed to manipulate time.

No. Not correct, she realized.

She wasn't allowed to *experiment* with time. No one was, not even her father's chief competitor, GraceLord T'Agave.

She walked down the line. "Some of these are centuries old." They'd obviously come from Nobles.

"The spell that captures the time flow doesn't work," T'Ash grumbled.

"You expect me to revitalize them?" Dufleur asked softly.

Passiflora was watching her keenly, too.

T'Ash lifted a shoulder. "You can do it."

She'd never Tested her Flair with T'Ash's Testing Stones. He hadn't been so established when she was seven and experienced her First Passage.

Tilting her head, she said, "I'm sure you intend that these go back to their Families." She touched the gilt crest tinted above the smoky door of one of the no-times. Hawthorn.

T'Ash said, "I just told them that I'd run across a charm."

"Did they believe that?"

A white grin flashed in his outlaw's face. His fingers touched the knife he wore at his hip. "People don't make a habit of disbelieving me."

Dufleur hadn't noticed the weapon. She knew he spoke truly. His story had been a sensation. Even her father had read the newssheets and commented on it to her.

Entire GreatLord Family murdered when T'Ash was a child by a rival. Boy growing up in the Downwind slums. Vengeance stalk. Helping Holm Holly during his Passages that included Death Duels. Mortal dueling. Questioning by the FirstFamilies Council. Acknowledgment of his lineage and Flair. Building a new, modern, home—

"My father consulted with you on your no-time storage."

He gave a short nod.

"You wanted twenty no-times, plus two no-time vaults, one a walk-in." She finally realized that was the gilt that had eked them through the last years of her father's life. Brows lowering, she said, "You wanted a no-time storage for roc—*stones*."

"That's right. The crystalline vibrations of stones go in cycles, and I wanted to store them at their peak." He grimaced. "But they didn't like that, so I no longer use that no-time. For stones, at least."

She didn't want to think about that. Stones were T'Ash's interest. Time was hers.

Shaking her head, she said, "And no one would figure out that you had Dufleur Thyme consulting with you today."

"I had T'Agave here yesterday."

Her stomach clenched. Once old D'Willow had announced her father was a dangerous fraud, his enemy T'Agave had made sure the lies about Vulg Thyme grew and spread throughout all of Druida, from the noblest classes to the lowest. He, too, had given interviews to the newssheets.

"Why do you want me to fix these?"

"Because you can. You should not deny your Flair."

"People would delight in smearing my name, as they did my father's."

"Is Celta to lose a great Flair because you are too cowardly to practice it?"

She clamped her teeth shut. Surely this man used his Flair to forge swords and knives and whatever into new patterns. Surely he *created* with his Flair every day. She was forbidden by law to try something new. She wouldn't bring that up, couldn't let him know that she might be breaking laws.

"Dufleur's personal creativity is for embroidery." D'Holly stepped between them, facing T'Ash. "Her art now hangs in my brother's gallery."

"I'll have Agave fix the things, then."

Dufleur snorted. The man might be able to do so. What did she know of his Flair? But T'Ash had spurred her pride. She stalked to the end of the line and popped off the side panel of the first one with an easy Word, looked at the tracery of the equation that activated the spell. It was old and clumsy, but would work . . . and continue to work for another century if she redrew it and recharged it with her own Flair.

Dared she?

Touching a faded symbol, she sensed the lingering Flair of a female ancestor who had crafted the spell. Modern no-times used the general spell her Family had sold linked to a time-gathering storage nut that producers could power themselves.

With a shrug, she fumbled in her pursenal for a writestick. She didn't find one, but her fingers closed over a large needle. Close enough. Perhaps even better for her. With a wave of her hand the antique no-time angled itself so she could work. Once again she studied the equation—one only a master or mistress of time could read.

She sucked in her breath, coalesced the particles of time spread throughout the room, bent them into a stream, and with her needle, created a new equation. Time sped up around her, and she was done with the job before Passiflora and T'Ash blinked.

She gestured, and the panel fit once more against the box.

T'Ash frowned. "Does it work?"

"Yes."

"Hmm." He strode to a table holding a caff mug, mumbled a word, and steam rose from the drink inside, then he came back and stuck it into the no-time. "I'll check it."

Dufleur raised her brows. "Do you want me to finish the others?"

"Please. Then I can return these to their owners."

After the first one, the rest came easy. Her eyes stung as she saw the different hands of her ancestors, female and male, their personal modifications of the spell when the units were new. Soon she was finished, and T'Ash nodded as he sipped his caff. "It works."

She started to put her needle away, when T'Ash held out his hand. "I can sharpen that for you." Dufleur and D'Holly followed him across the hall to his workroom. He gestured at the jewelry. "Take whatever you want, Dufleur. Passiflora, you'll pay me for that necklace." He opened a door and left them.

Passiflora looked at the diamonds and rubies she still held, noticed some softleaves and small boxes, and went over to wrap her choice. She sighed. "T'Ash is a very strange man."

Presented with a choice of everything in the room, Dufleur simply froze, still trying to puzzle out what the man was trying to say to her. That she should continue to experiment with time? No. That was *not* it.

"Yessss," said Fairyfoot, and once again began circling the tables. She touched a paw to a heavy collar of large square pieces of gold.

"No," Dufleur said.

Sniffing, the Fam went back to her small pile of stones.

As soon as Passiflora was done with her own selection, Passiflora picked up the two necklaces and earrings they'd looked at, then three more—smoky pearlescent beads, a trio of glisten chains woven together, and another of gold, silver, and glisten.

T'Ash entered and handed Dufleur her needle, with a tiny bit of cork on the end, placed in an equally small leather sheath.

"Thank you," she said, then decided to be bold. "What are you trying to tell me?"

"You do no honor to your father by not practicing your GrandHouse Flair."

Dufleur raised her brows. "All the old Family spells are well standardized and can be included by others into such things as new no-times."

T'Ash grunted. "The producers sketch the spells, but do not know the *reason* they work. I certainly don't know why or how a no-time works. But you do. We humans don't have such numbers on this planet to be sure of our survival. We need all the knowledge—all the expansion of knowledge, possible."

"Hmmm," Passiflora said.

Dufleur shrugged.

"The laws against time experimentation only apply to Druida," T'Ash said, his words rougher than his hands as they wrapped and boxed up Dufleur's selections and placed them in a bag.

"Yes," Passiflora said acidly. "Come spring Dufleur can leave Druida and blow herself up elsewhere. *That* will advance our knowledge oh so very much."

Dufleur decided saying nothing would be best at this point.

Fairyfoot meowed in demand.

They all looked at her. She sat up straight beside the green moonstones for her collar and a piece of black tinted leather. *When will My collar be done?*

"We begin our socializing the night after next," D'Holly said.

T'Ash bowed deeply, but his eyes glinted humor. "By the end of the week."

"Nooooo," Fairyfoot yowled. *I need them by Our first party!*

Looking at Passiflora, T'Ash said, "I wasn't aware that Fams attended balls and suchlike." He tilted his head as if considering his FamCat, the battered alley tom, at a social event. T'Ash shook his head.

Passiflora said, "It depends on the FamPerson and Fam, I'd imagine. I have accepted an invitation for D'Ivy's musical soiree, since my Journeywoman, Trif Winterberry, has been hired to play, and will be debuting several new pieces by both of us."

Ear twitching and big eyes from Fairyfoot. *I loooove music.*

With a smile flashing teeth, T'Ash said, "Danith has a new litter of kittens that need to be trained to mouse. You stay today for a while, return tomorrow and the day after, and I will have your collar ready by the end of your last session."

Fairyfoot huddled into herself. When T'Ash remained unmoved, she leapt from the table in a graceful arc, then stalked over to the door and glowered at him, turned her back, and flicked her tail.

I will teach, she said grudgingly.

As Passiflora and Dufleur left T'Ash Residence, she once again felt shock stealing her wits. T'Ash had gotten exactly his own way.

She was definitely over her head, trying to swim in these exalted circles. She almost longed for her old life back . . . except T'Ash *had* renewed her dedication to her Flair. She'd spend the rest of the day reviewing her notes and discover exactly what went wrong. Then she'd explore the notion she'd had yesterday of developing something new to please the nobility.

But when she opened the door to D'Winterberry Residence, anger and conflict rolled out of the place in waves, along with shouting and wailing.

Nine

♦

She shut the front door behind her. Upstairs another door slammed. Dufleur winced. Setting her packages on a table, she noticed it needed dusting again. Some of her Flair had been going to housekeeping spells. Her mouth curved wryly. She, too, was proud enough not to want D'Holly to see how poorly they lived.

With a sigh, she trudged up the staircase. Her own day had been delightful enough that she didn't want to smudge her contentment with unpleasantness.

An older man flushed with anger strode toward her. She barely recognized him—her cuz, Meyar, D'Winterberry's oldest son, Ilex's older brother. Before he reached her he stopped, sucked in a breath, and bowed. "Greetyou, cuz Dufleur."

Eyeing him warily, she sketched a curtsy. "Greetyou, Meyar."

He blew out a breath, and now he considered her as much as she was doing him. Though he'd returned to Druida a couple of months ago, she'd met him rarely, and never here, in the Residence. It was he who should be WinterberryHeir, not her mother. Dufleur figured that was what the shouting was all about.

His fingers fisted, then unclenched at his sides. "S'pose I should tell you I've decided to file an action with the Noble Council against my mother and yours, charging negligence." His spine stiffened. "They haven't kept up the estate. The Residence is nearly dead."

Dufleur flinched. When was the last time she'd spoken to the Residence entity? She'd spared Flair for housekeeping, that was pretty much all. Involved in her own concerns.

How could she have been so stupid? Relying on housekeeping spells to open and close the secret door to her laboratory. She should have used her own Flair for that, sparing the Residence even that low amount of power. If the Residence died, the door to her laboratory would probably become part of the all-too-solid stone wall.

She'd only done a brief scan when she'd discovered the room, to check the vibrations and see if there were any echoes of dark deeds that might have tainted the space and affected her experiments. Time was a tricky thing.

Now her guilt at draining the Residence of precious energy weighed on her. Horrible enough that the core Thyme Residence had never recovered from the explosion. Worse to kill a being from her own neglect.

"I'm an adult, come of age, and living here. I haven't given the Residence as much of my energy and care as I should have. Are you naming me in your action?"

His face softened. "You aren't D'Winterberry or Winterberry-Heir, responsible for the upkeep of this Residence, able to transfer power to it easily. You have no fault in this."

She did, but kept quiet.

He frowned. "Shouldn't you be D'Thyme? Why'd you let your mother take the title?"

"It was all she had left to her."

He nodded somberly. "But it was her mistake that she wed your father, that her life has been a miser—"

Dufleur stiffened.

"Beg pardon, that she believes her life has been a misery, or made it so herself." He ran his hands through his gray hair, grimaced. "Lord and Lady know that was rude. Anyway, I can't speak on that matter, either. I made a wife miserable enough to run off." He shook his head, hunched a shoulder. "Decades past." His eyes were shadowed. "Tell me, does this scheme to wed you to a wealthy lord and demand a large marriage settlement for the Winterberrys disgust you? I'll find a way to stop it."

"I don't care for the marriage part, but I'm committed to the social season for more reasons than for Winterberrys."

He nodded. "D'Holly." His lips thinned. "I don't like that they called on her, that they're using her. But I think the Holly Family still needs any help they can get." He made a half bow. "I thank you for your generosity."

More guilt bit at her for using his Residence for time experiments without his—anyone's—knowledge. Once again she curtsied. "You're welcome, and D'Holly has given me much more than I can ever repay." Her mind dazed as she recalled her embroidery hanging on the walls of an art gallery.

For the first time, Meyar's smile was easy. "Those First-Families can be benevolent, benevolent enough to roll right over a body."

Dufleur smiled back. "Right."

His brows dipped. "Do you mind staying here?" He jerked a nod toward the MistrysSuite a few doors down the hallway. "Living with them can't be easy. I can find a place—"

"No, thank you. My mother is a difficult woman when she's unhappy—"

"I just made her very unhappy," Meyar said.

"I'll stay," Dufleur said.

"Good." He turned around where he stood, surveying the surroundings. "I've felt your Flair in maintaining this place, and I thank you."

Again she thought that she'd received more from the Winterberrys than she'd contributed. "Whatever her faults, your mother took us in when we had nowhere else to go."

"Of course, you're Family." He bowed, looked over his shoulder again. "I don't envy you calming her down. Your mother." His jaw flexed. "Mine has already succumbed to a yarduan stupor."

Dufleur gave a little cough. "Why did you decide to fight for the title and estate now?"

All his anger disappeared. His face lit with joy. "My son and daughter-in-law gave me a Son'sSon last night. The birth oracle said he has great Flair." Meyar beamed, chuckled deprecatingly. "Though every generation seems to have greater Flair, and we Winterberrys have enough mixed blood from several lines that we don't have one overwhelming Family Flair. We'll have to wait and see what the babe's talent is."

"Consult T'Ash and his Testing Stones when the time is right," Dufleur said.

"It seems so. And for that, I need to be saving now. Merry meet, cuz Dufleur."

"And merry part." She gave the standard reply.

"And merry meet again." He nodded and strode past her, his step and manner lighter than when he'd slammed the door. At least she'd had a good effect on someone. Bracing herself, she walked to the MistrysSuite door and knocked.

"Who's there?" grated her mother.

"Dufleur."

"Come," her mother said on a grunt.

Dufleur entered. The stifling room reeked of yar-duan. She noticed a pot bubbling in the corner—potent oil being distilled from roots.

The heavy velvet curtains were drawn against the winter evening, and Dufleur wondered the last time the windows had been opened. She didn't want to stay too long. Just lingering in the atmosphere could affect the mind, and she still had things to do before she went to bed.

As Dufleur turned to her mother, she caught Dringal holding her stomach and straightening as if from a blow. Surprised at the show of feeling, Dufleur asked, "Can I help?"

Her mother's jaw worked a second or two, her mouth trembled in anger or hurt or both, her eyes sheened. Dufleur pretended not to stare, but she hadn't seen her mother so discomposed for a long time—since they'd asked D'Winterberry for shelter when their home was gone. Even Dufleur's father's death hadn't been as wrenching for Dringal as the loss of their home, and Dufleur found that hard to forgive.

"Our cuz, Meyar, has returned." Dringal nearly spit out the words. Her face set, and Dufleur realized she'd decided to be angry.

"I met him in the hallway." She kept her tone perfectly even.

"He accuses us—me!—of being negligent with this estate! After all I have done." She slid a gaze to D'Winterberry.

Yet her mother didn't look too exhausted by whatever energy she was sending to the Residence, and the last time Dufleur had visited Dringal's rooms, they'd been richly appointed and well tended. "Can I help?" she asked again.

D'Winterberry roused unexpectedly and laughed, then coughed with the harsh roughness of the yar-duan addict. When she was finished, she said, "Yes, you are central to our plan to remedy our finances." With a hand gesture that should have been a wave, but looked more like a flopping fish, she continued, "You just wed the right Nobleman, and all is saved."

Dufleur started to inhale deeply, recalled where she was, and said, "You two should not pin your hopes on that."

"Not very pretty," D'Winterberry mumbled.

Ignoring her, Dufleur said, "My creative Flair is valuable.

Mother, what of your tatting? Do you have any? It's lovely, especially set off against rich jeweltone velvets and silkeens. We might be able to talk Quert Apple into a mother-daughter show. That could be a draw, I think."

"My tatting," Dringal said. She turned her head and stared at the drapes enveloping the window. "Most of it is gone with our home. Fifty years of tatting up in smoke."

Dufleur flinched.

"You sent me some," D'Winterberry cackled, reaching to the table beside her for an elegant teacup that held her yar-duan, and sipping. "I never liked it. Looked too much like spiderwebs." Another little cough. "You can have them all back, if you like. I don't care. Ask old auntie where she put them." She licked her lips, finished the cup, reached for a bottle. "More'n fifty years worth of Nameday, New Year's gifts. Since we were children."

Dringal turned her head slowly and stared at D'Winterberry. Dufleur's heart squeezed. Depression and anger and fear whirled around the room. Hurt.

What could she do to make it better? She went to the scrybowl. It had a nasty film coating the water, but Dufleur disregarded that. She circled the tarnished metallic bowl with her index finger and said, "Scry Cascara Bank."

"Here," said the Bank's automated teller.

"This is Dufleur Thyme. Transfer a third of the funds I received this morning into the household account of D'Winterberry."

"Done," said the Bank.

"How much is in the account?" asked her mother.

The Bank told her.

Dringal staggered a step to a chair and sank down. "So much?" she whispered.

"Quert Apple is showcasing my embroidery in Enlli Gallery." Dufleur cleared her throat. "I sold a few pieces to him outright, but most are on commission. All of yours are on commission."

"Good."

Dufleur looked at her mother. "You and Winterberry use Cascara Bank, too, don't you? Authorize me to review the Winterberry account. I don't need to have access to it, but I want to know where the gilt is going."

Scowling, Dringal addressed the scrybowl and the Bank.
"Dufleur Thyme may receive information or statements on the
D'Winterberry account at any time."

"Done," said the Bank.

"Thank you," Dufleur said. "End scry." Turning to her
mother, she said, "I should have been able to address the Residence and have it form a link to the Bank."

"We just don't have the gilt to keep up all the housekeeping
spells."

"Now you do," Dufleur said. "Use it."

Dringal stood and shook her long tunic skirt out. "And now.
Now that *man* is suing us!"

"He was WinterberryHeir before you were. This is his home."
Dufleur tried to sound reasonable. But her mother was up and
pacing.

"*I* am WinterberryHeir now. This *was* his home. What is he
doing back here, and now? He should have established his own
home by this time in his life." She whirled and jabbed a finger at
Dufleur. "There will be examiners coming. We'll need your tes-
timony."

"The examiners will probably have truth-sensors with
them. I'll answer any questions." Pray the Lady and Lord they
didn't ask her about her own activities in D'Winterberry Residence.

"From what Meyar told me, if we can reenergize the Residence, we might be able to disprove the charges of negligence,"
Dufleur said half-heartedly. She wanted the Residence healthy
and safe, but thought Meyar would be a better guardian.

Dringal flung her hands in the air. "How can we do that?"

"The HouseHeart? I—" As ThymeHeir only she knew the
spells for their own, lost, Residence HouseHeart. "Shouldn't
you, as WinterberryHeir, know—"

"I don't," Dringal snapped. She shot a glance at D'Winterberry, who'd fallen asleep again, teacup in her lap. Dringal's
pacing got faster. "What a mess. All I ever wanted was a secure
home of my own. Is that too much to ask? Is it?"

"No," Dufleur said in a small voice. Her mind was getting
dizzy, her emotions becoming exaggerated. She didn't want to
hear again of her father's failings that were all too like her own,
of her mother's shattered ambitions. She couldn't think. The air
began to waver in rainbow patterns. Tongue thick, she said,

"Perhaps you should consult the HouseHeart. I must leave."
She went blindly to where she thought the door would be.

Dringal snorted. "Useless."

Dufleur didn't know if her mother meant the Winterberry
HouseHeart or herself. The thought that her mother sneered at
her was a lancing pain. Yes, her feelings were too sensitized.
She had to leave this room. How could her mother stand it?

Why had D'Winterberry ever turned to yar-duan? The drug
dulled the mind. How could anyone live that way?

She plunged through the door and pushed it shut, hard. It
slammed. Weak kneed, she hobbled down to her own rooms,
her sanctuary in this place. Flung the door open.

And was struck with the blatant sexual heat of a HeartGift.

"Light," she slurred the command, but her Word was loud
enough that her bedroom lit as if it was midsummer. On the carpet faded to shades of gray lay a vibrant red pouch. A pouch *she*
had made and embroidered.

Her heart thumped so hard she quivered with the beat.
"Wha—" Despite the fogging of her mind, she should be able
to deduce where the pouch had come from. Ancient Earthan designs that had appealed to her when she'd stitched . . . she'd
made it for the shop.

Fairyfoot grinned.

"Traitorous cat. I'm not paying for your collar."

He will pay for My collar.

Her Fam knew who her HeartMate was, even if she didn't.
Dufleur should have reasoned that out. "Go to him, then, and
don't come back."

Brain misty and with blurred eyes she stared at the Heart-
Gift. She remembered the filthy thing she'd thrown outside a
couple of nights before. She didn't see this pouch clearly, just a
rectangle of vivid red, but she remembered the septhours she'd
spent on the pattern. The care she'd taken with each stitch, using her Flair to create a piece she was proud of. She swallowed.
She couldn't fling this outside.

She couldn't think. Especially with whatever was in the
pouch emanating waves of sexuality that had her skin warming,
her thighs loosening, her body preparing for a man.

Dragging heavy feet, she moved to a safe in the wall. There
she fumbled with the spell words, cleared her throat, and enun-
ciated them again. But she was flooded with a huge longing to

hold and be held, for a man's hands to trail down her sensitized skin . . .

The safe gaped open. Moving as quickly as she could, she scooped the pouch up.

Bad idea. The silkeen caressed her hands, the silk embroidery pattern pressed against her fingers.

And she felt him come up to stand behind her, his hard body against hers, jolting her. It had been years since she'd had physical sex, and the entire act had been less than what she now experienced; heavy passion laced her breathing, the raggedness of the man's behind her. The sense of being consumed by desire. Yearning so bad . . .

The touch of her fingers on the pouch sizzled fiery need through Saille. He reeled three steps to the couch, collapsed upon it, gloried in the thought that she held his HeartGift—that which emanated from his deepest self. The small gift he'd made with exquisite care during his third Passage, his soul calling to hers.

He felt her weariness in mind and body and spirit and longed to go to her. But he was wary of pushing his suit too quickly and too hard. Instead he closed his eyes and savored her touch. Sent a wave of compassion, respect toward her. Her surprise jolted through the silkeen of the bag she'd made. Penetrated to his HeartGift and then came to him in the connection between their two creations. His lips curved. She sensed him. He opened the link wide between them.

She snapped it.

Ten

Ufin!" He couldn't prevent the groan. He'd have fallen if he hadn't already been lying down. His mouth dry, he swallowed, but gained no relief. Opening his lashes, his eyes slowly focused, and he saw the bar across the room, the crystal brandy decanter. With an out-flung hand he ordered, "Drink!" The glass stopper lifted, teetered, fell to the bar, then the floor. Liquid poured from the carafe to a snifter, the snifter flew into his hand. Lifting his head, he drank a few mouthfuls, felt the punch of it—as hot as his continued desire, as hard as the pain of her rejection. Why did he think he liked the stuff?

But it cleared his head so he could tamp his emotions, the rejection, and think. She hadn't thrown it into the street this time, to lay in the cold and be kicked or scavenged and dropped somewhere else, to circulate through the whole damn city. It was still in her rooms, in some shielded receptacle.

Progress.

Paws on his ankle. He looked down. Cat walked up his leg, settled on his stomach, purring. *You have treated Me well. You may call me Myx.*

Progress, there, too. Scratching behind the cat's ears, he said, "ResidenceLibrary, please recite the HeartMate Laws regarding HeartGifts."

"The HeartMate must accept a HeartGift willingly and without knowing it is a HeartGift . . ." the Library started. The voice of the Library, as the Residence, was now male, rich and rolling with an archaic accent—the very first T'Willow? When Saille had moved in, the tones had been female, what he thought was his MotherDam's voice when she'd been younger. She'd been egotistic enough to have all the personas of the Residence speak in her voice. Saille grimaced. He couldn't imagine living here for a long time, completely surrounded by his MotherDam. When he'd requested that the ResidenceLibrary and Residence recall and speak in the last male voice they had in their memories, the rest of his relatives had been startled but pleased at the change. He noticed they *listened* more, now, as if they'd often disregarded the previous admonishments.

But the ResidenceLibrary had stopped, and Saille's mind had been wandering. *He* had not been listening. "Please repeat," he asked.

"The HeartMate must accept a HeartGift willingly and without knowing it is a HeartGift before the other can claim them as a HeartMate and HeartBond with them. The punishment for telling a person they are your HeartMate is that the offending party must always be chaperoned while in the presence of the HeartMate—"

"Stop. I don't intend to tell my HeartMate who I am." It wouldn't be necessary. She still had the HeartGift. Locked away, perhaps, but still with her.

"Let's explore this HeartGift acceptance business. How long must the HeartMate keep the HeartGift until it is considered accepted?"

There was a pause. "I do not fully understand the question. One presents the HeartGift, the mate accepts it or not. No other options are recorded in my memory."

"Ah. I see." Nothing about a HeartGift circling around the city. He shuddered at that image, what he'd done, but he'd had no choice. He wondered if his action had been unique, as Trif Winterberry's had been, forming a charmkey and going house to house.

"Residence?"

"Here," a slight change in the man's tones, as if he were younger.

"Connect me with the Ship *Nuada's Sword*, and Supreme-Judge Ailim Elder. I have a matter of law I wish to consult her about."

"It is nearing RetireBell."

"But not quite yet. Connect me."

The Residence seemed to sigh, and Saille smiled. His Mother-Dam's previous parameters had been far too stiff and formal to allow the essential entity of the Residence to reveal personal characteristics. He thought the Residence itself welcomed the change. And that made him feel good.

"Ailim Elder here," said a young woman.

To Saille's surprise, a wooden panel in the wall of his ResidenceDen slid aside, revealing a glassy screen that showed the

SupremeJudge. He jacknifed up, caught off guard, far too casual, lolling on a sofa.

Myx hissed and jumped off the couch, disappearing under it.

"Pardon me." Saille stood, straightened his clothes, and bowed toward the screen. "I'm not used to the screen." More used to scrybowls that formed an image in misty water droplets above the bowl.

She just smiled and nodded. "You have a question?"

"Yes, a consultation request, top gilt to be paid—"

"Call me Ailim and just ask, Saille." She rolled her eyes. "No payment, no favor for favor. Ask."

"Ah. The HeartMate Laws."

Her gaze sharpened. "Oh, something interesting, excellent."

He raked a hand through his hair. "I'd better explain from the beginning."

"Always a good thing," she said, then she disappeared as a little girl burbled in the background. Lifting her child up, she said, "Dani Eve, this is GreatLord Saille T'Willow."

"Greetyou!"

"And you," he said.

"Not someone new. See you every week."

"Almost," Saille said.

Ailim frowned. "I didn't know that."

"I visit my MotherDam," he said stiffly.

The judge's expression went impassive. "Yes. D'Willow." Her lips tightened. "I try to forget she's a guest of the Ship's."

Dani Eve waved both hands. "Later!"

"I'll see you later," Saille said.

The small girl kissed her mother and climbed down from Ailim's lap, and now the judge was smiling, even when she turned to him, eyebrows raised.

He cleared his throat. "When I assumed the title I found that my MotherDam had hidden my HeartMate from me—"

"That can be done?" Ailim's eyebrows dipped.

"Only by one with great Flair in matchmaking."

She nodded. "I'll check the laws. I think that should not be allowed."

He shrugged. "I want my HeartMate beside me." Too many things had been withheld for too long, and he wanted the life he'd imagined for so long all at once.

Ailim nodded again.

Bracing himself for her reaction, he said, "I'd suffered through my third Passage last year and connected with my woman, sensed she was here in Druida, made my HeartGift. Two months ago I sent it out with a minimal spellshield to circulate through the city—"

Her breath caught audibly, and her eyes widened, but that was all. Well, the lady was a judge, used to keeping her thoughts behind a mask. Yet she covered a little cough with her hand and met his gaze. "A risky business."

"Had to be done." His voice was harsher than he liked. He followed it with a charming smile.

Ailim tilted her head in thought. "A risky business." A corner of her mouth curved upward. "Difficult for you, I'd imagine, but more discreet than a charmkey."

"That never occurred to me."

"Just as well. I can't see a FirstFamily GreatLord walking the streets, searching for his HeartMate."

He glanced down at himself. He wore clothes of the finest materials, imbued with Flair to keep them clean, modify the cut if fashion changed in a small way. But when he'd come to town, he'd worn commoncloth, looked like the bumpkin he was. He had walked the streets of Druida with complete anonymity. "In any case, I sent my HeartGift out to draw my lady—or be drawn to her. She found it within a few days, then it was lost again."

"My sympathies."

"Recently—tonight—she found it again. She senses what it is, of course."

"Of course."

"But she *has* kept it. Locked away behind a shield, but kept it—"

"For the moment."

"Yes," he said.

"She may or may not send it wandering again after some thought."

Oh, the lady was a judge, all right. He ignored her last statement. "I would like to know how long she must keep it in her possession in order for it to be considered that she has legally 'accepted' it."

A small line creased between Ailim's brows. "I don't know the answer to this." She looked at him for several seconds, then continued slowly, "But I think the HeartMate laws must include some obscure clause to deal with the fact. They were crafted by the fifth generation after the founders, and the fifth generation did like their laws."

Saille read her narrowed gaze. "I don't intend to enforce the letter of the law."

The judge eased a little. "It would not be right, since it is not in common usage."

He'd heard some FirstFamilies say the judge was too merciful. He'd thought it was continued grumbling for the events regarding her husband five years ago. But it wasn't, it was her personal character. He didn't know if he liked that or not. Probably only when the mercy applied to him. "I do not expect to enforce the letter of the law," he repeated carefully.

"But you might use it to exert a certain . . . pressure." Ailim sighed. "It's what any man would do, let alone a GreatLord."

He managed a stiff nod.

"I will study the HeartMate laws thoroughly and get back to you on this matter."

Saille suddenly wondered if he'd made a mistake. If there were laws that clarified the rights he had as a HeartMate, there were bound to be other obscure laws that protected his woman. But he'd already set the SupremeJudge on her course, and she wouldn't be deflected by a "Never mind." So, instead, he said, "Thank you."

Once more she fixed her gaze on him, and he kept from shifting uneasily. It was a weapon, that gaze. He'd heard she was telempathic. Let her sense his emotions, his desire, his *need* for his woman, his lover, his HeartMate. He didn't care that she knew his blood coursed swiftly through his veins, that his palms damped when he thought of Dufleur and claiming her—by fair means. He'd had enough of his MotherDam's capricious injustice in his own life to be scrupulously fair.

Apparently he passed judicial scrutiny, for Ailim smiled. "May I ask who your HeartMate is?" She raised a hand. "Sheer curiosity."

"Dufleur Thyme."

Again his words sent expression to her face, surprise, sympathy. "Your MotherDam spent some time and energy vilifying her father's name."

Saille's jaw tightened. "I know that. Another of her schemes to keep Dufleur from me, I believe."

"I observed D'Willow in action. Very carefully stated rumors." Ailim lifted and dropped her shoulders. "Very nasty, but they didn't illegally harm D'Thyme and Dufleur. And the newssheets interviews could not be called libel, so there was no action to be taken."

"Just hurt her in immoral ways. Emotionally," Saille said flatly and stopped.

With an inclination of her head, Ailim said, "I should be able to study this matter and scry you with the information tomorrow night. Ship, end—"

"Wait, one moment."

"Yes?"

Saille stood straighter. "I am uncomfortable asking favors I don't return. I have been in your husband's, Ruis's, company quite often over the last few months." And he never got used to being with the Null who stripped his Flair from him. "Being what he is, you can't know whether you are HeartMates. If I give you a personal reading, I could determine this. I am T'Willow, my matchmaking Flair is strong, but it isn't the sole tool I have at my disposal for my craft."

Ailim was smiling again. "Ruis and I are very content in our marriage." Her cheeks pinkened, her fingertips touched her flat stomach. "In fact, we are expecting another child. This one I think will be Flaired."

"My congratulations."

"Thank you." Once more she stared at him, then her smile widened, and she said softly, "But I think this reading of yours, and any good results, would be a lovely gift from me to Ruis. Why don't I deliver the information personally tomorrow after evening bell?"

"Why don't you and your Family join mine for dinner?"

Her eyes widened. "A very generous offer. Do you coerce your relatives into breaking bread with two Nulls?"

Like his MotherDam would? But Saille shoved the thought away. "My relatives are predominantly women." As he was sure Ailim knew. "But I think they'd be avid with curiosity to meet you, your husband, and your daughter."

Chuckling, Ailim said, "It's done then, a dinner date between the Elders and the Willows. Ship, note the appointment."

"Yes, ResidenceLibrary—"

ResidenceLibrary said, "I have placed the dinner and

appointment on a calendar sphere, which the household will consult in the morning."

"Merry meet," said Ailim.

"And merry part," Saille replied.

"And merry meet again—tomorrow." The glass screen turned dark, and the panel covered it again.

He stood there, in the low glow of lamps shining on rich surfaces of wood, highlighting the jewel tones of the rugs and furniture. All this was his now. Slowly he turned to gather in his good fortune. The plants behind the wall of the conservatory— bespelled against condensation so an occupant, no, *he* could see into the glasshouse—glowed green with health and pretty flowers.

This was his.

He had proven himself T'Willow. Already was carving himself a place in the strata of the FirstFamilies culture. He wouldn't have thought to attend the social season if Dufleur hadn't been doing so, but it was another milieu where he could learn of the men and women of his own class.

A small click came, then his mother's voice from a different part of the house. "Saille, you're still working? We purchased D'Holly's latest composition, I think you'd like it. Shall I set it to play there?"

Clearing his throat, he said, "Yes."

Wafting strains of powerful music filled the air around him.

"It's lovely," he said, knowing his mother still listened.

"We all think so. I have noted the dinner with the Elders, and we are excited. We haven't entertained in ages. We'll do the Willow name proud."

"You already have."

Her breath sighed out. "Thank you. I'll tell the others you said so."

"Please."

"Well, we all have things to wrap up before morning," she ended briskly.

"Yes."

She hesitated, "Don't work too hard. You've had a full day."

"Thank you. I'm fine. I love you."

"I love you, too. We all do. Good evening."

"Good evening. Blessed be."

"Blessed be." Her voice vanished, and the music continued

to lilt. He was smiling. Fiercely. This was his life now. And he'd fight to keep it if his MotherDam ever revived.

Striding to the bookshelf, he took the last three large volumes of the journals and set them in a stack on his desk. Then he put his hand atop them, gathered his Flair and commanded, "You *will* open to me. I am *T'Willow*, and all the records and journals are mine to read and evaluate. *Dispel. Unlock. Open!*"

The books flew out from under his fingers, spread themselves on the desk—chronologically. Pages flipped open on the earliest to where his MotherDam had bespelled it shut. The covers of the other two opened.

"Thank you," he said, then felt a little silly addressing the books.

With a firm step, he circled the desk and sat, pulling the first book toward him, and began to read.

A few minutes later he shoved back from the desk and poured another, larger, drink. Gulped it down. Sat again.

He stared at the words in the Family business journal. Bright red, they seemed to blur and move upon the page, though he knew it was his eyes and the horror that coated his stomach like the cold sweat on his body.

Eleven

*S*aille's gut clenched. The last decade of her life, his
MothcrDam's Flair had been erratic. The last few years it had
been gone—he didn't know why, only that if he wanted to learn
the reason he'd have to do a full day's ritual in the HouseHeart,
the core sentience of the Family Residence.

That wasn't what concerned him. He ran a shaking index finger down the list of the people she'd matched, saw the prices
she'd charged and *no* notes as to how the couple would suit. Not
like the beginning of her section, when she'd inherited the title at
seventeen. Those pages—and the pages of her predecessors—
held long notations about what divination tools were used in a
Reading, the ritual done, the results of the ritual, and the descrip-
tion of what the Reading determined about each person. Sometimes a holo was attached to the journal, showing aura patterns.

Just as he'd done with his own consultations—the few he'd
done in the country and those since he'd taken the title here in
Druida.

But in the last six years there was only the list with a few
words.

She should have retired ten years ago, when he'd been nineteen, but she couldn't bear the thought of a young *man* taking
her title and her status and her power, as she'd taken her
mother's, and banished her mother to the very estate he'd
grown up on. That had been in a brief, savage margin jotting.

He leaned back in the comfortchair, wiped his face with a
softleaf. Luckily her fees had been so great that she hadn't had
many clients. One free consultation to earn her yearly Noble-
Gilt, to the first person to present himself or herself at the Family Residence upon the New Year as was customary.

One client to earn her NobleGilt. It echoed in his mind. Her
Flair had been so very well respected. Two months ago at New
Year's, Saille had scheduled seventy free consultations over the
year to fulfill his duty for his yearly stipend from the Noble-
Council.

Cave of the Dark Goddess.

He took a swig of brithe brandy, but it didn't have the jolt to stir his thoughts. He could cross to the bar and get some whiskey, but his knees might just be too damn weak. She'd *matched* couples. He shuddered. Given marriages approvals though she had no idea whether the unions would be good or not.

Perhaps during her long lifetime, she'd have developed good observational skills, too? He could only hope. Their Family reputation was on the line. His gut burned. She could have destroyed the Family with her hubris.

With a groan, he looked at the page again. His jaw flexed as he noted the names. Somehow he'd have to meet these couples, see whether they were suited at all. What if there had been terrible mistakes?

Muttering prayers, he saw that all the names except two were outside the FirstFamilies who could so easily destroy their house—any house. The two were Tinne Holly and Genista Furze, who had married.

Just what he needed, to have the Hollys antagonistic toward him and his.

He had the Family to protect, not only their name and tradition, but his relatives, the innocent. Whom his MotherDam had betrayed.

Why had she been so foolish as to do a consultation with Holly and Furze? He found the reason two pages earlier.

Holm HollyHeir looked at me with a charming smile and impudence in his eyes. He withdrew his essence from my divination sticks—his Flair that had empowered them for a fine Reading. I found out later that when he'd done that, whatever was left of the echoes of Flair in the traditional sticks was gone, too. He impoverished me. If there is a way I can serve him ill, I will do so.

Saille's breath caught in his throat. His mind swam with dizzy realization. That was when his MotherDam had called him to Druida for a few weeks—after years of neglect. For *his* observations, particularly of the Hollys.

He recalled something more. *He'd* glimpsed residual traces of Tinne Holly's and Genista Furze's auras. Stretching his memory, he brought back the information.

The match had been acceptable for a dynastic marriage—two aspects of what was needed for a solid marriage had been fine—affection and sexual attraction. He'd sensed companionship, some shared interests, definitely a shared class. He would not have recommended the marriage for a regular client couple. But then, when a couple usually consulted with him, they considered themselves in love with each other. Not because they married for other reasons.

He deciphered one last item regarding the matter. *I requested the upstart imbue several sets of divination objects to "test" his Flair and skill. I don't know why he has my Flair, nor the strength, matching me in my prime. But I sent him away. Though his male Flair in the tools fit awkwardly in my hands, I will use them until their Flair is gone. Then I will use him again.*

Saille smiled bitterly. She'd used him, his Flair, taunted him the entire time he made his own sticks, and dice, and disks. But a tendril of relief shot out sprigs of hope. Perhaps all was not lost after all.

He'd have to meet the couples she'd matched, observe them, see how their marriages progressed. If there were problems, he'd have to steer them—somehow—into making their unions stronger.

Addressing the books, he said, "Show me any information on the Thymes."

Not a corner of a page stirred. So there was nothing in these journals. He only had the information Ailim Elder had given him. But he sensed that wasn't the whole story, not when it involved a bitter woman like his MotherDam who never wanted to relinquish a smidgeon of power, especially to him. She'd have written it down, or recorded it in a holosphere. She'd have hidden it from him, of course.

He'd have to find it.

She'd given orders for the MistrysSuite, the rooms belonging to the Head of the Family, to remain the same.

That would change. He'd have them cleaned—sterilized—and request any and all holospheres be given to him.

He was the master of this GreatHouse, this Residence, the Head of the Family.

By the Lady and Lord he'd protect it from *everything*.

One thing was for certain. He dared not visit his Mother-Dam in *Nuada's Sword* again.

If he did, he'd pull the plug on her.

Dufleur woke in the night, cramped, clothes binding, groggy. Something was different about her rooms. She checked the wind of time, it shifted and flowed in a different pattern, eddying around a spot.

The safe.

Memory rushed back. Fairyfoot had brought back the bright glowing object that was a HeartGift, and Dufleur had stashed it in a no-time safe. She heard the raggedness of her breath and realized the idea disturbed her on more than one emotional level.

First, it reminded her of when she'd found it two months ago. She placed her hand between her breasts over her heart. The surgery had left no scar, but just the thought of that time made her entire body go cold.

Before the new year, she'd found the object, and it had sent her Flair spiraling with pulses of lust, of only emotion, no thought at all. She'd been kidnapped, then she'd listened while murder was being done and been the subject of attempted murder herself, saved at the last minute by Fairyfoot calling her cuz Ilex. She shuddered. She hoped never to be so terrified again in her whole life. No wonder she didn't want to see it again.

Then there was the overwhelming sexual heat and passion that melted her insides and made her want to search down the man and pounce, roll wildly with him on a bedsponge. Or on a carpet. Or take him *anywhere*. Have him take her and pound into her again and again until the burning need was satisfied. Then start all over again.

Not rational, not controlled. She hadn't really thought about what a HeartMate might mean.

Someone who'd know her secrets. That was her first thought. She supposed if the man was a HeartMate he would love her, wouldn't he?

No, close that line of reason off, fast. She wanted to be loved too much. Didn't even know, exactly, what love was—not between a man and a woman. Sexual attraction, of course, but love? A couple of times she'd studied obvious Heart-Mates, and her chest would always constrict.

She wasn't even very sure what other sorts of love might feel like—reciprocal love—love *for* her. How she'd feel being an object of someone's love. Unknown territory. Scarier than time.

A HeartMate would know her secrets, the mind-emotion connection between them would reveal all.

That would be terrible. There was no one in the world she trusted to know she continued to experiment with time.

She didn't know love.

She didn't trust love.

She'd never trust a lover.

*T*he next day Dufleur spent with the Hollys, with her new gowns and jewels, determining several "looks." And practicing dancing.

Her partner was Holm Holly, recently reinstated as Holly-Heir, and quite intimidating. She got the idea that he wanted to spend time with and please his mother, so he danced with Dufleur.

He was the only one who didn't criticize, though Passiflora only offered gentle suggestions—both to Dufleur and to Trif Winterberry, who would be playing at the opening ball. All three of the FamCats watched the proceedings—Fairyfoot, Meserv, and Phyl. Their comments were vocal both audibly and mentally.

Because of her name, or because she was still irritated with Dufleur, Fairyfoot was especially smug and annoying. She "danced," too, weaving in and out of the line dance patterns, hopping and skipping and prancing as her inner muse directed. All three of the humans shared an eye-rolling glance when the cat had announced she would accompany Dufleur and Passiflora. The thought of the cat dodging fast feet seemed to concern the others as much as she, and Passiflora murmured something about human allergies. Fairyfoot countered, with a superior sniff, that Danith D'Ash had sent a spell to Dufleur that would envelop the cat. Seeing the wisps of cat hair floating gently around the Holly ballroom floor made Dufleur wonder how the spell was supposed to work. Holly Residence would have to clean the ballroom again before their own grand ball.

When Dufleur and Fairyfoot returned home, Dufleur exhausted, she entered her rooms to find a distasteful male odor.

"Residence, who has been here?"

The Residence didn't answer, and she sensed it was preoccupied elsewhere.

Dufleur looked down at Fairyfoot who'd wrinkled her nose and opened her mouth, curling her tongue in the extra sense cats had.

"My HeartMate?" she asked. Had he come to see if she still held his HeartGift?

No! Fairyfoot sounded indignant. *He smells *much* better, like good clay and green growingness.*

Hmmm. Dufleur relaxed a little. She should make more of an effort to return the gift, but Fairyfoot had refused to carry it back to the man. The small breeze of time still gathered around the safe and in a quantity that told Dufleur it had not been disturbed. Since she sensed the HeartGift even through the no-time vault's shields and its own small shielding, she was certain that the man might do so, too.

With slow steps she moved toward the safe, frowning as she realized she'd left its door translucent. Nothing else was in the safe, and the HeartGift glowed. A bit of knowledge came to the front of her mind. HeartGifts were naturally shielded during the creative process. Only the pair could easily see it, so to someone else the safe would look empty.

At that moment the secret door slid open, ordered by the Residence. *Intruder*, it whispered. *Sorry. Used new no-see-me spell.*

Dufleur's skin prickled. With a glance she saw her papyrus had been disturbed. She ran into the room, and the smell was stronger here; more, the wind of time that she'd gathered in the room was definitely tainted with some other presence. The molecules were agitated.

She took a deep breath and *shifted* into her Flair, into the wind of time that showed all things . . . if you knew how to look, as she was learning. She saw the dark, hulking form of a man shuffling through her papyrus, lifting them to read. She heard a rough chuckle. He turned, but she couldn't see his face.

Then the strain on her Flair became too much, and she let the past go, crumpling to the floor. Fairyfoot ran over to her, rubbed against her body. A small, rough tongue licked at her face.

Bad man. Bad, bad, bad.

Yes, I know. She rocked to her hands and knees. Much as she hated to do it, she used some of the Time Wind as energy and struggled to her feet.

Fairyfoot spat. *Nasty smell. Nasty taste. Nasty man.*

Dufleur pushed at her hair. "I know," and she knew who he'd been. Agave, her father's chief rival in time experimentation.

He continued to explore time illegally, too.

*D*inner with the 'Elders went surprisingly smoothly. Saille's relatives rose to the occasion and had engineered the whole meal to be served without Flair. There were odd bobbles and surprised expressions when someone instinctively used Flair as part of the conversation and it didn't work—which led to laughter. Saille had never been so proud of his Family.

Dani Eve was cooed over and praised and constantly surrounded by the Willow women, which led Saille to think more about his female relatives.

Ruis Elder had been stiff, but had also relaxed under the goodwill and ministrations of the ladies. Saille had been equally formal, since he'd never spoken with Ruis outside the Ship and the presence of his MotherDam, but he relaxed, too.

"Amazing," said Ruis in an undertone to Saille. "I'm rarely invited to a Residence, and I've never felt so welcomed." He eyed the ladies grouped around his wife and child and shook his head. "Your MotherDam trained them well to her needs."

"Yes. It occurs to me that I should do an in-depth consultation with each of them and see if they have HeartMates." Some of them were still of an age to have children. His MotherDam might have wanted to rule their lives and keep them single and childless to serve her, but he didn't.

"Ailim told me that your MotherDam had hidden your HeartMate from you." Ruis gestured to the women. "You think she might have done the same with them?"

"Perfectly possible. We all have matchmaking Flair. Even if they don't have HeartMates, together we can find them good, loving spouses."

"Which brings us back to the reason why Ailim and Dani Eve and I are here." Ruis sipped after-dinner caff. "You *can't* pick up any Flair from me to do your work."

Saille met his eyes. "No, but I can from Ailim. The fact that she never felt a HeartMate during her Passage is telling."

"Maybe it just means she doesn't have a HeartMate, and I'm just a husband."

Snorting, Saille said, "I've seen HeartMates less in love and loving than you two."

Ruis blinked, set down his cup. "You have?"

"Just because people are HeartMates doesn't mean they don't have difficulties in their marriage, differences of opinion, or argue." And he should remember that for himself, too. Just because he found his HeartMate didn't mean his wooing would go well. As if he had truly expected it to, though he had hoped. But his MotherDam had set more snares for him than he'd anticipated. No Thyme would like what she had done to their Family.

Saille pulled his mind back to the topic. He smiled. "But in the very beginning, when our ancestors had little Flair, they had other tools." He leaned closer. "They had *questionnaires*."

"Questionnaires?"

"Lists of questions about topics for matchmaking. I'll settle you in a nice corner of the conservatory, and you can start answering them while I consult with your lady."

Narrowing his eyes, Ruis said, "You sound too cheerful. What's the catch?"

"Well, there's only fifty pages of questions."

Ruis stared. "Fifty pages."

"That's right. I, of course, will be able to use my Flair with your wife and do the consultation in an hour or two. You can send your questionnaire to me when you're done."

"Huh," Ruis grumbled, then his gaze sharpened. "What of my daughter? Will you be able to match her when the time comes?"

"If I am still T'Willow, I will do my best."

"I don't understand."

"My MotherDam fully believes the Healers will find a cure for her disease and she will leave that cryonics tube. When she does that, she will endeavor to retreive all the power she was forced to abdicate."

Ruis grunted. "I wouldn't want her trying to match my baby." His lip curled. "She has no use for us Nulls, and I don't forget that she voted to have me executed." He glanced at Saille.

"You've already smoothed a bump in my relationship with my wife."

"What?"

"I thought Ailim had let her Flair and innate tenderness guide her decision and accept D'Willow as a guest in the cryonics tube. She thought I had taken the contract and disapproved. There were hard feelings between us until we sorted the matter out, and your call made us do that." His jaw flexed. "It was the Ship who'd negotiated the contract with D'Willow. The Ship is fascinated with learning and knowledge. I've had a discussion with *Nuada's Sword*. It will *never* deal with my enemies again without telling me. I rule my own realm."

Saille had no doubt about that.

"Meanwhile, we must honor the agreement."

Throat dry, Saille said, "Of course."

Saille's mother rose, signaling the meal was over. Saille and Ruis stood, too. Ruis said, "Show me this questionnaire, and I'll get started while you consult with my lady. I think my daughter will have five women for playmates, and that will suit her just fine." He clapped a hand on Saille's shoulder. "Should your MotherDam be released during your lifetime, remember that the FirstFamilies can be fought, and overcome. And I think you'll have plenty of allies on your side."

But Saille would never take a Family matter to outsiders. He'd never force his ladies to choose sides in Family civil war. He'd never fracture the Family. He cared too much for it, and for his relatives, to do that.

An hour and a half later, his consultation with Ailim Elder was done. It had been unexpectedly easy, and Saille didn't know whether it was that she already loved and had married her mate, her exceptional telempathic Flair, or that she was a First-Family Noblewoman. He'd have to make detailed notes so he could figure this out later as his career progressed.

Saille toyed with a writestick. "My conclusions are exactly what you found for yourself. You need a man who will allow your great telempathic Flair to rest. Had you not already been wed, I'd have looked for a Nobleman of the highest status and sensitivity, but with little Flair, to match with you."

She blinked. "Thank you."

"You are a very beautiful woman, inside and out," Saille

said. He'd rarely met anyone so innately ethical. "Captain Elder is lucky to have you."

Her face flushed from the reading and his compliments, Ailim said, "My thanks again." She gazed in the direction of the conservatory. "Though I can't read their thoughts, I can determine where they are by a . . . blankness."

"Everyone makes adjustments in marriage," Saille said. It was one of the standard phrases of his profession that he now used automatically.

Ailim straightened and, with the shift in her posture, became a judge again, authority. "Yes. Those who don't leave and break the marriage."

"There is no divorce on Celta." The very notion offended him, since his whole Flair was geared to bring people together in marriage and mating.

A corner of her mouth lifted. "It's rare, but I've seen perhaps three in my career."

Twelve

Saille frowned at *Ailim Elder's words.* "I thought the Councils had to approve a divorce."

"Here in Druida, certainly, and for anyone of higher status than Commoner, the Noble Council must be petitioned, or three FirstFamily Lords or Ladies must approve the action. But in far-flung towns and fishing villages—I was a circuit judge, you know."

"No, I didn't."

"I *do* think that we Celtans try harder to marry the right person, and work harder at our marriages than the old Earthans."

"After four hundred years, our birthrate is still low, our survival on this planet still in question," Saille said.

She tilted her head in consideration. "You with your Flair could be helpful to the circuit judges faced with divorce. The cases I heard invariably included a third person one of the parties wanted to bond with."

"Sounds interesting."

"Good. I'll inform the judges. You can travel with the Healer assigned to the case. We always call a Healer from Druida for the deep emotional, mental, and spiritual testing. A minimum of four days." She grimaced. "An expensive business."

"I would waive my fee," he said.

Her eyes widened. "Very generous." A thought flashed over her face. "Though I'd imagine when word hit a town that the great T'Willow would be coming, you'd have more business than you'd know what to do with."

Saille blinked. "I hadn't thought of that, but you're right. And since I'm new to the title, my rates are relatively inexpensive."

"Your MotherDam would never have done this."

"My MotherDam's Flair made great demands. She is a heavy woman and didn't often leave our home." It was hard saying pleasant words about a woman so selfish and proud she'd ruin her Family.

Ailim tilted her head, but only said, "You are kind."

He returned to the previous subject, figuring out how a country divorce would work. "The Healer would conduct the seven tests each person must endure to ensure that the marriage is truly broken, as well as weigh their Flair," he said.

"Do you check the seven points on each person of a couple to see if they meld and match?" Ailim asked curiously.

"It is a good preliminary indication," he replied.

"Ah, you have secrets of your trade," she said.

"Doesn't everyone? Besides that, I can't always describe the way my Flair works, every person is unique, therefore I tailor my consultations to each. Some 'tests' or observations are more revealing than others during my interviews. Sometimes I hear sounds, or see auras. I work with different tools." He shrugged. "It depends on the person."

Ailim nodded, then reached into the arm of her dress to the long sleeve pocket and pulled out a sheaf of papyrus. "This consultation has been fascinating." She smiled. "All the more so since whatever you determine, I know I am with a man I love and who returns my love. But I copied down the appropriate HeartMate laws for you." Her forehead creased. "They are not totally specific. If the HeartMate does not accept the HeartGift outright, she or he must keep it in their possession for a 'reasonable' length of time."

Saille's own heart began to beat harder. "What would you, as SupremeJudge, consider a 'reasonable' period of time?" He hoped it was three days.

"I've given the matter some thought and believe any judge or reasonable person on Celta would think that two eightdays would be eminently reasonable."

His triumphant mood deflated. He tapped his fingertips together. "I see." It would be difficult to wait that long to confront Dufleur. Actually, it would be difficult for him to wait until morning. He had to regain control over his baser self, which wanted to scoop her up from that cold and forbidding Residence Fairyfoot had told him of and bring her here into the light and comfort of his Family. "Two eightdays." He looked at Ailim Elder. Yes, she was softhearted, more liberal than most. He suppressed a sigh and stood, without looking at the papyrus she'd set on his desk. "Thank you for your expertise."

She rose, too. "You're very welcome." She hesitated. "I heard Ruis ask if you'd match our daughter. Will you?"

"Of course, if you wish. I will do my best when she comes to age." He crossed to the ResidenceDen door and held it open for her, then they walked down the corridor to the entry hall. "As I told your husband, if my MotherDam is revived, she will once again claim the title and power. I might have little choice in the matter."

Her face subtly hardened. "There have been a couple of cases lately regarding the proper Head of Household of a Family; Straif Blackthorn, for one, and now the former Winterberry Heir has filed an action of neglect." She slanted him a look. "You'd be interested in that."

"Yes." A sudden chill had taken him. "Has Dufleur Thyme been named as a party?"

"No. But it can't be a pleasant situation for her." She hesitated. "Nevertheless, I am pleased you will take your time wooing her."

"Yes," he forced out.

"So, if your MotherDam is revived, there will be some recent precedent." Lips turning down, she said, "Something I little speak of is that when I succeeded to Head of Household of the D'SilverFir Family I had to fight internal factions to keep my place. I know the fear of splintering a Family."

"I won't allow that to happen," he said roughly.

She set a hand on his shoulder. "Your Family obviously appreciates you as Head. That is a great benefit."

He straightened his shoulders. "I still won't have infighting."

Raising her eyebrows, Ailim dropped her hand. "Then we'll see what the law might do to protect you. Your MotherDam hid your HeartMate from you, and others of her Family. That's an abuse of Flair."

"Don't—"

All stern judge now, she said, "I will do what must be done to protect the innocent and bring them justice." She swept ahead of him, and as she drew closer to the knot of Willows around her husband and child, her manner once again altered. When she reached her husband, she kissed him on the jaw. "Greetyou, HeartMate," she said.

The Willow women beamed. Ruis Elder swallowed hard.

A glow of satisfaction warmed Saille at the little scene, but only lasted until the door closed behind their guests. Inadvertently he'd set events in motion. He had been as negligent and not nearly as discreet as his MotherDam. If the Nobles learned his MotherDam had charged extortionate consulting fees and had had no Flair to substantiate matches, the Family would be ruined.

*T*wo *nights later, Dufleur sat in her dark bedroom, smooth-*ing her gown—petting it—feeling the change of the pattern's texture from the heat of her fingers, or the small molecules of time that tended to cling to her.

She'd be leaving for her first ball in a few minutes, and she was close to petrified—when she should be concerned about far greater issues.

Such as Agave reading her notes. She'd spent the next septhour transcribing her work to her last, expensive, memory-sphere and setting a spellshield on it that no one could access except her. That wouldn't stop Agave from taking or destroy-ing it.

The disturbing taint he'd left in the air had required her to do a full cleansing ritual in the lab, and she found it had once been used as a ritual room. The energy of the Residence had been boosted, even as her own had drained.

Agave was a real threat. He'd looked over her notes, exam-ined her equipment. Now he knew her progress and her failures. She'd felt his contempt and a lingering malice.

He'd continue to be a threat in many ways. She'd have to watch her step.

Nothing was going right with her work. Sometimes fear gripped her and she lived through it, sometimes she was opti-mistic. Too many changes and emotions.

But she wanted to work instead of messing around with so-cial obligations—and that was ungrateful. Passiflora had changed her life forever for the better; the least Dufleur could do was provide a screen for Holly politicking.

Which led her back to the upcoming ball.

Since it was mid-Alder and their Family color was crimson, Passiflora had informed Dufleur that most people would be wearing a touch of that color for this opening ball of the social season.

Crimson didn't go with her coloring. It held blue tones, and Dufleur looked much better in red tones that held orange like scarlet. She snorted. Fussing about colors! But she knew the importance of making a good impression. So she'd bespelled her gown to a sheen of old gold and activated the wide embroidery around the hem to be crimson.

All dressed up. Her hair done by the spell the hairdresser had given her, along with her cosmetics. Color and shading to accent her eyes and slick over her mouth. The hairdresser had told her that she had lovely eyes and a charming smile. Right now, she didn't believe him. Anything he'd said.

She didn't believe anything Passiflora or Holm Holly said about her dancing, either; she still felt as clumsy as ever. She had a spell for that, too, but all the steps blurred in her head, the line dances both modern and antique, even the ancient waltz.

This was going to be a disaster.

Fairyfoot had gone back to T'Ash's to give a final mousing lesson.

After bolstering the front door with security spells, Dufleur had gotten ready. Too early, of course. She wanted to ensure her dress and jewels and hair and face were perfect. Biting her lip, she wondered if she should move through time just slightly, a few more minutes, no more than a septhour. In a quiet room where she anticipated nothing would happen, it wouldn't take much Flair, and would disrupt no other lives.

But who knew what she might need her Flair for later? Like teleporting to the secret room to hide. She called up the dimensions of her lab, the coordinates. Yes. A perfect sanctuary for escape.

She didn't recall ever being so nervous.

She *had* wondered if her mother would come down and check on her, wish her well in this enterprise that was all her and D'Winterberry's idea, but there had been no knock.

Softly, gently reaching out with her mind, she brushed her mother's mind. Sleeping. Her mother had gone to bed. Even in her dreams, Dufleur could sense her mother's doubt that Dufleur was capable of making a good match. A stray hope, but no real conviction. Worry about the upcoming examination on her fitness as WinterberryHeir. Worry that she might not be admitted to the Winterberry HouseHeart.

Dufleur withdrew her senses from her mother's mind, came back to the present reality of sitting on a hard chair in her bedroom. Waiting. Fulfilling others' needs—her mother's and D'Winterberry's, and D'Holly's.

Not her own.

But she couldn't truly categorize her current needs. They seemed amorphous. Her thoughts went to the HeartGift, flinched away from the idea of a lover and a mate. The only thing she knew she wanted was the peace and quiet and space and permission to work with time.

Biting her lip, she thought of the goal of her experimentation. To build a reverse-time vault that would not only stop time from passing, but turn it back, particularly reversing disease. That had been her father's goal. He'd fai—He hadn't been able to finish his experiments, to meet his goal, though she thought he'd been several steps ahead of what she was doing now. There shouldn't have been an explosion of such magnitude that it destroyed their home. Perhaps if she looked at the papers one more time . . .

She stood, and the loud knock on the front door that echoed through the house jolted her from her hypotheses back into reality. Where she was about to make a fool of herself.

No. She drew in a big breath, stood straight, lifted her chin. She would surprise everyone.

"Coming," she called, projecting her voice so the Holly footman she sensed outside the front door heard.

With a twirl, her new evening cloak settled warmly around her. She stepped through the door of her bedroom, climbed the stairs, and exited the Winterberry Residence into the winter night and to Passiflora's waiting glider.

*Y*ou look gorgeous." *Saille's mother straightened his wide* collar where it had gotten caught in the shoulder of his new crimson embroidered vest. "You are the equal of any GreatLord there. Remember that."

He stepped back and swept her a bow. "Thank you, madam. I will." He hesitated. "Did you tell the rest of our Family that I'd be pleased to do consultations for them?"

She looked aside. Her hand went to the folds of her long tunic, and he saw how she pleated the fabric. "Some of the Family have added their names to your schedule."

"And you?"

Shades of old pain drifted in her eyes. "My HeartMate's been gone to the Southern continent as long as I can recall. We connected, but he never searched for me." Her lips trembled as she met Saille's gaze and touched his cheek. "I cared for your father. You must believe that."

His father had been an arranged marriage by his Mother-Dam for her daughter, weak in character and in Flair, and weak physically, dying when Saille was an infant. But his father had brought much gilt and several estates into the marriage as the last of a GraceLord line.

Saille caught his mother's hand. "You can go after him. I'll hire a retinue for you."

"Me! Travel rough throughout Celta." She shook her head.

"Then I can send a message to him. Call him here."

She lifted her chin. "We never even met."

"He's your HeartMate."

She just raised her eyebrows. "The link is so small that I rarely feel it. He's had his life, I mine. Leave it be, Saille. Concentrate on your future." She tilted her head, placed her hand against his cheek again. "You have new problems. Will you tell me?"

He hesitated, but said nothing.

She sighed, stepped back. "Go enjoy yourself. Don't work too hard at the politicking. We do not need as many alliances as you think." She smiled. "No one wants to alienate a Family who can lead to marital bliss."

He just grunted as he donned his evening cape.

"Blessed be," she called as he left the room.

*D*ufleur *had never felt so awkward in her life. She,* Passiflora, *and Trif Winterberry had arrived early for the ball, so Trif could consult with the orchestra hired for the occasion. Now Dufleur tried to stand nonchalantly as other women claimed territory around her and Passiflora D'Holly. In the pit of her stomach, Dufleur was sure that there was some maneuvering and placement was key, but she didn't discern a pattern. The failure made her shift, and that caused her gown to caress her skin with a softness she'd rarely known—unless she'd been embroidering such material. She loved the gown, and now one of the glowing light designs bespelled was the correct shade of crimson.

She sipped small relieved breaths that she was neither the oldest nor the youngest member of a Family to be introduced this season. Still, she did notice that she held her body more stiffly than almost everyone else. The dancing lessons she'd had at T'Holly's hadn't cured her of that, though she was reasonably sure that she wouldn't be stepping on anyone's toes.

Her gaze slid to some of the men. They were fully as colorful as the women, though she noticed that earth tones were fashionable for them, particularly a rusty fox red. Bloused sleeves and trous legs were even more extravagant for the men than in regular day wear, and instead of knee-high boots, most noblemen wore ankle boots—including a dagger sheath and weapon.

"There are a lot of weapons in this room," she muttered to herself. Even some women wore jeweled sword or blaser belts. Dufleur considered herself a thinker, not a fighter. Nothing in all of Celtan society emphasized their ancient Earthan roots more than all those weapons.

"The weapons are mostly those made by T'Ash, another luxury decorative object to flaunt," Passiflora D'Holly said.

"I know T'Ash better now, and I'm quite sure that he doesn't craft mediocre weapons."

Passiflora gave a little sigh. "Very true." She watched the crowd gather, new arrivals enter the chamber, and Dufleur thought she shivered with delight.

How wonderful. Dufleur would much rather be back in her lab. But this was business for her—business and pleasure for Passiflora, but just plain business for Dufleur.

That was her last simple thought, as women surged toward them, greeting Passiflora and being introduced to Dufleur. Great excitement seemed to emanate from everyone, and only a couple of people "felt" malicious. More relief. She didn't think she had the skills to deal with mean people. She only hoped she could watch those more sophisticated than she so she could pick up some tips. Or maybe Passiflora's grace and charm would rub off. Dufleur suppressed a not-so-ladylike snort at that notion.

"Smile," Passiflora said, with a whisking of her eyelashes and a charming, amused curve of her lips that Dufleur knew she'd never be able to master. She grinned.

Passiflora blinked. "I've never seen such a . . . grim . . . smile."

With a burst of honesty, Dufleur said, "I'm being tortured here."

Rippling, lovely laughter escaped Passiflora, drawing many gazes to them. Dufleur cringed inwardly.

Then the lady patted Dufleur on the shoulder, her gesture at odds with her coolly lifted eyebrow. "All you must do tonight is enjoy yourself like your Fam is doing."

Dufleur repressed a shudder at Passiflora's words. If she wanted to enjoy herself, she'd be alone in her laboratory. Fairyfoot was currently inspecting the musicians and touching noses with Trif Winterberry's kitten, who sat upright in a basket.

Old GreatLady D'Alder had stared in disbelief at Fairyfoot, when the cat had insisted on an introduction in the receiving line, then used her as an excuse to retire. AlderHeir, her equally old sister, started, blinked, but her HeartMate had bent down and stroked Dufleur's Fam. AlderHeir just shook her head and waved the animal on, then stepped aside to a companion to mutter about antiallergy spells on the ballroom and dining room. She didn't seem to think the one Dufleur had bespelled Fairyfoot with would be enough.

"Truly, Dufleur," Passiflora said. "Converse a little, dance a lot. Listen to the music. I promise you, it won't be difficult. Here's Holm now to be your first partner."

Holm greeted his mother with a bow and a kiss on both her hands. "Darling Mamá." He winked at Dufleur, bowed with a bit more flourish as if singling her out. "May I have this dance?"

"Please," she choked out.

"My pleasure." He put her hand on his arm, looked around the room, and heaved a sigh. "The first ball of the social season and already I am taken for granted as HollyHeir again and old news."

His mother tensed beside him. "Thank you for making the rounds with your father and me to the New Year's parties."

Lowering his voice, he said, "Mamá, it was Lark's and my pleasure. I adore you. I love my father. Lark likes you both."

Horribly uncomfortable at overhearing this, Dufleur studied the guests coming in. Saille T'Willow finished his greeting to the hostess, stepped away from the receiving line, and met her eyes with an intense blue gaze. She found herself staring at him, his broad shoulders in the midnight blue coat, the bloused trous that could not entirely conceal the muscularity of his thighs. He looked different. Polished. Sophisticated. Out of her league.

She wrenched her stare away from him, looked toward the small stage set for the musicians. They stood or sat, watching the line of guests diminish. Trif Winterberry glanced uncertainly at Passiflora, as if she wasn't sure when to strike up the first dance.

But Passiflora continued to focus on Holm. He was saying, "Lark will be here later, I have her word."

"Tinne?" Passiflora asked.

"He'll be here, and Father will arrive a few minutes after dinner to take you ladies home, as we strategized," Holm soothed.

"Genista?" Passiflora said in a small voice.

Dufleur glanced at her. She'd never heard Passiflora so uncertain.

Holm closed his eyes, gave the tiniest shake of his head. "She didn't change her mind."

"Trif Winterberry needs your advice, Passiflora," Dufleur blurted, thinking she couldn't bear seeing the loving Hollys hurt.

Passiflora drew in a breath, relaxed, smiled with charm that even made it to her eyes. She glanced at Trif, then at the receiving line and the hostess, and lifted two fingers.

With a single note of her Flaired silver flute, Trif Winterberry alerted the guests that the dancing was starting. Six beats later she initiated a slow waltz.

The hostess and host, AlderHeir and her HeartMate, swept out onto the floor. They were the oldest of the FirstFamiles, and both seemed slightly frail, but as he whirled her onto the floor and she looked into his eyes, the HeartBond love they shared filled the room.

The waltz ended after a single playing of the melody, and the Alders stopped at one end of the floor. "We are pleased to announce that Passiflora D'Holly has graced us with a new Grand March. Let the social season begin!" AlderHeir declared, with a look at Trif Winterberry.

All the instruments sounded together in the first notes of the stately dance. Dufleur clutched Holm's arm. He patted her hand. "Easy, we all start dancing at the end of the first refrain."

Quert Apple, Passiflora's brother, owner of the Enlli Gallery, smiled at Dufleur and offered his sister his arm. Dufleur figured the Apple Family was completely involved in Passiflora's plan, too.

Couples moved to stand in the opening lines. Dufleur observed that they were all arranged according to rank. She sent a discreet glance around the room and saw that not all danced. Saille T'Willow had collected several people around him, including some young women, and was deep in conversation. That shouldn't have bothered Dufleur, but it did.

"Ready?" Holm asked, taking her hand.

Ready, said Fairyfoot, joining them and standing to the outside of Dufleur, whiskers twitching in pleasure.

"Trust me, your partner," Holm said.

Dufleur did a quick count of the couples in her head, recalled the pattern of the dance. "I won't always be with you."

He glanced to the head of the line and calculated. More by experience than arithmetic, Dufleur thought. His eyebrows raised. "Fast figuring." He squeezed her hand. "Then follow the lady two in front of you."

Fairyfoot lifted her nose. *Follow me.*

Dufleur smiled with gritted teeth. The Alders began the march. "Ready," she muttered.

Thirteen

$\mathcal{A}$s two septhours wore on and Dufleur continued to dance, she loosened up, and the situation turned out not to be as bad as she had feared. Young Laev Hawthorn, nearly sixteen, had spread the word to the teenage boys who'd been forced to attend that Dufleur Thyme was easy to dance with, because she laughed at her own mistakes and didn't laugh at theirs. So, she was popular with the youngest set, as teenaged girls gathered around her to meet the boys.

She'd just finished a fast reel with Antenn Blackthorn, when the musicians announced that the next dance would be a waltz. The boys streamed in a pack toward the snack table, even though this was the last dance before dinner. The Fams followed, sure of tidbits.

And Saille T'Willow, still cool and elegant to her flushed and perspiring, appeared before her.

Her nerves jolted. She took a step back and ran into the wall. He'd made her nervous before, with his attention, his presence in Dandelion Silk, but now she didn't know if she could even face him. There was a subtle air of power around him. He was a GreatLord, she should not ever have forgotten that, despite his previously casual manner and clothes.

"May I have this dance?" he asked.

Covertly, she scanned the room. She was far from Passiflora, who was flirting with T'Oak. Holm Holly's HeartMate, Lark, had just arrived and been claimed by him.

Dufleur swallowed, risked a glance at T'Willow. His lips smiled, but his eyes were all too serious. Which made her even more nervous.

"Yes," she said.

He held out his hand, and she placed her fingers in his and got the shock of her life.

He was her HeartMate!

She'd touched the HeartGift long enough to now recognize him. A small gasp escaped her.

One corner of his mouth quirked upward, as he spun her into the midst of other colorful couples. She couldn't let go of his hand, and with his other palm pressed against her waist, she felt the burn of his heat through the fabric to her skin.

While she still struggled with the emotions streaming between them, his deep satisfaction, her shock, bouncing back and forth, reverberating, as strong and potent as the winds of time, he whirled her around.

He moved fast, expertly. And she kept up with no misstep. There was no hesitation here, no worry that she'd make a fool of herself.

Her body followed his naturally.

All previous anxiety was crowded out by the sheer *feel* of him, his body powerful beneath her hands, his mind brushing hers. The vastness of his feelings for her, known and accepted by him, kept her mind off balance.

She could barely deal with this new realization.

"The HeartGift," she gasped.

His eyes met hers. "My MotherDam hid you from me. I sent my HeartGift out into the world for you to find. Anything she could do to hurt your Family and keep you from me, she did. She did not like the idea that I would succeed her in her power, her Flair, her position."

Too many lines of inquiry pushed at her mind.

He was her HeartMate.

He'd circulated a barely shielded HeartGift around Druida to find her!

She was the reason D'Willow had ruined the Thyme name.

Too much. She narrowed the link between them that seemed as wide and as rushing as a river to a mere strand.

His breath sighed out, but he didn't widen the connection.

Her wits settled a little, even as her body became most sensually aware of him. Heat flooded her as she recalled the times they'd connected in dreams and had loved. Now he was holding her, and she knew the touch of his hands, the scent of his skin. A few centimeters from her fingers on his shoulder was the thickness of his dark brown hair, waving under his earlobe.

In shared dreams she'd caressed his hair, his body, moved with him on a bedsponge.

Now she danced with him in reality.

"Dufleur," he murmured, and it went through her—the sound

of his voice in her dreams merging with echoes of the way he'd said it now and then when they'd met, resounding through time and space. Through her blood to her bone. To her soul.

When she shivered, he brought her even closer, caught.

"Not caught," he said, and she sensed the willpower it took him to loosen his grip. "Found."

The music began to slow.

"All too soon," he said. The last note sounded, and he took her to Passiflora's side.

Still dazed, senses overwhelmed by him, she thought she was still spinning. She stood in the circle of his arms a moment, sent a thought to him. *I do not think I could dance with you again tonight.*

His eyes narrowed. His mouth set.

She stepped away from him. *Please, let me consider the ramifications of this.* "Thank you," she said aloud.

"My pleasure." He made a punctilious bow, lifted one of her limp hands, and kissed it. "I'll call tomorrow."

Before she could deny him, he moved away and was immediately snagged by a GraceLady who said, "Can I discuss a delicate matter with you over dinner, T'Willow?"

After an instant's hesitation, he nodded and let the woman grasp his arm to lead him into dinner. He'd be seated near the head of the table with the other Heads of Households.

He was doing a good business here. That might have been the reason he came, Dufleur told herself halfheartedly. But she knew it wasn't. The thread that spun between them was strong. From only a dance. She didn't know how to act. What to think. How to marshal her emotions.

Tinne Holly coughed. She blinked up at him. He offered his arm. "I'm your dinner partner tonight."

That was right. His wife hadn't come to the ball, but he was here to support Passiflora. Dufleur cleared her throat, concentrated on the moment. "Thank you."

He smiled, but sadness lurked in his eyes. "My pleasure."

A lot of men had said that to her tonight. Only one had meant it sexually.

D*ufleur picked at the lavish display of food, as course after* course was set before her. Seated between a brooding Tinne and another second son—one of her teenaged partners focused on eating—her brain worried at the revelation of her Heart-Mate.

Saille T'Willow. She didn't even like to think of his name, the same as his MotherDam's. Her throat closed, and she waved away a dish of fowl.

Saille *D'Willow* had ruined her and her mother's lives. Focused a bright light on them in the depth of their grief. Coping with her father's death, the destruction of their Residence, their poverty and homelessness had been a thousand times worse when almost everyone they'd dealt with sneered at and ridiculed them.

D'Willow had seemed gleeful in her malice. Dufleur and Dringal and the ruins of their Residence had been on the front page of the newssheets for two solid eightdays.

With fast talking, Dufleur had been able to convince D'Dandelion to let them use a couple of small rooms above the shop where she'd been selling some embroidery. She'd promised to work in Dandelion Silk and accept commissions to embroider gowns.

The next day, Dringal had visited D'Winterberry and found them another home. Dringal, at least, had been pleased with the situation, especially since she'd immediately taken up the ordering of the household.

All a year and a half past. Dufleur still grieved. Sometimes her loss crashed down on her until all she could do was curl in on herself and wait for the pain to pass.

To her horror, tears stung the back of her eyes. She grabbed for her glass of wine.

Dear Dufleur, whispered Saille in her mind, sending her soothing compassion. She couldn't see him far up the table, and that made his touch even more intimate, like when they'd met in dreams to love.

Fairyfoot gently pricked her ankle, distracting Dufleur from indulging in her emotions. *He is a good man*, Fairyfoot said. *He has adopted a feral Cat, just as you did*, then, *A small piece of that furrabeast steak please.*

Dufleur gestured to a footman who served Fairyfoot as she ate beside her chair.

Now Dufleur thought back, the new T'Willow had first appeared in Dandelion Silk a few days after her attempted murder, requesting Dufleur embroider all his shirt cuffs with the bright green chain of willow leaves that indicated his title.

He'd attended the closed but vized FirstFamilies Council Sessions that judged those who'd attempted to murder her, had spoken in favor of death for the perpetrators. Had voted for death when most others had voted for banishment and incarceration on a deserted island. Because of her?

Ever since that time, he'd been in the store on a weekly basis, buying gifts for his many female relatives.

What would he expect from her?

Everything, she sensed.

The meal ended, and T'Holly arrived to take them home. Passiflora didn't want to press too hard this first ball. The Hollys had been seen, had socialized, that was sufficient.

A great weight seemed to roll off Dufleur's shoulders as she left the Alder Residence and hurried into the Holly glider.

She was free of burdens only for an instant, as she noticed the movement in the shadows, felt an inimical stare. Agave.

He watched, then he followed, disappearing only when the Holly footman opened the door of Winterberry Residence for her.

She couldn't sleep. Her eyelids felt heavy, her body weary from the unaccustomed exercise of dancing, but her mind nagged at the problems besetting her. The threat of Agave, her own fears about her work, the knowledge of her HeartMate and how he would want to change her entire life. Again.

What had he been thinking, sending his HeartGift out to circulate in the world? Wouldn't every time someone touched it have sizzled back to him through his link with it? Yech. How horrible. How difficult to endure. Yet he had. Why?

How could she convince him she didn't want a HeartMate? Didn't even want a husband or love.

Her body and her emotions called her a liar.

But her mind dismissed that. She had no idea how to relate to a HeartMate. She didn't think she could love or bond with a person, it wasn't in her.

Love was a great distraction, she knew, and she yearned to continue her work on time.

How would such a relationship, and him, affect her and the wind of time?

She bathed, dressed in her nightshirt, and shoved a complaining Fairyfoot from the middle of the bedsponge. Propping pillows behind her, arranging covers, Dufleur closed her eyes, summoned her Flair, and *stepped* into the gray landscape full of eddying wind that time ruled.

"Saille Willow," she whispered and two smudges of light appeared on the flat plane, in two different directions. One a small red glow, one a strong, sparkling rainbow of light.

Dufleur blinked. Ah, the not-quite-dead old D'Willow still faintly showed on the landscape. Still in the Ship, suffering from the disease Dufleur's father had been trying to reverse. One of the more simple but deadly viruses of Celta.

D'Willow had wanted to live and had been disappointed in Dufleur's father's experiments. That fact should have eased her disgust for the woman, but it didn't. Life cycled. Who was even a GreatLady to ignore that simple fact? Even now she burned as a red glow on the horizon, dying and nearly dead, sending out streaks of black-red and able to affect Dufleur and T'Willow.

Turning away from D'Willow, Dufleur moved toward her HeartMate, wanting to see how he looked here. From a distance he was impressive.

As she drew closer, she noticed he wore all white silkeen: shirt, trous, boots, and pondered what that signified. Purity of emotion? Of purpose? She didn't know, but a small thrill shivered through her. The color suited him.

For the first time she looked down at what she herself wore and gasped. A sheath of brilliant, glittering gold covered her, like ancient supple metal armor. Incredible.

Saille opened his eyes and looked at her. "Dufleur."

She just gaped.

He glanced around. "What is this place?"

She wasn't about to tell him it was the plane of the Wind of Time. "A construct of my Flair."

He nodded.

And she noticed something more. His garments flattened against him in the breeze, but his hair remained still. Here, he was not affected by time, no more than she was. He might even be able to manipulate time here, see into the future or the past, propel a wind in a specific direction to slow events or speed them up.

Setting his hands on his hips, he repeated, "A construct of your Flair. I wonder . . ." He swept his arm out in a wide gesture, and more people appeared on the plane.

Mouth flattening, he said, "The couples that my MotherDam matched in the last few years."

Dufleur wondered why that mattered, but now he'd populated the plane, she turned and noticed a few people, too. Some were together, some apart but looking at each other, several had turned their backs on each other.

None of them fared well here. They shivered or shrieked, they pummeled the air as if they could hold back time and age, they were flattened on the plane, holding on tight.

"Not good," Saille muttered, "but not as horrific as it could have been. My matchmaking divination tools must have helped some." He frowned. "I have a lot of work to do to persuade them to get emotional counseling." He looked up to find her watching him, and a smile curved his lips, but didn't reflect in his eyes. He waved a hand. "Note the HeartBonded ones. See how their auras merge, or consist of the same colors.".

Once he said it, she could see the glow of the individuals, or the couples. It was mildly interesting.

He was fascinating. Standing here, casually, unafraid. Using her Flair and this place to experiment with his own Flair.

But the fact that he was here led to all too solid conclusions.

He was her HeartMate, matched well with her.

If she tried to use the Wind of Time to push him away from her life, it would take great effort and Flair and likely damage them both.

He knew her too well already.

Still, she stood up straight and lifted her chin to inform him of a few points. "I do not think I am a good candidate for a HeartMate."

He stared at her, then laughed. "It is not something you apply for. Either you have a HeartMate or not." His face softened, he held out his hand and made to take a step forward, but couldn't.

Interesting. Her heart picked up beat.

His gaze sharpened. "What is this place?"

"T'Willow—"

"Saille." Now that she'd said his name, she realized how often she'd thought of him that way, since the first few times he'd visited Dandelion Silk. How telling that was, and how unobservant she'd been. "I'm not good with emotions. Definitely not good with love."

His expression sobered. "Then we have the absence of love in our lives in common. We lived as children in loveless homes. I've now been blessed with a Family who cares for me, reunited with my mother. I'm sorry you don't have the same."

His eyes fired. "But you will. From me, you'll have every shade of love. Affection, HeartMate love." His tone dropped. "Passionate desire."

She stepped back. "I wouldn't know what to do with all that. How to act." How to think with such distractions.

Stretching his hand, he said, "Please."

"I don't think I can," she said, and shifted back to the reality of lying in her bed, with Fairyfoot snoring beside her legs.

Still, his last words echoed. "I do think you can."

The strange plane vanished, but *Dufleur was still linked* with him. Saille waited until he was sure he could seduce her, then slipped into her dreams. Thinking of her had made him ready. His body hot and throbbing. Yearning. He placed his hand in the curve between her shoulder and her neck, brushing her cheek with his thumb—as he always preluded the lovemaking between them.

"Dufleur." He could finally say her name, hoped she would say his.

Suddenly she was out of bed and two paces from him, her face pale, her eyes wide and huge. Looking wary.

"I would never hurt you," he said.

Her expression didn't change. She sidled close to a bright blue energy field that rippled behind her. He sensed it was the plane, but she'd called him to it before, he hadn't gone on his own. She could escape, and he couldn't follow.

Fourteen

He kept a smile on his face, made no aggressive gestures.

What could he do that wouldn't make her slide into that otherness?

It occurred to him that his time with her had been like a dance—he approached, they touched, separated, she retreated. Watching her carefully, he made a formal bow. Held out his hand in a position to take the tips of her fingers in the most formal of the ancient dances. Much, much less than the dance of bodies in loving he wanted.

But his need to simply touch her raged. Hardly to be satisfied with the smallest grasp of fingers, but gaining her trust was uppermost. With slow, small steps he neared her. Inclined his torso in a half-bow. "Only a dance, Dufleur."

She tilted her head, eyes narrowed. And he knew that she, living with her parents, had been more isolated than he, banished to a country estate. There, he'd made friends, practiced his Flair among the countryfolk, become an excellent potter. He'd created a fairly contented life, even if he hadn't been able to fulfill his true potential.

Her parents hadn't loved or valued her, even as she strove to satisfy them. He saw that clearly in her aura of wariness. He forced his smile wider, sent her love in it. She stepped back.

"Simply a dance, Dufleur." He hummed a couple of bars of a pavane.

She snickered.

He winced, obviously his voice hadn't magically changed in this other place to become pleasing. He thought he was on key, she probably heard otherwise. But her fear had faded. His vulnerability had disarmed her? "You hum the dance, then."

Surprise flashed in her eyes. Had no one let her ever lead? She wetted her lips, and he nearly groaned, squashed his physical needs to the back of his mind. Earning her trust was more important. He kept that phrase at the forefront of his mind, chanted it to the beat of the dance he'd tried to vocalize.

Dufleur hummed the melody. Set her fingers in his.

A jolt of desire blazed through him. She glanced at him from the corners of her eyes, but when he only moved into the opening steps of the pattern, she relaxed and matched his steps. They sailed through the dance, experiencing their connection in this dreamtime much as they had a few hours before.

He wooed her with glances, touches, the warm steadiness of his hand. The last was her thought that came to him. What she liked most about him. The warm steadiness of his hand. He tucked the notion away to consider later.

Her body relaxed and became supple, responding to his even at arms' length. Her mind brushed against his, accepting the connection between them.

The dance ended. He bowed over her hand, dared to kiss it. Desire swamped him.

She withdrew from him, but her glance was less wary. "Thank you," she said, and vanished.

She'd known who he was and had enjoyed their time together. That was enough. For now.

Though he knew she'd retreat again the next time they met.

*D*ufleur woke with the buzz of an imminent headache and tears drying on her face.

Fairyfoot mewled about breakfast, so Dufleur overindulged the cat with a scrambled egg and watched the feline return to bed to curl up and snooze.

Dufleur's own breakfast was tense, as her mother whined about the estate examiners. And the fact that Dringal finally had gilt and was spending it on updating the Winterberry Residence spells. Dufleur only pointed out that as WinterberryHeir, Dringal had a responsibility to the Residence. Her mother retorted that she wouldn't be in that position if Dufleur's father hadn't blown up their own Residence.

And the headache came as Dufleur kept her jaw clamped shut to prevent angry words. She did, however, take a copy of the examiner's list of witnesses that had been addressed to her and opened by her mother. She looked at the names—Meyar and Ilex Winterberry, D'Winterberry and Dringal D'Thyme, and the Winterberry Residence itself were the main entities involved. With relief she noted that she had only a half-septhour slot and was listed with neighbors and other casual contacts and Tinne Holly who'd been adopted by D'Winterberry for a couple of weeks.

Two things were interesting about the form. There were no names under the "Clients" listing for D'Winterberry or D'Thyme. They couldn't be earning their NobleGilt—had they been collecting the annual income paid by the Noble Council for their services? That would be bad.

A special empath examiner would be admitted to the House-Heart, his memory later to be altered. Interesting.

Dufleur wanted to ignore the whole business, but even being on the outer edges of the situation, she couldn't do that.

What would happen to her mother if she was judged neglectful? The title of WinterberryHeir taken away? Would she and her mother have to find a new place to live? Meyar would probably let Dufleur stay in the Residence, but she probably would go wherever her mother did.

She'd let her subconscious fears rule her long enough, she *needed* to work. So she had to find another place, perhaps a small abandoned building near the docks. She shivered just thinking about the amount of winter traveling to and from such a location.

Her stomach tensed when she thought about what the Residence might reveal about her, so she did another cleansing ritual of her laboratory.

She hadn't begun to pack her equipment when she found a small old memory ball that she'd thought was blank. A paragraph of one of her reports caught at her and she sat to listen, pulling papyrus and writestick close to jot additional notes. She'd been planning on following in her father's footsteps, perhaps she should experiment with something very different.

It wouldn't hurt to do a few simple experiments, to feel herself in the Time Wind again. That would ease her fears, give her confidence. Her fingers flexed. She could re-create her first experiments, see where she'd change her hypotheses.

You are working in the hidden room! Fairyfoot covered the distance between the bedroom and her perch in the laboratory in several long bounds and sat upright on the velvet stand, turning big eyes toward Dufleur. Her purr rumbled. *Time to play with time.* She smirked. *I am very clever.*

Someone must have told her so lately. Too bad.

The next thing she knew, a tap came on her bedroom door, and Saille T'Willow called, "Dufleur? Your mother told me you were down here."

Fairyfoot jumped down, ran into the bedroom. *We are here!* she trilled. *Come in!*

He strolled in, a mass of fresh lilies in his arms, all colors.

Dufleur's mouth fell open. She could only think of her appearance. Her hair. *Her clothes.* She was dressed in one of her worn-out drab tunic and trous suits covered by her lab coat. Lady and Lord.

His lips curved as he took in the tumbled bed. "Restless night? Me, too."

Fairyfoot ran toward him, wound herself around his trous. He was dressed perfectly, stylishly. He looked incredibly male, and his aura blinded her senses.

"Good morning, Fairyfoot," he said.

She sniffed. *You have That Scruff Cat's hair on your trous.*

Saille lifted and dropped a shoulder. "He's my Fam. Adjust." He turned again to look at Dufleur. Gave a half-bow. "You're beautiful this morning."

She stared at him in horror. It must be after MidMorning Bell, the earliest time a social visit was acceptable. Her mother had admitted him. He was a FirstFamily GreatLord. One of the Twelve. Dufleur's mind scrambled.

With a flick of his fingers, a tall, exquisitely shaped porcelain vase of a deep blue green appeared on her writing desk in the bedroom. Filled with water. He put the lilies in the vase, stirred them around, and the bouquet appeared even more dazzling. Reds—scarlet—and yellows and oranges, coral, peach. All bright and cheerful when the day outside the windows lashed snow and ice.

"You're a Thyme," he said, gesturing to his floral gift. "You could keep these fresh forever with a syllable. What are you doing?"

Lord and Lady. Lady and Lord. Lord and Lady. Her *experiment*! She said a Word of Dismissal, but it wasn't enough, and a puff of black smoke appeared along with a trace of burnt pine she hoped was covered by the lilies' pungent fragrance.

Fairyfoot hopped behind Saille.

No use hiding her work. Try to be cool—when her body

warmed under his gaze—keep his eyes focused on her, not the scene behind her. She tried a weak smile. "As you can see, I'm not dressed for callers." She pushed at her hair, aimed a look at Fairyfoot.

Now he was frowning. "You don't have a suite. Not even a sitting room. Just a bedroom and a—"

Fairyfoot! Dufleur shouted mentally.

I will help. She placed herself in front of Saille again, put a paw on his boot, and looked up with an ingratiating smile. *Let's go upstairs to the Gray Sitting Room. There will be food.*

"Caff," Dufleur croaked. Twitched her lips in a smile again. What would Passiflora do in a situation like this? That thought sure didn't help. Passiflora wouldn't have been caught unawares, and Dufleur had no iota of Passiflora's style. She cleared her throat. "Please, wait for me in the Gray Room." Heat surged across her neck, up to her face, burned on her cheeks. "Thank you for the lovely flowers."

He watched her, sympathy lighting his eyes. "Since I'm discomfiting you, I'll go."

She sighed relief.

"To the Gray Sitting Room and wait for you there. How do you like your caff?"

"Um, milk and honey."

"Right." He scooped up Fairyfoot and cradled her in a broad forearm, unaffected by the fact she was leaving hair all over the wide sleeve of his fine blue jacket. His gaze went beyond her, to her lab, traveled down her dishevelment, and lingered on her lab coat. He nodded, and he wasn't smiling, now. "We'll talk. HeartMate." He closed the door gently behind him.

Oh, Lady and Lord.

Disaster.

*D*ufleur *entered the sitting room attired in one of her new* tunic-trous suits with the brocade tunic cut right at the knee and yards of shiny silkeen in the puffed trous gathered into cuffs at her ankles. The clothes were of her Family color of vibrant royal blue. She'd noticed that the cuffs of T'Willow's white shirt carried the bright green embroidery of his GreatHouse.

To her surprise, her mother was entertaining T'Willow and also dressed in new, very conservative, clothes. Dringal smiled and rose, excusing herself as Dufleur came in, sending her a direct look as if to tell her to do anything she could to keep this man happy. Including sex. Dufleur swallowed and nodded to her mother.

Dufleur stood, wordless, looking at anything but the man lounging on the dark green sofa. The room itself had been cleaned, the furniture polished, the walls freshly tinted a pale gray with a sheen of silver. Everything gave off a slight scent of minty lemon. The Residence was receiving a long-delayed sprucing up. Dufleur only hoped most of the funds she transferred to the bank account—and the gilt her mother got from Quert Apple for her tatting—went to helping the Residence and not to yar-duan.

With a wry smile, Saille straightened and made her a cup of caff, which her mother should have done, but hadn't. "I suppose you're thinking about everything except the fact that you're my HeartMate."

A shudder ran through her at his low voice and the words that she'd never be able to ignore. He held out a pretty, delicate china cup, decorated with tiny boughs of holly, and met her eyes. It was as if he was offering a great deal more. As if the cup represented his HeartGift that was residing in the no-time on the floor below.

She turned on her heel. "I'll get your HeartG—the . . . the object Fairyfoot brought in."

"Don't. Don't, Dufleur." His voice was quiet. "I'm not going to pressure you. In any way."

Cautious, she turned back to him.

His glance scanned the room. "You think I couldn't figure out what was going on? Why you're attending all the social events this year? Not because you want to. For D'Winterberry, D'Thyme, D'Holly, but not for Dufleur." He moved the hand cradling the cup. "I know what it's like to be ignored. Or pressured. You aren't going to get either reaction from me."

His hand remained steady, more, there was something in the way he held the china that she couldn't quite understand, as if he recognized the simple beauty of the piece and enjoyed it. Like his gaze told her he saw something in her that deeply satisfied him and that he enjoyed. "Please, sit. We can talk."

Scowling, she said, "Your MotherDam ruined my father's good name."

"She was good at being mean."

Dufleur blinked.

He laughed, not with amusement. "One of the reasons she maligned your father was because she wanted to make it as difficult as possible for us to meet, and learn each other, and love. She used her Flair to hide you from me. Are you going to let her cruel plans succeed?"

Her chin wobbled, and she hated that betrayal. "The hurt is still raw." She cleared her throat, glanced away. "The consequences of her actions are still affecting me—my mother and me."

She took the cup of caff with both hands and raised it to her lips, sipped. The combination of honey, dark caff, and cream sank into her taste buds. Perfect. He'd made the perfect cup of caff for her.

It was rare that she, with her mind usually on her work, even made a good cup of caff for herself. "Thank you."

"You're welcome." He didn't move to sit down, simply stood there looking at her with eyes of blue that deepened every second.

They observed each other for a minute. She'd listened to gossip about him last night and had despised herself for it. She *hated* rumormongering, since the Thymes had been the butt of it. Talk about him had been admiring. That wasn't so bad, she was sure.

Everything she'd heard about him confirmed what he'd told her. His MotherDam had scorned him, might have disinherited him, except he carried the most Family Flair. The less-charitable folks had muttered that the only reason old D'Willow *didn't* disinherit him was because if she ever revived she wanted to return to a powerful GreatHouse. Though most people spoke of D'Willow as dead.

Dufleur didn't think of the woman as dead, and she was sure the man standing here in front of her didn't, either. Shadows lived in the back of his gaze, there were faint strain lines around his eyes. His beautiful blue eyes.

He took a step forward and removed the cooling cup of caff from her hands. "You don't want to taste this," he said, and set it aside. "You want to taste me."

Firm fingers wrapped around her own, drew her toward him until their bodies touched. Her heart rate sped, her breathing went erratic as he pulled her into his embrace, against his strong body. He bent his head, and then they were sharing uneven breaths. His mouth brushed hers, gentle, tender.

He was right. Suddenly she craved to learn the taste of him. Their coming together in dreams hadn't included that sense. Taste.

And his tongue was slipping across the line of her lips, and she couldn't help herself, she gave a small moan of need. He pulled back slightly, and she saw his lips curve into a smile. His right hand moved to the back of her neck and sent a tingle to every nerve ending all the way down her spine.

She tipped back her head and opened her mouth in invitation.

His hand on her derriere pressed her close, until she felt the hardness of his erection against her. Another ragged moan tore from her as her nipples tightened, her core dampened, needing this man and what he could give her.

Her body swayed even closer, into the heat and hardness of his. His solid arousal pressed against her, evidence of his passion that created a twisting desire of her own. Hard chest, long, muscular thighs, firm belly. She gasped at the feel of him, and he took advantage of her open mouth to plunge his tongue inside.

The taste of him exploded through her. Man, deep earth, the last fierce winter storm before spring. The tang of him was already in her blood, settling into her heart, never to be forgotten.

Starving. Her body was starving for closeness, for a chest against her breasts, maleness to her female.

For the enveloping aura of someone who cared, the touch of a mind against hers that held attraction, delight, respect.

His tongue slid against hers, and her knees trembled and weakened, leaving her to lean against him, and the warmth and the strength and the hardness of him was all she'd ever dreamed of desire.

No thought. Only sensation. The breadth of his shoulders under her kneading hands, the tender skin of his nape under thick, soft hair.

He bowed her back in his arms. She'd never felt so supple.

His breath in her, sweeping through her like the most precious wind of time.

A loud cough came.

Trumpets shattered the throbbing silence.

They jerked straight. Dufleur whirled from his arms to face an older, blond, solid woman filling the open doorway. Dufleur blinked, then stared. The woman wore the livery of the Councils of Celta, blue and gold, and carried a cylindrical document holder. Her expression was solemn. She flicked a thumbnail against one of her brass buttons and the fanfare stopped. "Dufleur Thyme?"

"Yes?" She was aware that Saille was moving behind her, and he handed her the cup of caff he'd reheated with a word.

"I am the Herald of the AllClass Council. Here on official business."

"I don't understand." Why was she here? Was it the Winterberry estate dispute? Had someone deduced she was conducting illegal time experiments? Her throat closed.

Saille came to stand beside her, took her arm, and moved her to a couch. Dufleur sat.

"Herald, would you like anything to drink?"

The woman slightly relaxed her stance. "Thank you, Great-Lord T'Willow, black caff would be welcome. The day is bitter." She seated herself in a large, plush chair, placed the document cylinder on her knees, and watched Saille refresh a bowl of cocoa for Fairyfoot from the no-time caff cupboard, and pour a cup of black caff.

Saille glanced at Dufleur. "Not many Residences have such no-time caff areas. I take it you installed this one?" He handed the Herald her cup. Picking up his own, he joined Dufleur on the couch.

"Yes," Dufleur said. She'd fiddled with all the no-times of the Residence when she'd moved in, to keep herself busy in her grief.

"Ahem," said the Herald, placing her caff on the table and opening the tube to withdraw papyrus. Her voice softened. "I am here with a list of gilt and properties as reparation for your ordeal with the dark cult two months ago."

Dufleur jerked abruptly, her caff nearly sloshing over the rim of her mug. She squeezed her eyelids tight shut, a mistake, bringing the horrible memories back. "No," she croaked.

Saille's palm curved over her shoulder. "Please explain," he said coolly.

Fifteen

The Herald said, "The murderers were stripped of all assets, and they were set aside for reparations to the surviving victims and the lost victims' Families. It was determined that those involved be contacted in the same order as . . ."

The same order as the attacks. That would make Dufleur fifth.

Now the Herald was staring straight ahead, face grim. The events of two months ago had shocked all of Celta. No one remained unmoved.

Without looking at either of them, the Herald said, "Most of the Noble Families have refused any reparations."

"They can't have their children back," Dufleur whispered harshly. She'd been older than all of the other victims. Of six, only two had survived.

The Herald pushed the papyrus at Dufleur.

She locked her fingers together. "I don't want—"

"Take the reparation," Saille said. "You deserve it. You can use the gilt."

"No!"

He grasped the papyrus, glanced at the list, then up at Dufleur. His shoulders tensed, and his aura flamed with anger at what she'd been through, yet his eyes held a hard, considering look. "There is a piece of property close to here. A GrandHouse estate. Vacant now. Ritually cleansed of all evil nine times by priests and priestesses."

"I could not live there." Her words were jerky. Live in a place where someone who'd tried to kill her had once resided? She shuddered.

"There's a guesthouse. Little used, it says. It might make a fine . . . studio . . . for you."

She stared at him. A lab. He meant she could use the place as a laboratory.

What had he seen? What had he guessed?

She'd been working on her experiments, but there had also been obvious packing.

What did he know?

Through will she kept her fingers from clenching into tight, anxious fists. She stared into his eyes that were no longer warm and admiring but cool and impassive.

He said, "This would give you a separate workspace."

Forcing her mind away from Saille, she smiled weakly at the Herald. "Can . . . are there specifics on that property?"

Upending her cylinder again, the Herald shook out four holospheres and handed a black one to Dufleur. All too appropriate. When she settled the sphere in her palm, the holo began to run. It showed a fair chunk of land and a tall, narrow Residence with peaked gables, and an unattractive, squat building, long and low, off to one side.

Narrowing her eyes, Dufleur judged the distances. Using standard spellshields, even if the laboratory exploded, nothing else should be harmed, except . . .

"Is this a true Residence?" Dufleur whispered.

"I beg your pardon?" asked the Herald.

Dufleur swallowed. "Does the Residence live?" she asked in a whisper.

"No." The Herald smiled perfunctorily, as if Residential entities meant nothing to her. "The GrandHouse was a new upstart, only a few generations old, not even a century. The house is but a house."

"Take it, Dufleur," Saille urged.

Her mother would want the gilt the estate would sell for—though Dufleur couldn't imagine that with all the space in Druida anyone would want the property. She really didn't want it either, but she needed someplace to work.

If she tripled or quadrupled the shields on the guesthouse, or, better yet, modified the shields to *implode* the building, no one could possibly be hurt. She knew the exact force of the explosion that had destroyed her father's laboratory, then weakened their Residence until it collapsed and caught fire. She could defend against such an explosion.

"No one else has accepted reparations?" she asked in a thin voice, stroking the black holosphere with her fingers.

"Some gems. A country estate," the Herald said. "Nothing here in Druida." She bent a kindly look on Dufleur. "Only you and Trif Winterberry survived."

"It's a different matter for the other Families who lost some-one," Saille said.

"Indeed," said the Herald.

A thought struck Dufleur. "You go to Trif Winterberry after me."

"Yes."

Dufleur couldn't imagine that Trif, her husband Ilex Winter-berry, or any of the Clovers would want the estate with the guesthouse. Or much of anything. Her whole body chilled until her very lips felt blue, as memories crowded her mind with her experiences, with the horror and grief everyone involved felt. She cleared her voice, lifted stinging eyes, squared her shoulders.

"This is what I want. I personally want the estate with the guesthouse and enough gilt to reimburse Primary Healing Hall and the Healers who saved my life, and a reward to Hazel Guardhouse and Ilex Winterberry who saved my life." She waved a hand. "Others would know the appropriate amounts."

"None of that will be a problem," said the Herald, taking out a writestick and jotting notes on the back of the papyrus.

Dufleur sat up straight. "If, after you visit Trif Winterberry, there is still reparation gilt and properties available, I want it all to go into a trust for the Families of the victims, excluding my-self. Please ask T'Reed to create the trust and administer it."

"He will probably donate his services," Saille said quietly.

"Noted," said the Herald.

"This generation, these Families, may be too grief-stricken to want or need the reparations, but sometime in the future when the horror fades . . ."

"A very good idea." Saille squeezed her shoulder. "Good job."

To Dufleur's astonishment, the Herald immediately trans-ferred the property to her and had all the documents—and the keys to the house and guesthouse—forwarded to the Winter-berry collection box for Dufleur. Fairyfoot volunteered to get them. She was sure that an empty estate would have good hunt-ing.

Life-changing events once more progressed at a pace that made Dufleur's wits spin.

As soon as the Herald was gone, Saille placed his empty caff cup down with a click on a saucer and said, "So, what were you doing when I interrupted you this morning?"

The bond between them pulsed with curiosity from him.

Dufleur wasn't sure how to answer. She stood and walked to the no-time where the most time molecules lingered. Finally she met his eyes and said, "Even though we have a . . . link, I don't know you well."

He blinked. "I am glad that you admit to the link," he sent a burst of affection for her down it that warmed her, removing the cold of terrible memories, "but you deny the trust. And we're HeartMates."

Hearing him say the words aloud tightened her chest. "We barely know each other."

His eyelids lowered, his gaze became sensual. "Wrong. We know each other well."

Swallowing, Dufleur whispered, "We may have connected in bed."

The lust was gone in a burst of laughter. "Understatement. We've explored each other in linked dreams. Completely usual HeartMate behavior. All HeartMates I've known have dreamt of lovemaking with each other."

She found her teeth set. "I know nothing of any Heart-Mates."

With a tilt of his head, he considered her. She wondered if he'd push. She understood that he hadn't yet, and then wondered at his restraint. GreatLords weren't known for patience and restraint. "Dufleur?"

She dared not reveal her secrets to him. Not this man who was related to D'Willow, who was still finding his place in society, connecting with allies, vulnerable to scandal himself. She met his stare with a steady gaze of her own. "I know nothing of HeartMates," she repeated. "Don't know the weaknesses or strengths of that . . . condition." Her lips thinned, then she went on. "Even a loving marriage is outside my personal knowledge." She didn't like admitting that, but it was the truth.

His eyebrows raised. "Your cuz Ilex Winterberry is Heart-Bound to Trif Winterberry. You witnessed that."

A snort escaped her. "I've seen very little of them. My mother doesn't care to associate with the Clovers." Commoners. "They are a newlywed couple and happy, I think, and Ilex is learning to live with a large Family." She crossed her arms. And she'd been busy working on her experiments in the morning and evening after her day at Dandelion Silk, with little opportunity to socialize.

She tried a quick smile. "And the Clovers scare me. Such a big, loud Family." She'd spent a couple of hours on New Year's Day and Yule with them and had returned to Winterberry Residence with her ears ringing.

At that moment Fairyfoot pushed the door open and trotted in, pulling a large envelope that clinked with the new ceremonial Flair keys that had been made for the property.

Let's go see. Our new place.

"This will not be our home."

Fairyfoot sniffed. *Want someplace of My own.*

"Fairyfoot," Saille said mildly. The cat glanced at him, and her eyes rounded. Then she smiled.

"She's not blackmailing you, is she?" Dufleur asked, stooping to pick up the envelope.

"No, we simply have an understanding. Fairyfoot, if the new place is infested with rodents, perhaps my Fam, Myx, would like to hunt there, too."

Or foxes.

"That, too," Dufleur said. She sent an awkward smile to Saille. "Thank you for the lilies."

"I'm going with you."

"I didn't ask—"

"I want to ensure the place is safe."

"The Councils—"

"Dufleur, you never answered my original question. Don't be too stubborn."

"Or what?"

"You aren't the only one who knows you're my HeartMate, and the weight of Celtan culture favors my suit."

She gasped. "Who did you tell?"

"Your cuz Ilex Winterberry has known since you first found my HeartGift."

Her breath puffed from her. "Oh. Yes. I suppose. He hasn't said anything."

Saille stood, closed the distance between them, lifted her free hand, and kissed her fingers. "He knows that courting and winning a woman takes time and finesse."

Dufleur shrugged a shoulder, withdrew her hand. "I don't think—"

"Don't try and keep me out of your life, Dufleur." It was a silky threat.

"Can't I have some privacy? Some secrets of my own?"

He flinched, and his eyes flickered dark, those shadows coming to the fore. "For the moment. Everyone has secrets."

Now her curiosity was stirred. "Even HeartMates?"

"Until the HeartBond, I'm sure."

"You're the matchmaker."

He inhaled. "Yes. Yes, I am."

Later that evening as Saille dressed for socializing, he considered his HeartMate. Dufleur was keeping secrets from him, and he wanted her, so much. All of her, including her secrets. But he wanted her to tell them to him, trust him with them.

And as long as she still held his HeartGift, he was satisfied, since he thought the dreamtime loving between them would continue.

He wanted real loving. Wanted to feel the contours of her flesh with sensitized palms, wanted to probe her mouth with his tongue once more, wanted to sink his body into hers again and again.

The trip to the new, ugly workplace—laboratory?—had been made in silence, though he'd caught her quick looks at the glider, himself, and his Family driver. Saille had helped her from the glider himself, cherishing the feel of her fingers in his hand, tucking her arm in his. She'd only struggled briefly.

Now Saille donned more new evening clothes. He'd dance with Dufleur this evening, at least, though it had to be later. Business first. He must work on righting his MotherDam's errors. His own secrets.

Still, he knew he'd have Dufleur sooner or later. Celtan culture celebrated everything to do with HeartMates. That was on his side. He'd also sensed she'd been wary because of his name, the ruin his MotherDam had caused her Family. That had been a deep, aching wound in her, still bloody. The loss of her father, the Residence, the change in her circumstances. The lingering fear that she would fail to keep herself and her mother from poverty.

His mother rapped on his door and bustled in. "A new cloak." She carried it over her arm. He kissed her. "Have I told you today that I love you, Mama?"

She pinkened. "Yes, Saille. I love you, too." She looked away. "Yet I let *her* order our lives, keep me here, and send you away."

He gripped her hands. "I don't blame you. Or myself. Neither of us were strong enough to fight her, and doing so might have ripped the Family apart. She'd have disinherited us."

She shook her head. "No, I don't think so, because then we'd be free to live our own lives. But she'd have made our lives wretched. Even more awful than they were." Her smile was wan. "But I regret that I didn't insist on living with you."

"She liked you here, under her thumb."

"Yes." She blinked, took out the cloak and bustled around him to set it on him, smooth it over his shoulders. "You made excellent contacts last night." She sighed. "The first ball of the year."

He turned, grasped her hand. "Come with me tonight. Dance, enjoy yourself."

Her mouth fell open. "Me!" She made pushing motions. "No, no. I don't want to experience that crowd. I haven't been at such an event for years. *She* only went occasionally, and took my sister, who loathes such things most of all."

"Oh? Such a poor creature D'Willow was. Despite her power, such a small soul." He bowed elegantly over his mother's hand.

"Thank you for being the man you are," she whispered. "I am so proud of you."

He flushed. "Thank you."

She hesitated, looked aside. "You told us all how she might have hidden our HeartMates from us when you offered to find matches for us. Did she do that to you also?"

He didn't know how much to tell her. He loved her. He trusted her. He didn't want to tear at any loyalties she had or hurt her.

Sighing, she glanced back at him, her eyes shiny and chin quivering. "Your silence is enough. You were right. She was a very poor creature. In more ways than one. Had she been a different kind of person, we all would have loved her. But she preferred power and dominance more. Pitiful, really, and worse because we didn't stop her. We could have. I regret that more than I can say."

He waved a hand. "It's done."

She pressed her lips together, shook her head. "It isn't really. She still hovers over us like a malignant spider. I wish she were gone from our lives for good!" Her expression turned fierce. "She hurt us, but most of all, she hurt you."

"Shh." He hugged her.

She snuggled for an instant, then stepped back, wiped her eyes, and blew her nose on a softleaf she drew from her apron pocket. "You're very good for us." Her expression hardened. "It is quite a contrast. And I'm sorry that she hurt you." With a shrewd glance, she said, "It isn't only the wish to form good alliances and bring in business that you attend this social season, is it?"

He found himself smiling. "No, I've found my HeartMate." He shrugged, and his smile faded. "But D'Willow harmed her, so it will take some wooing to win her."

"I'm sor—"

Saille put a hand over her mouth. "No more apologizing. We are all sorry. But we'll deal with the past, only to move on to our future."

"You're right, of course."

Raising his brows, he said, "Don't tell me that too often, or I'll become as egotistical as D'Willow."

"Not possible. She was pampered and had her own way all of her life."

The calendar sphere dinged. And his mother took on her bustling housekeeper manner, heading for the door to hold it open for him. "The glider will be waiting for you." She stopped him as he exited for a kiss on the cheek. "Blessings, my son."

"Thank you. Blessings, mother."

A cold glider ride later, Saille studied Tinne and Genista Holly from across the salon. This was the first time he'd seen them together since the revelation of his MotherDam's journal. He'd accepted the invitation to this small gathering just to see them, knowing that Passiflora Holly and Dufleur were attending another large ball. Gossip was circulating that Passiflora was consolidating her HeartMate's position so that he could run for the Captaincy of the FirstFamilies Council. So she was concentrating on the larger gatherings. None of the Hollys had even hinted to him that they'd like his vote. But he was certain Passiflora knew of his obsession with Dufleur, and that would place him more on the side of the Hollys.

Tinne hovered beside his wife, who looked pale and listless, her mouth set in strained lines.

Saille ached for them. Even their physical cues spoke of a couple who hurt—separately and together. Everyone knew that they'd lost an unborn child just a couple of months earlier.

That was always a terrible strain on a marriage—even a HeartBond, which this hadn't been.

Shifting his weight slightly to fade even farther into the shadows so he could examine their relationship completely, he also shifted his Flair sight.

And immediately learned several things. The marriage he'd briefly consulted on three years ago had grown stronger than he'd anticipated. The couple had bonded on many levels. But the loss of their child had been a great blow.

Tinne lifted his head from speaking to his wife and turned a brilliant gray gaze upon Saille. Then the younger man stiffened and nodded. *We will talk later*, Tinne sent mentally.

Saille was a little dazed at the telepathy. No one else from the FirstFamilies had spoken to him mind to mind, and the intimacy and strength of that communication surprised him. He'd known the FirstFamilies, through centuries of ties and tradition, had their own shared "channel," but hadn't expected it to be so strong.

He returned Tinne's nod. A few minutes later, Tinne excused himself and his wife to their host.

Come, he said to Saille, not looking at him, as he led Genista from the room to the entrance hall.

Saille mentally ordered his Family glider to drive to the front door, bowed to his host with a few murmured words of appreciation for the pleasant evening, received a bow in return, then left to bundle into his coat and step out into the gray night of winter.

Tinne was handing his wife into a sleek Holly Family glider, when Saille's old clunky one slid behind the vehicle. He already knew that his chauffeur would be pressing for him to buy a model more like the Hollys'.

Shrugging, he lifted the door open with a grunt, then slid into the heat. His face tingled, as the quick chill to his skin warmed.

Tinne joined him on the cushy bench, snapped the door shut, and stared straight ahead. "You wanted to comment on our marriage, matchmaker?"

*W*ho is this?" *A* thin, blond woman let her haughty gaze slide down and up Dufleur, causing her to petrify. The lady was obviously of the highest class, a FirstFamilies GreatLady or GrandLady. She wore an incredible emerald necklace.

They hadn't been introduced, and Dufleur saw no indication of her House, so she was only miserably aware that she was outclassed.

The woman said, "Oh, it's Passiflora's little bit of baggage she's hauling around, so she can charm Holm into the Captain's seat of the Council."

There were four Councils that ruled Celta, but the woman clearly believed only the FirstFamilies Council mattered.

Dufleur wasn't used to handling insults. She glanced under her lashes, but no one she knew and liked was near to help out. She was all too certain that if she said what she wanted the woman would be highly offended. So she took a step back, and another woman bumped into her.

"How rude!" the newcomer said.

"ThymeHeir," the blond woman said in a disparaging tone. "She didn't even greet me properly."

"Oh, the mad Thymes, I suppose we shouldn't be surprised." The other woman's laughter was more of a bray. Dufleur knew this female. One of her mother's old "friends," a woman of lesser rank than the Thymes.

Sixteen

♥

Fire crawled up Dufleur's neck, heated her cheeks. She didn't know what to say. All she could think of was the facts. "I am not mad, nor was my father," Dufleur managed. She stared at the woman who'd pretended to be her mother's friend and had listened for years to her mother's complaints about her father. Were there many of these women around, spreading gossip about the Thymes? Dufleur's mother had not been wise in choosing her friends.

Or her husband. He hadn't been a good match for her, Dufleur admitted painfully. How could she think that she'd be able to be wise in choosing a man?

The man who was a HeartMate, ready to change her life.

Yet those thoughts barely snuck through her current humiliation. Swallowing, she lifted her chin. "But the Thymes are loyal. Like the Winterberrys. Like the Hollys. We don't feign friendship one day, then laugh at our friends and concoct rumor the next."

The woman's mouth dropped open, and *she* turned red.

The GreatLady sniffed delicately. "Your father was merely stupid then, squandering a fortune, blowing up his Residence." She smiled a frigid smile and swept away, beckoning the lesser noblewoman to attend her.

Dufleur trembled with anger. Her skin got hotter and hotter. She thought each follicle of the hair on her scalp was lifting.

She had to get away before she did something foolish. Before she began ranting about petty-minded people who couldn't see beyond their trifling concerns. Arrogant people who believed they had a right to dictate to others how to use—or not use—their Flair. Nobles who made decisions based on gossip and not facts.

She couldn't breathe.

Dufleur told herself she shouldn't pay them heed, they couldn't damage her. Except they already had—beyond this horrible humiliation. This anger. This doubt of her father and herself.

They had voted to make experimentation with time illegal.

Walking stiff-kneed away, she saw T'Agave smirking in the background, knew he'd primed the women somehow, though he was lesser than they in status. But obviously excellent at manipulation.

Her cuz Ilex was leading his wife, Trif, away from the musical group. Passiflora was deeply involved in flirting with a GreatLord. Neither of them were paying attention to her, both of them could be damaged if she made a scene.

T'Willow wasn't here. He was her HeartMate, would he have defended her?

She left the ballroom, jogged around the turn of a hallway. She shouldn't care what people said. Nothing they said would stop her from her work, would only make her more dedicated to proving them—and all of the FirstFamilies Council—wrong, wrong, *wrong*.

But she didn't have the skills to avoid the women the rest of the evening. Sit at a table with them and pretend nothing happened. She had to leave.

No one would miss her. She was a very minor noble. ThymeHeir.

Glancing around to see she was alone, she visualized sanctuary . . . not the old lab in Winterberry house, but the new one she'd moved her equipment into that afternoon. She imagined how it would look, dark with a filtering of half twinmoons' light coming through the windows. The night was cloudy.

And found herself in blessed, warm silence.

She *yearned* for her work, the solace of it. More than she feared it, feared failure.

This was a new place with new possibilities—and excellent shields. Here she could be her essential self.

She was alone, whatever she did could harm no one except herself.

But if she wanted to work, she had to *settle*. Emotions had churned her up, affected her thought processes.

She spent some time arranging her equipment, touching it, feeling the residue of the Time Wind. The lab had already gathered more molecules of the wind, just by her being here today and setting up her instruments and tools.

Then she lowered the light, sat in her old chair and prayed. For peace, for insight, and renewing her dedication to her Family Flair. Her words faded and her feelings subsided, then her mind quieted too as she centered herself and opened herself.

The Time Wind swirled around her in a blessing. Tension drained from her body and she opened her eyes, ready to work again, knowing she *could* work again.

Saille didn't answer Tinne but asked, "Where should I tell my driver to take us?"

Tinne's face went blank. "Genista is again spending time with her Family. Whom she doesn't care for much. But she likes them a lot better than *my* Family." He glanced at the long strip of mirror attached to the front window of the glider and met the chauffeur's eyes. "Take us to the Mistletoe Club."

As the glider smoothly engaged, Tinne met Saille's eyes. "You haven't accepted membership in the Club yet, have you?"

"No." Saille cleared his throat. "I don't recall an invitation."

Hunching one shoulder in an offhanded shrug, Tinne said, "FirstFamilies' Men's Club. Should have been automatic. Your MotherDam, being female, would have belonged to The White Lady's Club." He grimaced. "The ladies ever wanted the clubs to be separate, and now it's tradition." Once again Tinne's gray gaze cut to Saille and back. "Your MotherDam gave her approval of my marriage," he muttered, then fell silent.

"Privacy shield," Saille said, and an invisible soundproof wall solidified between the front bench and the back. "Yes, she did."

"You scanned us with your Flair tonight. I felt the touch."

"Very true. I congratulate you."

That had Tinne jerking his head to meet Saille's gaze. "For a dynastic match, it is a good relationship. You are well suited."

Tinne blinked. Opened his mouth. Shut it. Inhaled through his nose, then said, "We both strove to make the marriage sound."

"It will need more work to stay healthy."

Tinne's laugh was bitter. "The marriage is not as solid as it was. Nothing in the Holly Family is as solid as it once was." He clenched his hands. "But I will do my best."

"That is all anyone can do." And he was greatly relieved to

know that neither he nor his MotherDam had made a mistake in advising this marriage. Saille had appointments with the rest of his MotherDam's clients—those he could reach. Two couples had separated with one of the partners leaving Druida.

The glider stopped, and Tinne opened the door and stepped out, but Saille made no move to exit.

Face less haggard, Tinne asked, "Do you come?"

"No, I am continuing on to the Aspens' ball."

With a nod, Tinne said, "Thank you for your reassurance. I'll double-check that you are on the membership list of the club."

"Appreciate you doing so."

The door descended, and Saille vanished the privacy shield. "To the Aspens."

His chauffeur, a kinsman, murmured, "Yes, Saille." He hesitated. "Did you speak of HeartMates?"

"No. It is not proper for Tinne to think of his HeartMate when she is wed to another man, and he to another woman."

"I do not think D'Willow knew who Tinne Holly's Heart-Mate is."

"That is not our business."

"Aren't you curious? It's said he knows."

Saille was curious. "It's not our business. Tinne and Genista spoke vows."

"I doubt any Holly is going to break a vow anytime in the future, though marriage vows aren't the same as HeartBonding."

"To the Aspens," Saille ordered in a tone ending the conversation. And to his own HeartMate.

*D*ufleur *stared at her* Fam, *who had just arrived from the* ball. "I didn't want to stay and listen to insults. And I don't want any from you, either." She picked up the cat and looked into big eyes. Fairyfoot glanced away. "I've heard that cats can be snotty, but your behavior is beyond cat selfishness. A Fam should not be a traitor to her FamWoman. A woman and her Fam should be companions."

Fairyfoot twitched her uneven whiskers. *We belong with Fam-Man. Winterberry House hurts my nose, always. Stings my eyes.*

The yar-duan! Of course. It must have a different effect on animals than people, though its effect on people was all too awful. If she learned how to reverse time—no, she was only trying to affect the debilitating virus inside a person, kill it, perhaps reverse some of the most dreadful effects through the virus. Yar-duan addiction was a choice, not a disease, and she didn't think she could make a Healing Time Tube that would stop the deterioration of an entire body, not just the virus and its immediate surrounding tissue.

Fairyfoot wriggled in her arms. *Put me down.*

"Of course. I'll speak to D'Ash. See if there's some sort of spellshield that would protect you from yar-duan fumes." She winced at the thought of more expense. Today she'd purchased layer upon layers of spellshields for this place and had little gilt again.

She set Fairyfoot down on her cat tree, and Dufleur's gaze was caught by her neatly stacked papyrus, the results of her experiments. Once again she thought of her earlier notion of following a different path than her father had, using another virus to work with than he had. He'd experimented with one for years, but she still didn't understand the virus.

Maybe something simpler as a base. Perhaps not a pinecone, either, but something more fragile, a leaf. What would be better would be some diseased rats or mice. She might be able to spread the word to Fams that she would pay for such. She could communicate with the rodents on a very minor level—impress upon them that their bodies were disintegrating and request their permission to try and stop that disintegration.

She wondered if D'Ash easily communicated with rodents; if so, Dufleur herself could make her wishes known to them. If D'Ash couldn't speak with rats, perhaps Dufleur could trade her knowledge for Fairyfoot's spell. Or D'Ash might want to help her just to learn more, as Dufleur did. Even D'Ash couldn't Heal all the diseased rats out there.

But first, leaves. She'd have to visit a flower grower.

FamMan has a nice, warm conservatory.

Dufleur wasn't asking for Saille T'Willow's help. He was getting too close to her secret. The more he learned, the more he could deduce that she was continuing with her father's experiments.

She and her father had gone to the Horehounds when they wanted leaf specimens. She glanced around the laboratory. The place would look better, less sterile, more welcoming in the winter, with plants.

And that idea would never have occurred to her father.

Dufleur set her shoulders. She wasn't her father. She wasn't his assistant anymore. She'd always had a line or two of her own inquiry going, with his absentminded, grunted blessing. She crossed to the minuscule no-time she'd set in the heaviest bespelled corner. If disaster struck, this corner and the area around Fairyfoot's perch should be spared.

The corner held her greatest secret, her most important discovery.

A minuscule no-time that kept a living thing in stasis. One leaf at a time.

She set to work.

Later, her calendarsphere began chiming, pulling Dufleur from her studies.

Fairyfoot stretched and yawned on her perch, licked her paw, and groomed a bit of hair near her ear. *Home now.*

Dufleur put down her writestick, sighed, straightened, and stretched. The first three experiments with the leaf and its virus that mimicked the one Dufleur actually wanted to study had gone well. The results were promising, even better than the experiments with the pinecone. "Did you program my calendarsphere?"

Another lick, another swipe at sticking-up cat hair. *Winterberry Residence did.*

"Oh. Well, that's a good sign that it is recovering."

Fairyfoot sniffed. *Getting better. Let's teleport back.*

For a moment, Dufleur's stomach clenched. Did she have enough Flair energy left to 'port? That was one thing she'd forgotten. If she didn't, she wasn't dressed for even a walk to the nearest public carrier plinth. And she didn't know the carrier routes or schedules. Stupid!

She was too accustomed to working in the same premises as she lived. She'd have to put a bed in here, and a small wardrobe. Rolling her shoulders, she took stock. Just enough energy to teleport to her bedroom. Good thing she'd only done simple spells tonight.

Stripping off her lab coat, she adjusted her ball gown, which had been more comfortable than anticipated, picked up Fairyfoot, and teleported to her bedroom. She received a jolt when she found it crowded with people, all as appalled as she that she might have 'ported on top of someone, in*to* someone.

"What's going on?" She clasped Fairyfoot tighter.

"You disappeared from the ball," Passiflora said, worry lines crinkling around her eyes.

Dufleur had meant to send her a note, but hadn't. Guilt nibbled at her. "I'm sorry." She lifted her chin. "I'm a competent adult."

"If not a courteous one," her mother said. One glance at Dringal told Dufleur that her mother was infuriated. And scared.

She scanned the room. Passiflora D'Holly was there, so was Saille T'Willow—Dufleur's heart twinged in her chest Dringal, and three other people she didn't recognize.

Worse, the door to the secret room was open!

Fear clogged Dufleur's throat.

But first things first. She put Fairyfoot down and swept a deep curtsy to Passiflora. "Please forgive me. I teleported to my new studio. I've sketches for the Temple tapestry." That was true enough. She *had* managed to work on that lately.

Passiflora smiled. "You had me worried."

"I'm sorry."

With a nod, Passiflora said, "I'll leave you all to your business, then. My glider awaits."

"I'll escort you to the door," Saille said in a neutral tone that warned Dufleur that he, too, was angry.

"Thank you," Dufleur said, her own voice rough with emotion. She darted a look at the second chamber. It didn't look or smell badly. In fact it was pristine from the cleaning Dufleur had given it in the afternoon. More, there was a scent of sage. She'd also returned the battered altar and religious instruments that she'd found in the room back to their places. It looked like the ritual room it was designed to be.

The question was, who believed that?

Not Dringal. One glance at her mother's tense body told Dufleur that. Dringal would know for what purpose Dufleur had used the room.

Not Saille T'Willow, as he returned to the bedroom. His expression gave little away, but the blasted link between them told Dufleur that he recalled there was no altar in the room when he'd seen the chamber that morning.

Dufleur moistened her lips, looked at the three strangers. "I'm sorry." That was getting to be all too familiar coming from her, and she got the notion that she'd be saying the phrase a few dozen times more. "Can I help you?"

The young woman bowed. "We are the examiners assigned to the Winterberry legal case."

Staring at them blankly, Dufleur said, "But why are you here?"

A small, thin man with bushy eyebrows gave a little cough. "For your convenience. We realized our schedule didn't take into consideration the fact that you were attending the social season this year, and your Mother and GreatLady D'Holly indicated that late at night would be better for you. We came at the time designated in our revised schedule."

Winterberry Residence had saved her by putting the appointment on her calendarsphere, and Fairyfoot by insisting they go home.

"We waited for you upstairs, but our charge is to examine every room in the Residence, and WinterberryHeir suggested that we come down here."

Something her mother was definitely wishing she hadn't done now, Dufleur was sure. Dringal had expected Dufleur's rooms to be innocuous. Full of thread and cat hair, no doubt.

"My fault," Dufleur croaked, "for 'porting here instead of using the designated teleportation pad upstairs." And that was a lesson she'd never forget.

Heart thumping, she continued, "I'm not comfortable being interviewed in my bedroom. Shall we adjourn to a sitting room upstairs?"

The small man—the empath, Dufleur concluded—entered the secret chamber. "Twice cleansed," he murmured, sounding slightly approving. Then his forehead wrinkled. "There's something strange." He shifted his shoulders. Dufleur felt his Flair brush hers, as if he was sensing layers within the rooms. She stood very, very still as if that would stave off discovery.

"Yes, something strange . . ."

The larger man with soft features sent a sharp glance to Dringal. "You're a Thyme, aren't you?"

Dringal jerked in surprise, straightened to her full height. "I am Winterberry by birth, Thyme by marriage."

"Marriage to Vulg Thyme who blew up his Residence. So you have taken the title of WinterberryHeir and D'Thyme," the man persisted, then stared at Dufleur. "That would make you a

Thyme and ThymeHeir, and these are . . ." He turned to his colleague. "These are Thyme's rooms—consider . . ."

There was an intruder. The words that saved her came from the Residence.

Yes, an intruder, Fairyfoot piped up. *Nasty-smelling man. When we were gone to the Hollys.*

"Someone penetrated the security shields? How did that happen, I wonder?" Saille murmured. "What level of spellshields are there?"

The woman placed her hand on the threshold. "New ones, here, done by ThymeHeir."

I do not know who came. There was a no-see-me spell, the Residence said.

"When did this intrusion take place?" demanded the bigger man.

"Yesterday," Dufleur said, then touched fingers to her temple. "No, three days ago, I think. Many changes have occurred in my life lately." She managed a smile. Probably still as grim as D'Holly had noticed. But grim wasn't out of order here.

"We should definitely question D'Winterberry and WinterberryHeir about their spellshields."

Saille said smoothly, "And I would remind you that Dufleur has had a difficult day. The Council Herald visited her today with reparations for her ordeal at the hands of the black cult."

Shock rippled around the room, and suddenly no one was looking at her. As if they'd all just recalled what she'd suffered and were hideously uncomfortable. One of the two survivors of a series of horrible murders.

"She was, of course, living here in these rooms when that happened," Saille added.

They couldn't get out of her chamber fast enough. The empath looked back and sent her a sympathetic glance from under his heavy brows.

Wishing to be anywhere else, Dufleur changed into an old tunic trous set that was casually drab.

Fairyfoot grumbled a little. *My name was not on their list.*

"Be glad. And you've only been here a couple of months."

I could tell them much. But I won't. She lifted her nose, sprang onto the bed, and curled up in the middle. *I will stay here.*

"Of course." Dufleur trudged upstairs. The examiners awaited her in the gray sitting room, and Dufleur could tell through her bonds with her mother and Saille that he soothed her in her suite. Dufleur rubbed her temples. Her neck was tense. Actually, all of her was tense.

But better to get it over with.

And because Saille had reminded the examiners of her past, they treated her lightly as she recounted the tragedy of losing her home and her father, getting work at Dandelion Silk, coming here. Her mother's grief and how she had become more emotionally stable when she was named WinterberryHeir. How they tried to help the failing D'Winterberry. Reluctantly she admitted that she hadn't seen the former WinterberryHeir, Meyar, until a few days before. That she hadn't met the second son, Ilex, until more than a year after living with D'Winterberry.

The stark little tale reflected poorly on the whole Winterberry Family.

They didn't ask anything about her rooms or her actions in them, though she had said truthfully that she'd embroidered in them often, using Flair.

They noted that she'd helped the Residence and the entity was fond of her. And she said she was deeply grateful to it. The empath watched her with half-closed eyes, but all of Dufleur's emotions were true, and she knew he sensed nothing but them.

She was released after half a septhour and nearly stumbled with exhaustion to the door, which Saille opened from outside. No anger radiated from him. He was back to feeling steady, solid and reliable to all her senses.

The examiners trooped to the teleportation pad and left, and Dufleur's deep sigh matched her mother's, who stood on the landing to the second floor.

"Thank the Lady and Lord that's over," Dringal said. "Dufleur, I want to speak with you."

The relief that had filled Dufleur vanished, and she tensed again.

"Dufleur's had a wearying day," Saille said. "And so have you. It's late and I thought the examiners said they'd be back tomorrow?"

Heavy silence from Dringal. "Yes. Yes, this has been *very* trying. Tomorrow, then, Dufleur."

"Goodnight, mother," she said. But she didn't rid herself of Saille so easily. He followed her into the bedroom, glanced at the plain wall that hid the second chamber, and Fairyfoot snoring gently on the bed, then turned Dufleur into his arms.

"Rest a moment." His hands stroked her back, circled the nape of her neck.

"You were angry with me."

"I was, and no doubt will be again. Did you think HeartMate connections were always smooth? But tonight is not the time to speak of . . . secrets. No, don't tense up. Lean against me a moment, Dufleur. Let me try . . ."

He took her weight, and a moment later, Dufleur felt more than comfort from him; a surge of energy flowed through her, making her catch her breath. It was as if a tide had come and washed away her ills.

She'd occasionally received energy before—once when she was sick from her mother, sluggish but strong. Her father and she had exchanged energy when they worked sometimes, and his had been quick and impatient, hard to hold and integrate.

This was completely different, and felt so good it frightened her. Everything about him was too tempting.

"I thought that might work," Saille said in a low voice.

"Thank you," she said stiltedly, pressing her palms against his chest, ready to step away.

He frowned, touched her cheek. "I did it correctly, right?"

That surprised her, and she blinked. "Yes." She cleared her throat. "Excellent." She hesitated. "You didn't ever do that before?"

"No. There was no one I linked well with at the country estate; MotherDam saw to that," he said matter-of-factly. "And there's been no reason to link with my mother or other relatives here." Then his jaw clenched. "The only time I would have wanted to do this was when you were . . . taken by those murderous fliggers, and we'd barely connected. Not enough for me to find you, to save you."

Now she touched his face. Somehow his anger for her helped lessen the awfulness of her ordeal. "They hurt you, too," she murmured. "They didn't only hurt Fairyfoot and me, but you."

"We weren't linked."

"But they hurt you emotionally all the same."

His eyes fired. "I wanted to kill them myself."

"They paid for their crimes. I've heard two have already died."

"Not enough."

"Shhh." Now she was comforting him, feeling the rage running through his muscles.

He took a breath, let it out, one side of his mouth crooked. "Something else we must deal with. But not tonight." Covering her hands with his own, he took them from his face. Squeezed her fingers. The golden bond snapped into glittering substance between them.

"Spend the night with me." His voice was intense, his face was set in that easygoing smile, but his eyes belied that, as did his clenched jaw.

Seventeen

T*hrough their bond he knew what she was feeling, had felt* since she'd arrived home. The shock, the outrage, the sense of invasion, and underlying all that, the relief. Too many huge, surging emotions for her to easily handle.

"I'll take care of you." Again his body seemed relaxed, yet his muscles were still strained.

The offer of help, of comfort, sank into her like a balm . . . but there was more. He was offering more.

No, he was *wanting* more.

"I want everything you have to give. I want all of you." He answered her thoughts, and the room that had been noisy with voices now seethed with silent emotions. Their link snapped between them, almost tangible, definitely visible, a golden cord.

He lifted a hand. "I'll give you whatever you need. All of me."

Desire shivered through her body at the timber of his voice, the heat in his eyes. She didn't know what to say. What to do.

What she wanted.

"Come with me." His hand was still palm out. "I promise you can have a guest room."

But his mind flashed a suite. The consort's suite of a Great-Lord.

She stepped back.

His mouth twisted. "I'd rather have you in my bed. With me. But I'll give you whatever you need. Tonight and always."

It sounded like a vow. Again she felt trapped—by the immensity of his feelings for her, acknowledged and accepted by him.

"I don't know what I need." Her voice came out small, and she hated it. Hated that she was so confused.

But the pleading note in it did affect him. He smiled, more truly. "We can figure it out together."

"What I need?" Disbelief now.

"Of course. I said I wouldn't pressure you."

"Just being here is pressuring me."

"I had hoped I helped." The tone of steel was back. Oh, yes, he was learning to be a GreatLord quickly. "You've had enough to deal with today."

Including their kiss.

Now he held out both hands. "Come with me. For rest."

Rest. She couldn't recall the last good *rest* she'd had. "I don't want anyone to know I'm with you."

Hurt flashed across his face, and she wanted to bite her tongue for the rude—honest but rude—words.

He inclined his head.

She cleared her throat. "This Heart—this business is so very personal. Must all my faults and feelings and personal business be put on display?" More plaintiveness in her voice that she despised. She turned away.

He followed. The next moment had him behind her, cradling her against him, arms around her, his warm breath near her ear as he said, "The sitting room of my suite has a wide sofa you will find comfortable. I would offer my own bed, but I think you wouldn't accept."

A dynastic bed. No. Definitely not. Bad enough that she was allowing weakness to overcome her. But he felt so fine. Warm. Solid. Comforting.

Sexy.

"We'll 'port on three." A detailed image of the sitting room, shadowy furniture, and slivers of bright light from waning twin-moons came from his mind to hers. She settled against him. Could sense the even thump of his heart.

Wait! Fairyfoot zoomed from the corner of the bed to squeeze between their feet.

"I didn't invite you," Saille said coolly.

The little cat jerked in surprise just as Dufleur had.

I am her Fam.

"You haven't been taking care of her. You haven't been loving."

Fairyfoot hissed.

"And you still owe me an apology for being disloyal," Dufleur pointed out.

"So you are not invited. You can stay in these cold and sterile rooms tonight. Furthermore, I haven't yet paid T'Ash for your collar, and I'm not going to."

"Neither am I," Dufleur said. "I don't reward traitorous cats."

More hissing.

"My cat sits on my lap and purrs. He keeps me company. And he's quiet. Not too demanding. One. Two. Th—"

Sor. Ry. It was loud and more snide than not, but the right words all the same.

"I think that's the first time I've ever heard of that a cat actually apologized," Saille said. "I'll have to tell Danith D'Ash for her record books."

Fairyfoot growled. She'd hate that. Hate all the other cats knowing she'd had to apologize.

"Cats are not allowed to manipulate people," Dufleur said.

"People should not manipulate people, either," Saille said. "But under no circumstances are *companions* supposed to manipulate their friends. Are we clear on that, cat?"

Dufleur found herself smiling as Fairyfoot sniffed sulky agreement. Spirits lightening, she leaned back against Saille. He'd already given her comfort. Perhaps she could trust him.

"One. Two. Three."

And they were in a spacious sitting room, scented lightly with lavender and the underlying earthy fragrance of Saille. A large bouquet of colorful flowers rose from an exquisitely shaped porcelain vase.

"Lights," ordered Saille.

The room looked like him, biscuit-colored walls, bookshelves, large leather sofa, armchair, and twoseat in dark brown.

"Rrow." It was soft and unassuming and came from a cat trotting through the open door from the bedroom. A cat that was even less distinguished looking than Fairyfoot. Bigger and scrawnier, though.

"Good evening, Myx. Dufleur, this is Myx, my FamCat. Myx, this is my HeartMate, Dufleur Thyme."

Tingles ran up and down her spine. She wondered if she'd made a bad mistake, giving in to his sweet talk. His dazzling offer. His tantalizing body.

The cat slipped in, then stopped outside reach of a kicking foot. That saddened her.

Myx wrinkled his nose, stuck out his tongue. *I know your smell.*

Dufleur blinked.

The tomcat cocked his head. *Same smell as odd place near little white round temple. Interesting smell-feeling-air.*

Her pulse leapt. Thyme Residence! Or the ruins of it. Near Brigid's Temple. The interesting smell-feeling-air must be the lingering motes of time that had tended to gather around the Residence as she and her Family worked. Or the soot of the fire and explosion.

No good prey there. No mice or rats.

"Oh." Now her spirit was weary again.

Fairyfoot, Myx said neutrally, then grinned. *Fairyfoot had to apologize to her FamWoman. I heard my FamMan say so.* Myx made a cat snicker. He lifted his nose. *Fairyfoot was not an acceptable FamCat.*

With a growl, Fairyfoot shot toward him. He leapt nimbly aside, then headed out of the suite through a cat door low in the wall. Fairyfoot followed.

Saille rubbed his hands up and down Dufleur's arms. "I think that will put an end to any misbehavior by Fairyfoot."

"I'd imagine so," Dufleur murmured, but her words nearly stuck in her throat. She was all too aware that he hadn't released her. Heat generated between their bodies. He was aroused, and that knowledge kindled yearning in her, reminded her of all the times they'd met and mated in dreams. Her breath came faster.

"Anything you need, Dufleur," he repeated.

Had anyone ever offered her anything without expecting payment in return? She didn't think so. Didn't want to think what Saille might expect from her.

"Everything," he murmured. His tongue slid down the curve of her ear, his teeth closed gently over her lobe, and she quivered. "Everything for you. Everything from you." His hands, loosely clasped in front of her, flattened against her.

She wondered if he would trail fingers downward where her need stirred, but his palms flattened against the slight curve of her stomach, slid upward. He cupped her breasts, thumbs slowly caressing the nubs of her nipples, sending a rush of pleasure through her to her core. Her head fell back against him.

He kissed her neck, soft brushes, a touch of his tongue as if he tasted. His lips pressed against the corner of her mouth. "Lover," he whispered. "How I've wanted you with me. Finally, with me." She turned her head and opened her mouth to his probing tongue, as she knew she'd open her body to his. As she wanted to feel him with her, in her.

Standing this way wasn't enough. She turned, letting her body rub against his, feeling the muscularity of his thighs and chest, the thickness of his erection, until they were together front to front. She twined her arms around his neck, played with the hair at the nape of his neck, and smiled when his body arched into hers.

His eyes were wide, only a rim of blue showing. Color flushed his cheekbones.

Nice.

She tipped her head back, licked her lips, which seemed hot and swollen, needing his kiss again. She put her mouth on his, traced his lips with her tongue, penetrated his mouth so she could draw in his wonderful taste again.

He groaned, and she sucked on his tongue, and he grabbed her bottom and pulled her tight, and she gloried in the heat and the tide of delicious sensation that swept her mind away.

She shifted so her aching sex would cradle his hard length and moved against him. They moaned into each other's mouths.

He lifted his head, breath ragged. "No clothes," he ordered and a cool breeze whisked around her, and she was naked.

So was he.

Skin to skin. And it was very, very fine, the slide of their bodies together. His rough velvet, hers smooth.

Their mouths met, parted, tongues tasted, probed, duelled. Her hands roamed the planes of him, the curve of his thigh, the hard roundness of his backside. She slid a leg up around his waist, locked it, moved so that most needy part of her could welcome the heated length of his erection.

"Hot, wet," he said, setting his teeth in her lower lip and arousing her to the edge of ecstasy, until only fulfillment of her driving need mattered. She whimpered.

He shifted and thrust, and she gasped as pleasure speared her. *I want* . . . it was hardly a thought, more a demand from her body, her heart, her soul to him. There was a change in space, in position, and the cool leather of the couch met her back, and he came down on her and into her, and it was hard and good.

Then fast. He pumped, and she writhed, wanting, yearning, needing. Too fast. The slick slide of him took her too high, too quickly, unbearable.

One. Last. Thrust.

She screamed her completion, and it echoed through her head and her heart and through time itself.

He grabbed her close, arched, shuddered, and his groan was but a whisper that wrapped around her and pulled her into madness once more. Shattering. Falling.

Resting. Damp, fragrant skin against damp skin. Warm entwined bodies.

"HeartMate," he said, and it was the last thing she heard before lush sleep claimed her.

She awoke, then realized it was the sense of time passing while she was in a cocoon of comfort and safety. Tiredly, she understood that she didn't trust comfort and safety, had gotten used to being wary, even in sleep. What did that say about her, and was she becoming like her mother? She sincerely hoped not.

But Saille still held her in his arms, between the back of the sofa and himself. Surrounded by him.

She didn't know how to escape. And she had to, because she wanted him so much. The scent of him, of them, promised everything.

So much different than being at Winterberry Residence, or before in her own home. Love. She was afraid of it. A huge emotion that changed everything.

Here in T'Willow Residence she was safe—as long as she was the embroiderer, not the time experimenter. The Residence around them pulsed with life. It was strong itself and housed no less than fifteen other Willows—not to mention the FamCat, Myx, sleeping on Saille's bed, or Fairyfoot snoozing in the lush verdant air of the conservatory.

None of those entities would want her working with time.

Saille opened his eyes and snared her with his gaze. Awake, though she'd known he'd been sleeping a moment before.

His arms tightened, and he frowned. "Do you always run away?"

She flinched. "I'm still here."

"You were thinking of leaving, would have if I hadn't been holding on to you."

"I don't know what I was going to do, would have done." Her

mouth flattened. "Such pretty words for a morning after . . ." She couldn't finish the sentence with "sex," which is what she wanted to say but wasn't truthful. She couldn't bear to call their coming together "loving," which was what settled in her mind. That was too scary.

"You're right." He brushed her lips with his mouth, fuller from kissing. "I should have pretty words for my HeartMate the morning after we finally made love in the flesh."

He slid his body against hers, and she became aware that his flesh was hardening and stirring and her own body melting for his.

When he slipped inside her, she was ready, the sheer thickness of him pleasured her. Fulfillment.

His thrusts were slow and measured, and he looked down at her with bright blue eyes, and she couldn't escape his gaze, couldn't hide.

Intimacy.

They climbed to the pinnacle together, and he held on to her when they fell together.

The aftermath was fully as lovely as the first time, so different from her other limited experiences, when either she or the man left soon after sex.

Several minutes later, Saille pushed her hair away from her face. This time his gaze wasn't demanding, but concerned.

"I looked for you as soon as I arrived at the Aspens' ball last night. What happened?"

She wanted to ask why he hadn't come at the start of the ball, wanted to know, but actually saying the words would reveal too much—that it mattered whether he'd been there. That she wished to know more about him. That she might even probe into his secrets.

She was still formulating a reply when he said, "Passiflora D'Holly heard that you had been the object of unkind words. She was concerned when she couldn't find you. It became obvious that you'd left." His voice was rough from sleep.

She pushed up. This time he didn't hold her, but let his hands slide down her arms. He followed her to stand beside the sofa. Now she felt mussed—hair sticking out in different layers, damp with perspiration. Not at all attractive.

He squeezed her hands a little. "Stop that. You are beautiful. And you're looking everywhere except at me."

So she met his gaze. It was unwavering, but didn't seem as judgmental as his first words. Straightening and pushing her shoulders back, fighting down a flush, even though it was too dark for him to see, she said, "I owe Passiflora another apology. I shouldn't have allowed my hurt feelings to dictate my actions." Though she still shuddered at the thought of facing down a lot of strangers of the highest noble class who judged and gossiped about her Family. She grimaced. "I hate doing something stupid."

"Everyone does." Once again he squeezed her hands, and a gleam came to his eyes as he smiled. "But loving—and being together like this—is far from stupid. It's simply right. Don't you feel it?"

Their link was wide and the feelings he sent—wonder, affection, joy—wrapped around her like a blanket. So hard to deny her own feelings. So difficult to step away, but she did, and he followed. She took another pace back, tugging on her hands, and he let them slide from his own.

"I'm not running away."

"No? It seems like you've been running from me since I first started visiting Dandelion Silk."

Her chin shot up, she swept a hand around the room. "Look at you, a FirstFamily GreatLord, and me, a lower-class noble. Tell me whose life will change the most if we . . . if . . ."

"If you HeartBond with me? I can promise you that I'll do everything I can to make your life change for the better."

"Ha."

He tilted his head. "I've been poor, and now I'm rich. I like rich better. You'd have your own suite of rooms—"

"—and expectations of fulfilling responsibilities of Great-Lady Willow. D'Willow." The idea of taking the title of her enemy caused a ripple of disgust to go through her. She raked her fingers through her hair. Her brain hurt. "I can't do this."

"We can talk about responsibilities," he paused, "expectations." He strode to the undraped window, glanced down, then back at her. Hands on hips, he said, "A year ago if I'd been offered the title and the status and the wealth and a good home and a loving Family and my HeartMate, I would have known all my dreams had come true." His jaw hardened. "That should be true for anyone. What dreams do you have that can't be fulfilled by those things? By whatever I can give you?"

Suddenly cold, she picked up a throw and wrapped it around herself. "You want honesty?"

"Always."

"Me, too. I prefer honesty."

"That's progress."

"I don't care about titles. Much. I want to be D'Thyme. That's important to me, and it will come to me eventually. But now it is not a very respected name, because of both my father and mother. I want to remove the tarnish from that name."

"I can help."

"How?"

"I don't know, but we can find a way."

She sighed and sat and rubbed her face. "I only know one way to restore the name."

She heard him pace to the window and back again, then felt the slight shift of the couch when he sat beside her. He didn't slouch.

He didn't touch her. "You mean the continuation of the experimentation with time."

Eighteen

$\mathcal{D}$eciding he was right, she'd been cowardly, she turned to face him. "Yes. The illegal experimentation with time. And to clear my father's name, I need to prove that my—our—studies are valid." She laughed harshly. "Provide something of value to the FirstFamilies at least, if not all society."

He set his hands on her shoulders. "You can do it."

"I think I can. But not without working, illegally, with my Flair."

"How dangerous is it?"

Her heart started thumping hard. "You're the only one who's ever asked me that." She swallowed. "Everyone else just believes it's unsafe."

His hands tightened, let go of her. She missed his touch. "I can't say that I want you doing anything dangerous. But I can understand why." She sensed he fibbed there. More like he might try to understand why, but even that was something. And there was no feeling from him that he'd betray her in any way. Only enough emotional support that it made her want to weep.

"I don't know what happened in my father's lab," she said baldly. "He didn't often work at night, and none of our projects were dangerous." She lifted her chin. "The Family has worked with time since our founding. It's our specific Flair that brought us the title. Nothing like this has ever happened. Because of one tragedy . . ."

"And the help of my MotherDam," he said quietly.

"Yes." Her lip curled. "She was a moving force in the vilification of the Thyme name."

"But you must admit that Druida is more populated than ever before. An explosion . . ."

She looked aside, at the windows where the light of the twinmoons was being swallowed up by the rising sun. "The Thyme estate is on the edges of Noble Country, but we have a good-sized land parcel. No one was harmed except the . . . the Residence itself. I had a good home."

He shifted and put an arm around her. "And that's an additional grief. It's odd how a person can become attached to a house entity. I am already to the Willow Residence."

"Willow Residence is not my home."

"It could be. And your mother's."

He didn't say that it appeared her mother would soon need another home.

"My mother can be a difficult woman. In that list of yours, status would be her first priority."

"Living here, she could move in the highest of social circles." His tone was neutral.

"As the mother of a GreatLady. I can't think of that." She rubbed her face again. "She would be wild for me to marry you."

"Additional pressure on you."

"Yes."

"I like Winterberry Residence." She reverted to the previous topic.

"It obviously likes you." Again the dry note in his voice.

"Because it kept my secrets."

"Plural? Is there more that you aren't telling me?"

She stared at him. "No. But you have secrets, too."

He hesitated.

"I don't need to know them."

Rubbing a hand over his heart, he said, "That hurts."

"I'm sorry. Back to your list of wonders. Having gilt is good. I've been poor, but now I'm—we're—doing better. And it's good to know that my embroidery will sell well."

"Your embroidery is art. I've always thought so."

She closed her eyes. The man was too good to be true. There must be something wrong with him. He didn't like her working with time, practicing her primary, Familial Flair. His words and the feeling behind them were too cautious.

"As for a loving Family . . . I have Ilex and Trif Winterberry. My mother loves me in her way. I know you believe your Family would accept me . . ."

"They'd adore you. So modest and talented and undemanding, and you make me happy."

Dufleur sniffed, and it was more watery than she cared for. "Nevertheless, they're strangers. All of them. I've had to watch my step with so many strangers lately. And your Family is not going to be pleased if I smudge your title or status with my actions."

His grim smile was as good as her own. "We can fight any dishonor together."

"My father wasn't dishonorable! He wasn't mad, or stupid, or a fool like those women said last night."

"So that's what you heard."

"That's what was said to my face. I'm not used to highborn nobles insulting me at social events—"

"Especially since you didn't want to attend the social events in the first place."

Some of her anger drained. "No. But now I'm stuck, and I must admit Passiflora has been wonderful, and I repaid her poorly last night." Her lips pressed together, then she said, "I'll do better, but D'Birch and her friend were spreading all the lies and rumors again throughout the room. I didn't want to face it. You were right, I was cowardly and ran away."

"HeartMate." He put his hand on her cheek and stroked it with his thumb, and her blood fired once more, and she nearly despaired. They'd just loved, and he aroused her once more with a small touch.

She was overwhelmingly aware that he was naked, and as her pulse ignited with passion, it cycled to him and returned to her with the taste of his own desire. She couldn't resist. Morning light was filtering in the window, another clear, chilling day, she should be home for breakfast.

"Saille," she breathed out, knowing his name roused him further, but wasn't the word he wanted to hear. She added more, echoed what he'd said earlier. "Lover."

And he used that word as a basis . . . his gentle fingers caressed her, his lips pressed against her skin in tender kisses. She strove to keep the mood, to return his gentleness, and allowed herself to slow and explore him, cherished his low moans and quivers.

Once more he tucked her under him and met her eyes. This time his looked blurry with desire. Though he kept the loving slow, it cost him in his ragged breathing. The pleasure inside her slowly spiraled until the ecstasy heightened and she arched to shattering completion and took him with her.

The late dawn of winter brightened the windows before she wriggled from under him.

He groaned again, swept out a hand, and caught her wrist. "HeartMate," he said.

She grabbed his hand with her free one, slipped from his grasp, kissed his fingers. "Lover." She hesitated. "I can give you that much. Lover."

"I have never had such loving," he mumbled. He opened his eyes, and they were less than sharp. She bent and kissed him on the lips.

"Neither have I."

"Another temptation for me to give you."

"I must go." She grimaced and dressed. "Apologize to Passiflora and my mother. She'll expect me for breakfast. I can just manage a quick waterfall and change of clothing."

The FamDoor flapped, and Fairyfoot appeared. She looked at them critically. *You noisy. As noisy as Cats.*

Dufleur felt a flush heat her neck. Saille put an arm over his eyes.

"I'm 'porting on three," said Dufleur.

Fairyfoot leapt, and Dufleur caught her. No extended claws. Good. "One, fabulous Saille. Two, my sweet lover. Three, see you later." And they were on the teleportation pad of Winterberry entryway.

Dufleur dropped Fairyfoot, who made a startled sound. *Rug. No cold stone floor.*

Glancing down as she hurried to the steps to her level, Dufleur saw Fairyfoot was right. An old but beautiful rug—clean as the entryway was clean—now filled most of the chamber. It helped muffle her steps down to her rooms. Good, her mother and D'Winterberry were spending more gilt on the Residence.

A few minutes later, she left Fairyfoot eating furrabeast and walked into the breakfast room.

Her mother was waiting at a small table covered with pristine linen and studying household documents. Grateful for a little respite before a scolding, Dufleur took cheesy eggs and porcine strips from the buffet and ate, refueling herself after the wonderful activities of the morning. She shifted a couple of times in the wooden dining room chair. It had been nearly two years since she'd had sex, and her body twinged.

Several minutes passed as Dufleur ate. She knew her mother

was aware of her, and hoping the anticipation would bother
Dufleur, but this morning she was hungry enough to only concentrate on the food and not worry about her mother's mood.

"Dufleur," her mother finally said in a tone that sent chill
slivers of ice down her spine. Definitely a mother tone. A disap-
proving mother tone. Nothing to do but keep her back stiff and
face expressionless and take whatever berating there would be.
No getting out of it. No defense allowed. The action had already
been judged a crime and eternal nagging punishment was about
to begin.

"Yes, Mother." She set down her silverware. She wouldn't
be able to eat further. Just looking at her cooling eggs made her
queasy.

"GraceLady Caraway scried me this morning." Dufleur
cringed inwardly. That was the name of the woman who'd been
Dringal's false friend. "Already, this early in the morning." Dringal's nostrils pinched. "And told me you'd been rude to D'Birch.
D'Birch of all people. She's not a woman you want to rile. And
that you revived the old gossip about your father and the
Thymes." Muscles clenched in her jaw.

No use in telling her that Agave had primed the women. Especially since Dufleur knew miserably that she'd fueled the fire by
leaving.

"I'll scry Passiflora and apologize," Dufleur said.

"Of course." Dringal waved that away. Shook her head. "Why?
Why did you have to misbehave at this particular moment? The
night before the opening of your show at the Enlli Gallery."

Dufleur froze. She hadn't wanted to think about the gallery
opening, so she'd forgotten. Lady and Lord, it was tonight!

"Mother, it's for you, too."

Dringal went on as if Dufleur hadn't spoken. "You can deal
with the talk on your own tonight. I'm not going."

"But Mother—"

"Absolutely not. I am not going. I've been the object of
enough pity and scandal for the rest of my life."

Now Dufleur knew where she'd gotten the instinct to run and
hide. From her mother. How awful. She hoped she didn't become more like the woman.

"You can deal with the gossip and consequences of your
actions. I'm sure Passiflora will help." She sounded as if she
didn't care. Dufleur knew otherwise. Her mother had anticipated

playing the artist. Had purchased a new dress. Dufleur would pay for ruining this moment of her mother's life forever. She should just forget trying to be a good daughter.

"Worse, Dufleur." Dringal's voice lowered, and Dufleur wanted to bolt for the door at the ominous sign. "You have been experimenting like your father. With time. Downstairs in that room, in the foundation of the house." She lifted a hand to stop any protest, but Dufleur was far beyond that. Her mouth was so dry, she thought opening her lips would peel away skin.

"At least your father had the good sense to use one wing of Thyme Residence. It's all that saved our lives. How dare you put us in danger here, after all D'Winterberry has done for us! After all I have done for us."

Anger freed her, overcoming good sense, and Dufleur snapped, "There was no chance of any danger to you of the Residence." But her mother caught the little flash of guilt.

"Dufleur!"

"It was a very minor eruption. Nothing more than one of the pops that occurred in the old lab."

Her mother paled, and Dufleur realized she'd never understood what went on in the Thyme laboratory.

She hurried on. "Hardly more sound than a noisy teleportation. And I stopped working here immediately so there would be no harm to you or the Residence or D'Winterberry. Now I have an outbuilding on the new estate to work in. With maximum shields."

After staring at Dufleur for a couple of minutes in silence, Dringal obviously gathered her composure and said bitingly, "I wondered about you taking reparations. I didn't think you'd have such sense. But now I know you weren't thinking of me at all, only your work. Again. Still. Just like your father. If you believe I'll live in that house near the laboratory—maximum shields or not—you are very, very wrong." Dringal had put down her silverware and pushed her plate away.

Eyes wide—eyes the same shade of smokey blue as Dufleur's—Dringal said, "Dufleur, I want to see you settled."

Distracted by a husband and children and Residence and social life, Dufleur understood. And her mother was telling the truth. Dringal loved her, in her own way. Dufleur swallowed hard, reckoned her fingers were steady enough to drink her tepid cup of caff.

"I know, Mother."

"I just want you to have a more satisfying life than my own."

Dufleur released her breath slowly. That was true, too, but now Dringal would begin a standard recitation of her woes and who was responsible for them. Dufleur's father used to be at the top of the list, now it was Meyar Winterberry, Ilex Winterberry, then Dufleur. Dufleur was only glad that she hadn't taken first place. She listened with just enough attention not to be reprimanded. Her input in this portion of the discussion wasn't necessary. She wondered if Passiflora would have arisen. It was past WorkBell, but still relatively early, especially for those who'd stayed up much of the night.

"I know it's early yet, but has any young man shown interest?"

Jerking her mind back to the conversation, Dufleur made sure her expression went from attentive to blank.

Dringal tssked. "I thought not. Not even that young man who escorted Passiflora here last night?"

"Saille T'Willow." She kept her tone offhand, refused to remember how she'd lain in his arms a couple of septhours ago.

"Willow," Dringal said with loathing.

"Yes."

"That old besom's Heir."

Another person who didn't think of D'Willow as dead.

"Yes."

Dringal's fingers clenched and unclenched. Then she narrowed her eyes, glanced at the newssheets. "He seems well regarded."

"I saw him occasionally in Dandelion Silk, buying gifts for his Family. He is nothing like his MotherDam."

"Well." Dringal tapped a forefinger on the newssheet absently. "They were estranged, I heard. And he is of a different generation, probably would not ally with those close to D'Willow." She studied Dufleur, then her mouth twisted down. "You seem tired. Try and get some sleep today. That might help your looks." She went back to pondering. "Still, he did escort Passiflora here." She reached for a biscuit. "He defended you to the examiners last night."

He'd done so much more in bed, but sex could be easy. Standing steady for her before authorities could be harder. Even if he was one of those authorities himself.

If she were a GreatLady . . . Don't think of that. That way lay temptation, and there were plenty of instances where First-Family Lords and Ladies had been chastened lately.

Why, the whole Council who'd condemned Ruis Elder had had to walk in ritual robes barefoot in autumn and kneel to him and publicly ask his forgiveness. All of Celta, including Dufleur, had watched the viz in fascination. Hadn't old D'Willow had to do that, too?

Oh, she would have hated that. Dufleur smiled.

"Pay attention, Dufleur, you are as irritating as your father." Her mother's sharp tones brought her back.

"Good, now I have your attention, I think the fact that he defended you is quite telling," she said.

"Telling?"

Dringal smiled. "He has an interest in you."

"Maybe he's softheaded and would have defended anyone." Dringal snorted.

"He's new to his power as a GreatLord. Maybe he's trying it out."

Now her mother looked more thoughtful. "Perhaps. But perhaps he's interested in you." She closed her eyes in near bliss. "To be part of a Great household." Yearning throbbed in her voice. "The best of everything."

Dufleur's stomach tightened. Taking her mother into the Familial warmth of the Willows. Could it possibly soften her? No. She would probably irritate them all. Ruin the comfort that permeated that Residence. Familial love and respect. What a concept.

Another reason to be wary of what Saille offered her.

Her mother tapped her finger on her lips, once again studied Dufleur, shook her head. "I wonder what he sees in you." Then the same finger waved the notion away. "He's a matchmaker. He would know his own mind. And the FirstFamilies marry for much more than beauty and charm."

Behind her pleasant mask, Dufleur winced.

Suddenly her mother's eyes rounded. She glanced around the room, lowered her voice, leaned so far toward Dufleur that her large bosom touched the table. Dufleur leaned forward, too, though there was nothing she'd keep from Winterberry Residence, which knew all her secrets.

Dringal licked her lips, glanced around again. "You don't

think he suspects how much you—the Thymes—can manipulate time?" It had been drummed in both their heads from when Dufleur's Father'sFather was alive that no one must learn how much the Thymes could affect time, how much a weapon controlling time could be. All Thymes, whether born or married into the Family, took long and complicated Vows of Honor to use time in an ethical manner.

Dufleur was sure Saille knew she could manipulate time greatly. He'd been in the construct of her Flair, had seen her lab. But even her mother didn't know how much Dufleur could affect time. Nor had her father. Dufleur wasn't even certain herself. She hadn't totally tested her limits.

"If he were interested, it wouldn't be because he believes in time manipulation. That's a detriment right now, with the laws."

"You will encourage him."

"Mother—"

"If there is any possibility that he might want you, we want to be nice to him." She sent Dufleur a hard look. "You may go now."

"Thank you." She slipped from her seat and left, and muttered at herself for being so concerned about what her mother thought, for staying with her. She should leave this place.

But couldn't when her mother and D'Winterberry were still under examination for fitness.

Once back in her rooms, Dufleur couldn't settle. Certainly not into any embroidery on the Temple Tapestry, or even anything for the gallery. Her fingers held a fine trembling that would make a mess of even a mousie for Fairyfoot. She did scry Passiflora and make another abject apology for leaving her without word the night before and was, of course, graciously forgiven. Which made her feel even more guilty for her cowardice.

She knew her mind was too distracted to start on the new experiments, though she'd outlined a series the night before. She had no social obligations this morning, found herself pacing her bedroom and stopped. Since her temper was riled and it seemed like a morning for confrontations, she decided to go to the root of her current problems.

T'Agave. He'd reminded D'Birch of the gossip around her father and her Family, then stood aside and smirked. And though Dufleur had taken precautions to shield her work from him, she had no doubt that he would continue to make trouble—to interrupt her work or spy on her. Better she should face him.

So she dressed in new, stylish tunic and trous of dark blue, suitable for a minor noblewoman who practiced her profession, bundled into a new coat, hat, scarf, and gloves, all of a rusty, foxy red, and took the public carrier to his street. As she walked the block to his house, she observed the neighborhood. Old, settled, minor nobility rowhouses made of various colors and textures of stone that blended together in a welcoming whole. One or two of the buildings had the general aura of a Residence—a house becoming a sentient entity through the Flair and nurturing of the Family.

She frowned. They were very close together, and though it lent cohesiveness to the neighborhood, it also meant that damage from fire or explosion could spread easily. Her teeth gritted at the memory of her own Residence, about the size of two of these, and set well in the center of a half-block lot. Neither of the Residences on the other side of T'Thyme Residence had been harmed.

Stopping at the yellow door of Agave's home, Dufleur strove to recall details of her competitor's life. No wife, Family grown and moved away? She thought so. A son who had more of his mother's Flair—for holospheres—than interest in time. No other Family who lived and worked in the house—it wasn't a Residence—as staff.

After knocking briskly, she waited for a couple of minutes before a grumbling woman wearing a housekeeper's apron opened the door. Dufleur stood straight. "ThymeHeir to see T'Agave."

"Huh." It was the only thing the lean woman said before leading Dufleur through a long hallway of the house to a back addition that was obviously a laboratory. With the workroom, the house took up nearly the entire space of the lot.

The housekeeper touched a gleaming crystal. "ThymeHeir here to see you." She nodded to Dufleur and left.

Small sounds came from behind a sturdy door. With her Flair, Dufleur tested the shields. Security shields were strong. The protective shields were minor. Just the opposite of the

Thymes's practice. Finally, the door opened, and as soon as there was barely enough space for her to slip inside, Dufleur did so. She had to brush Agave's thick, paunchy body, and he scowled. "Why don't you come in?"

Nineteen

❤

$\mathcal{T}$hank you." *She gave him her sweetest smile. He frowned*
harder. Well, she didn't have much in the way of sweet smiles.
Tilting her head, she said, "Don't you think it's counterproduc-
tive to your own studies to inflame gossip about the Thymes?"

He grunted. "I'm not doing anything illegal."

She didn't believe that for an instant. She scanned the room.
His equipment was the finest, his long table less scarred and his
papers and memoryspheres organized tidier than hers. She went
to the table, put her pursenal down in a suspiciously empty spot
the size of a standard no-time, and leaned against it, watching
him.

"What do you want?" he muttered.

"I want you to stop the nasty talk once more making the
rounds about my Family." It took all her control to look relaxed.

"Too late, even you should realize that, and the wonderful
thing about such talk is that it isn't rumors, it's fact." He grinned,
and she noted one of his eyeteeth overlapped another. Since that
was a matter easily corrected, he must have had a preference for
keeping it that way.

Mist parting.

A young woman laughed, Dufleur could swear she felt the
vibrations in the table, but instead she recognized time gathering around her—more motes in this laboratory than usual, even
in her own. Had he been in the middle of an experiment when
she'd knocked on his door? If so, why had he let her in?

"Angusti, your mouth is sooo luscious," the woman said.

Dufleur blinked, and a younger, fitter Agave grinned past
her.

*"My new table needs to be initiated. It has some wonderful
built-in spells,"* he said. He was aroused.

Dufleur jerked to stand straightly, letting go of the table. Her
Flair wasn't for telemetry, sensing emotions from objects. The
time eddies . . .

"What do you think you're doing?" he demanded.

Surprised, she stared at her own hand. She'd been stroking the table, feeling the saturation of time within it, affecting it.

"What did you just learn?" he snapped.

She lifted a shoulder. "You know how time is. A little glimpse into the past."

He stared at her. Then said, "Your father meddled with forces he didn't understand and blew himself and his Residence up." He grunted again. "You and your mother were lucky to get out alive."

Now her grim smile was back, with teeth. "Like this place, our laboratory was attached to one side of the building." Her grip went tight on the table edge behind her.

"I'm not going to have any *accidents*," he said.

"My father knew what he was doing. He was twice the scientist you are. Three times," she said.

Color came to his cheeks, his nostrils widened, but he only said, "You can't know that. You don't know me or my work."

"I can extrapolate. A man who is secure in his own theories doesn't go spying on others."

His lip curled. "You can't prove that."

She lifted her own brows. "No?"

He shrugged. "No. If you could have, if the Winterberrys could have, I would have spoken with a Guardsman by now, eh?"

"Don't think that you will be able to enter my laboratory ever again."

"I heard you moved to another place. Got a windfall of a property."

Shock swept through her. That he had no concept what she'd suffered during the attempted murder, that she would welcome the reparation.

"But that place doesn't come near to what you Thymes had." He glanced around with satisfaction. "Now this is the premiere time laboratory on Celta. The person who discovers how to reverse the progress of disease will be remembered on Celta forever."

"Is that why you're duplicating our studies and not pursuing some other inquiry regarding time?" She made her voice scornful.

He snorted. "I'm working on that for the very same reason

your father did. Gilt. A decade ago D'Willow offered a reward to anyone—Healer or other—who could cure her. The virus is a simple organism; if time can be reversed in any living thing to destroy it, that virus is it. The time Families have been experimenting with reversing or speeding the flow since our Flair was discovered. Why shouldn't I be the one to find the secret? Your father failed."

Her father had never worked simply for the gilt, but she wouldn't waste her breath. "Perhaps he miscalculated." She hated admitting it and kept her voice steady. She spent a long moment scanning the room again, observing his instruments, letting the wind of time whisper by her. "But it's obvious why you stole into the Winterberrys' to read my notes. You aren't close to any consistent results. Any successful result at all." Her tone quieted, serious. "And I'll give you several warnings. Heed your own words. Don't meddle in something you don't understand."

Bright spots of red appeared on his cheeks.

"And I won't tolerate any lies about my Family. Be careful what you say."

"I'll follow D'Willow's example," he sneered.

That hurt, but she didn't let it show. She picked up her pursenal, stared pointedly at the empty place, then looked at another door to the room that appeared to be to a vault, insinuating that his experiments weren't worthy of hiding. "Don't *ever* come near my laboratory again. I'll know if you do, and remember that my cuz is a Guardsman—even without proof he'll listen to me."

He looked uneasy, then said, "Stick to your embroidery needle, Dufleur." He grinned again, once more in control, superior. "Better yet, let that pretty boy, Saille Willow, take care of you." He snorted. "Must be giving old D'Willow nightmares, how he's panting after you." Agave raked her with a look. "His interest is probably just rebellion because she hated you Thymes."

Dufleur threw him a disdainful look as she shoved the heavy door open. "If that's a sample of your reasoning, it's no wonder you're so far behind us in experimenting with time. GreatLord T'Willow must make good alliances, and now you've started the gossip about the Thymes going around again. I am not the kind of woman he should take as a wife, am I?" In a show of

Flair, she teleported to D'Winterberry Residence. No doubt Agave conserved Flair as she did, keeping it for his experiments. But she wouldn't be doing anything more important than dancing for the rest of the day.

When she entered her bedroom, Fairyfoot sat in the middle of the bed, radiating love and purring loudly. Dufleur stared, then finally figured out that she was looking at a reformed cat, a true loving Familiar companion. For the moment.

She sighed and undressed to put on more casual clothes, shabby trous and a long work tunic with slits to the waist. She stared uneasily at the safe that still held Saille's HeartGift, then flopped onto the bed, making Fairyfoot jump aside. The cat started to hiss, cut herself off, and smiled instead.

Fairyfoot gave a little cough. *The MistrysSuite in T'Willow Residence is looovely.*

"I don't want to hear about that Residence, or that man." Dufleur wriggled around until she was comfortable and folded her arms under her head.

Where have you been? Fairyfoot sounded conciliatory.

"To Agave's."

Fairyfoot sputtered. *Nasty man. I should have gone, too.*

"You weren't here. You were about your own business."

Learning about our FamMan, she said slyly.

"Huh," Dufleur said, more interested in her conclusions about Agave.

Fairyfoot climbed on Dufleur's stomach, curled around, and stared at her. *What of the nasty man?*

"I don't think he is nearly as competent with time as my father."

Or you. You are better than your father. And nasty man is an upstart.

"The Agaves have more than a century of Familial Time Flair, that's not upstart."

Compared to Thymes, from Discovery Day.

Dufleur smiled. "Not quite. I think the oldest records in the GuildHall put us as recording our Flair and our Family name and GrandLord title at seventy years after colonization."

Old.

"Um." She shifted on the bed. "The more I think about it, the more I believe Father mentioned a partner . . ." Her memories of shortly before the tragedy had been fogged with grief. "He

seemed more secretive than usual. And I think we had more gilt."
She thought of her mother; Dringal hadn't known about any income. "At least enough to buy a few new pieces of equipment."
Following that notion, she said, "But now that I've spoken with him, I'm sure Agave wasn't Father's partner. If he had one."

Don't know. Fairyfoot stopped mid-sniff and purred again.

"No," Dufleur said, petting her cat. "You weren't my Fam then. I'm glad you're here." The few hours' sleep she'd gotten between the examiners and waking in Saille's arms now felt all too short. Drowsiness crept upon her. "Glad you've decided to be reasonable."

FamMan loves Us.

The twinge of alarm Dufleur felt at that statement wasn't quite enough to keep her from falling asleep.

*W*ith no matchmaking appointments, and a restlessness at wanting to claim Dufleur and being unable to do so, Saille dressed warmly and walked the estate. Set in Noble Country, that portion of Druida where most FirstFamilies had their Residences, it was large with several outbuildings. He tramped the grounds to one corner near the cliffs overlooking the Great Platte Ocean and wondered if Dufleur would like the view of the sea and the sky and thought she would. It would be a wonderful change from stone walls or the bland view outside the windows of her new laboratory.

Then he considered if the ground was solid enough to withstand an explosion.

The very thought of it gnawed at his gut. He didn't want Dufleur involved in anything so dangerous that it would harm her—let alone his Family, Residence, and estate. But he recalled how he'd had to hide the fact that he practiced his own Flair in the country from his MotherDam. It was easy to remember how he ached to use his gift to the fullest. What beautiful china he'd made with his creative Flair when his greatest Flair had been stifled. Rather like the beautiful embroidery Dufleur had hanging in Enlli Gallery.

How much did she experiment with time? How dangerous was it really? He shivered and knew it wasn't solely from the cold, clear day. And what an odd and wonderful Flair to have. Time.

He had no clue about the nature of time.

But he knew Flair and the strength of it, and knew Dufleur's was powerful. That eerie gray plain he'd visited. A construct of her Flair, she had called it. Something to do with time. He'd seen her garbed like a golden Lady, the Lady who controlled time? Another shivering thought. He didn't know what she'd seen, or how he'd appeared, but he recalled the clarity of the dream-place, how he could use his own Flair there to discover the problems in the matches his MotherDam had made.

He didn't know who he could talk to about this. Who he could possibly consult. Who he could trust.

There was a tiny whoosh of air behind him, and he stiffened, understanding he was no longer alone. He waited.

"Hello, T'Willow," said a boy's light voice.

And then Saille knew, even without turning around. Why he'd come here. Why this person had come when he had questions about the past and the future. The Lord and Lady had directed him, directed them both.

"Greetyou GreatLord T'Vine," he said to the prophet, a boy of eleven or twelve.

"Call me Vinni."

He turned slowly, and when he met the boy's gray eyes, a blinding flash erupted in his mind—his Flair recognizing the power in the child, knowing that the boy would never be one of his clients. He already knew his HeartMate.

"You have great Flair," said Vinni, appearing smaller and less formidable when Saille blinked. The boy's smile was crooked. "And we're connected somehow, a past life perhaps." He tilted his head. "My son will marry your daughter."

For a moment Saille couldn't speak. He processed the words. "You're a lot younger than I am. And despite everything it is still usual for a man to be older than his wife. Sometimes much older." He wondered if what the boy said was a fixed, true future and what it meant for him and Dufleur. Did it mean that he lost her and waited a long time before taking a wife instead of a HeartMate? Fear clutched his throat.

Vinni joined him and turned to look at the ocean, the white-capped waves whipped up by the wind. Saille muttered a word to increase the warmth of his clothing. He'd never been good at weathershield spells and felt that lack as cold was raw on his face. He cleared his throat. "What do you know of time?"

"I try not to think about the aspects of time. It makes my head hurt." The boy glanced up at him, eyes green-brown. Saille had heard about the boy's changeable eyes and it was as disconcerting as talk said.

"Hazel," Saille said, and a tremor of Flair pulsed through him.

"My HeartMate is Avellana Hazel, you're right. Should she live to bond with me, which is undetermined." Now he appeared far too old for his years. "Her survival is precarious, especially during her Passages." He brooded, then glanced at Saille. "We have already deflected one threat from her. Your HeartGift played a part in that, so I owe you."

Saille narrowed his eyes. "How?"

The boy kicked a rock hard, sending it sailing over the cliff and into the sea. He didn't look at Saille directly. "One of Avellana's futures was to die the youngest victim of a black magic cult."

Breath whooshed from Saille, he had to force words from a tight throat. "Instead, because of my HeartGift's effect on Dufleur, she fit their profile better, and they took her."

Vinni turned his back on the sea and started back to the main Residence. "That's right. I'm sorry." That sounded oddly muffled.

Despite his twisting gut, Saille put a hand on the boy's shoulder. Vinni turned his head away.

Words came from somewhere deep inside Saille. "You can't hold yourself responsible for every outcome that you see. I'm sure there were . . . several. Avellana's how old?"

"Five." Vinni sniffed wetly.

Saille stopped in his tracks. He thought of the horror Dufleur had experienced, something he'd wished he could have banished from her life, taken on himself. Then he thought of a young, Flaired, girl child in murderous hands. More words tore from him. "You shouldn't feel guilty for being glad it was Dufleur instead of Avellana or Trif Winterberry instead of Avellana." He sucked in a breath. "Anyone would prefer that an adult who could attempt to fight back or did fight back be in that situation instead of a helpless child. *Anyone.*"

Clearing his throat, Vinni looked up at Saille with clear green eyes. "Avellana's not exactly helpless, but she doesn't know her Flair or the strength of it."

"She's a baby."

Vinni snorted. "Only because you're so old."

"Twenty-eight is not old."

"Not compared to your ancient MotherDam." Vinni paused. "And that's whom you're always compared to. By yourself as well as others, right?" He didn't wait for an answer but went on in a musing tone, "I guess everyone who knew my ancestress, my predecessor, will compare me to her. She was a good woman and an excellent seer, but I'm not like her."

Those simple words sent a jolt through Saille. His Mother-Dam was a selfish woman and a wretched matchmaker in her last years, but he was *nothing* like her. He could definitely lead the Family in a different direction.

"Why are you here, Vinni?"

"You don't want a formal consultation, say, to learn if your MotherDam will be revived in your lifetime?"

Another blow. The boy certainly knew Saille's weak points. Saille thought he might know everyone's weak spots. No wonder most people avoided him.

"Pointing out my deepest concerns is not endearing to me," Saille said drily. "If you don't want to be avoided, take my advice and don't prod people's tender areas."

Vinni scowled. "You think that's why some folks evade me?"

"One factor."

"Oh." He chewed on his lip. "Um. I'll think about that."

A trickle of relieved sweat slipped down Saille's spine. He'd sent Vinni's attention away from himself and any prophetic visions. Perhaps he was like most people who thought if they didn't hear an accurate prediction of their future, they'd be able to change the event. Which brought him back to time. But he repeated his question. "Why are you here, Vinni?"

"I dunno." Vinni shifted his shoulders. "I just felt that I should come. And you're a new GreatLord, and I hadn't met you yet, and there's all that stuff about alliances, too."

Saille stared at him, knowing the boy was the strongest Flaired person of his generation. Obviously his Flair gave him great insights, but he was still a boy with limited understanding. They'd reached the outbuilding closest to the Residence, which Saille had had remodeled into a studio with his potting wheel and a kiln.

"Come in," he said abruptly, placing his hand on the palm-plate and reciting the couplet that would drop the security spellshield. "You can have your choice of my work. I have two creative gifts: pottery and perfumery. I've been concentrating on pottery lately."

Vinni gazed at him.

"Why?"

Shrugging, Saille said, "Because of that link between us. Because I think I like you. Because I want you to consider an alliance between our Families." He frowned a moment, not remembering. "Did you send me a gift upon my ascension to the T'Willow title? I can't recall."

"I don't know, either. My Family, like yours, is mostly women. They would have sent something appropriate, but not personal." Vinni had entered first and was looking at the range of items on the shelves. Made from various clays, there was everything from a wide and shallow scrybowl of earthenware to a small, nearly translucent cup of porcelain. In this one area, his mother had supported him, ensuring whatever he needed for his creative Flair was sent to him. Saille didn't know what that had cost her with *her* mother, the old D'Willow, but knew that there would have been a price.

"We aren't our predecessors," Vinni said softly.

Saille might have thought that he was speaking idly since he had lifted a set of deep purple glazed runes incised with gold, tools for both of them, or personal divination for both of them, but the remark once again resonated against his spine.

"No, we aren't," Saille said and thought it another similarity between them that they were both following a very strong female Head of the household.

"I like these," Vinni said, clicking several of the fired pieces between his fingers.

"They're yours."

"Thank you." He looked at the worktable with interest, walked to the potter's wheel and stared at it, glanced toward the door to the small building that housed the kiln. "Interesting Flair you have here, T'Willow." He grinned. "Have you considered exhibiting your work in the Enlli Gallery? It would make a nice contrast with Dufleur Thyme's embroidery."

Saille just closed his eyes a moment. The boy knew his

HeartMate was Dufleur. Ilex Winterberry knew, so his Heart-Mate, Trif of the Clovers, probably knew. SupremeJudge Ailim Elder knew and had no doubt told her husband. At this rate, soon all of Druida would know, and pressure would be applied to Dufleur to wed with him. He preferred to do his own wooing, finesse his own bride.

It was on the tip of Saille's tongue to ask Vinni how soon he'd be successful in his suit, but Saille kept his mouth shut. He wanted this courtship to be right. That he win his lady honorably and with no cheating. He was not his MotherDam.

"Take the runes, Vinni." Saille handed him a pale green velvet bag to store the pieces in.

The boy gave him a cheeky grin and tumbled the runes into the pouch, his fingers lingering on one or two. Vinni's obvious pleasure in the gift made Saille smile in satisfaction.

"So, why did *you* want to see *me*, GreatLord T'Willow?"

Twenty

I *was thinking of time,"* Saille said.

"I'd imagine you'd often be thinking of Thyme."

Saille frowned in admonishment. "The nature of time."

Vinni sobered, tilted his head, then shook it. "I don't know the nature of time. I don't manipulate it. I simply see visions. Futures. Options. Paths." His brows dipped. "Yours grows darker ahead. In every instance."

Saille's mouth dried. He cleared his throat. "I don't think I needed to know that."

"I think it's best to be prepared, not to be ignorant."

They were never going to agree on this, Saille thought. Vinni might never agree with anyone on this. He recalled being on that plain that was Dufleur's Flair construct, how she stared as if seeing what he couldn't. "Do you see the past as well as the future?"

Vinni's eyes—still green—widened. And Saille felt satisfaction at surprising the young GreatLord. "No. Only the future. Though I know that Trif Winterberry can see past events, call them up. But I think she is like me and the other prophets and oracles of Celta. Our Flair sends us visions, we do not see through the past or future or manipulate time. You think Dufleur Thyme can sense time?"

He wasn't about to imperil Dufleur in any way, leave her open to any slur, any injury. "I don't know."

Vinni's eyes changed, took on a silver sheen. "Isn't that odd," he whispered. "When I look at you, I can see some of your paths. When I use your link with her to look at her, everything is fluid, like she is always in motion." He stepped back, bumped into the worktable, sent Saille a shaky smile. "I'm not as skilled as I thought."

"Always good to understand our limitations." Saille's voice came out rougher than he'd anticipated.

The boy nodded. "Yes." Then he grimaced. "But I don't like it."

"No one does."

"I think I should go. Take care, T'Willow." Vinni squinted. "I saw . . . traps."

"Traps?" Saille said sharply.

"And shadows on your path." He hesitated. "And turning back."

"Turning back?"

Vinni shrugged. "Turning back, or over and over. I don't know what it means. But take care." He made an elegant bow and 'ported away, taking the set of runes Saille had specifically made for him. Over the years he'd made runes for every First-Family. Vinni was the first to accept them.

Scratching came at the door, then a yowl, reminding Saille that he hadn't made a Famdoor for Myx yet in here. He'd definitely keep the kiln off-limits to his Fam. He went over and opened the door to Myx.

Greetyou. It was more growl than polite salutation. But Saille noticed snowflakes melting in the cat's fur. Going to the window, he saw clouds had swept in while he and Vinni had been talking.

"Do you need a towel to rub you dry?" The building had a waterfall room, hot-square and several food no-times, a small apartment if he wanted to stay there.

No towel. Myx's back rippled, then he sat down and groomed his whiskers. He glanced at Saille and started a loud, rusty purr. *Sensed you upset and needed Me.*

Saille squatted by him and stroked him gently. Both Vinni and Myx had felt he wanted them. Saille wondered what sort of aura or Flair signals he was emitting. Then wondered why Dufleur hadn't perceived the same. But knew the answer to that question immediately. She'd narrowed the link between them, not breaking it, but not completely acknowledging it, acknowledging him as her HeartMate, either.

She hadn't accepted the HeartBond during their lovemaking. In fact, he was sure that was another thing she hadn't perceived. Every time they'd joined, bodies, emotions, minds, he'd thrown her the golden HeartBond. It had simply bounced off what *he* sensed was an impenetrable shield around her heart.

That had hurt, a dull, aching agony that hadn't fully diminished. Was anything so painful as being rejected by a HeartMate, a person made to complement you? Saille didn't think so.

And experiencing this hurt would make him better at his work, he was sure, but he'd just as soon as not endure it.

Dufleur hadn't even noticed the HeartBond. Probably didn't even know anything about HeartBonds, how they were formed, when they were formed.

Only that she didn't want one.

She didn't seem to want anyone to be close to her in her life. Why not?

He could only believe that it was rooted in her childhood, as most wounds were. Her life with her parents. Her mother was certainly a self-absorbed woman. He wondered about her father, the father she was determined to prove was sane and honorable. How close had she been to him?

She had the Thyme Flair for time. Of that he was sure. She was breaking the laws of Druida, set in place after her father's death at the urging of Saille's MotherDam. What a mess.

Myx hissed. *You pulled my hair out.*

"It was a matt. It wasn't attached too much."

You didn't feel it.

"I apologize."

Myx grinned. *FamMan apologizes well. Not like stup Cat Fairyfoot.*

Saille cleared his throat. "How's Fairyfoot doing?"

She has lost face. She must be a very loving Fam to recover.

"That will help Dufleur."

"Yessss." *I have always been a loving Fam.*

"For the few days we've known each other."

Always, Myx agreed.

Saille raised his brows. "Which means?"

Myx gave a little cough. *I should have a collar.*

"I see."

Stretching his body under Saille's hand, Myx said, *You could make beads.*

"I could."

In History of Cats on Ship, I saw bright blue beads. Myx projected an image.

"Faience." Tin-glazed clay.

I would like beads like those.

"Our color is scarlet."

Blue.

"Very well." He thought of the dusty brown cat wearing

bright blue faience beads and shuddered. Another cat without taste. He supposed he should be grateful for a Fam at all. And this one was loyal to him.

Good. Myx butted his head against Saille's hand for more petting. *I am good at walking in shadows.*

"What?"

I will walk in the shadows with you.

He'd wanted to forget Vinni's prophecy. Now he knew he wouldn't. "That's good of you."

"Yesss."

*S*he was awakened by the low, repetitively irritating tune of her scrybowl. How had she ever thought that music lovely? Certainly wasn't a Passiflora D'Holly melody. Groggy, she squinted at the bowl, saw multicolored swirls of blue light. D'Sea, the mind Healer, was calling. Dufleur's stomach knotted. She wanted to curl up in a fetal ball.

"Dufleur," said the melodious voice of the FirstFamilies GrandLady. "Please answer the scry. I know you're there, though I'm sorry I woke you." Of course she would know, they still had a telepathic link between them, likely always would. "I'll wait, Dufleur."

The message cache was large. Seven minutes. D'Sea would wait that entire time. Then call back. They'd been through this pattern before. Dufleur heaved herself from bed, noting that Fairyfoot still snored gently on her corner of the bed.

As she wobbled to the scrybowl, Dufleur picked a hairbrush off a table and pulled it ruthlessly through her hair, feeling the new shorter style fall into place. That was something.

She tapped the side of the scrybowl, and the tune stopped. Taking a deep breath, but forbearing to paste a smile on her face that D'Sea would see through, Dufleur answered, "Greetyou, D'Sea."

"Merry meet, Dufleur." D'Sea appeared as calm and serene as ever, middle-aged heart-shaped face interestingly lined, compassionate blue green eyes. "I heard that the Councils' Herald visited you and wondered how you were doing."

"Did she reimburse you?"

Hauteur chilled the pretty face, and thin, brown eyebrows lifted. "I donated my services and will continue to do so. It's the least I could do." Her eyes sharpened. "I also heard that you had accepted reparations, and believed that was an excellent step, but then thought that circumstances might have forced you into doing so." In the holo image formed by water droplets above the bowl, D'Sea tilted her head to study Dufleur and gave a slight sigh. "You look weary and strained."

Dufleur tried a weak but genuine smile. "I'm not used to the social season." She coughed, felt her face settle back into a serious expression. "Rumors about my father were rampant at the ball last night. All the old gossip." She grimaced. "I didn't handle it well. I was accused of running away."

"By whom?"

"Uh, a new friend."

"Resistant to counseling as usual, Dufleur."

"I'm sor—" she remembered not to apologize for something she wasn't really sorry for just in time. Another pattern. "I haven't been an easy patient."

That rewarded her with a faint smile. "No you haven't, but I think I made some errors in your treatment, and that only added to your problems. I apologize for that."

"You've been very good."

"Nevertheless you were glad to stop seeing me. I do understand, but at least I know I helped you some."

"You helped a great deal."

"No flashbacks?"

"None." There'd been a few nightmares, but that wasn't the same.

D'Sea sighed again. "It's a pity the emotional distance therapy didn't work as well as usual. I still don't understand why."

Dufleur thought she did. She was aware of the wind of time in every cell of her body. Convincing her mind that the events that had taken place a couple of months ago were decades old didn't really work. She smiled again, this time more gently. D'Sea was a very nice and competent woman. "It seems as if more than a year has passed, at least."

D'Sea frowned. "That places your attempted murder in the same time frame as your father's death. Not good."

"I'm doing well enough."

"I'd like to schedule you for another session."

"I'd rather not."

After a searching gaze and a touch of Flair on Dufleur's

mind that she endured, D'Sea nodded. "I'll consider it." They both knew that if D'Sea decided Dufleur needed more treatment, no one would gainsay her, and Dufleur would be back in D'Sea's client comfortchair. "I'll decide tonight when I see you at the opening of your show at Enlli Gallery." Her face softened. "I'm very proud that you are exhibiting your work, Dufleur. It's a wonderful opportunity for you."

"Thank you," Dufleur said, trying not to look nervous at the reminder of the show. The evening would be nothing but socializing and being personally talked about, and right after last night when stories of her father would still be circulating. Definitely something she'd prefer to run away from. She stiffened her spine. "It will be good to see you there." D'Sea liked her, Dufleur knew, would be on her side if sides were taken. Somehow Dufleur couldn't imagine Quert Apple tolerating any scene in his gallery. That notion cheered her. "It truly will be good to see you," she repeated, unable to think of anything else to say to express her feelings.

"Thank you. And how is Fairyfoot doing?"

A bright light of realization burst in Dufleur's head. Fairyfoot. Fairyfoot was being difficult, and it might relate to her experience with the black magic cult, too. Of course. "We're relating better." In the last few hours.

"Good. I hope to see her, too."

"She'll be there." Dufleur had no doubt about that.

"Merry part," D'Sea said.

"And merry meet again, tonight," Dufleur ended the standard saying.

The water in the scrybowl rippled, and D'Sea vanished. Dufleur walked with shaky legs to her bed and sat. It was midafternoon, too late to go to her laboratory and work on the next phase of her experiments. Too early to prepare for the showing.

She reached out and pet Fairyfoot, savoring the softness of the cat's fur, healthier now that she wasn't living on the streets. Dufleur stood, then picked up Fairyfoot. The cat shifted in her arms, looked up with sleepy green eyes, and purred.

"We're going to scry Danith D'Ash," she informed her Fam, who scowled.

Hate scrybowl! D'Ash is mean.

"That's what we're going to talk to D'Ash about."

Fairyfoot's whiskers twitched, and a gleam came to her eyes. *You will tell her how wonderful I am.*

"We'll talk to her."

Walking over to the scrybowl on its table, Dufleur made sure to angle her body and Fairyfoot away from the bowl. "D'Ash," she projected her voice, so her breath disturbed the water.

"Here." D'Ash answered the scry after a few seconds, looking a little harassed. She blinked at the sight of Dufleur and Fairyfoot. "Is anything wrong with Fairyfoot?" she asked, concerned.

"Not physically. But I think some of her behavior lately has been because of the horrible . . ." An image came of a black room, being tied to an altar, Fairyfoot beside her, linked hands holding a knife over her chest. Dufleur stopped and breathed through the memory. Not a flashback. Not quite, and why had D'Sea put that idea in her head anyway? Just a memory. She continued her sentence and hoped D'Ash hadn't noticed the couple of seconds of hesitation. "Because of what we went through just before Samhain."

"Ohhh." Danith D'Ash smile was as gentle and compassionate as D'Sea's. "Of course. She has such a large, courageous personality that we tend to forget that she was a victim, too."

Fairyfoot emitted a pitiful mew, accompanied with big, round eyes.

"And she tends to manipulation," said D'Ash.

"More than tends," Dufleur muttered.

D'Ash tapped a finger on her lips. "Let me think what we can do."

"You're The Animal Healer."

"Yes," D'Ash said, "and I worked with Fairyfoot at the time both physically and using distancing Healing, but we should have expected additional time to heal, the poor soul."

Fairyfoot mewed.

"But I don't often try to mend animal minds. They aren't, after all, like ours." Her expression turned grim. "There were more victims of that cult than humans. Even though the Fam-People died, the Fams survived. Six Fams survived. I've kept in touch with all the new human companions." A small line knit between her brows. "Oddly enough, the Fams that are the most stable now are those that your cuz, Ilex Winterberry, questioned during the investigation. You might ask him to work with Fairy-foot, if he hasn't?"

Did cuz Ilex ever talk to you, Fairyfoot? asked Dufleur.

Only when he brought me to you.

"No," Dufleur said to D'Ash. "That's a good idea. He'll be at the Enlli Gallery tonight. Perhaps he can take a few minutes . . ."

"I'm sorry, Dufleur, we can't make it—"

Dufleur flushed. "I didn't think you . . . that is, I expected that you have other plans."

D'Ash smiled. "We do, and we're not much for the social season. In fact, we don't go, but Holm HollyHeir persuaded us to make an exception for their ball next week. Who can miss a ball at Holly Residence? I think it's the first in decades."

"Ah, yes. I'll see you then."

"Earlier than that. Ruis and Ailim Elder are opening part of the starship *Nuada's Sword* for a ball. No one can miss that, either?"

"I imagine not." Dufleur didn't like the Ship, the Time Wind was a little odd in it.

An angry child shrieked in the background of the scrybowl. D'Ash winced. "Nuin is not happy. I'm sorry, I must go."

"Of course."

"And if Fairyfoot has any continuing problems, bring her to me. Oh, and I'll remind the cat community that she and her FamWoman nearly died at the hands of the black cult. Fairy-foot, no more punishment, but you must continue to help your FamWoman, she needs love as much as you. Blessed be." D'Ash signed off hurriedly.

Fairyfoot gave a little wiggle in Dufleur's arms then purred even louder. *Life is good.*

"For the moment," Dufleur said and thought she could get a little work done in the lab after all.

*D*ufleur hurried from the Residence the moment she sensed the Holly glider drive up. She was nervous enough to run down the steps and barely wait for the footman to open the glider door, even so an excited Fairyfoot jumped in first.

"Where's Dringal?" asked Passiflora.

"She's ill."

There were a few instants of silence as if Passiflora was considering the lie. "Ah. Well." She glanced out the window at the lights that flowed by. "I should not say it, but I prefer your embroidery to her lace. It's very good, but not quite good enough to be featured in the Enlli Gallery by itself. Still, a mother-daughter show with similar Flairs, that hasn't been done too often." She let out a long breath. "And after all, you are here."

"Yes." Dufleur endeavored to insert a little sincerity into her grim smile.

Passiflora laughed. "Better."

I am here, too, Fairyfoot said. *People will want to see Me. Especially now I have My Collar.* She swiveled her head so Passiflora could admire it.

"The collar arrived a few minutes ago, since we decided on more stones. You're the first to be shown it." Dufleur smiled.

"I'm honored," Passiflora said, then put a gloved hand on Dufleur's locked fingers, and Dufleur met her eyes. "You should truly try to smile genuinely more often, Dufleur, your real smile is . . . radiant."

My FamWoman is beautiful when she smiles, Fairyfoot agreed.

Dufleur stared.

Rolling her eyes, Passiflora said, "Surely you know that."

"I always thought people complimented me on my smile because I'm plain and it's something else they can say." She lifted her hands and let them drop, another awkward conversation. The whole day had been talking, talking, talking, and she was getting worse at expressing herself. Lady and Lord knew how she'd handle the gallery opening. Smile. Small talk.

"You are *not* plain. You are attractive. And your smile is incredible. You believe that, Dufleur."

"Yes." She'd agree to anything. She was glad she hadn't eaten a heavy meal.

"You're nervous." Passiflora patted her hands. "As I was during the first reception after the soiree where my first composition was debuted. Dufleur, your embroidery is gorgeous. Can you believe that?"

"Yes." She knew it. She just wasn't used to people looking at it as art, or complimenting her on her work.

"Remember that I am here to support you. This is your night, Dufleur, your moment." Which meant that Passiflora wouldn't be doing any obvious politicking, Dufleur supposed, then felt ashamed at the thought. Her emotions were too vivid, not under control.

I am here, too. Saille T'Willow will come. Ilex will come, though I do not think his fox will come.

"I don't think foxes like gallery openings," Dufleur said.

They are not as civilized as Cats. Trif will come. Mitchella and Straif T'Blackthorn will come. D'Sea will come.

Dufleur didn't know whether the list helped or not. She breathed deeply, settled into her center. For a moment she wished that her real work was more social, she'd know how to handle people better.

"All the Apples will be there, and all the Hollys. Even Genista, Tinne's wife." Passiflora hesitated. "I promised she could have her pick of your work, or that we would commission something special for her, whatever she liked. I think the idea of being with beautiful art and away from T'Holly Residence soothed her spirits."

"I'd love to embroider something for Genista. She's a lovely woman and complements anything she wears."

Passiflora eased beside her. "Yes, she is. If you would say that to her, I'd be grateful. She's had a hard time lately."

"Of course."

The glider stopped, and they were there.

Twenty-one

♥

$\mathcal{D}$*ufleur's breath came rapidly.*

"Calm." Passiflora put a hand on Dufleur's arm and drained away the nerves. Dufleur closed her eyes in gratitude. "Thank you."

"I've perfected the calming spell. I use it often enough on my journeywoman, Trif."

Dufleur smiled again and let it widen at the Holly footman as the door opened and she stepped from the glider. He blinked and appeared a little dazed.

"I told you that your smile is potent," Passiflora said.

"Surely I've smiled at him before."

"I don't think so."

Fairyfoot purred at him in appreciation, then hurried up the cold stone walk to the door. An Apple doorman enveloped in a weather shield held back one side of the arched wooden doors, and warm air laden with the sounds and scents of the gallery rolled over Dufleur.

"We're fashionably late, as an artist should be," Passiflora said as they left their outerwear with another Apple. Without letting Dufleur drag her feet, Passiflora linked arms with her and brought her into the showroom of her and her mother's work.

Breath caught in Dufleur's throat. The presentation of her pieces was dazzling. Her embroidery was lit in subtle ways that accented the time Flair in her stitches so the most Flaired pieces appeared three-dimensional.

As soon as he noticed them, Quert Apple, Passiflora's brother, surged to them, kissing Dufleur's hands, tucking one into his arm. He led her to a tall, older gentleman with shaggy gray hair, a handsome face, and intense turquoise eyes the same color as Passiflora's.

"Dufleur," Quert said, "may I introduce you to my father, T'Apple."

Dufleur froze. The greatest artist of Celta.

Fairyfoot pranced up, pawed at T'Apple's shiny leather dress shoe, opened her green eyes wide, smiled, and sent loudly, *You may paint Me in My beautiful collar.*

Quert looked stunned, T'Apple surprised, and a ripple of laughter came from Passiflora that made Dufleur smile.

T'Apple's eyes narrowed on Dufleur's face. "That smile." He rubbed his fingers together. "That smile has Flair." Then he, too, smiled. Glancing down at Fairyfoot, he said, "We'll see. My portrait appointments are filled for several months." He made a half-bow to Dufleur. "I admire your work."

Dufleur stared at him. Passiflora nudged her with an elbow. "Thank you," Dufleur squeaked.

T'Apple took her hand from Quert's arm and shifted it to his. "I have a question about technique . . ."

From that moment on, the evening passed in a daze. She thought she found words to explain her creative Flair to T'Apple, without talking about time. He nodded and muttered to himself, then she was passed back to Quert Apple who introduced her to others who had purchased more than one piece of her work—including D'Birch.

That interlude stood out, the GreatLady smiling coolly, apparently condescending to forgive Dufleur her rudeness the evening before because she was pleased with a small tapestry Dufleur had done of a slice of Noble Country—one that showed the entrance to the Birch estate. As Dufleur suspected, no rumors about the Thymes came to her ears, and she doubted if it circulated.

Saille Willow had been in the gallery before Dufleur had arrived, and she watched him with sidelong glances. The link between them was strong and, to her, evident, but she hoped she was shielding it from others. She shrank at the thought of even more gossip. Still, she knew that he watched her even when she felt him turn his mind to business. In some way, his presence both energized and eased her. Unqualified support came through their link, as did an underlying desire, anticipation of the night to come. She hadn't thought she'd spend the night with him, but he had no doubts.

She would rather he stay with her in Winterberry Residence, but didn't know how to manage the bed, though the couch they'd slept on the night before wasn't quite as wide as her bed. Perhaps she could convince Fairyfoot to sleep at T'Willow

Residence. The Fam had taken a particular liking to the conservatory.

Fairyfoot and her collar were praised, too. An Apple had been assigned as a companion to "honor" the cat, though Dufleur figured Quert didn't trust the Fam with embroidery and lace.

Her meeting with D'Sea was very pleasant, especially since her Mind Healer had purchased a couple of her pieces. Smiling, Dufleur chatted with D'Sea, and when the woman nodded decisively and complimented Dufleur, she knew that she was spared another appointment. Even as she watched the older woman walk away, she felt perspiration dampen her palms. But it was warm in the gallery.

By the end of the evening, Dufleur had sold all of her work, and her head buzzed with compliments. When someone spoke of a commission, she referred them to Quert Apple. As the gallery emptied, she took one last look around and found that most of her mother's lace had sold, too. She sighed in relief. Her mother would be pleased and would avidly check the newssheets for reports of the event the next morning. Dufleur was a little interested in what they might say, too.

"I have accepted three commissions for you." Quert Apple beamed in satisfaction as he approached with Passiflora. Everyone else—except Saille Willow—was gone. "I had requests for more, but I know you have other commitments, and I want to ensure your exclusivity." His smile broadened further. "We have a waiting list."

"Good," Dufleur said faintly. She thought she had an idea of the new rhythm of her own life factoring in the social season and would have to sit down and make a schedule—for experimenting with time, working on her embroidery, resting.

Playing with Fairyfoot, the little cat added, prancing up, moving her head so light caught her collar and everyone could continue to admire it.

"I'll take Dufleur home." Saille T'Willow joined them.

Dufleur frowned at him. "You didn't commission anything, did you? You have a great deal of my work as it is."

"Does he really? I'd like some unsold pieces." Quert sent him a glance.

"Not for sale." He picked up Dufleur's hand, made a small bow, and kissed her fingers. "No. I didn't commission anything more." His eyes went half-lidded, his mouth quirked at the corner. "Though I'm considering an embroidered comforter for the Willow generational bed."

"The Willows have such a bed?" Quert asked. "They are very rare. Usually made in the first or second generation of colonization." A considering look came to his eyes. "I wonder if I could do a show—" He stopped himself. "No, I'm sure no First-Family would loan such a wonderful object."

"You must be mad," Dufleur blurted, folded her arms across her chest. "I will *not* embroider a bedcover for a man who has a FamCat sleeping on his bed."

Myx would ruin it, Fairyfoot added.

Saille winced. "Oh. Good point."

Passiflora raised her eyebrows at Dufleur. Quert looked away, as if something had caught his attention. And Dufleur knew beyond a doubt that she'd revealed too much.

Saille said, "No, GreatSir Apple, I would not loan my bed. As you said, it's too valuable. As for other FirstFamilies." He shrugged. "I don't know who else might have such a bed. Every Family has secrets."

Just that easily he'd asked them to keep quiet, Dufleur realized with wonder.

"Very true, very true," Quert agreed.

Passiflora's smile held a trace of melancholy. "And some Families' affairs are known and gossiped by all."

Quert put an arm around her shoulder. "You're tired, my dear. I know Holm sent your glider here an hour ago. You've been doing a great deal—"

"My health is perfectly fine." Passiflora freed herself from her brother. She lifted her chin. "In fact, the Healer, T'Heather, scrutinized me while we spoke earlier." Her smile softened as she looked to Dufleur. "He wanted to convey to me his thanks once again for the softleaves you embroidered for his lady, and notes that they have now become quite valuable."

But Dufleur reacted to the first part of her speech. "You're not the only one who had an interesting talk with a Healer. D'Sea was here."

"Oh." Passiflora's eyes filled.

Dufleur managed a smile. "My health is fine, too." But she felt closer to Passiflora than she had for a while.

Quert took his sister's arm and led her away. "Holm will be waiting for you, you know. You're overtired."

"This social season is important to us."

"I know, and you have been such a good HeartMate . . ." A door closed.

"My glider awaits, too," Saille said. "Come, Dufleur."

She eyed him warily. "No comment about HeartMates."

"Of course not."

They looked at each other. A half-smile was on his lips. Their link was wide and pulsing with emotions—affection, pride, desire.

Fairyfoot rubbed Dufleur's ankles back and forth, circling her, sending love and pride and purring. She crooked her tail. _We spend the night at Willows's._ Her whiskers twitched. _Food here is acceptable, but Willows give Me cream before bed._

Dufleur stared at her cat. She wouldn't be small if she kept that habit.

With smugness, the FamCat sat and looked up at Saille. _You should put Fam door to the other rooms, so I can use them._

"Other rooms?" Dufleur asked.

"I'm using the consort's rooms. They're equal in size to the head of household's."

"But, that bed . . ."

"MotherDam had a special bed made for herself. She put the old Willow bed in storage, I had it moved to the consort's suite."

She couldn't prevent the small, fake smile from flickering on and off her face. That bed scared her, it spoke of generations. Of all the time of the Willows. "So Fairyfoot wants to use the head's suite as her own."

Saille smiled. "Cats don't have a problem with self-confidence."

"No." She smiled, too, though she knew she was all too full of self-doubt.

He gazed down at Fairyfoot. "Dufleur has invited me to stay with her."

The cat flicked her tail. _Bed is small._

"Very true. I wondered if you'd like to stay in the Willow conservatory."

Fairyfoot purred louder. _One or two mice there in from the winter. Fresh mouse as snack. Then cream. Then sleep in glass house smelling like summer._ "Yessss."

"Then I'll—" He lifted a hand as if to 'port her, but she had already popped from view.

Saille shook his head, then he scanned the room and eased. "It has been difficult pretending that you aren't my HeartMate, that we are casual acquaintances. That I might be thinking of wooing you and not that I'm ready to HeartBond tonight and wed you tomorrow."

Dufleur took a step back, stopped. "I didn't ask you to do any of those things."

"No. But I promised not to push. I suppose that means rushing you, too."

"You are moving at the speed of light."

"Not time?"

She dropped her voice. "This is not the place to speak of time."

"Or *the* time?"

She closed her eyes. "You're going to be difficult."

"Over the fact that you are breaking the law? Perhaps." He took her hand again. "Or perhaps not. Being able to practice your Flair is important." He glanced around. "Though I wish your primary Flair was for embroidery. It would scare and confuse me less." He reached for her other hand, brought both to his lips. "You are a very talented person, and I am a lucky man."

Her heart jumped in her chest. "I don't think so."

His blue eyes went from dancing to serious. He dropped one of her hands and sighed. "Let's go."

She led the way. "The garment storage is here."

Then she fell silent, and he didn't speak, and instead of being uncomfortable, she felt relieved that she didn't have to think of things to say. More, he was letting her unwind from the event that had focused on her, until she wondered how to hold her hands, where to place herself in relation to her "art."

They stopped at a piece, and he gestured. "I like that. I bought it." It was a large tatting of her mother's, worked in silver thread. It *did* look like a spiderweb.

"A very beautiful spiderweb." Saille answered her thought. He helped her on with her coat and frowned. "This seems light for a winter like we're having."

She shrugged. "I use a weathershield."

"Dufleur, I know you've been as busy as Passiflora Holly with all your various—projects. That takes energy. You're tired, and a weathershield can be draining. Get some gloves and a hat and scarf."

Chuckling, she said, "The weathershield is a very minor bit of Flair for me. Hardly noticeable."

"In that case, I don't think I'll tell you that I've never mastered it."

"Oh." A flush crept up her cheeks.

His eyes heated. "I like seeing your flush, it's lovelier in more intimate settings, though." He brought her hand to his lips and nibbled on her fingers. "Maybe I'll reconsider gloves. You can keep my hands warm with your weathershield, and I can taste your—fingers at any time."

The imago he was sending to her weren't of her fingers. She swallowed. "Your glider awaits?"

"Yes." He led her out the door into the breath-catching cold. She slammed the weathershield around them.

He hummed with pleasure. "Nice. Warm." He gestured to the massive old glider sitting on its stand a few feet away. The driver waved to them, but didn't exit the warm vehicle to lift the door. No footmen.

"My Family is predominantly women, and my MotherDam discouraged men from staying in Druida and working at the Residence. A couple came back when I took over the title, but I think several more are waiting to see what happens." He opened the door, put his hands on her waist, and raised her the couple of feet inside. He followed her in and shut the door without taking his arm from her waist.

"No light," he whispered, and the soft glow in the back dissipated until it was dark. He turned his head and kissed her.

Her mouth opened on the press of his lips, and she accepted his tongue. He tasted of the sparkling wine punch that had been served. His body angled over hers, and she noted he was very aroused and that—and the passion flooding down their link—caused her to melt.

They kissed, and he stroked her breasts. She sensed that he liked the thickness of her garments. He savored anticipation.

Her mind swirled away under the tide of sensation—his hands on her breasts, his leg between hers, and the knowledge that *she* had invited him to stay with her.

The drive was far too long, since he'd spent every moment arousing her to fever, and then, finally, they were in her bedroom.

He pulled her gently into his arms, and she became aware of

his solid erection. It caused her knees to loosen. He chuckled, rubbed his cheek against her hair. "Yes, I desire you. I always do. The most basic fact about HeartMates is that the sex will always be superb."

His hands framed her face, and his blue eyes met hers. "But I want more than sex."

"Everything," she whispered.

"Yes." He hesitated. "And I would give you everything in return. Dufleur, why don't you trust me?"

She tensed, but kept her gaze locked on his. "I don't know. I think much of it is that I don't trust *me*." But she probed at his question as if it had been a scientific hypothesis. "I don't . . ." She sent her confusion, more, her bone-deep conviction that no one could get close to her. After all, her parents had never gotten close to her. She didn't have close friends. Something must be lacking in her.

"Dufleur, nothing is lacking in you."

Then she showed him what she thought of as a closed door in her.

"What?"

"The horrors of the past. The explosion of the lab, my father's death, the demise of the Residence. When I was kidnapped by the black cult and my attempted murder. I try not to open them for myself. Can you live with someone who has such terrible events closed to you?"

"They will open in time."

But she doubted.

Saille was impatient. He wanted all of her now, despite any doubts. Her irrational doubts. All she needed to do was to trust in the HeartMate bond.

And trusting was the matter of the emotions, you couldn't rush it, and it was obvious from what she'd just shown him that she didn't trust him yet. Instead of a heavy sigh, he let his breath out slow and easy.

Think of his triumphs. He'd found her. She hadn't formally accepted his HeartGift, but she hadn't thrown it out into the street again.

He had her in his arms. They'd loved physically before and would do so again. And that was the last thought he had before he began to persuade her that he'd be a good mate in another fashion.

Before he'd been too hasty to savor lovemaking. Not tonight. His hands still curved around her face. He loved looking at her. Her wide brow, blue-gray eyes that seemed to see everything, weigh everything. Her lips that always tempted him because they plumped up so wonderfully with passion.

He lowered his head and brushed her mouth. Didn't even allow himself to taste. "Slow and easy. Tonight I'll show you exactly how close I can get to you." He nibbled her lips, swept his tongue across them to taste.

Dufleur. Rich. Sexy. With an exotic flavor of no other. Time.

"I'll get close. Inside you. Physically, emotionally, spiritually."

His hands caressed her soft skin, went to the tabs on the shoulders of her tunic, and opened them. He slid the garment down her, feeling the full roundness of her breasts, the indentation of her waist, the nice curve of hip and butt and stomach. Then the long tunic fell free, and he set his fingers at her waist and the tab there. He peeled it back and pushed her full trous down, down, down her long, sturdy legs. Legs that had wrapped around him as her body demanded release.

Twenty-two

♥

He slipped his hand between the silkeen cloth of her pantlettes and her skin, knew his fingers trembled, his breath came short, his own trous tightened over his groin, as his cock grew in anticipation of fulfillment.

Her folds were damp and plump. "Low light," he growled and looked at her face. Yes, her lips were fuller, too. Her eyes were wide and had lost the piercing intelligence. He stroked her, coaxing more slickness from her body, slid a finger into her, and she arched. Her stomach caressed his shaft, and his groan mingled with her whimper of desire.

"My clothes off," he ordered and felt the rush of the spell around him as his clothes fell to the floor, his shoes and liners broke away from his feet.

He stood naked and ready, and she was still garbed in her breastband and pantlettes that showed a thick transparent white against her skin. One of his arms supported her back, and he saw her breasts with aroused nubs of nipples. He looked down her and saw his fingers around her, holding her damp sex. His skin heated, his own sex throbbed with need. Memories of how wonderful it felt to slide into her, feel her legs clamp around him, her hands go to his butt to pull him even deeper inside made him shudder with desire. He withdrew his fingers from her only to rip her pantlettes off. She gave a flinch, but her mouth curved.

Her breasts tempted. With a quick jerk, her breastband opened and fell away. His lips tasted her right nipple, and he laved it, sucked it. A different taste here from her lips. Sweet. He moved to her left nipple, indulged himself in the softness of her breast pressing against his mouth, the fullness of her flesh in his mouth.

She gave another whimper of need that fired his brain, set her hands on his shoulders, lifted herself, and slid down on his waiting cock.

Fabulous. So incredible. He freed her breast to gasp. She'd

taken him by surprise, his hands clamped on her bottom, and the feel of her firm flesh in his hands, of her hot, wet sheath surrounding him snapped his control. He took a pace to the side, another, and his leg touched the bed.

Then she was on her back, and he was thrusting into her, giving her all of him. Each stroke wound the tension tighter and tighter, until he spun off the edge of the world and into pure sensational pleasure.

Several minutes passed before he could piece himself together. Touch returned first. Her body was damp against him, her breasts cushioning his chest. He rolled from her, came up against the wall. They'd sleep close together. Good.

He tucked her under the covers, yanked the linens up.

She said nothing. He sensed her mind was still dazed, and he smiled, then he held her until she fell asleep, and he slipped into the darkness, then the dreams, with her.

There was a horrible bang, an awful flash against her eyelids that woke her, all her senses screaming with fear. The scent of smoke was everywhere.

She stumbled from the bed, dragged on trous and tunic, shoes, ran downstairs from the Family wing and through the house toward the laboratory, and as she ran she heard her mother screaming in her brain, felt the horrible emptiness of the link to her father. He barely lived.

As she came closer and closer to the lab, heat mounted. She stopped in horror to see flames devouring the last of the portraits along the corridor from the laboratory to the main building. They jumped into her mother's salon. The way to the laboratory was blocked.

"Call the FireMages!" she screamed to her mother, mind and heart and soul.

She dared not 'port to the laboratory. No way of knowing what shape it was in. So she 'ported to just outside the front door of the main Residence. Her heart clutched in her chest. Her throat closed.

The laboratory was a ruin. It appeared as if there'd been an explosion. She ran to the tumbled walls of the lab, depending on the link to her father to tell her where he was. His life force was thready. The heat burned the soles of her summer workshoes, and she sent precious energy to shield them and keep them cool, was glad she didn't wear sandals. She didn't recognize anything of the lab. If it wasn't for the main Residence, she wouldn't have known even the alignment. Stopping over a place that felt more of her father than anything else, she probed. He was under there! Buried. She didn't have the strength or the Flair to move the rubble atop him.

Desperate, she did something she'd never attempted. She drew the Time Wind around her, rich in this place of centuries of experimentation, and moved backward into the grayness of the past.

She was in the middle of the lab. Huge deadly shadows moved like threatening enemies. Her father was on his hands and knees. Dufleur couldn't understand it. The lab was still whole. Then her father staggered to his feet. Took a pace toward the outer door.

BOOM! The room rocked. Dufleur staggered, grabbed her father. Held his solid, living body tight. But when she stepped back into the future, her father vanished from her arms, and a cry tore from her soul. After her eyes cleared she found her experiment hadn't worked. Her father was not alive and well. The paradox of time was something even Thymes didn't understand. But her experiment hadn't been a complete failure. Her father was no longer buried but burned and broken at her feet. His head showed an ugly, bloody dent.

"Father," she screamed and knew her screams were lost in her mother's, in the shouting of the FireMages as they battled the fire that devoured the Residence, in the Residence's screams itself. No! Dufleur knelt, put her arms around her father, teleported to Primary HealingHall.

Where they tore her father from her arms.

She struggled and found herself battling Saille Willow. Her breath came in panting gasps.

"Dufleur," he said, and when she looked at him, his expression of concern, the comfort of their link seemed so precious that she couldn't face it. He was so whole. She was so fractured.

Saille let her pull from his arms. They were weaker than he cared. The nightmare—the *memory*—had been so terrible.

She left the bed, gave him a sad smile, turned away to dress.

"It could have been worse. It could have been a nightmare about the dark cult." Her gaze lifted to his. "If you stay with me, you'll get to experience that, too. Unquestionably." Her beautiful mouth turned down.

He was more shaken than he wanted to admit, even through their link. The horror she'd gone through that night, pulling her father from the flames, 'porting him to Primary HealingHall, then returning to her hysterical mother and watching their home burn down.

"I thought your father died in the explosion."

"He didn't. He lingered three days. Burned over most of his body. Brain damage."

"Shouldn't your night ills be less? I thought you went to a Mind Healer."

Another of those smiles that wasn't a smile. "I did, D'Sea herself. I *am* better. But the Mind Healer's best tool is distancing Flair—as if a great deal of time has passed. That doesn't work well on me."

"Because you experiment with time."

"Yes." She didn't look at him and drew on her coat.

"What are you doing?"

She grimaced. "The best way to settle myself . . . Actually, the only way I've found to settle myself is to go to the Thyme Residence." A shudder passed through her. "I've never been able to sense the HouseHeart, but I can't give up." She straightened. "I can't give up on many things—finding the HouseHeart, experimenting with time, which is illegal here in Druida, clearing my father's name as a madman, trying to have my mother love me." Shaking her head, she met his gaze with hers in the briefest of slanting glances. "I am not a good candidate for a HeartMate."

"You're mine," he said roughly.

But she opened the empty chamber that had been her secret laboratory and walked to the center. She looked at him with hollow eyes. "I don't expect you to come."

It was like a body blow. Before he could find his breath, she'd teleported away. He couldn't find his clothes.

"Lights!" he commanded, pounced on his clothes, and dressed in both the elegant suit he'd worn to her opening and his outer gear.

He didn't know the location of the old Thyme Residence

well enough to teleport to it. He swept the fearful knowledge that Dufleur continued her father's work to the back of his mind so it wouldn't petrify him.

Dufleur had said this had happened before. Probably many times. There'd be another who had accompanied her.

Fairyfoot! he shouted mentally, followed his link with her to find her sleeping on a mossy bed in the warm humidity of the conservatory. *Prepare to be 'ported.*

An instant later she was hissing in his arms. Claws set in his forearms, and he ignored the small pangs.

"Dufleur has had an awful nightmare about the loss of her father and the Residence. She's gone to D'Thyme Residence."

Fairyfoot's hissing subsided. Her face wrinkled in a cat-frown. *Nothing there but ruin.*

"Nevertheless, I want you to give me a good image and co-ordinates so I can teleport us."

Shivering, Fairyfoot said, *It will be very cold.*

"Yes, but I don't want her there alone."

Weathershield, Fairyfoot demanded.

"That is not one of my skills."

She spat. *The nice scarf with warmth spells, then.*

He dragged the scarf from around his neck. "A belated New Year's gift from me to you."

Purring, she snuggled in. *Good FamMan.*

The fine knit would not withstand her claws, and the scarf would be wrecked for his own use. "An image, if you please."

It formed in his head. A mid-sized estate on the south edge of Noble Country, snow covering the dips and protuberances of ruined walls. He took the image, tested it with his Flair. "Very good."

I 'port very well. Not like some Cats.

Was that a slur on his own Fam? He hadn't explored Myx's talents. "We will teleport on three . . . one FamCat—"

Just 'port.

So he did.

*I*t was late, but the weather was clear—and bitterly cold. On the far edges of Noble Country, the ruins of T'Thyme Residence showed as broken columns and piles of brick and stone in the dark. As broken as her heart at the sight of her lost home.

She'd lost two people she'd loved that horrible night. Her father and the Residence.

Her hands fisted. Despite what the rest of the nobles thought, her father would *never* have put the Residence or the rest of them in danger if he'd suspected his experiments threatened them. *Never.* He always did his trickiest work in a cabin in the Hard Rock Mountains—a place they'd had to sell after he died. A place that had had four owners and was currently vacant, called Time Passes. Dufleur suspected that the time currents around their cabin, which had been used by Thymes for centuries and rebuilt every generation, had warped. No doubt it would take her or her descendants, should she have any gifted in great Time Flair, to put right. No one had asked her, though.

She smiled at the thought that GraceLord Agave had purchased the place and had not been able to mitigate whatever was wrong. Well, the Agaves hadn't been working with time for three and a quarter centuries.

She walked up to a ragged column that came to her chin. The last time she'd seen it, it had been a dingy gray, now it was as white as she remembered from her childhood, when the Residence had been pristine. She touched fingertips to it and found the color came from frost, not the scouring of weather, which had cleansed it.

Tears froze on her cheeks. A Residence established in the first years of the colonists had long become sentient, a member of the Family. Her father wouldn't have imperiled it. Or her. Or her mother.

Swallowing hard, she boosted her weathershield so she wouldn't be clumsy. She carefully picked her way over the rubble, smoothing her way with Flair. Teleporting was Flair she was using more and more often instead of hoarding her power.

Her lack of work with her Flair made her heart ache, too.

Though ruined, she knew every inch of this land, and picked her way to exactly above the hidden HouseHeart. The passages to the ancient, sacred place were caved in, as was the room itself, and the altars to the elements—the hearth fire, the fountain, the air vent, the rich loam of the earth.

She could only pray, as she had for the last year and a half, that the HeartStone had been spared.

Seeing T'Ash earlier in the week had reminded her that his childhood home had perished, too, yet he'd rebuilt. His House-Heart must have survived. With Passiflora there, and the matter of HouseHearts so sensitive, Dufleur hadn't approached him to ask about it.

After the first shock of her father's death had worn off, she'd visited here, and several times thereafter, mostly on holidays. She'd searched D'Winterberry's library on HouseHeart information, had even gone to the PublicLibrary and asked for help, but little had been found.

She'd last been here just before the turn of summer into autumn, calling for the HouseHeart. Hearing no reply. Then there had been tufts of grass and other sturdy plants showing green. It hadn't been as wrenching as this place on a dark winter night. She wouldn't come here again this winter. But she was here now.

Coughing to clear her throat, she dragged in barely warmed breaths and surveyed the landscape. Blinked again and again. Settled her emotions. She lifted her arms to the twinmoons, slivers, near new. Summoning her Flair, she said the opening rhyme to enter the most sacred and protected place of a Residence, the HouseHeart.

Nothing.

She steadied her voice and her Flair, ignoring the winter night that pressed in upon her, circling her spells like a snapping beast. Said the words again, with feeling.

No reply.

For the next attempt, she relaxed her tense body and centered her Flair, deciding to end the request for entry with a hard mental knock. Again she said the prayer, punching it up with Flair. Then continued with a long benediction that she would have said once inside the HouseHeart itself.

The faintest stirring. *ThymeHeir?*

Her breath stopped in her chest. A tiny voice. She couldn't even tell if it was the Residence voice she knew, or one that came before her time, or one that had evolved since the explosion. With soft, warm thoughts, she sent, *Thyme Residence?*

Yessss. Falling on a sigh.

"Dufleur!" Saille said.

She spun, tottered, caught herself, grumbled a couple of swear words.

He stood outside the rubble of the Residence, hands on his hips, frowning at her. Fairyfoot sat wrapped in his scarf on his shoulder. He looked cold, but determined.

What should she do? How did she dare reveal her House-Heart to him?

How did she dare walk away from a HouseHeart that might be crippled or dying?

"Dufleur?"

He wouldn't go away. She knew that about him now.

Dufleur? asked the HouseHeart; perhaps it had withdrawn only to the HeartStone.

Do you need help? she asked.

The Residence sobbed.

Oh, Lord and Lady.

Help. Dark. Cold. Too QUIET! Alone, alone, alone.

She looked at the ground where the HeartStone was buried in a building that had collapsed around it. She wondered how much of the Residence's mind survived. Could the Residence Library also have endured?

"Dufleur?" Saille stepped over the first line of bricks.

"Stay there. Please!"

He halted.

Placing her hands palm down, she sent Flair questing to her Residence's soul. The HeartStone was whole, had sent additional parts of itself into the marble cobblestones that had surrounded the lapis lazuli slab. Perhaps six stones in all.

Saille was her HeartMate. He could help. If she dared.

Dufleur, the Residence whispered.

"I'm here, and I'll help. Now." She met Saille's eyes. "I've finally discovered that Thyme Residence lives."

He nodded. "A blessing."

She watched him. He didn't come storming across the debris to take charge. He honored her request that he stay where he was—though she had no doubt that if danger threatened, nothing she could say or do would keep him from acting. He knew the sensitivity of the HouseHeart, the HeartStone—a Great-Lord would. So he kept watch.

But she could almost hear the Residence dying under her feet. She moistened her lips, then regretted it as the cold wind kissed them. She'd let all her spells go when trying to reach the HouseHeart and hadn't even noticed. Now the frigid cold wrapped her until she trembled in the embrace. Not at all like Saille's embrace when they'd loved together.

Not at all like the hours she'd spent in the womb warmth of the HouseHeart as a child. She locked gazes with Saille. *Will you help me save the Thyme HouseHeart?*

Triumph blazed in his eyes, but his reply was steady, solid. *I would be honored.*

A huge step, trusting him with the HouseHeart. But before she could do any further analysis of her emotions, he was by her left side, holding out his hand—his bare right hand. His face held a half-smile, but she thought she could still see that light of success flashing deep within his eyes.

She'd willingly lowered the barriers she'd set between them. For a good cause.

He'd been clever enough to place himself exactly where he'd be needed for great Flair work, taking this seriously. She put her hand in his. His fingers closed cold over her own chill ones, but natural attractive energy spurted between them, warming them.

Taking her seriously. She should have realized that he'd follow her.

She liked the energy cycling through them, the strength of it and of him. With a shaky smile, she met his gaze. They would work great magic together, and that would bind them together, too.

Everywhere she turned, he was there, tying them together. With sex. With dancing. With the mind link. With Flair.

She took his hand, the scent of him, healthy soil, fresh breeze, drifted her way. But she couldn't let him distract her during this, the most important venture of her life. Saving the Thyme HouseHeart, the kernel of the Residence itself. More tears stung her eyes, dried on her cheeks under the weather-shield.

We can do this, Fairyfoot said with supreme confidence, stepping from Saille to Dufleur, managing to make the transfer still wearing the scarf like some elegant garment. Wasn't the collar enough? *Focus.*

Twenty-three

❦

So she integrated Fairyfoot's energy flow and strength into her own, squeezed Saille's hand. He squeezed back, and she stitched the three of their Flairs together.

Then she submerged herself in memories of the House-Heart. Herself with her father as a small child, holding tools as he taught her the rituals of the Thymes. Learning the couplets to unlock the door, the way to the secret passageways, how to manipulate a few molecules of time to enter.

Celebrating rituals herself there. Suffering through her first and second passages as her father held her, helped her, there.

How it looked, like a rounded cave cut out of rock, but with small white lights providing constant illumination. The tiny bubbling fountain, the equally small firepit, the soughing of the winds—the atmospheric wind of air and the rich wind of time—through specially made crevices. The small deeply soft chinju rug. Barely enough room for three, but her mother had always preferred Family rituals in a spacious room of the Residence.

All gone.

Dufleur sniffed, pushed the tears aside.

The HouseHeart lived in the HouseStone. All the Residence's personality, its life, its memory flowed from the HouseStone. The ResidenceLibrary, the knowledge garnered by the Residence and by Thymes and stored with the house entity, was an extension of the HouseHeart itself.

The heart and soul of the Residence came from the Heart-Stone. Dufleur thought the HouseHeart itself had been the entire floor of the cave.

Now broken.

She visualized the smooth slab that was the HeartStone, a deep blue lapis lazuli with silver sparkles and one discrete streak. As thick as her little finger. As wide and deep as both of her hands together.

The Thyme HouseStone.

Thyme, Thyme, Thyme. Time, time, time. Mine, mine, mine.
She whispered, she lilted, she sang to it.

Yours, it whispered back. *Thyme's. Time's.*

*No longer alone. No longer without energy or strength or
light or Flair.*

The stone whimpered.

Hanging on hard to Saille's hand, she said to the Residence,
I am going to probe around you. Are you whole?

Whole, well-protected once.

And you will be again. You are six stones?

Withdrawn to six. Lost much, many, lost . . .

I am here, and my HeartMate, and my FamCat.

She sensed the HouseStone focusing on her, something outside itself and its tragedy. *HeartMate for the ThymeHeir. Blessing.*

Yes, a GreatLord. Willow.

There came a hum of approval, of hope. *A GreatLord with
great Flair is here. I sense him!* More hope and a touch of joy.
Send me the arrangement of the six stones.

Probing, she found the location and relationship of the stones
to each other. They were tumbled and at odd angles. A weakening spellshield kept them in a pocket of space. She murmured a
prayer.

Saille said, *It will be difficult, but we can do it.*

We can do it! echoed Fairyfoot, lending her purr to the hope
and rising Flair around them.

Each stone wasn't as distinct in her mind to know them well
enough to teleport them, so they'd have to be slid through the
ground. Dufleur rolled her shoulders and set to work.

It was hard. The stones in their weathershield were slippery.

They were afraid. She pushed earth out of the way, created
space, hauled the stones. Her breath came in ragged pants. She finally reached the last meter of earth—fused earth from explosion
and fire. She probed one way for space. None. Another and another and another.

Flair slipped from her grasp. She couldn't bring them up.
Couldn't shift or shape the earth enough to move it aside to free
her HouseStone. She would fail! And if she left this cold wintry
night, the HouseStone would relinquish hope and perish.

Then Saille was there, taking control of the spell. *He* knew
how to shape earth, with his potter's hands. How to mold it.

How to force it to curve. He knew the weak parts of the ground. When he reached a blockage, he slipped around it, forced another path.

Pop!

Several meters from them the ground broke.

Cold! screamed the HouseStones.

Dufleur yanked at the first warm thing that came to mind. Her thick velvet, bespelled heated dress cloak. Stumbling with weak legs, she brought Saille to the HouseStones, turned them over into the cape, covered them, crooned over them.

They whimpered back. *Safe. Safe. Safe. Wrapped in Thyme love. Thyme does love us. Thyme did come. Thyme did not abandon.* And the stones sent a tiny thread of love.

Dufleur leaned against Saille.

FamCat and FamWoman and FamMan saved the House-Stone, Fairyfoot said smugly. *I am a hero again.*

They were done. And the task was very well done. The HeartStone and its subsidiaries lay shrouded in the heavy velvet of Dufleur's new dress cloak.

Saille had helped her in this most delicate task as he'd promised.

The sweat on her body slowly dried, the trembling in her limbs subsided, and she leaned down and gathered the stones close to her body. Somehow she was regenerating energy faster than she should have been for such a major undertaking. The sharing of the project with her HeartMate? Partnering with him? No wonder FirstFamily rituals were powerful enough to change the world, it was FirstFamilies who found and wed with HeartMates most often.

Had any studies been done on how much stronger a Heart-Mate couple was than the individuals who made the couple?

"What next?" Saille asked matter-of-factly.

But she felt the surging satisfaction in him. He was binding her to him with many threads: dreamtime connection, common past experiences, affection, sex, gratitude that tumbled from her to him because he'd helped her save Thyme HouseHeart, which she cradled in her arms like a baby. More—a shared great working of Flair, ritual. Secrets.

Though she thought he kept some of his secrets to himself.

"What now?" he repeated even more quietly, putting his arms around her and the bundle of velvet she held.

In spite of the weathershield, she felt the cool tracks of tears on her face. She gulped.

Saille took a linen softleaf from his pocket and dabbed her eyes, smiling gently. He held it to her nose. "Blow," he said.

But she couldn't let him do that. Such a disgusting bodily function. She shifted the HouseHeart and heard the components clank. Then she took the softleaf from Saille, turned and blew her nose, adding a little "clearing" spell, and the aftermath of her weary joyful tears was gone. With a small spurt of energy, she sent the softleaf to the clothes cleanser in her rooms.

We go home? Fairyfoot asked.

Dufleur cleared her throat, and her eyes dampened again as she stared at the ruins around her. "What would be best would be a no-time safe. We used to have many old ones that had worn out and only needed a renewal spell." Frowning, she said, "I think I rehabilitated all the ones in Winterberry Residence, and they are in use." That would be one thing the examiners would find right.

"T'Willow Residence, then," Saille said.

Better! Fairyfoot said.

His arms tightened around Dufleur, and before she could protest, he'd built a detailed imaged of a teleportation pad in his mind, checked it for use, and they were there.

"Low light," Saille said, and the soft golden light reminiscent of the Earthan sun flickered on in graceful porcelain lamps painted with sprays of flowers. A rosy, comfortable room patterned in floral chintz was illuminated. Overstuffed twoseats and chairs were grouped for conversation. It wasn't a formal parlor but a well-used chamber well loved by the Family. It radiated soothing hominess, and primarily from one woman.

Pretty, Fairyfoot said, claiming a large chair.

Dufleur listened to the tenor of the house. Saille's stamp was strong and masculine, but recent and didn't reach to all corners of the house. Beneath that was a cold, demanding, formal polish—the old D'Willow, and *she'd* left her mark on everything. But there was an additional undertone, one more layer, more basic, that had kept the Residence and its inhabitants sane and held them together. A loving undertone that matched the Family name and nature. Willow. That which would bend to the harsh wind, but not break, and ultimately survive.

"Mother," Saille said, and for an instant Dufleur thought he was identifying the source of that layer, but he was calling his mother through their link and the Residence.

"Saille," Dufleur hissed in a horrified whisper. "It's four minutes to Transition Bell." That time of the always-dark morning when most people left their lives and moved on to their next on the Wheel of Stars.

"Here, Saille," responded a female voice matching his in calm.

"I need a nonfunctioning no-time brought to the teleportation pad."

"What size, Saille?"

"A mid-sized safe."

"I'll bring one down, unless you need me to 'port it transnow?"

"No, save your energy, though an anti-grav spell will have to be set on it."

"Most certainly. I'll see you in ten minutes."

"Thank you, Mother."

Dufleur just stared at Saille.

"What?" he said, taking her hand and leading her to a twoseat that was so cushy she sank deeply into it. Saille slipped his arm around her waist.

"You woke up your mother at Transition Bell."

He shrugged, snuggled closer, so the length of their thighs touched. "She's the T'Willow Residence housekeeper. She'd know the inventory of the Residence."

"She did. She knew you had a mid-sized no-time safe and where it was located."

"She's a very efficient person," Saille said. Dufleur wondered at the word. Did he think of his mother as a housekeeper first? Why?

Perhaps it wasn't she who'd provided that underpinning of love and flexibility and sanity for the Family.

Saille said drily, "My MotherDam would never accept anything less than perfection."

They sat in silence, while Dufleur wondered if her own mother had known of every object in T'Thyme Residence. Somehow Dufleur didn't think so, and she was certain that her mother didn't know the inventory of D'Winterberry Residence.

"My mother has lived here all her life," Saille said.

"Always?"

"Yes. Occasionally she'd visit me on the country estate—perhaps once a year when I was a child—but otherwise she's always been here. Of course she'd know everything." His lips brushed her hair. "But I think I should get a show of appreciation for my help this evening." His voice lilted.

She turned her head, and their lips were a millimeter apart, she could taste the heady whisper of his breath. Her lips tingled.

The door opened silently, but Dufleur felt the change in the air, she rose quickly. Saille followed her up, one of his hands capturing hers.

A plump, round woman with Saille's blue eyes, a pleasantly attractive face, and dark brown hair beginning to gray walked in. She was dressed in a pristine housekeeper's T'Willow scarlet tunic and trous, with a white apron, the ancient symbol of her office. Dufleur didn't know what she'd expected, but it wasn't this tidy woman, who echoed of the sweet undertone of the Residence. Or it echoed of her. Dufleur realized she was staring at Saille's mother.

"Mother, Dufleur Thyme. Dufleur, my mother, Arbusca Willow."

"Merry meet." Dufleur held her cloak tight and managed a nervous curtsy.

"Merry meet," Arbusca said, flashing a smile as soft and as warm as her eyes. A secret smile that made Dufleur all the more jittery because she was pretty sure that Arbusca knew Dufleur was Saille's HeartMate. The woman had a strong Flair, and for matchmaking, after all.

Fairyfoot hopped down from the chair where she'd been snoozing. *Merry meet, GreatMistrys,* she said, spoiling her courtesy by yawning.

"Merry meet, Fairyfoot."

The cat glanced around the room. *Pretty, but I like the plant room better.*

Arbusca held the door open for Fairyfoot to trot out. The little Fam stopped on the threshold. *I will see you later. I am a loving cat and will stay, but I left half-eaten mouse in plant room.* She sent a sweet smile to Arbusca. *GreatMistrys doesn't like half-eaten mice.*

Dufleur shuddered. "She's not the only one."

D'Winterberry Residence stinks too much of bad smell for mice.

"Small blessings," Dufleur murmured. She waved at Fairy-foot, "Go finish your mouse or bury the remains in a place that won't upset the gardeners."

"Too late," Saille said.

Dufleur winced.

"Where do you want this?" Arbusca gestured to the half-meter, large square box that glided beside her. Definitely an old no-time safe, built approximately fifty years ago. Perfect.

Dufleur glanced around and saw a worktable set against one wall. It was piled with picture-framing materials.

"I . . . uh . . . we can just take it home, and I can work on it there—"

"I think the need is sufficiently pressing and important that you work on it here. That table," Saille nodded.

"Of course," Arbusca said, not seeming in the least discomposed that her own projects would be set aside for Dufleur's needs.

Dufleur squirmed inside, but Saille was right. Best protect the HouseHeart immediately with the strongest of spells. "We should have cleaned the table off while we were waiting," she muttered. She simply hadn't thought of it. Wasn't thinking clearly. Too many things distracting her—the proximity of her beloved HouseStone, Saille, being in T'Willow Residence, Saille, meeting Saille's mother, and Saille.

"No matter," said Arbusca; with a wave of her arm, the materials on the table disappeared tidily. Dufleur wondered where they went, then hurried over to the table where Saille was positioning the no-time. He said a word that gently removed the anti-grav on the unit, and it sank to the table.

"Will you trust your bundle to me?" Saille asked.

Arbusca turned curious eyes on the gathered cloak but kept her questions to herself.

Dufleur hesitated. He helped her save the HouseStone. He was her HeartMate. But she made the decision on what would be best for the HouseStone. It would do better, held by a living person than placed atop a table—for now.

She offered the cloak. Saille took it with the care given to the most fragile of newborns. She made sure he cradled it well, then managed a smile. She shucked her coat, summoned the needle she'd used before at T'Ash's from her rooms, and popped off the side panel where an ancestor's equations swooped in curving flourishes to capture and still time.

Dufleur lost herself in time, in her Flair, as she retraced the equations and coated the box, inside and out, with time. No one and nothing could touch the safe without alerting her. Then, drawing strength from Saille, she set an invisibility spell on it. Only she would be able to see it.

She opened the door to the no-time and, with infinite care, took her cloak and its contents and placed it in the box. Then she shut and pass-coded the safe.

The Thyme Residence seemed to sigh. She heard a little shifting, a stretching, a rearranging into a particular pattern. *Good*, it whispered to her mind. *Very good.*

The HouseHeart liked being surrounded by time molecules; it would have always been accustomed to that. Time merged with Flair would have been what had sparked its sentience.

It was only after she relaxed her concentration that Dufleur was able to focus on anything but the HouseHeart and her own concerns, and then she became aware of the slight constraint between Saille and his mother.

Dufleur frowned. Saille didn't seem to be aware of the emotional distance, but his mother certainly was.

She told herself it wasn't any of her business.

She told herself not to get involved between mother and son.

She told herself that trusting her instincts and following them through was a bad idea, hardly ever worked for her. She did it anyway.

Twenty-four

❤

Looking at Arbusca, she said, "You hurt Saille, and he hasn't forgiven you."

Saille flinched. Arbusca merely smiled sadly. "I know."

"You need to tell him you're sorry." What was she saying! She was the last person on the planet to be able to give advice. But perhaps she was the only person on the planet who could see the tension between the two.

"I have told him, more than once," Arbusca said, still calm, still completely undefensive.

"Dufleur!" Saille's cheeks matched the color of the rosy room.

"He couldn't hear you, then, past the hurt," Dufleur pressed on, flushing herself, miserably uncomfortable but sensing this was as important as the HouseStone. She went to Saille and stood before him, snuggled back to him, brought his arms around her waist, and held on to him. Their breathing synchronized. So did their hearts. She *sensed-saw* the large, aching bruise on Saille's heart, sent the hurt warmth, understanding, caring.

She turned her gaze to Arbusca. "Apologize again."

Saille shifted behind Dufleur, but she kept her grip on his arms tight.

Arbusca straightened, looked directly at her son. "I should have been stronger. I should have taken you away from this place." She sent an image of her standing in an entryway with stacking trunks ready to be teleported, grasping a small boy's hand—a five-year-old's?—and leaving.

"I should never have let her separate us. I was a coward and took the easy way out."

Dufleur flinched.

"It's something I regret every day, my son." She came forward and put her hands on Saille's shoulders. Dufleur tried to slip out from between them, but Saille kept her where she was.

"I didn't protect you, then I disappointed you. I'm sorry."

"It's in the past." Saille sounded strangled.

"That's true, and I think I am stronger now."

"She always abused you emotionally. You didn't have the chance to grow strong on your own here. I know that."

"Thank you for the defense." A smile trembled on Arbusca's lips. "But a person always has choices. I'm sorry, Saille, more than you can ever know. I love you, so much."

This time Dufleur escaped, went over to busy herself with reactivating the anti-grav spell on the no-time, while Saille hugged his mother and she wept. Keeping her face turned aside, but her link with Saille open, she understood that his mother's tears were finally healing his old hurt.

"Mother," Saille said. "I think that mask of your livery is no longer needed. I'm not MotherDam. Please dress as you choose."

"Saille." Arbusca's tears renewed.

When the pulsing emotion of the atmosphere eased in the room, Dufleur said, "I'll leave you two, now. Saille, you belong here the rest of the night." With a Word, she bespelled the no-time to follow her.

His forehead creased. "You have it?"

"Yes. Thank you for your help." Her chest went tight. "I don't think I could have done it on my own." She forced a smile. "Even with Fairyfoot's help." Dufleur dipped her head at Arbusca. "A pleasure meeting you, GreatMistrys, and I couldn't have done this without your help. I apologize for waking you and thank you for your generosity."

"I am always pleased to help," Arbusca said.

I think you should stay here for the rest of the night, she sent to Saille. *Your mother needs your presence near her.*

Yes, and I thank you. He held out his hand to Arbusca, a corner of his mouth lifted in a smile. "One last request, Mother, we need energy to teleport Dufleur and the no-time to Winterberry Residence."

Arbusca joined hands with him, and Dufleur linked her fingers with his on his other side. A surge of warmth and strength rolled from Arbusca—gentle and potent—through Saille and to her. Easy and familiar.

After a last curtsy to them both, she went to the no-time, embraced it, and teleported to D'Winterberry's.

Suddenly weary, she eased the safe into a corner of the room between the end of her framed bedsponge and the wall. She thought that Fairyfoot would sense it, too, enough to avoid any harm from the edges.

Dufleur put her palms on the top of the no-time, sent her mind to the entity inside. *Sleep. Recover strength. Gather Flair from me and the Fam and the atmosphere around you . . .*

A thought occurred. "D'Winterberry Residence?"

"Here, Dufleur Thyme." It seemed actually proud to be using energy to issue words aloud instead of telepathically.

"You know I brought in Thyme HouseStone and that you now house it."

"Yes. It is welcome here."

"It needs rest and safety and energy and Flair."

"The energy and Flair will not be too much for me to give. Minuscule."

"I trust you to know your limits and what is needed for another of your kind." And who better than D'Winterberry Residence who had nearly perished itself?

It is safe and well protected. Dufleur heard the words in her mind and felt them on another wavelength. D'Winterberry Residence speaking to the kernel of the D'Thyme Residence.

I sleep, whispered D'Thyme Residence.

Then Dufleur sought her bed herself, the scent of Saille rose from the linens. The bedsponge was warmed, another new housekeeping spell. Then her mind swirled away into sleep.

*S*aille woke, stretched luxuriously, and reached for Dufleur. She wasn't in his large bed. Yet.

But she would be. Last night had been incredible in many respects—the great sex, the saving of the D'Thyme HouseStone—he made a mental note to find a good place to put a medium-sized no-time safe until they could rebuild the Thyme Residence—and finally the falling away of the last of his anger at his mother. It had taken a long time for that ache to heal.

It had taken Dufleur.

He was so lucky to have her in his life. She had given him the gift of rediscovering his mother. A weight had been lifted from him that he hadn't known he carried.

Breakfast was excellent, as usual, and his first morning appointment went very well and put a nice amount of gilt in the Family bank account. Though snow once again sifted in large flakes from a gray sky heavy with its icy burden, his mood—and his mother's—remained fine. She smiled more, and her natural grace showed more, now that his lingering resentment was gone. He'd never seen her so centered, and thanked Dufleur mentally again.

He was feeling fine enough to visit his MotherDam's rooms and hunt for her personal memoryspheres. The all-too-familiar old-powdery scent of her dimmed his spirits a little, but he proceeded with determination, not liking searching her rooms and irritated that she'd made him.

She'd done *nothing* to help him as the head of the household and everything she could to hinder him. He found his teeth gritted and stopped at the end of one shelf of the bookcases that lined her sitting room, full of mementos, boxes, bottles, tools, and anything else her avaricious soul had wanted near, and decided to quit for the day.

But he wanted to know her alliances, and she hadn't recorded them in the Family business journal where they belonged—not for a decade. And alliances shifted, as the First-Families Council reformed when someone retired or died and their heir came into power. Saille was sure that D'Willow had allied with old D'Vine in many matters, but D'Vine had died and left a young boy as the new T'Vine. Saille's MotherDam would certainly not have approved or trusted Vinni.

Bucus Elder, also dead and a former Captain of the First-Families Council, had probably also been an ally. Ruis Elder would have been considered an enemy—if she hadn't needed him and *Nuada's Sword* for her plans for life extension.

Saille closed the doors of her suite behind him and descended the stairs, thinking of the ebb and flow of politics. Straif Blackthorn had taken his place as a FirstFamily GrandLord. The Hollys' fortunes had ebbed, then recovered, and Passiflora was endeavoring to mend them. Saille didn't want to be surprised by any unexpected favors called due. Traps.

*M*idday *meal wasn't as cheerful. The snow continued to* sleet down, more icy than pretty fat flakes, and the pace of the city was slow. That wasn't the problem at the table, though. A couple of his cuzes were suffering from the lack of sunlight and grumpy at being kept inside as the snow mounted into deep drifts around the Residence and the estate. Saille offered the glider and when grumbling continued about the weather, told them to visit the conservatory. But they didn't want any "damn green flowery garden."

On the verge of losing his temper, he asked what they *did* want. They stared at him, and he felt once again that they wondered how far they could test him, trust him.

"They want a solarium, dear," his mother said, setting ice cream with cocoa sauce on his plate.

"A solarium?"

One of his cuzes explained, "All glass, like the conservatory, but not only for plants. A pool or pools. And some miniature suns."

"Miniature suns are expensive," Saille said.

"Yes, but they are wonderful for the emotions of those who don't get enough sunshine during the winter."

His mother gave a little cough.

"Yes?" asked Saille.

"We drew up an estimate and preliminary plans last year and presented it to D'Willow. She, too, suffered from lack of sun depression. However she did not approve of the plans or the expense."

That was almost enough for Saille to authorize them right there. He sighed. "What's my afternoon schedule?"

"Your first appointment canceled because of the snow."

"Very well, you may give me the file on the solarium."

"*Thank* you, cuz Saille."

He regretted it when he found a thick stack of papyrus and several holospheres on his desk. The papyrus mostly dealt with figures. He winced at the cost. It would have kept him for a decade at the country estate. He flicked a holosphere with his thumb, and a room bright with yellow sunlight appeared—very much contrasting with the gray day.

"This is the north view of the proposed D'Willow Solarium," said a throaty voice he recognized as Mitchella Blackthorn's, the designer favored by the younger set of the FirstFamilies. She knew her job, the room entranced.

He was lost in a daydream of a golden room against a snowy

sky with a couple of turquoise pools when he heard it, screams of rage, shattering china, the snap of a marriage.

He froze, despair coating his gut. He'd met with someone from each couple his MotherDam had matched in the last few years—two of them had already separated—and made slight links with them. Another bad match was finished.

The marriage was dead.

He scried them immediately, and the GraceLord himself answered, jaw tensed and white-lipped. "Is there anything I can do?" asked Saille. "I am available for a free consultation, as I stated before."

"No," the man said, rubbing a hand over his face. A cut welled blood above his eyebrow. "We're finished here. My wife is moving back to her parents. Where they will support her the way I can't, emotionally, financially, completely in every little thing." Then he reddened. "My apologies, GreatLord," he said stiffly. "My wife has this seasonal sunlight yearning thing. Your Mother-Dam made this match, but we have truly broken it. There is nothing you can do." He disconnected.

Saille wanted to argue. Wanted to do more, pound his fist on the desk and rail at the stupidity of his MotherDam. He'd been sure, *sure* that he could have matched both of those individuals well. Not to each other.

Now they were stuck. Despite what SupremeJudge Elder said about divorce in the countryside, Saille knew that the social stigma against it would prevent most people from ever considering ending a marriage.

And Saille was of the opinion that people only joined together when they were well matched and ready to work at a marriage and Family.

But these two had been matched by a Flairless, mean old woman who only cared that she fulfilled the most superficial terms of her GreatLady responsibility so she could draw her yearly NobleGilt.

He opened the drawer and took out the list of the names of his MotherDam's last clients. He drew a line through the matching that had just failed.

Another line.

When would the gossip begin?

When would someone put together the pieces that his Mother-Dam had abused her name and title and responsibilities?

Cold sweat pebbled his brow.

He'd spoken with every person except Genista Holly, committed to helping them. Two couples had taken his advice and were in counseling. They might make it.

There were so few on the list. He was doing his absolute best with his work and his Flair. Perhaps the Willows would get lucky and no one would ever know of his MotherDam's mistakes.

He stared at the pretty solarium projected in the dim room. He wanted that.

He wanted sunshine and warmth.

He wanted Dufleur.

"Calendarsphere," he commanded, and it winked into existence. "Status of my next appointment."

"Canceled due to the weather."

"Dismissed."

He teleported to D'Winterberry Residence. It was even darker than his own. When he sent a probing thought toward Dufleur's rooms, he found them empty, except for the slight trace of the contentedly sleeping Thyme HouseStone.

Dufleur!

Hmmm? It was a very absent reply.

His mind traced her.

She was working in her new lab. The one with the many shields to implode.

Just last night, they'd found the shattered remnants of an entity that had been nearly destroyed by her father's experiments in time.

Today Dufleur was conducting her own studies.

It was time to discuss the situation.

*H*e *found her hunched over a worktable, closing a tube* over something. A dead rat?

Fairyfoot said, *Diseased rat. He volunteered. For food. For pain ease.* The little cat didn't turn around, was as focused on the experiment as Dufleur.

"Dufleur?"

"Ummm."

"Dufleur."

"Minute."

"Dufleur!"

"Not now!" A tool clattered, the rat moaned, twitched, died. "Dammit!" Dufleur stood, rolled her shoulders, turned; frustration was on her face. "Do I interrupt you while you are matchmaking?" she asked in a low, furious voice.

"I'm not doing something illegal. Dangerous." He looked pointedly at the rat. "Deadly."

Rat was dying anyway, Fairyfoot said.

Dufleur ran her hands through her hair, tugged at it. "No, you can just ruin lifetimes."

He flinched.

FamMan ruin experiment, Fairyfoot sniffed. She still didn't look at him.

Dufleur's inhalation and sigh was ostentatiously audible. "I apologize. I know your Flair is great and that you use it for good." She walked up to him and kissed him on the cheek. "You saved the Thyme HouseHeart last night."

"We did it together."

"I couldn't have done it alone."

Saille couldn't look away from the dead rat. "You experimented on that rat and killed it."

Her face went stiff. She took a step back, put her hands in her lab coat pockets. "I am an ethical scientist. I abide by all the laws of Celta regarding experimentation. I sent word through the feral community for volunteer diseased rats. Some came. Like Fairyfoot said, they get out of the cold and damp, get good food and pain ease. You make me forget my duty." She turned and went to the tube. She studied it, passed her hand over the cylinder, and it opened. With a word, her hands and upper arms were coated with a yellow-tinted molecular shield.

She was taking care of herself in that way, at least. She examined the dead rat, treating it gently and with respect, wrote down her notes, marked the rat's left ear with an intricate pattern, said a blessing over the corpse, and teleported it away.

"Where does it go?" He was reluctantly fascinated.

"To death grove of feral animals."

"Haven't heard of that one."

"There's a small order of priests and priestesses who run it, with some low-level Healers for corpses found by citizens. I always mark my subjects with the disease it had and how it died." She looked away, her lips firmed. "Human error."

Fairyfoot licked a paw. *It would not have lived long anyway, a day or two.*

"They come to you. But what do rats know of living and dying?"

"I don't know. They know what I can give them."

"With the winter we've had, I'm surprised you don't have a stream of rats coming to this place.

"They know rats come here and never come out. It takes a sick and desperate rat to come here. Sometimes they don't have what I need to work on." She shrugged. "I house them anyway."

Snow today stopped them, Fairyfoot said. *Good.* She sniffed again. *They are sick rats. I do not get to play with them or eat them, or I will become a sick Cat. It is hard not to play with them.* She hopped down from her embroidered velvet perch and went to a closed door, sat in front of it, tail twitching.

"It's always hard to go against instincts, isn't it, Saille? You told me once that your MotherDam forbade you to practice your Flair in the countryside. What did you do?"

He unclenched his jaw to say, "I disobeyed her, but she really didn't care that 'yokels' were getting the benefit of Great-House matchmaking Flair. What do you work on?"

Her eyes widened. "You don't know? My father had been studying a reversing time spell that would only affect bacteria or a virus within humans. His beloved younger brother died of the same virus as your MotherDam as a child. When your MotherDam heard that a Time scientist instead of a Healer might find a 'cure' for the virus, she offered a huge prize. That's when Agave started the same research, I think."

Saille felt the blood drain from his head. His fingers went chill. "You want to kill my MotherDam's virus, revive her." He couldn't even move. "That could tear the Family apart."

Twenty-five

❧

Saille continued, *"Some of my Family have come to prefer* me."

"Of course they would. Anyone would."

"I've only been in power a little over five months. If my MotherDam were revived, the FirstFamilies Council could decide she should retain the title after so long. They are more familiar with her." Another breath in and out. "I'd fight. It could get very messy."

She looked aside. "You can be easy on that, anyway. I've had no progress with that virus. It is too virulent. I've changed to another."

Relief weakened him. He went to the worktable and hitched a hip on a free space. The room contained only one chair and Fairyfoot's perch. Sterile in the extreme.

Fairyfoot hopped to her feet, nose sniffing at the crack under the door. She growled. *There is a healthy rat in there. He lied.* She sent a narrowed look to Saille. *Rats lie.*

"I don't," Dufleur said, her gaze steady on his. "I don't lie. You came here to say something specific, Saille."

"I want to protect my HeartMate!" He took a breath and held it, released it. "You have plenty of other responsibilities— embroidery for the Enlli Gallery and the commissions. To Passiflora. Why must you continue this endeavor that could tear you apart, as it did the Thyme Residence!"

Her eyes were big and blue. "Because practicing my craft feels good. It's something for *me*." She put a fist on her heart. "It fulfills *me*. For good or ill, embroidery is not the pleasant pastime it once was. It's how I support myself and Fairyfoot and my mother. You forgot to list my responsibilities as a daughter, and what I am or should be doing regarding the legal case against my mother and D'Winterberry."

He closed his eyes. "I'm sorry." He opened his lashes on another sigh. "I saw how you reenergized that no-time last night, why can't you limit your skills to that?" He knew that limiting primary Flair was tough, a person wanted to know the extent of their capabilities. He knew what he was asking was unreasonable.

"A no-time repair person. Doesn't sound like a successful career." She crossed her arms. "There's a ban on researching time. Your MotherDam saw to that after my father died without a solution to her problems. Punishment, perhaps."

"If I asked you to stop for a while, until spring, would you do so?"

"I won't lie. I don't think I could, Saille." Her eyes fired. "The law against my craft is wrong. And convincing the First-Families Council to lift it, to clear my father's reputation, is right."

"Your father killed himself and destroyed his house, impoverished you and your mother."

"And he paid for that. But it must have been a freak accident. He wouldn't have continued to work somewhere that would hurt others."

Dufleur didn't, either, Fairyfoot said.

"You had a problem!" he roared.

Fairyfoot tilted her head. *Seared My whiskers.*

"I want to protect you."

She came up to him, put her hands on his chest, lifted her face. "I've been very careful, Saille."

"You've been careful of others. Not of yourself." But he'd caught her scent. His body instinctively remembered loving her, sexual tension tightened his muscles.

"I am not good with people, Saille. I make bad mistakes."

"We have a difference of opinion here," he said steadily, wanting nothing more than to 'port her to his bed.

"I can't promise to stop my experimentation," she said in a small voice.

"I don't like that at all. But I understand it. I don't accept it, and we'll consider options."

Her eyes narrowed. "What options?"

"I don't know. There must be a compromise."

She shook her head. "I don't think so."

"I'll find one." He set his hands on her shoulders. "You must promise me to be especially careful."

"Yes," she said.

It wasn't enough.

He teleported from *Dufleur's* laboratory back home. *He'd* been aroused and irritated, and she'd shown no interest in sex. He hadn't been in the mood to persuade her, not to mention the laboratory had no ambience whatsoever. He'd taken some hits in the pride and the heart, and anxiety still buzzed in his brain at the thought of any threat to his HeartMate.

The day, which had started out with such promise, had become frustrating. The breaking of a marriage and his worry that his MotherDam's botched matches would come to light and harm the Family, the argument with Dufleur. Both had weighed on him.

More, he couldn't get the Thyme HouseStone out of his mind. Residential entities seemed to be playing a part in his courtship with Dufleur. He had freed his from the constraints his MotherDam had set upon it. Dufleur's mother was accused of neglecting an estate and a Residence and could have her home taken from her. Dufleur and he had rescued the core of a Residence last night.

That was one thing he would never regret and an accomplishment that would always give him pride. And that nudged him into thinking of his own Residence. It was standard lore that a head of household should spend at least a day's worth of time in the HouseHeart every month. He hadn't.

So he made that his priority.

His steps slowed as he reached the HouseHeart. He'd barely been in it since he'd become T'Willow. His MotherDam had never admitted him to this place, never taught him the right words or rituals. She had merely ignored the fact that her previous heir, her older sister, had imparted the knowledge to him. When he'd taken the title, he'd named his mother as his Heir and shared everything with her.

Despite all his personal and professional successes two floors above him in the ResidenceDen, and the acceptance of his Family and the FirstFamilies over the last two months, this being was the core of the Family. Would it accept him? He'd been loath to put it to the test.

He'd accused Dufleur of being cowardly, of being too aware

of others' opinions. He should have aimed that argument at himself.

So he took a big breath, shucked the robe he was wearing, and placed both palms on the ancient wooden door that had hardened with age and spells into stronger than steel. Softly, he recited the pretty poetry spell one of the previous many *D'Willows* had crafted and felt the door swing away from his hands.

A tendril of warm, scented air drifted out, redolent of generations of female Heads of Households, spring flowers mixed with a hint of musk. The scent of the Family itself. Nostrils widening, he caught the faintest trace of masculinity. It was enough to have his shoulders easing.

Welcome, Saille T'Willow. You have not spent as much time here as you should.

He strode in. "My apologies." The thick rugs, angled many ways and a blur of competing colors and patterns, caressed the soles of his feet. He walked to the center of the octagonal room and stood near the altar. The room was well lit with bright natural sunlight from hidden shafts on the property, set precisely in the four directions. Physics and Flair and mirrors. Saille thought a male Willow had contributed that.

Why are you here?

"As you said, I haven't spent much time here as the Great-Lord." His jaw flexed. "I *am* the GreatLord, T'Willow. I want that acknowledged."

It is acknowledged, the HouseHeart voice sounded mildly amused.

Saille closed his eyes and let out the breath he'd been unconsciously holding. His spine straightened. He hadn't realized he'd been a little hunched, either. "Thank you."

Perform the empowering ritual, T'Willow. No humor now.

He tensed again, shot his Flair around the chamber, up into the Residence, checking for weakening, for loss of energy. There was none, but with the example of Winterberry and Thyme Residences before him, he was all too aware of the need to keep the essential entities alive. With blood pulsing faster because of the scare, Saille bowed toward the altar, blew the dangle of nearby windchimes, enjoyed the light sounding of lovely random notes, then spent the next septhour reinforcing all the spells needed by the Residence. When he was done

he was barely able to slip into the hot, bubbling tub that wa_
the "water" portion of the four elements. He sat on a ston_
ledge and relaxed, head back. He was sure that this luxury
wasn't included in most male-dominated HouseHearts. Bles_
the ladies.

All is as it should be, the HouseHeart said, as if it had been
doing its own check.

"Thank you," Saille murmured.

Better than even your predecessor at her prime.

That sent a little spurt of interest through Sallie but no_
enough for him to open his eyes. "Each generation has more
Flair," Saille said lazily.

The Residence is well maintained for the next quarter. Approval hummed in the HouseHeart's voice.

"Mmm." The water—there was some faint scent to it—
soaked stress from his muscles.

*You are T'Willow, the GreatLord. Only your predecessor be-
lieves herself to still be the Head of this Household.*

That woke Saille up. "She *does* believe that."

She is the past, the HouseHeart said simply. *One cannot
dwell in the past.*

It occurred to Saille that the HouseHeart had seen many
generations of his Family come and go, yet still looked to the
future, and he had another distracting thought that time was
very often spoken of casually by all and understood by none.
Except Dufleur.

Before he could comment, a soft yowl came, then a cat-
expression of horror. Myx sat, whiskers twitching wildly, a few
feet from Saille. Another plaintive mew. *Your Whole Body is in
WATER.* The cat shuddered.

"I like it," Saille said.

Welcome, Fam Myx. You do the Residence honor, the House-
Heart said.

Myx preened. *Nice place.*

If you would be so kind, FamCat, to do me a favor, said the
HouseHeart.

A shrug rolled down the cat's back, but a gleam of curiosity
sparked in his yellow eyes. "Yesssss?"

Here. The slide of a wooden panel, clinkings. *These have
been kept for Saille T'Willow.*

The noises stirred enough interest in Saille for him to shift and watch, as Myx picked up a small leather pouch and trotted with it to within Saille's arm reach. The cat dropped the pouch and retreated to a safer place, purring.

Saille picked up the small bag of fine-grained leather and opened it. There were two objects. One was a pottery leaf inset with a red jewel on a cord of braided gold. His heart began to thump. The Willow ruby. He'd heard of the prize possession, but never seen it.

The first T'Willow was also a potter.

Saille closed his hand over the pendant, received a jolt, a rush of impressions of many of his ancestors holding it as he did. Generous women. Honorable men. A few smears of selfishness, of dislike of the simple token, of a wish to remount the stone. He dropped it back into the pouch.

It should be worn. YOU should wear it. The Flair it holds multiplies then.

"Ah." He coughed. His throat had clogged.

Myx grinned at him with smug, narrowed eyes. *I could wear it.*

Saille pulled the pendant over his head.

Purring loudly, Myx smirked. *Or I could have a ruby set in a willow leaf for a collar. From T'Ash. It would look good on Me.*

It would certainly accent the drab browns and blacks of his fur.

"I thought you wanted blue faience beads."

Cocking his head, Myx grinned. *I want both.*

Naturally.

The HouseHeart said, *There is another object in the bag. I had great difficulty preventing your predecessor from disposing of it. I had to cloud her mind.* The thought contained echoes of old suffering at disobeying a head of the household.

Saille looked into the pouch, a gleaming circle of gold showed. He plucked out the ring. A very delicate band, with even more elegant and delicate etched flourishes. Oddly enough, only male resonances came from it.

It is for your mother. Brought to her by her HeartMate. Given to D'Willow who never told her of it.

Shock cascaded through him. His fingers reflexively curved over the ring, protecting it, keeping it safe for his mother.

When he managed to speak, his voice was rusty. "Not a HeartGift." He wouldn't be able to see it if it had been.

No. But a gift from the heart nevertheless. The maker's mark is T'Ash's but he was commissioned by your mother's Heart-Mate.

Myx trotted over, keeping a wary eye on the tub, and looked at the ring.

Now Saille knew what it was, he could sense more of the man. He'd have been good for his mother.

The ruby on his chest flashed. Myx hissed, hopped back, slipped . . . envisioning sharp swiping claws, Saille sent a burst of Flair at his Fam that rolled the cat away from the tub.

"Grrrrr. *Too much water!*" Myx rose to his paws and stalked to a corner to lick away the five droplets that dewed his fur.

All thought of relaxation gone, imbued with renewed dedication to his Family, Saille rose from the tub.

Thank you for your gifts, HouseHeart.

One has always been yours, the other your mother's. Safely kept.

"But that's done and past. Now they should be used."

Yes, the HouseHeart and Myx said together.

*T*he function that night was at the starship, *Nuada's Sword,* and hosted by Captain Ruis Elder and his wife, Supreme-Judge Ailim Elder. Every year Ruis reported to the Councils on the state of the reconditioning of the starship, and a gathering and a tour was part of that. This year he'd scheduled it as part of the social season.

Some people wouldn't attend, because Ruis was a Null—a person who suppressed the Flair of others, as well as Celtan spell-technology. So he was uncomfortable to be around. On the other hand, there was the Ship itself. An entity like the Residences, but one that was centuries old and had traveled from Earth itself. And everyone loved the Ship's great greensward, the third of the Ship that nourished growing things—including the plants that gave Celtans their names, some of which only survived on the Ship, not having adapted to Celtan soil.

The invitation stated that this year the cryogenics room would not be a part of the tour. Because one of the tubes was inhabited by D'Willow.

On impulse, Dufleur called ahead and spoke to Ruis Elder to see if she'd be allowed in the cryogenics room before the gathering began. She'd been prepared to argue the matter, but Captain Elder had just stared at her from under lowered chestnut brows and agreed.

Fairyfoot was already at the Ship, playing with the other cats and SupremeJudge Ailim Elder's dog.

Saille had not offered to take Dufleur to the event. He was still upset—angry—at her. Or pulling away because he felt he might be hurt. She knew that just from the tenseness that ran down their bond. And as he'd said of her earlier, she understood his feelings, but she didn't like the situation.

He wouldn't like her visiting his MotherDam, either.

The Ship wasn't far—just a couple of blocks to Landing Park, then across the width of the park—but the snow was too bad to walk there, so Dufleur received permission to teleport to the north airlock, which, like the cryogenics chamber, was one of the places where Flair worked in the Ship. But the Ship was six kilometers long, and it would take time to walk from the airlock to the chamber.

She arrived a half-septhour before the official time of the gathering. Passiflora would be fashionably late as always. Dufleur had noticed Passiflora D'Holly always arrived twenty minutes after the gathering started unless her protégée was playing music for the function.

So Dufleur dressed in the royal blue of the Thyme house colors and found herself surrounded by metal walls. Everything here was different than any other place on Celta.

The whole ship gave her the shivers. More so than most Celtans, she thought, though the "curse" had been broken a few years ago by Ruis Elder.

It was the Time Wind, she realized. The foam metal floor beneath her not only wasn't *Celtan soil*, it was from a time and place more ancient than she could imagine. The Time Wind had been different on Earth. Or perhaps had changed—warped—during the long spacefaring journey.

Her soles buzzed from small electrical charges. The atmosphere around her tingled, heavy with age, time trapped in crannies of this strange entity. If she could tap it, use it, how would her Flair be magnified—or different? A scary thought, but a tantalizing one.

Captain Elder's voice came. "Merry meet, GrandMistrys Thyme."

Dufleur blinked. He gave her the noble salutation, as if she was of the same status as he was. "Merry meet, Captain Elder."

"I am sparing you my presence. I understand that you know the way to the cryogenics chamber, but there are maps on all the corridor walls. Should you have any questions, just ask Ship, or, if you prefer, I can stand ready to answer them."

"I wouldn't dream of bothering you as you prepare for the gathering."

Elder chuckled. "Most of the work is done, but I am in the greensward. The FirstFamilies do like to look at the sacred trees."

"Thank you again for your courtesy," Dufleur said.

"My pleasure. I'll see you later."

"Yes." Dufleur pressed the button to open the iris door and stepped into the long hallway. As she walked toward the center of the Ship, her Flair *changed*. She thought others might feel a diminution of their Flair, but for her, it was as if the Time Wind buffered her a little, but the wind itself felt different.

After taking a couple of omnivators, she found herself in the cryogenics room, surrounded by tubes that had held the founders of the colonization—the ancestors of the FirstFamilies. The crew of the Ships had lived and died for generations during the long voyage.

All the tubes were empty except one. There was a slight glow near the far wall and a small hum. "Ship?"

"Yes, GrandMistrys Thyme?"

"Flair works in this chamber." Her feet had stopped tingling.

"We have modified the atmosphere and the molecules of the walls, ceiling, and floor to accommodate both Earth and Celtan technology."

She supposed that was an answer.

Ship went on, "Your 'Flair' is operative here, as well as in Sickbay B, which will also act as the nursery for the Flaired little one, a gathering area for the leaders of your world just beyond Landing Ramp Six, and in what is now designated as the North End Airlock."

With slow steps, she went over to see D'Willow. A faint white fog filled the cylinder, sometimes parting so Dufleur could see a portion of the nude woman. She stepped back.

It should have given her some satisfaction to see the woman who'd defamed her father lying helpless and near death.

It shocked her.

Why would anyone hold on to a miserable life so long, a life riddled with disease, instead of seeking rebirth on the wheel of stars? Life was precious, and to be savored each moment, but the great adventure of crossing the threshold of death should not be seen as so fearsome.

Dufleur didn't understand it. She considered what might be the basic motivation of such a person, a woman who had been pampered and powerful all her life.

Greed. That was exactly what drove this woman. She was greedy—for food, for life, for power, for all the things her rank could give her, this time around on the wheel. Did she fear her next life? Dufleur snorted, if she'd lived the way D'Willow had, she'd dread karma and the next life. How often was a person born to great Flair and rank if they abused it? How often, if not? Too many philosophical questions. She was a scientist, she should think on the ethics long and hard, be sure that she followed her own ethical standards—as she did just by continuing experiments now considered illegal—but she wasn't a priest or priestess to ponder all the vagaries of reincarnation.

She put a hand on her own chest, felt the bump, bump, bump of it. She, too, had been close to death, her heart fatally damaged, yet she had been saved and lived. She could only think that it had not been her time to die. Could she take that as a sign her work was valuable and should be continued? It would be nice to think so, but was simply rationalization of her wishes.

All the huge feelings for Saille set her philosophizing too much.

"The Fams have joined the human gathering, including Fairyfoot, though there is a special anteroom for the FamAnimals." The Ship prompted, sounding proud. "Samba, Ship's Cat, is offering rides on her saucer."

Dufleur laughed. Cats *lived* every moment. She left the greedy old woman who'd ruined lives and now lived a half-life of her own, to join others who were in the prime of their lives.

Tempted by the odd Flair and Wind of Time, and knowing Saille had arrived and was still displeased with her, Dufleur didn't go directly to the party in the landing bay but followed the disappearing Flair until she found the epicenter, the Captain's Quarters.

Ruis Elder stepped from the door.

Dufleur gasped, caught rambling the Ship alone. By the Captain.

Twenty-six

❤

$\mathcal{H}$e raised an eyebrow at her. "The fact that my Nullness is spreading throughout the Ship and that it emanates from my rooms is in my report. My reports of the last three years."

Heat slid over her cheeks. She ducked her head. "My apologies." But she was tempted again. Turning aside to ostensibly study the marred door of the Captain's Quarters and the fascinating Earth writing, she gathered the slippery Time Wind and sent to Ruis mentally, *Thank you for letting me visit the cryogenics chamber.*

Watching from the corner of her eye, she saw his startled expression. "I haven't heard any mental talk since I was a young child before my Nullness grew. How did you do that?" he asked in wonder.

She faced him again. "Magic." Another name for psi powers, Flair.

He considered her. "Could you boost someone else's Flair to overcome my Nullness, even here?"

Since she thought he had a specific experiment in mind and she'd already used most of the Time Wind in the area, she said, "Probably not here."

"But in a place that was equal non-Flair and Flair? Or one mostly Flair?"

"I could definitely allow Flair to operate around you on Celta. With effort. And on the Ship." She didn't want to give away any secrets. "But areas with more Flair would naturally be easier to use."

"May I ask a favor?" He'd taken her arm, and they were walking briskly toward the landing ramp where the social event was occurring.

"You've already done one for me," Dufleur said.

"I would like you to link with someone so he could use his powers on me. That can be done?"

"That would be easier, yes. Why?" Ruis Elder had carved a

strong and essential place for himself in Celtan society and was a member of the FirstFamilies Council.

"I have this awful, interminable questionnaire . . ." He waved, then spoke, "Ship, please request my HeartMate and Saille T'Willow meet me and Dufleur Thyme in Ailim's blue sitting room."

Ship said, "I have relayed the message."

"Thank you."

A few minutes later, when Ruis waved a hand over a plate set in the metallic wall and the door slid open on either side, Dufleur saw that Saille and SupremeJudge Ailim Elder were already there. Ailim smiled at her. "Greetyou, GrandMistrys Thyme."

Dufleur curtsied deeply. "Merry meet."

Saille bowed formally. His expression was impassive.

"Merry meet, Saille," she said softly.

Beaming, Ruis went over to his wife—had he called her his HeartMate? How could he have known without Flair?—ah, Saille. Dufleur shifted from foot to foot. Ruis drew his lady into his arms. She looked amused at the public display of affection but went willingly enough. "Sweeting," Ruis said, nuzzling his wife's hair. "GrandMistrys Thyme can use Flair around me. I thought she could link with T'Willow, and he could read our auras for a brief HeartMate consultation."

"I already told you that I believe you to be HeartMates," Saille said.

"It's the questionnaire," Ailim Elder said. "It intimidates him. He's only halfway through."

"I've been attending to my duties and helping Ship plan this event," Ruis protested, then grimaced. "It's an awful, intrusive questionnaire."

Dufleur held out her hand to Saille. "Shall we link?" They already were, more than physically.

Stiffly he took her fingers. "Prepare yourself. Your Flair won't work in the usual manner, and I will only be able to repress Captain Elder's Nullness for a brief time." *Only for as long as I can hold the Time Wind in this room.*

"Repressing Nullness that suppressed Flair," Ailim murmured. "A double negative? That sounds odd."

"Ready?" Dufleur asked. Saille's fingers were impersonal, but she felt his mind and body prepare.

She drew the Time Wind to her, filtered the strength of it to Saille, and sent it whirling around the couple in front of them. Ailim Elder was smiling, leaning her head on Ruis's shoulder.

Saille made a noise, she felt his initial confusion, then the surge of his Flair. "The colors are all wrong," he muttered. He squinted, drew strong on Dufleur's energy, as she'd used his the night before. She fed him power.

"Yes," Saille said, then dropped her hand, ending the connection. "Yes, you two are definitely HeartMates."

"I know our courtship was before your time, Saille," Ailim said gently, "but you should know the story, that it wasn't easy and that Ruis nearly died."

He sent her a dark look. "I don't like thinking about Heart-Mates in danger."

"That's right. You voted for death for the black cultists."

"Yes. And I'd do it again."

He strode to the door and out.

The three of them stood in a frozen tableau. Then Ruis shook his head, squeezed his wife. "Why don't you mingle among our guests. I want to speak with GrandMistrys Thyme."

"Why?" asked Ailim.

"Our daughter, Dani Eve, is a Null. There will be situations where GrandMistrys Thyme—"

"Please call me Dufleur," Dufleur said, "both of you."

Ruis dipped his head. "Dani Eve may need someone to help her during her life. The new babe, too. I want to ally with you and your Family, Dufleur."

"You are wonderful," Ailim kissed him on the cheek, smiled at Dufleur, and glided out the door.

Dufleur stared at Captain Elder—Ruis. Her first request for an alliance! And with such a powerful man. She didn't even hold the title of D'Thyme yet. But she would. She would prove herself, and clear her father's reputation, and her wishes in that direction would continue to alienate Saille. She didn't want to make a choice.

*S*aille returned to *L*anding *B*ay *S*ix, still in an unsettled mood, despite the awesome setting. A wide entrance gaped in the northeast side of the Ship. As he'd approached, the space had shone through the snow. Now he could look through the slight waviness of the atmosphere that separated the night from this place and see the mounds of snow, the black sky beyond, and the glittering, starry sky.

It wasn't a weathershield keeping the elegantly dressed Celtans warm, but some force field generated by the Ship.

The open area of the Ship was as large as any ballroom, but the sides were a curving, polished silver. Steady light came from panels in the ceiling, unlike any Saille had ever seen. The whole place throbbed with *otherness*, alien to Celtans. Earthanness. Just as he suspected the Elders had anticipated.

Ailim Elder circulated throughout the room, dressed like any fashionable FirstFamily lady, in a long ball gown. Ruis had worn clothes of a different cut than those of a Nobleman of Druida, again harkening back to their ancestors. Saille had liked the style. No bloused sleeves or trous legs with extra fabric that showed a man's wealth, but form-fitting sleeves and legs. Had to be easier to work in.

As he sipped brithe brandy, he studied the crowd. All the twenty-five FirstFamilies heads of households and their consorts, and about a hundred more of the most politically important GrandLords and Ladies and GraceLords and Ladies of the Noble Council. A good venue for Passiflora D'Holly to campaign for her husband to become the Captain of the FirstFamilies Council, and therefore all the Councils of Druida. Only the FirstFamilies could vote, of course, and one vote for each couple, but all had alliances.

Saille's gaze appreciated Passiflora then automatically went to her side. But Dufleur wasn't with Passiflora. She was speaking to Ruis Elder in the room where he'd verified the Elders were true HeartMates. Because of their melding bright pink colored auras. That un-Celtan color still left an afterimage on his eyelids.

He'd known Dufleur was already on the Ship when he'd arrived. And he quickly realized where she'd been. The cryonics room. Studying his MotherDam. He didn't know why. He hadn't dared go to that room. He kept the anger he felt for his predecessor under control, but now and again it surged to blindside him. He wondered if he'd live with this feeling of limbo all his life, and, if so, *how* he would live with it.

A small mew attracted his attention. Myx crawled onto his dress boots. The Fam looked even more a low-class feral cat than usual. His whiskers drooped. He'd been excited to be invited to the Fam get-together in the Ship, but now he appeared less than enthusiastic, his mottled brown and black fur dull.

Don't like it here, he said and yearned to be picked up. So Saille did, cradling him in his arms. He had a certain smell.

Whole Ship feels funny. Don't like. Samba gave Me a ride on Her saucer, and I puked. Don't like.

Why don't I 'port you home?

Yesss. My pad under the couch in ResidenceDen.

It was done in an instant, but it left Saille with the feeling that despite the fine clothes and the title he donned, he was still an outsider. How many of these people would give power back to his MotherDam if she were revived?

A tingle came between his shoulder blades. Slowly angling his body, Saille was surprised to see GrandLord T'Yew staring at him. With a hard glance, T'Yew jerked his head toward a curved place by the wall.

It wasn't difficult for Saille to figure out that the man wasn't pleased with him and wanted to speak with him. His gut churned. There'd been one cryptic note in the Family journals about T'Yew. Enough so that Saille got a bad feeling that another trap for him had just been sprung.

He crossed the room leisurely, speaking a word or two here and there, and stopping by the drink table to set down his empty snifter and take another as a prop for his hands. Finally he leaned casually against a metal beam.

A little while later, T'Yew joined him. "I've heard you go about with Dufleur Thyme. Your MotherDam would not approve of you associating with that one," he sneered.

That relieved Saille of one worry. Whatever relationship his MotherDam had had with this ally of hers, she hadn't told him that Dufleur Thyme was Saille's HeartMate, or that she'd hidden Dufleur from him.

"She isn't here." At least down here in the Landing Bay. Saille kept his tone mild, though he was completely on guard.

T'Yew grunted, then said, "The Thymes are noted frauds and deceivers."

Saille raised his brows. "In what way?"

"Before he blew himself up, the dead one took your Mother
Dam's gilt and gave her nothing but empty promises."

Saille pretended to blink in surprise. "Strange. I saw nothing
in our Family accounts indicating that. Are you sure?" As he felt
his way in this conversation, he decided playing the stupid fool
might be his best option. T'Yew wore arrogance like a cloak.
No doubt he believed very few people matched his birth and
breeding.

"Nevertheless, she told me so," T'Yew said in a tone that
made it clear he wasn't surprised that D'Willow hadn't told her
Daughter'sSon.

Swirling his brandy, Saille said, "It's odd. There are all these
accusations against T'Thyme, yet the stories are all second- or
thirdhand. I haven't seen nor heard of any solid proof."

"Man blew himself and his Residence up. How much more
proof does anyone need to know he was a crazy incompetent?"

Since Saille agreed with the underlying fact of that, and it
angered him, he said nothing, though he stared at T'Yew and
the powerful ladies and lords around him and thought of bad errors.

Had T'Yew never made any mistakes? Committed any misstep that could have taken his own or others' lives if it had gone
wrong? Saille couldn't believe it, but had no doubt T'Yew never
thought he was wrong. Hubris.

But he did have a point about T'Thyme. Much as Dufleur,
and Saille himself, would wish to deny it, the man had endangered his Family—Dufleur—and almost destroyed a living
Residence. Saille didn't think he could forgive the dead man for
that—and for not cherishing his daughter as a father should.
"The daughter should not pay the price of her father's mistakes," he said.

Yew stared unblinkingly at Saille. "Every Family is judged
by each of its members. That's how it's always been, and should
always be." His jaw tensed. "I wondered if you would throw
your hand in with those young upstarts like T'Ash and T'Blackthorn." The men were a good generation older than Saille, but
he did agree with their ideas more than with anyone else's. He
kept his face impassive.

"New ideas. Lenient ideas. I don't hold with them," T'Yew
said.

Obviously not.

Leaning closer, T'Yew said, "Don't vote for T'Holly. He doesn't deserve the Captaincy after the mess he made of his life."

"The general consensus is that T'Holly lost everything because he was so prideful and unyielding," Saille replied, thinking that the words described T'Yew even better. T'Yew had no dashing charm.

"The man lost everything because he stupidly and rashly made a solemn vow of honor." T'Yew's lip curled. "Always impulsive, those Hollys. Never careful."

Never so cagey as this one.

Another slight shift of the shoulders from T'Yew. "When a new FirstFamilies Lord and Lady takes their title, like you did, alliances can shift. I am evaluating my connection with your House."

That wasn't a surprise. Saille didn't think he and this man would ever see anything in the same light.

"Particularly since I have not received the spell your Mother-Dam promised me when my wife was sixteen and a half. I've been patient, but your Family is now in default."

Everything inside Saille chilled. "What spell?"

He thought he heard T'Yew grind his teeth. The man stiffened even more, sent a haughty glance down his nose. "I have trained my wife as your MotherDam and I agreed. Lahsin will, of course, renew her vows to me after she is seventeen, but your MotherDam said there was a spell in addition to the herbs that would make her more . . . pliable."

The air stopped in his lungs. The atmosphere around him took on nightmare tones. He could see the good repute of his Family smeared, his relatives shattered as they were shunned by others of their class. How had Dufleur stood it? Because she had to. Even now, when faced with the direst of threats, his thoughts spun to her.

He wrenched his mind back. If Saille didn't handle T'Yew correctly, the older, powerful GrandLord might try and destroy the Willows. Weighing every word, he said, "Since you were in her confidence, you must know that she had no great opinion of me. She left me little guidance with regard to any of our Family affairs."

T'Yew's mouth tightened.

Saille continued. "And I saw nothing in our business journals regarding a transaction between you and my MotherDam."

"It was a favor between allies. Off the books, a favor for a favor. Which I paid. I want the compliance spell."

Definitely a trap for his unwary feet. "My MotherDam's methods are not my own. I know of no such spell. Perhaps you should consult the Roses or the Spindles, both deal in love matters." And both of those Families were very ethical.

T'Yew hissed. "This isn't love, this is business. My wife is the strongest in Flair of her generation. I'll make a tidy sum from her talents. And I want a son. Your MotherDam said that was probable, too."

Saille widened his eyes in mock surprise. "How could she know? Sometimes the match can generally indicate children, but to be certain of such things you would have to consult a prophet like GreatLord T'Vine."

Glaring, T'Yew shook his head. He had paled. "Useless. You are useless as a matchmaker, and I'll not put any of my Family concerns in the hands of a child like T'Vine." Saille wondered if T'Yew was as nervous about being in the prophet's company as everyone else. The older man began to turn away, anger radiating from him.

"If my MotherDam had wanted me to help you, she should have left me the tools to do so," Saille murmured, then, "One moment, sir. I honor my Family commitments."

The man stopped and eyed him.

"I cannot give you whatever spell my MotherDam created, but I could repay you in other ways . . ." He waited a beat. "If you can tell me what favor you did for my MotherDam, I can judge how to compensate you."

T'Yew narrowed his eyes. "This is not the place to continue this conversation." He glanced toward Dufleur and the Hollys who were watching them. "And I will think on your offer." His nostrils flared. "I wanted the spell."

Without waiting for Saille to answer, he strode away to his middle-aged daughter and Heir who was talking with a knot of the most conservative nobles.

Saille had managed to spend enough time in the company of the Hollys and the Furzes to know they held no grudge against his MotherDam or the Willows for D'Willow's approval of

inne Holly and Genista Furzes' marriage. Each Family had
ained in that alliance, and Tinne and Genista had been pleased
ith the marriage.

Saille had thought the worst threat to his Family had been
odged.

He'd been wrong.

Twenty-seven

❦

$\mathcal{D}$ufleur *felt the tension in Saille wind tight and observed th*
aristocratic older man stride away from Saille to join a woma
who resembled him. Dufleur probed through their link, caugl
that Saille was in turmoil and not willing to share. "Who is he?
she asked Passiflora.

Passiflora sighed. "T'Yew and his Heir. I don't like hir
much, but he has gathered around him the most powerful an
conservative of the FirstFamilies Council members, so we'
have to meet and greet and be polite." She slid a gaze over t
Dufleur. "He was an ally of GreatLady D'Willow."

Dufleur tensed.

But before they took more than a few steps toward the clus
ter of conservatively dressed people, a girl of about sixtee
dressed expensively but unflatteringly in pastels hesitantl
pushed through the force field and walked to T'Yew.

"You're late," he snapped, towering over the young girl.

"His wife," whispered Passiflora to Dufleur, who stopped t
stare in shock.

"My deepest apologies," the young woman said instantly
then added, "If we're late, it's my fault, not the driver's."

"Of course." T'Yew looked down his long, arrogant nose.

"The kind of Noble who gives all the FirstFamilies a ba
reputation," Passiflora murmured.

Licking her lips, the girl said, "We left exactly when my cal
endarsphere alarmed."

T'Yew lifted a brow in patent disbelief.

His Heir said, "Unlikely, as you're always late and alway
blame it on the calendarsphere. I don't suppose you have it witl
you."

With fingers that trembled, the girl held out a small calendar
sphere so antique that it was an actual sphere and not a disk tha
could project a hologram. She peered at it. "The time reads sever
forty-five."

"Nonsense, give me that," the middle-aged woman, T'Yew'

Jaughter and Heir, said loudly, drawing attention to the group, and took the sphere from the girl.

The Ship said, "The time is twenty septhours, two minutes."

"No, it isn't," Dufleur said absently.

"What?" boomed the Ship.

Everyone fell silent. Dufleur realized what she'd said, wished she could take her words back. People were turning to stare at her now.

She inhaled, let her breath out quietly, and said, "At the moment you spoke it was only nineteen septhours sixty-six minutes of the day. Not twenty septhours two minutes, as you called the time. Your figuring is five minutes fast."

A whispering as if a sussuration of many voices lasted a few heartbeats, then quieted. Someone said, "I have twenty septhours ten minutes, eight ten at night."

"It's nineteen septhours sixty-eight minutes," Dufleur said.

Captain Ruis Elder checked his antique watch. "I have the same time as the Ship, but that is not surprising."

Captain of the Councils, GreatLord T'Hawthorn looked at his wrist timer and said, "I have the same time as stated by GrandMistrys Thyme, who," he added drily, "I see is *not* consulting a timer or calendarsphere."

Others called out their time.

"It is the third month of the Celtan year, Alder, the fifteenth day, the twentieth septhour, four minutes and fifty-three seconds," the Ship said.

"No," Dufleur said. She closed her eyes, felt the gentle wind of time. "You are five minutes and fifty seconds fast." She opened her lashes.

Everyone had crowded around her, looking at timers, checking their calendarspheres.

Dufleur met T'Hawthorn's lavender gaze. "Captain of the Councils', T'Hawthorn's, time is correct, because it is synchronized with the Guildhall timer, which a Thyme calibrates every year at zero hours Birch, the first day of the new year. Or as necessary." Her gaze slid to Ruis Elder, who had spent some time in the Guildhall and whose Nullness had completely stopped the Guildhall timer. He grinned back at her.

"Ship, I challenge you to calculate the rotation and revolution of the planet Celta and apply the mathematics to our human time and date constructs."

"Whatever the time," young D'Yew said with the trace of a smile and a slight lightening of the shadows in her eyes, "it wasn't anywhere near the time on my calendarsphere, which was quite slow." She gazed pointedly at the old object that YewHei had not given back.

There was silence for a full minute.

"Calculated that way, it is the time you have named," Ship admitted reluctantly. "But with some additional Earth equations—"

"They don't apply here," Dufleur said.

"I don't like this," the peevish voice of an old man said, and he shook his timer in one hand and his calendarsphere in the other, as if that would correctly set the time.

"I am the Ship!" the Ship boomed. "My time should be the standard."

Dufleur kept her mouth shut.

"No," said T'Hawthorn, gazing at Dufleur. She thought this was the first time he'd ever noticed her and didn't particularly like it. Didn't like this whole business. He scanned the area and a half-smile curved his lips. "I see we have a quorum of the FirstFamily Lords and Ladies. I move that GrandMistry D'Thyme, here, continue to calibrate the Guildhall clock with the correct time, as determined by her Flair. Which she obviously has been doing. That time will be the standard. Ship can set its time by the clock. If there is ever a discrepancy, the current Thyme will be the authority." He gave her a hard, sardonic look. "I suggest you apply for your proper title."

"That doesn't help me," said the old man. "Neither of these are correct, nor is my official Residence timer!"

"I'm sure GrandMistrys Thyme can regulate all timers and calendarspheres to conform with the Guildhall timer," Saille said smoothly from beside her. "For a fee." He was smiling.

She glanced around the room. Most people appeared fascinated. T'Yew and his coterie left, and as she watched them, she noticed Agave in the shadows, hatred on his face. Directed toward her.

But Saille was drawing her to a desk and chair that was being set up at one side of the room for her use by a grinning Ruis Elder.

She knew through their bond that Saille was sure this would

keep her busy enough that she'd stop her experimentation. He was probably right, and her spirits sank. She'd get more gilt but less free time to research. And she'd brought it on herself.

*D*ufleur *arrived at* D'Winterberry *Residence from* Nuada's Sword exhausted and with a massive headache. People had come to her to have her align their timepieces. They'd paid a very nice fee set by T'Hawthorn directly to her bank account.

She'd only recalibrated those small items they had with them. Contacting Residences through the Ship was a cumbersome process, and it would be better if she went on site for those. As for general whole-house timers, she thought she'd write up instructions and sell them for a small fee for people to be able to set their timers correctly or link to the Guildhall timer.

But she had a sinking feeling that it had just become very fashionable to have Dufleur Thyme herself attend a Family and reset their household timer. This was the additional project she'd been wanting, but though it would plump up her income, she didn't know as it would do much in rescinding the law about experimenting with time or clearing the Family reputation.

So she had just enough Flair to teleport to D'Winterberry's. Fairyfoot had left earlier, which was a blessing, because Dufleur didn't think she'd have had the extra smidgeon of Flair it would have taken to teleport her, too. Her knees weakened, and she stumbled to lean against a wall and barely staggered downstairs to her rooms, shoved a snoring Fairyfoot from the middle of bed, and fell into sleep.

The next morning, she'd decided to prioritize her time so she could do her serious work in the mornings. She'd make her timer alignment very exclusive and do only one house/Residence per day and a couple of sets of personal timers and calendarspheres. Or a full set of timers and calendarspheres from a household over several days. Her first appointment was with T'Hawthorn, the Captain of the Councils.

When she teleported to her laboratory, she let out a huge breath. This place was hers, no goals or expectations to meet but her own. She'd spent some gilt and Flair in purchasing some Celtan plants that thrived on the Time Wind and lined two walls with them, staggering the heights, setting them behind invisible shields that kept the lab safe and clean. These living beings, too, would not suffer if there was an explosion.

Fairyfoot studied them critically. *Not as nice as Willow conservatory.*

"Of course not. This is a lab. My father would have been horrified with them."

They fine. Fairyfoot sneezed.

Dufleur studied her. She drooped.

"You have a cold. You've been doing too much. You shouldn't be here. You should be back in bed." No wonder she'd gone back to Winterberry's early the night before.

Fairyfoot sat up straight, blinked eyes that appeared a little runny. *I am good. I can be Time Cat. Told the other Fams at the Ship yesterday that I would be Time Cat soon.*

Closing her eyes, Dufleur prayed for patience, opened her lids again. "Fairyfoot, these experiments are supposed to be secret."

They know now about the timer stuff, Fairyfoot pointed out.

"Did you say anything about the experiments?"

No. She looked away, then glanced back. *Only to Samba and the dog. And they are Elders and our allies. Nothing to the others, and nothing to Black Pierre, T'Hawthorn's Fam.* She grumbled under her breath. *He had cold.* Her sniff was loud and wet.

"I think you should teleport home. If you don't have the strength, I can—"

But Fairyfoot leapt for her perch—and missed. Dufleur grabbed for her, snagged her, got scratched for her efforts. They fell. The table's edge and the carton of expensive, fragile image memoryspheres rushed toward them.

Instinctively, Dufleur acted. She stopped time, slowed their fall, moved through the heavy press of time to set her feet under her.

It wasn't enough. The memorysphere she'd been using for her notes rolled off the table, hit the floor, and cracked. *Fligger!*

She started time again, but the damage had been done. She couldn't afford to lose that memorysphere. "Quiet!" she snarled at a hissing Fairyfoot, moved with the cat to the far corner of the table. Staying in the gray place, she walked several steps back into the past, just long enough to catch the memorysphere and tuck it in her lab coat pocket, then *jumped* forward in time a full five minutes and hoped for the best.

Stepping out of the Time Wind, she and Fairyfoot were still alone in the laboratory.

Interesting, Fairyfoot said.

"Yes. I shouldn't have done that, but it harmed no one." Except her energy level was now too low to work. She had just enough Flair to teleport herself back to Winterberry's.

Fairyfoot licked her chin, purring. Dufleur grimaced and put her down. She strutted back over to her perch and hopped gracefully up. *I have traveled through time. I am the Time Cat.*

"Yes," Dufleur muttered. She hurried over to the worktable. "Let me check this memorysphere, see if *its* travels through time distorted anything."

You should not have bought balls so easy to hurt.

"I wanted the best, and the new ones hold more information."

But they are easier to break.

"Yes, yes. Quiet a minute here." She thumbed the memorysphere on, watched her last experiment.

Fairyfoot gave a little sniff.

"Looks good."

Fairyfoot sniffed again.

Dufleur's head jerked up as she registered the sound. She carefully opened a drawer and put the memorysphere in a small nest. Then she scrutinized Fairyfoot.

The cat's eyes were bright. Her nose didn't look runny. "How do you feel?" Dufleur's voice quivered with suppressed excitement.

Fairyfoot set her claws in the blue velvet and stretched luxuriously. *I feel GOOD!*

Could it be?

"Cough for me."

Fairyfoot rolled big eyes, emitted a tiny cough.

Striding over to the scrybowl, Dufleur activated it with an impatient whisk around the rim. "D'Ash's Office."

"Here," D'Ash answered a minute later.

"Fairyfoot needs a quick consultation."

"Is something wrong?" D'Ash asked.

"I think she had a cold."

D'Ash frowned. "I'm sorry, Dufleur, but I don't have time to
see Fairyfoot for a cold. There's nothing we can do, anyway."

"Can't you do a very quick scan of her with your Flair, it's
important," Dufleur pressed. "A minute, two at the most."

"Very well."

"She's 'porting to you."

Blinking, D'Ash said, "You aren't bringing her?"

"Frankly, I can 'port there, but don't have the energy to get
to Winterberry's." Though her pulse was beating fast and adren-
alin was kicking in.

With a sigh, D'Ash said, "I'll send you home in a glider."
She raised a finger. "*After* you reset my personal calendarsphere and timer and all my office timers."

"Done! We'll be there transnow." Dufleur looked down at
Fairyfoot. "I don't think you have a cold anymore."

Fairyfoot lifted a smug nose. *I don't. I have succeeded at the
experiment. Me, me, ME!*

"This is secret, Fairyfoot! Please 'port with me on three to
D'Ash's office suite teleportation pad." Dufleur knit her brows,
trying to recall the space.

A very clear and detailed image came from Fairyfoot.

"Good," Dufleur said.

A half-septhour later, Dufleur crawled into the Ash glider.
She'd managed to align all the timers and calendarspheres that
D'Ash had placed before her after a two minute examination of
Fairyfoot that pronounced her cold-free.

Fairyfoot hopped into the glider, purring loudly.

I have done it.

"We," Dufleur said.

We have solved the problem.

"Yes."

She'd killed the cold virus with the manipulation of time—
progressing back and forth. But not through a device. By using
her personal Flair. It seemed her father's way was not entirely
her path.

If she could do it with one disease, she could probably do it
with all. That wasn't what she'd intended, but if it was a big
enough victory, it might get the ban on experimenting with time
lifted, and that's what she wanted most. She could continue her
previous work on actually reversing the growth of the virus

later. And figure out how to make a time tube that everyone could use. The work of a lifetime.

Two. Her father's and her own.

It was a victory. But she knew she couldn't proclaim it to the world, couldn't even tell Saille and get a good reaction. So the triumph wasn't as wonderful as she'd always thought it would be. Not sharing the joy with Saille made it less.

He'd grown important to her.

Too important. She couldn't visualize a future without him in it.

And he disapproved of her Flair.

S*aille waited a good three days, during which time he and* the household renewed the search for his MotherDam's personal memorysphere journals, before T'Yew contacted him.

The man's cold, set expression told Saille everything. "I have scried to give you one last chance to fulfill your obligations to the Yew Family." He didn't use Saille's title, which fired a spurt of anger. Saille hadn't wanted to confront another First-Family Lord in the first months of his career, before he had solidified his own base, but there was nothing to be done. With a slow inhalation, he kept his face as impassive. "GrandLord T'Yew." Saille inclined his head slightly. "I have double-checked the Willow business records. They show no transaction between yourself and the former D'Willow."

"The current D'Willow."

Ignoring that, Saille said, "I have only a brief notation that you both went from a casual alliance to swearing formal alliance two years ago." Two years and four months ago. Saille didn't miss the shifting of Yew's eyes, the sudden flash of wariness. The man's reaction only confirmed Saille's impression that the exchange of initial favors had been on the shady side of legal. Surely his MotherDam had left *some* record of the alliance. He'd wager that she would have transcribed any ill she knew of him, too.

A muscle in Yew's jaw jumped. "Then you are worthless to me. I hereby cancel my alliance with the GreatHouse Willow. I will inform the FirstFamilies Council clerk that there is an outstanding debt of six hundred thousand gilt to Yew from Willow."

Cold chilled Saille's gut, but he smiled pleasantly. "Please do that, I will file a formal request for all reckoning from you to verify the debt."

Fury contorted Yew's aristocratic features. "You do that," he rasped, but Saille sensed the man couldn't provide what would be necessary. That was the problem when two immoral people made a deal. "I will ruin you," T'Yew said.

Saille didn't know if he could, but wouldn't put it past Yew to use underhanded methods. The problem with dealing with an immoral person. "If you wish to claim insult, I am happy to meet you on the dueling field, or we can formalize a feud."

Yew jerked in shock, masked it. "Worthless." Strong fingers snapped, and he cut the scry connection.

After blowing out a breath, Saille said, "Residence, inform the clerks of the FirstFamilies Council, the Noble Council, and the AllClass Council that the formal alliance between the Great-House Willow and GrandHouse Yew has been severed at the request of T'Yew. That Yew states there is an unpaid debt from Willow to Yew but has provided no proof, and the Willow Family records state nothing." He was sure there must be something, but what? And what harm would it cause the Family that was now his responsibility?

"Done," said the Residence. It hesitated. "The FirstFamilies clerk states that Yew is now transmitting the same information."

"Let me know if the debt is stated." Saille's mind raced. He'd bluffed, and he'd pushed. He'd do more. "Tell the First-Families clerk that I will open the Family business records for review if a debt is claimed in the interest of fairness." That would definitely ruin the Family, a gamble.

"A debt is noted by Yew. One million gilt," the Residence said hollowly. "The review of the records is accepted by Yew, and the FirstFamilies' clerk will schedule an auditor. Probably GreatLord Reed."

"Then also request in the interest of fairness that T'Yew open his Family business records to T'Reed."

A minute's silence while the Residence, the clerk, and T'Yew consulted outside of Saille's hearing.

"T'Yew refuses."

"Request that T'Yew's refusal be noted and passed on to all the Councils and a request for a legal determination as to whether his records should be reviewed."

Saille waited tensely, watching an antique timer tick away the seconds.

"T'Yew withdraws the request that the Willow records be reviewed." Thirty more seconds. "T'Yew withdraws his claim." Ten seconds. "The FirstFamilies Council clerk cancels the review of the Willow records."

Saille sank to the chair behind his desk, his muscles trembling in reaction. There should be some way to ensure the safety of his Family until he discovered what his MotherDam might know of Yew. He rubbed his temples, unsurprised when he found his scalp damp with sweat. Slowly he said, "Inform the FirstFamilies Council, the Noble Council, and the AllClass Council clerks that there is conflict between the former allies Willow and Yew and that Willow stands ready to defend his House and position with his body in duel or feud." He leaned back in the comfortchair, let the spells on his shirt and the chair take care of the sweat on his back.

"That is done," the Residence said, tone richly satisfied.

Saille wasn't pleased. He was young and had some arms training, Yew was old. Both of them had older, female Heirs who probably would not fight. Though from what he'd seen of YewHeir, she was a prideful woman who might very well carry on a feud, or hire mercenaries.

If Saille had had any allies formally sworn to *him*, they would have backed him, fought with him, feuded for him. Probably best that he brought no one else into this matter, but he felt as if he were a lone man fending off a snapping, rabid wolf.

For anyone else but an arrogant FirstFamily Lord, the precautions he'd taken would stop any further action. It wouldn't stop T'Yew.

Saille had made an enemy. He just didn't know how bad.

Twenty-eight

❦

Over the next eightday, Dufleur worked in her laboratory at least two septhours a day as soon as she arose.

Now that she was doing verification experiments, her work went faster. She'd repeated the experiment with five rats, then seven, found that a future-then-past jump was the quickest and most effective way to kill disease, using the least Flair and disrupting the Time Wind the least. She could pinpoint the bacteria or the virus, infuse their cells with the Time Wind, move them through time, and eradicate them.

The effects of the disease—various diseases infecting the rats—remained, but some of those could be Healed, as demonstrated by a reluctant Danith D'Ash.

Dufleur was sure the same procedure would work on humans.

The social season picked up pace, with more than one event in the evening and night. Passiflora's gentle politicking had also increased as the date for the vote, the next full twinmoons, the first day of Saille's month, Willow, approached. So his household was preparing for the full twinmoons ritual and the holiday of Imbolic, which fell during his month. This would be his first month as the spiritual leader of the FirstFamilies.

She saw Saille at social functions and spent sensual nights with him in her bed or his. Something was bothering him, but a coolness had come between them, and since she valued her own privacy, she didn't ask. Though she found it a thorn in her heart that he didn't reveal his concerns and let her comfort him. Nor did he ask about her work other than the timer alignment or her embroidery.

She didn't tell him how an inimical Agave watched her, either.

Saille had, one wintry afternoon, requested she take a formal Sabbat meal with his Family. It had caused her much dampness of palms until Arbusca had welcomed her with warm smiles and offered her timer for Dufleur to set. After that, it was easier, and oddly soothing to be in the midst of so many interesting and cheerful women, fulfilling a need in Dufleur that she hadn't realized she had. All of them must have known she was Saille's HeartMate, but only the keen excitement in their gazes pressured her. By the time she left, after catching several significant looks among them, she had the nervous feeling that they were going to plan an Imbolic wedding, too.

The thought both tempted and scared her. With the success of the last experiment behind her, one she'd meticulously recorded with an expensive memorysphere, it was time to make a decision on how to proceed.

She wanted to talk with Saille about it. She wanted more than just sex and affection and passion.

"Dufleur, dear," Passiflora D'Holly said, in a tone that told Dufleur the GreatLady had tried to get her attention more than once.

"Yes?" She looked at D'Holly, who had stress deepening the lines around her eyes. "I'm sorry, I was daydreaming."

Passiflora's mouth quirked. "It's nice to know you *can* daydream."

Heat rose to Dufleur's cheeks.

"I was saying," Passiflora continued, "that I believe the Birches' ball tonight will be the crucial event."

Dufleur's mind went blank.

Continuing, Passiflora explained, "My Family will be at the ball, even Genista. She's becoming slightly more social. T'Hawthorn will be at the Birches, too." She shifted. "I think the matter of the Captain of the Council will be settled."

Staring, Dufleur said, "In the Birches' ballroom?"

A long ripple of laughter came from Passiflora. "Yes, indeed. All the FirstFamilies will be there, so we can see the shifts in the groupings—a straw poll, as it were."

"Oh." Dufleur drew her cloak closer. "I'm glad it's you who needs to do all this."

"Yes, I know," Passiflora mocked gently. "You hate the social scene."

"T'Ash will be there, too?" Dufleur had come to think of

him as an indication of those events that were absolutely necessary. He wouldn't attend otherwise.

"Everyone." Passiflora smiled. "T'Ash is formally allied with us for three generations. My dear Holm called to remind him and D'Ash of the gathering."

"Ah."

"Anyway, you will be more on your own tonight. I just wanted to let you know."

"I've been doing all right," Dufleur said stiffly.

Passiflora squeezed Dufleur's hand. "Yes, you have."

Then the glider pulled to a stop and the footman lifted the door. Passiflora slid out, and Dufleur followed, smiling at the Holly who held the door.

He winked at her.

So Dufleur entered the ballroom with a dignified step.

As usual, she danced with all the younger men and Saille. His body was more tense than usual, and she saw him watching T'Yew and the more conservative set.

The energetic country dance ended, and she began, "Saille—"

He flashed her a practiced smile. "We're parched. I'll get us something to drink."

Well, that was true. He read her well physically, and emotionally, and she was learning to do the same, she just wasn't sure how to interpret her knowledge or act upon it.

A feeling still lurked inside her that she was going to wreck this somehow.

While Saille crossed to the snack table, she observed the flow of people around her.

Passiflora was taking a break from her gentle persuasion to lead the small orchestra in another dance.

Near Dufleur's corner, T'Holly and T'Hawthorn drifted together.

Everyone seemed fascinated to see the old archenemies in conversation. Power and great Flair radiated from them.

T'Hawthorn swirled brandy in his glass and glanced at T'Holly with a mild expression. "Well, Holm, do you intend to put your token forward to become Captain of the Councils?"

With equal mildness, T'Holly said, "Yes."

A rare smile graced T'Hawthorn's lips. "Then I will leave

it to you." He shook his head slightly. "The Captaincy was a heavier burden than I'd anticipated, especially with those murders a couple of months ago." He frowned, and lines dug into his face. "Filthy business."

"You handled it well, Huathe."

T'Hawthorn shrugged. "I much prefer my business, cinnamon trading. At least people do as I say when I request it."

The man was formidable, Dufleur couldn't imagine anyone with two brain cells to rub together going against him.

"You'll have an easier time of it, Holm. More diplomatic." A rare smile softened T'Hawthorn's face. "My Son'sSon has passed his apprenticeship and will be studying as a journeyman with me."

T'Holly smiled, too, genuinely. "A blessing for you."

"Indeed."

The two men separated, because grief shadowed their Flair. T'Hawthorn had lost his son in the feud he'd started with T'Holly, killed by one of T'Holly's son's, a bitter blow. T'Holly had lost his first Son'sChild in the womb because of his pride . . . all stemming from the Hawthorn-Holly antagonism.

Now the men were on an even footing and linked by a Heart-Mate marriage of their children, but Dufleur sensed they would never be more than distant acquaintances. Too much past and grief and Flair for each.

Passiflora had been right. This was a decisive moment. T'Hawthorn would not oppose T'Holly's bid to become Captain of the Councils. Probably none of T'Hawthorn's allies would do so, either. Dufleur hadn't heard of any other First-Family Lord or Lady who wanted the job.

When the FirstFamilies Council voted, T'Holly would be Captain of all the Celtan Councils, the most powerful man on Celta.

Dufleur's purpose in providing a front for Passiflora was no longer necessary, but the pretense would have to remain. She would be expected to finish the social season.

"GrandMistrys Thyme?"

Blinking, Dufleur smiled in the direction of the thin man who'd addressed her. It took her only three seconds to identify him as one of the Examiners in the Winterberry case. She was getting better at this social business.

"May I have this dance?"

She sent a discreet glance in Saille's direction. He was watching T'Yew, T'WhitePoplar, and the Birches who were scowling at T'Holly. Those were the ones who'd vote against T'Holly.

But she didn't want to think of politics, so she offered her hand to the man. "Thank you." They made up the last couple of a set, and a fast tune and the need to watch her steps whirled her mind away.

When the dance ended, her partner bowed, glanced at his timer. "I need to move on to my brother's soiree." He pulled a face. "Vocal music, not dancing. I like to dance, and may I say that you are a wonderful partner."

"Thank you. I like to dance, too." That was the truth, she realized. A gift this forced social season had brought her, the knowledge that she loved dancing, would always love it, especially with Saille.

Stepping closer and keeping his voice low, the Examiner said, "We have made a decision in the Winterberry case and will announce it tomorrow. I'm sorry." With a brief nod of his head, he disappeared into the crowd.

Dufleur's shoulders tightened. She didn't know the full details, of course, but just that sentence from the Examiner was enough to understand her mother would not be pleased. Ructions ahead.

At that moment, thirteen-year-old Antenn Blackthorn bowed in front of her, wiggling his brows. "Help, that Arcta Uva Ursi is after me." He took Dufleur's hand with little short of a snatch, and placed it on his arm.

Sure enough, a girl not quite grown into her height was watching them with narrowed eyes.

"Antenn—"

"I've already danced with her, I swear. But this one is a waltz, and that means we're together the whole time, and she talks too much."

One more check of Saille. He lingered in the shadows close to T'Yew, ear cocked. Yew, his heir, and the Birches seemed to be having a quiet disagreement.

Dufleur looked down at Antenn and smiled. She definitely liked this option better. Antenn led her out on the floor and waltzed a little faster than the correct beat, turning often. Dufleur was proud that she kept up with him and neither of them trod on each other's feet.

They ended a little out of breath near the door. A table with full water goblets was within easy reach. Both Antenn and Dufleur took one and gratefully sipped the icy water. Antenn bobbling the drink a little. Right on D'Birch.

"My apologies," Antenn said, bowing, and spilling more.

"You!"

"Antenn Blackthorn," he said.

"I know who you are. That common Moss boy."

"GreatLady, you're overheated." Dufleur nabbed a goblet and offered it to D'Birch, whose face and décolletage were certainly flushed, though probably from anger instead of dancing. Dufleur shifted a little in front of the young man.

"I don't want water. As for that Moss boy, he's the brother of a murderer. I won't have him in my house." D'Birch's penetrating voice carried through the ballroom.

Dufleur flinched. Slick nausea coated her stomach, her throat, as she thought of those who'd tried to kill her. As far as she knew, all the relatives of the cult murderers had left Druida in shame. Several broken Family members had visited her, begging for forgiveness for their relatives. It had been hideous.

Behind her, she felt Antenn hunched as if petrified. He wasn't associated with the cult at all. Then she recollected that Antenn's brother had killed several people in a FirstFamilies council meeting. Of course only the FirstFamilies murders years ago would concern D'Birch, not the killing of children of lesser nobility a couple of months before.

D'Birch raised a hand to summon a footman. To show Antenn out? How humiliating. Dufleur would not have been able to stand it. But here she was, in the middle of the scene. And where was Straif Blackthorn or Mitchella Blackthorn?

This time, she stepped back, forcing Antenn back, too, then placed the goblets down and moved to his side. She put her arm around the young man's shoulders. She knew Antenn to be painfully honorable.

"D'Birch, please," she said, not knowing where to go after that.

Mouth pinching, D'Birch glared at Dufleur. "GrandMistrys
Thyme."

There were two seconds of silence before D'Birch opened her
mouth again and Dufleur rushed into speech herself, hoping the
notion that came to her would work. "Thank you for inviting me,"
Dufleur said. "But I must go now. I've realized I'm behind on my
embroidery commissions and am certainly unaccustomed to the
social season. Please give my compliments to T'Birch. Oh, and
since my schedule is so full, I'm afraid I must tell you that I won't
be able to fulfill your commission." It was a tapestry featuring the
birch grove seen from the center of the great labyrinth.

Greed warred with insult on D'Birch's face. "I promised the
hanging to my husband as a Nameday gift."

Dufleur shrugged. "I'm sorry. My schedule is too full," Dufleur repeated. This was taking all her meager social skills,
fancy phrasing was impossible.

"I'll see you never sell another piece," D'Birch hissed.

"You'll have to speak to Quert Apple about that."

"I'll do that." But caution appeared in her gaze. She glanced
around at people observing the scene or studiously pretending
not to. Apparently D'Birch didn't mind circulating rumor but
didn't like to be the object herself.

"Shall we go, Antenn?" Dufleur said, dropping her arm from
his shoulders and turning toward the room that held the teleportation area. She thought he could teleport.

"Yeah," he mumbled, ducked his head at D'Birch. "Merry
meet," he started the formal greeting, caught himself and
flushed painfully.

Passiflora swept up to them with a bright smile. "I'm sorry
we must leave so soon, D'Birch." She turned to Dufleur and Antenn. "I've ordered the glider around."

Dufleur stared, hoped her mouth wasn't hanging open.

*We do have a bond, Dufleur, and you're my protégée. I
wouldn't abandon you,* Passiflora chided gently.

"You're not leaving, Passiflora?" D'Birch sputtered.

Raising her eyebrows, Passiflora said, "You don't seem to
understand that you insulted my nephew."

Dufleur blinked, looked at Antenn who lifted and dropped a
shoulder. She couldn't recall the connection, but all the First-
Families were a tangled mess of interrelatedness anyway.

"Your husband's nephew's wife's ward," D'Birch said tightly.

"My HeartMate's nephew's adopted son," Passiflora corrected. She put her hand on Antenn's shoulder.

D'Birch swallowed. "Stay." She glared at Antenn. "You, too." Then she switched her stare to Dufleur. "I'll expect that tapestry on time." She turned on her heel and walked away as cheerful, louder-than-usual dance music swelled from the musician's platform.

"I'd like another dance, Antenn," Dufleur raised her voice to be heard.

He nodded, grabbed her hand, and took her to the end of the line, which soon became the middle. She glanced at Trif Winterberry who led the musicians.

"Trif Winterberry is my cuz," Antenn said, as he made the opening bow and Dufleur curtsied. That's right. Mitchella Clover Blackthorn, Antenn's mother, was cuz to Trif Winterberry. Who was married to Dufleur's cuz Ilex. Connections and connections.

"Mine, too," Dufleur said. "On the other side. Small world."

Antenn rolled his eyes. "Oh, yeah. Especially among the FirstFamilies, and they're weird, too."

Then they separated and went down the line of dancers. When the music stopped, Antenn bowed again, grinning. "Thanks, Dufleur." He buffeted her on the shoulder.

"You're welcome."

He walked jauntily to the snack table, and Dufleur stared after him. He'd fight the stigma of his brother's crime for the rest of his life. As she would never be able to shake the gossip that her father had blown up T'Thyme Residence. Not much they could do about their circumstances except hold their heads high.

"Very well done," Passiflora murmured, handing Dufleur a glass of cold water.

"Thank you," Dufleur said. She met Passiflora's eyes. "I would have left."

"I know."

"It wouldn't have been running away."

"No." Passiflora smiled, waved to a friend. "Your leaving would have been a statement, and the right thing to do."

Dufleur tilted her head. "You would have left, too."

"Yes." Passiflora let out a little sigh. "D'Birch lives for gossip. She's a bored, dissatisfied woman who likes to stir up trouble. I doubt Holm will get the Birch vote for Captain." She shrugged.

"How's that going?" Dufleur asked, suddenly curious.

Passiflora chuckled, patted Dufleur's arm. "Very well. I've watched everyone tonight. I think we'll only have two or three against, an excellent majority. Ah, here's Saille."

Saille bowed to them. He held no drinks and looked chagrined. "I'm sorry I was derelict in my duty."

Dufleur was, too. He would have stood by her. But she hadn't needed him to rescue her or Antenn, and that sent a spurt of satisfaction through her. "You're going to vote for T'Holly to be Captain, aren't you?"

Passiflora's eyes widened at the blunt question.

Putting his hand over his heart, Saille sent Dufleur an amused look then said, "Passiflora has only to smile at me, and I would do whatever she said."

With a shake of her head, Passiflora said, "Flatterer."

"That wasn't an answer," Dufleur pointed out.

"Yes," Saille said. "I will be voting for Holm Holly Sr."

"Good." Dufleur nodded.

"Speaking of smiles," Passiflora said, "you each have the most charming I've ever seen, male and female."

They stared at her as she glided away. Then they stared at each other.

Smiled.

Dufleur sighed. "She's right, your smile has impact."

He took her hand and bowed over it. "And your smile is just one of the reasons why I am so very attracted to you." His voice was low.

Dufleur let him pull her close for the lilting waltz. She let a contented breath escape, then said, "I wanted to ask *you* to dance tonight." Murmuring into her ear, she said, "Seduce you tonight."

"You have. You do."

"Later," she whispered. "Let's make love in your conservatory."

Their bodies moved to the music, their gazes locked, and the distance that had come between them, that would undoubtedly return, was banished for the moment. As it was every night.

Even as prickles of desire slipped through her blood, Dufleur felt the fine tension of passion imbue his muscles.

"Let's leave early," he said, breathing a little roughly.

"Yes."

Twenty-nine

❦

"Dufleur," Saille whispered in her ear.

"I agreed."

"I need you." His yearning, through words and their connection, went straight to her core. And with a wide, sweeping turn, he danced them out of the door, across the hall to the teleportation area. The small room was empty.

She was still moving in his arms when he teleported them to the conservatory. Dufleur stumbled, was hauled close. They stopped.

"A little awkward," Saille said. "I need to make room."

"Awkward to dance," Dufleur said, sliding a hand down his shirt and opening the buttons with a spellword, "not to love."

His shirt hung open, and she ran her hands up and down his lightly haired chest, feeling the flex and play of his muscles under smooth skin, the breadth of his shoulders, how his torso narrowed to his waist.

With every touch of him, she aroused herself. She aroused them both.

He caught her hands in his and kissed her fingers, a gesture he hadn't done for five days, something she'd missed. But his mind and body was focused on her. He led her to an area of thick, soft moss, pulled her into his arms, then down. She had a brief worry about her gown, and then it was gone, and his hands covered her breasts, thumbs circling her nipples.

"Saille." She could barely breathe it, moved to touch his lips with hers, seduce him into opening his mouth, probing with her tongue, sucking on it, receiving the pleasurable jolt of the taste of him that she seemed addicted to and needed every night.

The air around them was heavy and scented with growing plants and flowers. Sleet snow spit against the windows. The contrast was wonderful, as wonderful as his murmurs of soft loving words and the power of his body, his strong, hard erection.

She curled her fingers around him, and he shuddered,

moaned. With a little push, she had him on his back, slithered over him, let his arousal prod at the needy entrance to her body.

Wait, she said. *Savor. Us together.* And he quivered under her, his hands went to her bottom.

She'd never had a lover like him, ready to explore with her, to please her as much as she needed to please him. Yearned to come together mind and body and soul.

All her barriers against him, all her self-doubt, were slowly eroding.

When she couldn't take the anticipation any longer, she raised herself and slid down on him and whimpered in pleasure at the feel of him filling her. Slowly she moved upon him, over him, enjoying the thrust of his hips upward, his fingers rolling her nipples, tugging gently with their movement together.

Then the blindness of ecstasy hit her, and he groaned, and they merged together.

When her mind cleared, she was held close, and her body was sated, but her heart ached. Neither of them had offered the HeartBond to the other. Perhaps they'd been caught up in the physical moment.

Perhaps.

She thrashed out of the nightmare to find Saille's arms around her, soothing coming from his bond, holding her close and warm, lovingly. Yet alarm remained, tweaking every nerve. Finally her brain cleared enough for her to understand. She pulled away from Saille, jumped to her feet, gathered her clothes, and dressed quickly, using Flair shortcuts. "Something's wrong. I feel the breaching of a spellshield." Not the old T'Thyme Residence tonight. The new laboratory. Agave.

Saille was with her, dressed, too. "Agave."

"Yes. I've been working on something—"

"Not now." Saille's warm hand closed over hers. "We 'port on three. One. Two. Three."

They were there, in the lab. Agave whirled, his shadow large and hulking in the flickering travel light that was clipped to his body. "Not again," he growled.

And finally realization burst upon her. She froze. "You. You were in my father's lab that night. Searching for his notes."

"Taking his notes. He discovered me. We fought. Lately

I knew you'd found something." Agave's sneer changed to a snarl as Saille's body hit him, and they fell.

"To me!" Spreading her fingers, Dufleur called her bespelled memoryspheres. They flew to her, and she managed to catch one, then another and another without harming them. She sent them to Winterberry Residence.

The men were rolling on the ground, and she scolded herself for thinking of her work first. She ran toward them, saw Agave fling Saille off him.

"He who rules time, rules all," Agave said.

Dufleur stared at him, realizing he was just beginning to move through time.

Agave reached for a silver box. A bomb.

No! she shrieked. *Saille, link with me.*

Always linked with you.

'Port him to his lab. Frantically, she shoved the image into his mind. They grabbed a struggling, writhing, mad Agave and flung him away. His thumb pressed.

They still "heard" the concussion of the explosion.

Dufleur flung herself into Saille's arms. "You're all right? He didn't hurt you?"

Saille held her close, wiped away blood from his cheek with his shoulder, replied in panting breaths. "Not much, though he had a madman's strength."

"Yes, a madman. Well, my notes are safe."

"And so are you, which is more important." Saille kissed her hard.

"We must go to his lab."

"I suppose so."

She stepped back, and Saille's arms dropped. "The first thing everyone will say is that he was experimenting with time and blew up his lab," she said bitterly. "And it was him all along. At my father's lab and here—" she waved to another explosive device, a small silver box, unarmed. "And at his house." Walking toward a corner, she took the image sphere that had recorded everything from the wall.

"You anticipated this?" Saille's voice was hard. "And you didn't tell me?"

"I knew he was trying to break in and that he might succeed. You've been keeping your own secrets, Saille."

And the small distance between them widened.

He ran fingers through his hair. "We have to tell the FirstFamilies."

Of course he'd think of them first. "Yes, and the guards. My cuz the guardsman, Ilex Winterberry, is still assigned to the FirstFamilies. To you," she said with a brittle smile.

Saille summoned his heavy winter coat from his home. "Tell him we'll meet him at Agave's."

The rest of the night was long. Dufleur had to explain again and again—to Ilex and his superior, Chief Sawyr. To GreatLord T'Hawthorn and T'Holly as representatives of the FirstFamilies. How she'd later recalled seeing odd shadows in her father's lab the night of his death. How Agave had smeared her father's reputation, kept the gossip alive.

She brought her mother's old friend into the story, and D'Birch. Probably lose the commission after that. Too bad.

How Agave had watched her, tried to intimidate her. She handed over the image sphere, let them see for themselves the fight in her lab.

Finally, even SupremeJudge Ailim Elder was called, and to Dufleur's surprise, stated Dufleur should be dismissed. So she was sent to Winterberry Residence in a guard glider.

She stood in the waterfall a long time, washing off the events of the night, the feeling of violation by Agave, which only triggered the memories of the horrible time with the dark cult. She stayed in there until Fairyfoot's demanding mews drew her forth, and she had to tell the story once again to her Fam. Fairyfoot, at least, was firmly on her side.

Then she dried herself with the last of her Flair and crawled into bed, once again trying not to see Saille's face as he accused her of keeping secrets and she'd flung the same back at him.

Trying not to notice that their link seethed with irritation and anger on both sides, and had narrowed to a thread.

*W*ailing woke Dufleur the next morning. She blinked blurry eyes to see Fairyfoot yawning in her face. "Urgh."

Your mother unhappy, Fairyfoot grumbled, planting her front paws on the bed and stretching luxuriously. *Dance and hunt with fox all night and help you after Agave, and D'Thyme wakes Me with crying.*

"We didn't tell her of Agave," and she wouldn't care, much,

since even the truth of his part in Dufleur's father's death wouldn't stop the deeply held beliefs that T'Thyme blew himself up.

Dufleur glanced at the windows. They let in bright sunlight, beyond she sensed a clear, cold day. It was late morning.

Sobbing filtered to her mind. The wailing wasn't physical, but mental. Her mother. Shock and fear. Suddenly she remembered, the Examiner's decision must have been delivered.

She grabbed a looserobe, dragged it on over her nightshirt, and hurried up two flights of stairs to the MistrysSuite. Not bothering to knock, Dufleur flung open the door.

D'Winterberry sat as usual in her chair. She didn't move, and Dufleur couldn't tell whether the woman was awake or not. She appeared mummified.

Dringal had collapsed into a chair, hands over her face. At her feet were several papyrus, one with an official-looking seal. Dufleur cleared her throat of morning stickiness and said as gently as she could, "Is that the Examiner's report about Meyar's suit?"

"That good-for-nothing man. Abandons his mother years ago, and what does he get for it, the whole estate."

Since she didn't think her mother wanted any physical comfort—they'd never been a demonstrative family—Dufleur picked up the papers and scanned them. "Meyar has a trial period of six months to prove he will be a better head of household." She swallowed. "Ilex is named as WinterberryHeir. D'Winterberry receives the title of Ex-D'Winterberry and must be cared for by the Family."

Lifting a blotched face, Dringal pounded a fist over her heart and said, "They gave nothing to me. Nothing."

Dufleur licked her lips. "That's not quite true. One of the measurements of how Meyar will be judged is his treatment of you—a home and a stipend."

Dringal threw up her hands. "That could mean anything! He could put me in those little rooms of yours."

"I don't plan on moving out soon." The very idea gave her jitters. Where would she go?

She thrust the thought of the Willow Residence from her mind.

It had been tough, learning to live here, when she'd spent her whole life in Thyme Residence. She'd always thought she'd live there forever. Then they'd been accepted here.

Two months ago she had been saving to move out and rent rooms, then the kidnapping and attempted murders had happened, and she just hadn't had enough courage to go live in another unfamiliar place with strangers. Now there was Saille. He loved his Family. He was a FirstFamilies GreatLord.

If they ended up together, he'd expect her to live with his Family on T'Willow estate in Noble Country. Many more new strangers to cater to, please, judge her.

Dringal said, "This is all your father's fault."

"Maybe so, but assigning blame doesn't help. And have you seen the newssheets this morning?" Surely they would contain information of the night's events.

Staring at her, Dringal said, "What?"

Dufleur knelt by her chair, took her mother's hands. "Agave died last night."

Her mother stiffened. "Blew himself up like your father, did he?"

Even her mother doubted. "No. In fact, it was he who killed Father, bombed his lab. For father's notes."

"What? What? What?"

Dufleur told her.

Halfway through the recounting, Dringal wrapped her arms around herself and rocked, tears running fast down her cheeks. "He didn't do it. My Vulg wasn't so careless as to kill us."

"No." Dufleur was shaken by her mother's emotions. She must have loved her father a little, at least. Thank the Lady and Lord.

Dringal fumbled for a softleaf, and Dufleur handed her some. Her mother blew her nose.

"I think I'd like to lie down for a while."

"Yes." Dufleur helped her to her rooms.

Sniffing, Dringal said, "They probably won't put us out today."

"I'm sure not."

"You're certain about this Agave situation?"

"Yes."

There was a moment's silence. "Vulg has been vindicated in his time experiments, which is what you wanted." Dringal was back to her bitter self. "That doesn't alter the fact that Vulg put all our gilt into his work. We can't purchase a house of our own. He'd have protected himself and his laboratory. But he impoverished us."

"Mother, I promise you that I will always take care of you, that you will live in as much luxury as I can provide. But I'm weary of hearing you harp on my father and his faults. I loved him. I don't want to hear you talk about him so."

"Conditions to your love, Dufleur?" Dringal said, looking at her from a stack of pillows, mouth turned down. But Dringal had always been the one who'd put conditions on love.

"No, Mother, but conditions for my company." Dufleur inhaled a breath she thought she could feel fill her to her toes. This event had been a long time coming, but finally the right moment was here. "I'll make sure that you are well cared for, but I won't live with you anymore."

"You're as dry as that damned Examiner's Decision." Dringal gestured to the papyrus Dufleur had nearly forgotten she held.

"I'm sor—" Dufleur halted. She wasn't going to apologize to her mother anymore for her words or actions or feelings, either. Now and then something might habitually slip out of her mouth, but she was tired of her mother putting her in the wrong, too. "Do you want to hire an advocate to appeal this decision?"

Dringal shrugged, said petulantly, "That wouldn't do any good."

Undoubtedly true.

"Then we must abide by it," Dufleur said. "Do you want to remain here?"

"In a Residence that welcomes my enemies? That will never be mine?" Dringal snorted. "No."

"Then wash your face and bundle up into some warm outer gear. We can visit the house on the estate that I accepted as retribution. It's three stories." Tall and narrow. "And it sits on its own on a good piece of land."

"What of that laboratory of yours?"

"It was a workshop and is on a corner of the estate. Not close to the house. Meyar is supposed to see to your abode. I have an idea to make him pay." That phrasing would please her mother.

Sniffing, Dringal said, "Very well." Then she threw a wary glance at the windows of her room. The heavy drapes were only open enough to gauge the weather and let in a little light. With a small shock, Dufleur realized she didn't know when her mother had last left the house. Surely it couldn't have been Yule, could it have? Dringal'd never liked the cold. Dufleur said lightly, "It's a beautiful, clear day outside."

"But cold."

"Yes, but it's a blue and blue day." The sun burned like a blue star in a deep blue sky. "Meyar and Ilex can meet us at the house and go through it with us. I haven't toured it. At *our* convenience. Now. If the house Flair and spells are low, they can power them."

A gleam came to her mother's eyes. "It's nearly MiddayBell. Ilex will probably be working at the guardhouse, Meyar strutting around preparing to move in here. Yes. They can meet us at our new house."

The snow around the house was drifted deep, but showed new tracks of fox and cat—Ilex's Fam and Fairyfoot playing. Dufleur anticipated complaints about cold paws and snowy ice between her pads when they returned to D'Winterberry—no *T*'Winterberry Residence. The little loneliness at the lack of a home expanded. She didn't know how she was going to take care of herself, of her mother, reestablish D'Thyme Residence, and have enough gilt to experiment. And she'd better make embroidery and her commissions a priority. Soon.

Dringal and Dufleur stood on the wide, covered wooden porch of the veranda. Dufleur had spent some of her nervous energy on Flair to sweep away the snow and provide a small weathershield.

Meyar and Ilex teleported to just below the front steps. Ilex waved, but their voices were muffled because of the shield. Both stood, hands on hips, and surveyed the outside of the house. It was more charming than Dufleur had recalled from the holosphere, of mellow redbrick, with sharply angled porch roof and roof of a pale green—Winterberry colors, which her mother preferred.

But Dufleur dreaded going inside. She'd used the outbuilding as a lab, but she hadn't come to the house. The previous owner had been a single man, the last of his line, as occurred on Celta far too often. He'd tried to murder her. Surely the blackness of his spirit would still be a smudge in the atmosphere, no matter how many ritual cleansings had been done.

The men tramped around the place, making a nice, well-defined path from the stairs along the front walk to the gliderway. They didn't go all the way to the street, but they did make a circuit of the house, accompanied by Vertic and Fairyfoot, who made the men smile. Ilex actually scooped Fairyfoot up and onto his shoulder. Oh, yes, she'd complained about her paws.

Finally they mounted the stairs and joined Dufleur and Dringal on the front porch. Meyar closed his eyes and sighed at the warmth, and Dufleur recalled that he'd spent time in the south of the continent, where snow rarely fell. He removed his gloves and snapped them against narrow-legged, working trous, dusting off snow.

Staring at Dringal, he said, "What do you want?"

Dufleur cleared her throat, and his gaze met hers. His face softened, and he ducked his head. "Merry meet, Dufleur."

"Merry meet," she replied, though with the anticipation of going inside the house, her voice had come out on a high note.

"Merry meet, Dringal and Dufleur." Ilex made a half bow.

Her mother mumbled something. Dufleur sent a strained smile to him. "Merry meet, Ilex."

He considered her, then nodded abruptly. "I'll do a quick check inside for evil emanations."

She cleared her throat. "Thank you." She reached into her pocket and handed him a slip of papyrus with the spellshield code couplets on it. Ilex took it, used the code, and went inside. Dufleur turned to Meyar, but he was looking at the snowy grassyard. "Nice-sized place." He sent a brief, sad glance to Dufleur. "You paid too much for it."

That was the only reference he'd ever made to her ordeal. She swallowed. "I know."

"The house is sound physically. I sense that it is at full power. Probably from whoever cleansed it."

"Ah," she said. "How is the new baby?"

His face lit up. "Wonderful. He already hovers in his sleep. A sign of good Flair." He glanced at the silent Dringal, looked away, then at Dufleur again. "My wife, Lady and Lord Bless her wherever she is, had good, strong Flair."

The front door opened, and Ilex emerged. "Let's go inside and discuss our options."

Everyone else tensed.

Ilex said to Dufleur, "The house has been cleansed by the highest. I'd say the Priestess and Priest dedicated to the Lady and Lord. I also sense the Flair vibrations of the FirstFamilies."

Dufleur blinked. "The FirstFamilies?"

"They must have done a powerful cleansing ritual." Ilex's eyes narrowed. "These places belonging to the murderers must have held a vileness that couldn't be allowed to exist or spread. They took care that evil wouldn't." He smiled. "And it smells nice."

Shivering from an inside cold, Dufleur searched his eyes. "You're sure?"

"Didn't he just say so?" Dringal snapped. "Let's get inside out of this winter."

Thirty

I agree," Meyar said and went to hold open the front door.
His smile was forced. "You see, cuz Dringal, we can come to an
agreement on some matters."

Without saying a word, Dringal swept into the house. Ilex
followed. Meyar patiently held the door for Dufleur. The entryway was dim. In fact, the whole house seemed dim with only
the infrequent windows providing natural light. The entryway,
hall, and the slices of the other rooms that she could see were
all empty of furniture. But it wasn't cold, and there was no
musty smell. Taking a cautious breath, Dufleur sniffed the air. A
lingering mixture of odors teased her nose and her brain, until
she understood that twelve sacred woods had been burned
within the house. Ilex was right, the house had been cleansed by
the most dedicated spiritual Priestess and Priest and by the
FirstFamilies as well. She cautiously let her emotional shields
down. There was not the tiniest taint of evil.

One more test. With the utmost care, she gathered her
Flair—and checked the Time Wind that sifted through the
house. It was laden with more power than usual, from the strong
FirstFamilies Lords and Ladies and the equally potent magic of
the Priestess and Priest. But the quantity of the flow seemed the
same as in any house of such an age. Not disrupted. As her Flair
mounted, she knew that if she wanted, she could see shades of
the past. But had absolutely no temptation to find the shadow
that would pulse evil. "Is he dead?" she asked suddenly, her vision clearing and gaze locking on Ilex.

"He was the one who committed suicide when he was
caught."

Dufleur pressed a hand to her stomach, feeling a little
queasy. "Of course he was. I don't know why I didn't remember." Because she never wanted to remember. Never wanted to
think of that day.

"Only one has survived her stay on the deserted island. She
is not anticipated to live to the spring equinox."

The punishment for the three who had been caught and lived to stand trial had been banishment to an uninhabited island off the coast in the south. And fixed with suppressflair collars. Dufleur shuddered. She couldn't imagine living without Flair.

Meyar had walked ahead and returned. "We have some extra furniture in the attic that you are welcome to have, Dringal."

"I can get some donations from the Clovers and their furniture business," Ilex said.

"I won't take charity," Dringal said tightly.

"Not charity at all," Ilex said, looked as if he was going to explain more, then wisely kept silent.

"With Mother living here, you won't have to find her a place to stay or pay her room or board. In exchange, I want you to buy the best spellshields available for the house."

The men looked at her, Meyar appeared pained. "That's going to be costly."

"The best spellshields," insisted Dufleur. "They will ease Mother's mind. And if you wish, I will move from T'Winterberry Residence, to Midclass Lodge perhaps."

"You're welcome to stay, Dufleur," Meyar muttered with a tired, lopsided smile. He shook his head, sighed. "The best shields for this place that is only housing one person."

"What do you mean?" Dringal said. "There will be two of us. My cuz D'Winterberry will be here, too."

"My mother?" Ilex asked faintly.

"Of course. She depends upon me. I'm sure we can ensure that some rooms upstairs are remodeled to look very like her suite now. I'll take care of her. We should stay together. And I certainly won't entrust her to your care."

Dufleur hoped her stare wasn't as surprised as Meyar's. He seemed to recover first, expression turning cheerful. "We'll see to your remodeling needs." He glanced at Dufleur. "And I'll get those shields up today."

Ilex gave a small cough. "The Clovers are expert in building, too. They've been working on that compound of theirs for years. With their help and our Family Flair, we can get the rooms in order during the next couple of days. Mother will keep all her own furnishings, of course."

No one would want such yar-duan saturated possessions.

Dringal inclined her head. "Good of you." She glanced at Dufleur. "This will do."

"I'm glad," Dufleur said.

Dringal went into the sitting room to the right. Her voice floated back. "There is a small area here perfect for teleportation." Dufleur and the men followed her in, found her behind a half wall near a window.

"Good choice," Ilex said. "Shall we designate this as the official teleportation area?"

Meyar shrugged. "Yes. But I'd just as soon do the heavy 'porting of the furniture directly from one room to another. Dufleur, will you be available to help?"

"Of course she will," said Dringal.

"Of course I will," Dufleur said at the same time.

Dringal set her hands on her ample hips and looked around again. She appeared—hopeful. Here was a house she could make the way she wanted it. That was important to her, Dufleur knew. Some bitterness eased from Dringal's expression. She nodded. "This will do very well for my cuz and me."

*D*ufleur *regretted her words when she teleported to her* laboratory that afternoon. She couldn't settle. She sensed this was also the right moment to press on with her own goals. After the previous night, rumors and gossip and false tales would be flying around Druida. She'd already had several appointments for timer alignment canceled. She was obviously out of fashion.

She wanted to continue her work, especially now that Saille was growing cool to her.

She couldn't hide her discovery of a cure for disease. That was too large. She'd spend the rest of her life, if need be, figuring out how to make a device that would trap time and mimic her own actions. Several equations came to mind, and she noted them down.

She'd been reminded all too cogently the night before at Birches how powerful the FirstFamilies were, their edicts and prejudices.

If she really wanted to prove herself, it would be to triumph over her enemy and revive old D'Willow.

But curing rats was one thing, healing a GreatLady was another.

Saille would hate that she revived his MotherDam, but

Dufleur didn't know if anything less startling would get her amnesty for breaking the law. If she spoke to T'Heather, the Healer, and offered to treat a patient, how many times would he insist on her help before he accepted that she could do what she said? And how much would that cost her in energy and Flair? How often could she repeat the practice? Not very often. Despair crept into her thoughts. If she could summon the Flair for this, say every six months, it could take years for her to prove the worth of her experiments. She'd definitely have to leave Druida.

But Saille would win any confrontation with his Mother-Dam. Her brain went around and around, considering the problem, and she paced her laboratory.

She wanted to consult with Saille but knew he couldn't rationally speak with her about this.

And the more she walked, the more she yearned to do this. To dismiss once and for all the stories that went around about her father.

She set her shoulders and teleported to D'Willow Residence, was admitted to Saille's ResidenceDen immediately. He leaned against his desk, arms crossed and with a wary expression that told her that the discussion would be harder than she expected.

Keeping her gaze level on his, she said, "Saille, I've found a way to kill disease. I want to prove that time experimentation is a worthy pursuit."

His smile was faint, his arms relaxed. "That's good. Tell me how I can help."

"I want to revive your MotherDam and cure her."

"No," he said, eyes going blank, more as if he refused to believe what she said, than refusing to support her.

Pain was ripping inside him, flowing down their bond.

"I said I would help you in everything," he said slowly, went behind his desk, putting it between them. "I aided you with the Thyme HouseStones. Tell me what you plan."

She swallowed. "It's the only way I can see to do this. I . . . I am calling a gathering at T'Winterberry's to request this of the FirstFamilies."

He just stared at her. Anger leapt in his eyes. "You ask a lot."

"Saille . . ."

"She's evil. She lost her Flair but continued to be a match-maker, approved Tinne Holly's and Genista Furze's marriage. Conspired with T'Yew to do something equally venal, I don't know what."

"Those secrets you've kept from me," Dufleur said.

"I spared you my problems."

"But you've seen all of mine. I wanted to comfort you."

He laughed, and it wasn't pleasant. "I couldn't tell you, either, that I suspected she was your father's secret partner."

"That makes sense." She didn't know why she hadn't thought of it. Denial.

"My MotherDam does not deserve to be revived."

Dufleur's stomach churned. "Then she deserves to be judged."

"It would ruin my Family. You know how that is, don't you? How Family members tear at each other when ruin comes upon them?"

Oh, that hurt. They were hurting each other. She couldn't speak, couldn't find the words, could only think this was the beginning of the end. Stared at him.

He swore, then said, "I can't persuade you. I never could. Any more than I could persuade *her*."

Worse and worse.

"Inform me of the time and place of your gathering. Please go." He didn't move to touch or kiss her as he would have even the day before.

She left wondering what she had done.

She could, of course, decide not to do this, live with rumors the rest of her life. Move to the country in spring, live far, far away from Saille and everything she knew. Uproot herself.

She could give in to Saille. Would that be cowardly? She didn't know, but she remembered how she felt when she couldn't work, when she was denied her basic nature. It wouldn't take long to go mad.

She'd stood up to her mother. Now she should go further. Since she was having such success with being courageous, she contacted several FirstFamily Council members, beginning with T'Ash. His formidable blue gaze and serious expression stared out at her from the water droplets above the scrybowl.

She swallowed. "I can Heal disease through time, and I want permission to revive D'Willow and prove it."

"I'm listening," T'Ash said.

She gathered a select number of FirstFamily Heads together in the Gray Sitting Room, including Saille, but not only those friendly to her. There was T'Hawthorn and T'Holly—and Passiflora—of the older generation, T'Ash and T'Blackthorn, upcoming leaders. D'Grove, D'Hazel, SupremeJudge Ailim Elder, Healers T'Heather and his Daughter'sDaughter Lark Holly. She had Winterberry Residence initiate a link to *Nuada's Sword* and Captain Ruis Elder. Her ally.

Someone she didn't invite, but who had shown up—the youngest FirstFamilies Head, T'Vine, the boy prophet, sat perched on a chair.

They all partook of beverages from the no-time dedicated to caff drinks, seemed impressed with the device, and Dufleur thought she might at least receive orders for such units even if the rest of the afternoon was a failure.

When everyone was settled, she addressed them. "I can kill disease, viri and bacteria, through the use of time. I want dispensation to use the technique on D'Willow who is housed in one of *Nuada's Sword*'s cryogenics capsules."

"Have you been experimenting with time?" T'Hawthorn asked.

"When was the last time each of you practiced your Lady-and-Lord-given Flair?" she countered. She knew the answer for all of them would have been "today."

"And how would we feel if we couldn't practice that Flair?" SupremeJudge Ailim Elder murmured.

Dufleur offered her memoryspheres and image spheres. "I swear by my most sacred Vow of Honor that these contain true, unedited experiments."

They watched in silence. Again and again.

"Impressive," T'Hawthorn said. He looked at the Healer, T'Heather.

Heather grunted. Stared at Dufleur, then with a wave of hands, produced a small housefluff, a pet that was a combination of Earth rabbit and Celtan mochyn. "My youngest

Daughter'sSon's pet. It has a cold." His large hands stroked the animal delicately.

Adrenaline shot through Dufleur. "I can Heal it."

"Her," said T'Heather.

"I can Heal her." She lifted the housefluff gently. The creature was soft and boneless. She went to an empty corner and sat. "As you all know, this chair has been vacant since the beginning of our meeting. The housefluff and I will be traveling slightly through time, both past and present." She hadn't explained any further or in exact detail how her process worked, and they hadn't asked.

She drew the Time Wind to eddy around them—this Residence would always attract more than usual of the Time Wind, since she'd lived and worked in it.

Preparing herself, she mentally reviewed the steps, gauged her own energy and Flair, the housefluff's—who was not a Fam—and the virulence of the cold—minor. She moved into the Time Wind, snagged the virus, jumped forward in time, then back thirty seconds. And relived those thirty seconds.

The housefluff perked up from its previous limpness, wrinkled its nose, hopped from her lap and over to T'Heather. He scooped it up.

Everyone stared at Dufleur, wide-eyed.

Saille left without a word, emotions churning through their bond.

"You hurt him," SupremeJudge Ailim Elder murmured.

"We've hurt each other."

"What do you want?" T'Heather asked abruptly.

"As you know, the former D'Willow lies in a cryonics tube in *Nuada's Sword* and set a prize for whoever Heals her." Dufleur waved a hand. "I'm not interested in that. I would take nothing from the Willows." Except Saille's heart. "The point is that the former D'Willow has already agreed to be experimented on."

Ruis Elder spoke from the screen. "Ship has been observing this meeting, too, and states that Dufleur Thyme has met the conditions the former D'Willow set for reviving her."

Healer T'Heather grunted again. "Ship's right."

Vinni T'Vine, the young seer, nodded seriously. "I advise we allow this."

They all stared at him. Dufleur could only pray that he wouldn't let her ruin her own or Saille's life.

"What do you want?" This time the question came from the Captain of the Councils, T'Hawthorn.

"I want the ban against the Thymes working with time lifted."

"Just against the Thymes?" T'Hawthorn followed up drily. He knew all about business competition.

"The Agaves are no more." She set her teeth, sent each a hard look. "It is my belief that the law forbidding the use of a natural Flair talent contributed to GraceLord Agave's desperate actions and the destruction of his House."

She waited tensely, her gaze drawn again and again to the housefluff T'Heather petted, until Fairyfoot jumped in her lap and purred. Her FamCat had promised to be quiet the whole of the meeting—for her own large room in the new house. Where Dufleur didn't want to live.

"There's more than just results that need to be considered," Passiflora said. "D'Willow was the head of the Willow household for decades. Saille T'Willow has taken on the responsibility for less than six months. Many might consider him an upstart and give the power back to D'Willow." Passiflora gave a little cough. "If the Family can't settle it themselves and it came to a vote in the FirstFamilies Council . . ."

"Even if the Family chose young T'Willow, the FirstFamilies Council might—"

"No," said SupremeJudge Ailim Elder. "Many of our laws have been bent and broken recently. We will not interfere in a Family unless illegality or abuse is shown."

"The Family prefers T'Willow," Dufleur said. Studied them each again. "And if the matter somehow came to the attention of the FirstFamilies Council, I believe that Saille would still win. I could ask those of you here who would support him. That would be a consideration for me in attempting to revive her."

"I wouldn't support her," Ruis Elder said cheerfully from the screen that showed him lounging in the Captain's Quarters of *Nuada's Sword*. "I am formally allied with you, Grand-Mistrys Thyme. Besides, she voted to execute me."

Others of the gathering winced. It was the blackest moment of the FirstFamilies Council in a century.

"I'm glad to say that no one else here wanted me dead," Ruis said.

"Our vote would go to T'Willow," Ailim Elder said.

And the discussion deteriorated into politics. Dufleur watched, tense, as they debated who in the FirstFamilies would vote for or against Saille as T'Willow—if it came to that. And she reached out to him through their bond. He did not answer.

After each FirstFamilies prospective vote was discussed, and a straw poll taken that showed Saille being backed by a solid majority, Passiflora said, "If it is D'Willow's time to die, if Dufleur finds a way to extend that life, would more people be greedy for more years? Would it undermine one of the key spiritual bases of our culture?"

And ethics was debated for two septhours.

Finally, finally such talk was done—easier for them, she thought, than this other decision.

They asked her to leave the room, and that Winterberry Residence keep their discussion completely confidential. Both Dufleur and the Residence agreed.

So she paced outside in the corridor, passing the teleportation area, thinking she'd made a mistake, thinking she was doing the right thing, thinking she wanted Saille.

After thirty-five minutes, she was called back into the room.

"We agree to your experiment," T'Hawthorn announced. "We have informed the rest of the FirstFamilies." Which meant Saille, too. She'd felt nothing from him in her bond.

Dufleur and the committee hammered out the details of the experiment, with input from the Ship. The date and time—tomorrow after MiddayBell—and the procedure. When the Ship would take D'Willow off life support, the quarter sept-hour Dufleur would have to attempt to eradicate the disease, when FirstLevel Healers T'Heather and Lark Holly would arrive to examine D'Willow, what they would do if the experiment was a success. Or if it failed.

They left, and the Residence was silent, even though their voices and arguments seemed to buzz in her head long after they were gone.

She tried all evening to reach Saille, first through their narrowed link, then by scry. Arbusca gently told Dufleur that Saille was spending the night in the Willow HouseHeart.

So she had to stop calling. That was a sacred commitment she couldn't violate.

Fairyfoot offered to teleport to T'Willow's and check on Saille, but Dufleur resisted temptation. She knew with a heavy heart that he wouldn't come to her tonight. Wouldn't ask her to love in the mossy conservatory.

Midevening she took a mild-sleeping tisane and went to bed.

By tomorrow night it will be all over, Fairyfoot said, smug in her conviction that everything would turn out all right.

By tomorrow night Dufleur's life would be changed entirely by success or failure.

*T*o distract herself, Dufleur helped her mother supervise the Winterberrys and the Clovers refurbish the new house in the morning.

Then she prepared herself as if for a great ritual.

Nuada's Sword in Landing Park wasn't far from D'Winterberry Residence. Just a couple of blocks. Since the Residence didn't border the park itself, it wasn't in quite such a desirable location, and the neighborhood had declined since the Residence was built. Even her new property a few blocks away on a different side of Landing Park was considered more upscale.

All these thoughts crowded her head and kept her outwardly calm as she walked to the Ship. It was a cold day, but her new coat, hat, and gloves were bespelled for warmth, and she'd put a little weathershield around her face. Fairyfoot had been hunting and had decided to go to the ship just before the experiment began. Dufleur wanted to look around once more so she appeared completely in control. She *was* in control.

Saille caught up with her in the anteroom to the cryonics chamber.

Thirty-one

♥

Saille's hands curved over her shoulders. His face was sterner than she'd ever seen it, lips compressed, a cold chill in his eyes. "Don't do this."

"Is that an order?"

He gave her a tiny shake. "I don't give my HeartMate orders. Don't do this. You will ruin a Family."

"Mine has already been ruined—"

"Yes, by that woman in there. Would you return life and Flair and power to her?"

"I would vindicate my name—and my father's. I would prove our work is valuable and should be *legal*." She spat out, her voice rising. This was not the place to argue so, but she couldn't control her anger anymore. She poked a finger in his chest. "You, a GreatLord, can practice your Flair openly, are valued for it—"

"That wasn't always so. I told you I understand how you feel."

"How can you? Look at you, noble and admired and with a home of your own and a loving Family." She pulled away, rubbed her hands over her face. "And how low I am to resent you so, because your circumstances have changed."

"Your circumstances have changed, too. You have gilt from your work, are garnering fame from your art. You can have my Residence and my Family, the warmth and comfort of them, too."

"It is not the same!" She whirled at him, knowing her face was in ugly lines. Her whole being felt ugly. "Not being able to use my natural talents and Flair openly is eating me alive." She flung out a hand. "Sooner or later my unfriends or enemies or even well-meaning but frightened people will discover what I am doing. The Ship could report my violations to SupremeJudge Elder, and I could be banished from Druida for the rest of my life." She shook her head. "Maybe that would be for the best. If

I was on a country estate. I should simply go away. Find a place and go away."

"You would leave me?"

"Saille, I never had you. Or you never had me—saw the real me—always ignored what I was doing."

"Untrue. I know you. I value you."

She laughed, and it sounded as bitter as any of her mother's. "Look at us, fighting. Feel the tension between us." She waved a hand between them. "I knew this connection was foolish. Wouldn't work." That she'd be too selfish and demand more than he could give. That she'd ruin any sort of relationship. Now it had happened, and at least the end had come and she didn't have to anticipate failure every minute.

Her anger was gone, shot out like fireworks in the previous moments. Hurting her. Hurting her. "I'm not good for you."

"I will go away with you," he said. "We have several country estates. Choose one."

She stared. Managed to keep another ugly laugh short instead of a long peal. "You would do that for your Family. Your Family first. Then me."

He strode to her and cupped her face in his palms. His eyes were blue and steady. "I would do it for you. For us. You had only to ask."

"I don't believe you."

He swallowed. His face went impassive. "I know. You don't believe me. More, you don't believe in yourself. Which is why you never accepted the HeartBond." One side of his mouth twisted. "Which is one of the reasons you have to prove yourself with this action that will have bad consequences for us all."

"It will restore our Family reputation. It will get the laws against experimenting with time repealed."

"Will it?"

Perspiration cooled on her skin. Did that mean he would speak against her? She had just enough sense not to voice that thought. And realized that he'd narrowed the link between them enough that he didn't hear/feel that doubt. She'd already hurt him too much.

He strode to the door leading to the cryogenics room, pressed a hand to plate. The door opened. "Go. Do what you feel you must do."

All the anticipation and excitement of the moment, the triumph at proving an enemy wrong had vanished. She hesitated. Perhaps she should abort this experiment. Take Saille up on his offer to leave Druida. Believe in him.

The Ship chronometer pinged. "The artificial life support on GreatLady D'Willow has been removed."

Dufleur met Saille's cool gaze. "I want it all," she said. "I want the Thyme Residence to live in Druida again. I want a good name. I want to experiment with time here." She licked her lips. "I want you."

He said nothing. So she walked through the door with a sinking sensation in her stomach that she had just lost the most important thing in her life.

*T*he door slid shut behind her. Closing him out. Closing her in with machines and tubes that once held and cherished life but now only housed one spiteful old woman. An enemy once of great power. She told herself that Saille was wrong. Reviving his MotherDam would not harm his Family. He was too much the GreatLord for that. He was too well loved by them all.

"Ship, you assure me that I can use Flair in this chamber."

"I have monitored the cryonics room, and Captain Elder and I have modified the fields surrounding the chamber so that native Celtan psi power is accessible and that his innate Null powers that suppress your Flair do not encroach upon the room."

"Thank you." Keeping her step brisk, she went to one of the largest cylinders. To accommodate the bulk of old D'Willow. The transparent top had cleared of all mist, showing a heavy, old woman with self-indulgent lines carved in her face.

No, this woman had already lost her Family. Her overreaching hubris in believing she would never be denied anything had already cost her everything.

And all these thoughts and rationalizations and justifications were mind games for Dufleur, staving off the deep hurt imbuing her down to blood and bone. With an underlying panic and despair. If she let it, a fine trembling would overtake her body.

She had to set all emotion aside and do what she'd planned. Clear her father's name. Restore her right to use her own Flair openly.

Triumph over an enemy.

So she shut emotion away so she could *think* and act. She was much better at that anyway.

After a deep breath, she pressed the key to slide open the top of the capsule and placed her hands on the woman's flesh. She was alive, and so was the virus.

Dufleur gathered the motes of the Celtan Time Wind around her, sent them into each virus nucleus. Then she *shifted* into the Time Wind and brought the cells with her, sped forward two minutes, accelerating time and the virus's processes, then *jumped* back a full five minutes.

The virus died.

She leaned heavily on the cryonics tube, letting it support her. Even now there was no joy. At the success of her experiment. At the knowledge she could duplicate it. Even though she believed she could form an equation to have time follow her steps and make a device that Healers could use.

She could save lives. And she was sure that this process could be duplicated with other viri. She'd cleared the Thyme name; her father's reputation and her own were now shown to be brilliant and honorable.

And it was all hollow.

Somehow, in the last few weeks, she'd become more than Dufleur ThymeHeir, the researcher of time, whose work was more important to her than anything else.

She'd become the loving HeartMate of Saille T'Willow. And nothing was more important than loving him, and being loved by him. Why had she discovered that so late?

The door opened, and she whirled. He'd come back!

No. FirstLevel Healers GreatLord T'Heather and Lark Holly walked in.

T'Heather quickened his stride. "You're done? Ahead of schedule?"

Dufleur tottered to a nearby built-in bench. "I began as agreed, when the Ship removed Willow's life support."

"Open the tube," T'Heather commanded, and Dufleur watched dully as the top of the cylinder slid away. He placed a hand on Willow's chest. "She lives." He frowned, glanced at Dufleur. "The virus is dead."

Lark Holly walked over to Dufleur, put her hands under Dufleur's chin, and forced Dufleur to meet her eyes. Dufleur felt a surge of energy as Lark transferred some of her own strength to her. Lark had been her physician after the attack, and there wa[s] a bond between them. "You are very low on energy and nee[d] rest. I will call a glider to take you home." Lark rubbed Du[-]fleur's shoulder, then went to join T'Heather and revive Willow to full consciousness.

Home, where was home? She had none. Not Winterberry Res[-]idence, which was readying itself for the new Family of Meya[r] his son, daughter-in-law, and Son'sSon. Not D'Thyme Resi[-]dence, which existed as a kernel. Not the house that had once be[-]longed to a murderer.

Not Willow Residence.

Saille didn't want her now.

With snorting breaths and sputters and a series of groans, th[e] former D'Willow awoke. It took nearly a half septhour befor[e] she was helped to a sitting position by the Healers. At that, Du[-]fleur looked away. The Healers might be used to nudity in al[l] kinds of patients, but Dufleur wasn't. Great Flair demande[d] great energy, and sometimes people overate to compensate.

After a bout of coughing, Willow said, "I am back. I *knew* [I] would be revived. And here are old T'Heather and his Daughter'[s] Daughter, not appearing a day older. How much time ha[s] passed?"

"Five months, one eightday, five days, twelve and a half septhours exactly," Dufleur said automatically.

"Who's that?"

"Dufleur Thyme, she who destroyed the virus in your body with a manipulation of time," T'Heather said.

Willow coughed again. "Interesting. I didn't know I'd left any of old Thyme's notes when Agave and I paid him that last visit."

That propelled Dufleur to her feet. "My Saille was right. It was you. You were my father's silent partner."

"And a poor partner he was, too. He didn't get the job done, did he? So I demanded he give his notes to Agave, who was showing more signs of success."

Dufleur stared, pulse racing, horror creeping over her. "You were there when Agave and my father fought."

"I had the passwords to Thyme Residence, so Agave and I could get the notes."

"It was you all along."

"I paid your father good gilt for his worthless work."

"I think you should keep quiet now, D'Willow, for your own sake," T'Heather said grimly.

"All because of you. You brought Agave into our home, demanded my father's studies." Oh, yes, she could see the whole scenario now, and it sickened her. "Agave and my father fought, and the lab exploded. Then you blamed my father for the explosion. Vilified his name. What have I done?" She wrapped her arms around herself. Her knees gave out, and she fell again to the bench. She'd been wrong all along. Saille had been right. This woman wasn't worth saving.

This woman would always cause problems, with her determination to get her own way, her selfishness, her hubris.

T'Heather and Lark stepped back from the tube. "The virus is gone, but the effects it had on your health are not."

Willow commanded, "A robe if you please!"

"We didn't bring one," Lark said. "You should be able to Summon one from T'Willow Residence."

"I am *D'Willow*."

"No," Dufleur said. This much at least she could do to protect the Willows from this tyrant. "T'Willow is Head of the Household now. Your Daughter'sSon. I think the best way to determine who retains the title is . . . is to Test each with T'Ash's Testing Stones. That will show who has the best Flair." She had no doubt Saille, her Saille, would triumph.

Triumph. The word tasted like ashes in her mouth, dry, dusty, dead.

"In my medical opinion, the strain of being D'Willow, Head of a FirstFamilies GreatHouse, would be too hard on your health," T'Heather said briskly.

"No!" Willow shouted. She put a hand over her chest. Her color had been high, but now grayed. "No robe. What a miserable place this is. What lack of foresight you all had." She breathed so heavily Dufleur could easily hear her.

"Calm, GreatMistrys Willow," Lark said coolly, using the title for a lesser member of a FirstFamily.

"No! I am D'Willow. I will remain D'Willow."

"I don't think so." Dufleur stood, shaking, from anger, from grief, from disgust, from horror. All mixed together. "It's obvious you have little Flair." One of her Saille's secrets. His Mother-Dam had lost her powers. When? The consequences of her practicing her craft without Flair staggered Dufleur. That was some of the business Saille had been pursuing, and Dufleur hadn't given him the comfort he needed, when he'd always given her tenderness.

Yes, she felt sick. A wave of nausea had her folding on herself. Lark Holly was with her. "Steady." Her tone, as well as her arm around Lark's shoulders, was warm. At her touch, the sickness subsided.

"What have I done?" whispered Dufleur.

"Followed your craft."

Willow screeched. "It's this Ship! This cursed Ship has stolen my Flair!"

"D'Willow," T'Heather said.

She batted his hand on her arm aside.

With a muttered oath, T'Heather produced a voluminous robe and shoved it at her.

"I will sue this Ship. I will ruin—"

"That's enough." SupremeJudge Ailim Elder swept in, looking stern, scanning the room with one glance, blinking.

Dufleur knew the telempath sensed T'Heather's frustration, Lark's concern for Dufleur, Dufleur's sickness of the heart.

The SupremeJudge put both hands in the large opposite sleeves of her purple judge's robe. "GreatMistrys Willow, this Ship is a curious, rational, and methodological being. It can measure an individual's Flair almost as precisely as T'Ash's Testing Stones. And of course it keeps records. It will have a reading of your Flair when it contracted with you to use the cryogenics tube."

Willow gasped, flushed once more, and donned the robe.

"Furthermore, T'Willow and I had a conversation a while ago about your hiding the HeartMates of his Family from them, which, in my *judicial* opinion, is an abuse of Flair."

"What?" said Lark, appearing fascinated.

"I must go," whispered Dufleur, wondering how she could fix this mess. It appeared as if Ailim Elder might mend it legally, but morally Dufleur still had the responsibility of helping Saille and his Family deal with the angry *GreatMistrys* Willow.

She could do it. Face an unhappy FirstFamily that had suffered from her actions.

She would do it.

As soon as she recovered her strength. She wobbled to the

door with Lark's help, ignoring T'Heather's rumbling admonishments to the former D'Willow.

"We have a glider waiting to take you to T'Winterberry Residence," SupremeJudge Elder said kindly.

"Thank you."

The judge glanced at T'Heather and Willow. "I think we've given her enough to think about. I'll accompany you out."

Moving slowly, regret in every step, Dufleur left the Ship, defeated.

The glider was new, with Meyar T'Winterberry's arms tinted on the side. Fairyfoot waited inside, whiskers and tail twitching in irritation. *I was too late. Ship started the experiment before We agreed and then would not let Me inside. I should have been there. I am Time Cat now. We were right, We were right. We were right!*

But as soon as the door shut behind her, Dufleur let the sobs come, fumbled in her pursenal for softleaves.

Fairyfoot purred and curled on her lap. *Why do you hurt?*

Saille didn't want me to revive his MotherDam, and I did, and now I have lost him.

We will get him back. His feelings are hurt. He is a good man. You love him. You will make it better.

She hoped. *If he gives me a chance.*

He will.

Dufleur cried harder, letting all her pent-up emotions out, and barely had time to blow her nose and mop her face before the door opened and Ilex helped her out. "How did it go, Dufleur?"

She twitched her lips up. "I succeeded in killing the virus. The Healers revived her. She is an awful old woman, Ilex." She grabbed and held on to him and let him lead her to her rooms, murmuring soothing words—and sending her calming Flair as well as energy through their Familial bond.

He seated her on the bed and sat next to her when she didn't let go of him. She gulped, swallowed, and met his smoky eyes. "D'Willow was Father's silent partner. That night . . . the night of the explosion, she let Agave into our Residence, demanded Father's notes. She was the cause of the fight, the explosion."

Ilex stiffened, his face fell into guardsman lines. "She knew the security passwords to T'Thyme Residence?"

"She said so."

"To you?"

"T'Heather and Lark Holly were there. I think the Ship wa
recording the experiment. The SupremeJudge came in later
She might know now, too."

"Agave answers to the Wheel of Stars and his next lives an
is out of our reach. GreatMistrys Willow is not."

Dufleur hugged him for using Willow's new title.

"Do you want to prosecute?"

"I don't know what the charges would be." Tears bega
stinging behind her eyes again.

"I'll figure them out. Consult with the SupremeJudge. Th
old hag will pay," Ilex said grimly.

Dufleur sniffed. "As long as it is she, personally, not the Wil
lows. I don't want the Willow Family harmed by this."

"I'll see what I can do." He stood, looked down at her, hesi
tated. "Anything else?"

"Saille broke our HeartMate bond."

"You mean he narrowed it to a filament."

Dufleur started, checked. "Yes."

Ilex raked his hands through his curly gray hair, strode
across the room and back. "It seems we of the Winterberry
blood are clumsy with our lovers."

"I always knew I was no good with relationships. That I'd
fail at it."

"Don't say that!" He squatted in front of her. "You may be
inexperienced with good relationships, so you make mistakes.
If you want the man enough, you will correct the mistakes." His
eyes were steady, unflinching.

Dufleur dropped her eyes. "I want the man enough."

"Then you'll do your best to correct your mistakes."

"I can't kill D'Wil—GreatMistrys Willow."

"No. I think you've broken enough laws."

She winced, put out her hand. "I'm sorry. I couldn't tell you.
You're a guardsman. You would have tried to stop me, and that
would have—"

"I understand." But he was obviously not pleased.

"I apologize for not telling you."

"Accepted. My temper will be raw over this for a while, but
it will fade. I love you as a cuz, Dufleur."

"I love you, too."

"So you've apologized to me, and the hurt will fade. Go do

he same to T'Willow." Ilex strode from the room, and the door snapped shut behind him.

Ilex right, Fairyfoot said and began washing herself.

"I know." Dufleur got up and rinsed her face, then made some herbal tea that would help the aftermath of crying, and drank it.

She had to go to Saille.

She was afraid of doing so.

Thirty-two

❤

Saille walked for a long time, hurting and trying not to. Trying not to think, either. He strode the full width of the two-kilometer Ship, then through a path cleared of snow in Landing Park. For a while he pressed a hand over his heart, feeling like it had been ripped from him. Then he shuddered. Dufleur had barely survived the attempt to pull her heart from her body. Despite being linked to her and experiencing her black moments, vague unpleasant dreams, and that awful nightmare, he hadn't made allowances for that. Or that she'd lost her father hardly more than a year ago.

Or was he making excuses for her? He *knew* her shield around her heart had been weakening, hadn't she gently refused the HeartBond last time they'd made love? She'd known it was there, had even held on to it for a moment, then refused it.

Why? They both had miserable parents—and, yes, time to admit he had resented his mother for not doing enough to protect him from his MotherDam, for not fighting for him, her child. But he'd always loved his mother, recognized her weaknesses, forgave her. In his head, his heart had taken a little longer to follow.

As Dufleur's would?

He was impatient and wanted his HeartMate now. That didn't mean she followed the same timeline. And he smiled grimly at that. Dufleur and time. He'd never use common phrases about time again without thinking of her.

Was she right? Had he willfully ignored what she was doing? To a small extent he'd wanted to pretend her greatest Flair was for embroidery. But he knew who she was, what she valued. Had learned of her and their similarities and differences. True, he'd had doubts, he'd hated the danger he thought practicing her Flair would put her in. But he'd always supported her.

His offer was good. He'd have gone away with her. That didn't mean he wouldn't have lobbied for a change of the law in the city banning time experimentation, would have brought her back when that had happened. He couldn't help but think bitterly that it would have been easier to prove her Flair if she legally and openly experimented in the countryside. And loving her, living with her, taking her away from the places that echoed with her father's death and his MotherDam's cruelty, might very well have mellowed her. He should have thought of that before. Before she became so entrenched in this particular line of experimentation. Before she was obsessed with proving to D'Willow that she was wrong to smear the Thymes.

Too late.

His feet dragged, and he discovered he was tired, more spiritually and emotionally than physically, but weary all the same. He looked around, saw a library, and entered to use the small teleportation area and go home to tell his Family that their worst fears were about to be realized.

*H*e teleported into his suite, and as he changed into casual clothes, he sighted a gleam of red on his old-fashioned bureau. His hand hovered over the gift the HouseHeart had given him, the ruby set in a leaf. That was his, never his MotherDam's.

Avoiding his busy Family, he went to the conservatory and strolled. He'd changed the Residence greatly since he'd moved in a few months ago. He'd changed himself.

He was a better GreatLord than his predecessor had been a GreatLady. Squaring his shoulders, he accepted the fact that he would have to face the cruel old woman and fight her. It wouldn't be easy or pleasant, and when he'd asked Dufleur not to revive her, he'd been thinking of himself rather than the Family.

At that moment the Residence said, "There is a viz from SupremeJudge Ailim Elder from *Nuada's Sword*."

His gut clenched. Dufleur had succeeded then. The SupremeJudge wouldn't be calling if his HeartMate hadn't triumphed. Pride for her mixed with dread for his Family.

"I'm going to the ResidenceDen. Please have my mother bring the Family symbols there, the ceremonial sword and blazer, and my finest robes of T'Willow." He already wore the ruby. The former D'Willow would swear a loyalty oath to him, or he'd banish her to the country estate where he'd grown up—even though he'd sworn an oath to her.

"Tell everyone else that we are having a Family meeting in the ResidenceDen in a quarter-septhour."

"It will be done," said the Residence. The air around him moved in a slightly agitated manner.

Saille strode through the trees, the flowering shrubs, and arrived at the ResidenceDen before his mother, leaving the conservatory door open. It would drain the plant room of heat and humidity, cause more work for the Residence and the Family, but he wanted the scent of life and living things, and would pay for that indulgence.

The panel covering the glass screen viz to the Ship had already slid aside. "Here," said Saille, and the glass lit with the image of SupremeJudge Elder. She looked serene as always, and he couldn't read her expression. Apparently his Mother-Dam hadn't been too nasty already or the telempathic judge would have appeared more strained, wouldn't she?

Only one way to find out. He bowed formally. "Merry meet, SupremeJudge."

Her face softened. "I'll remind you to call me Ailim. I am reporting on behalf of the Ship, *Nuada's Sword*, and the Healers T'Heather and Lark Holly. Your MotherDam, the previous D'Willow, the current GreatMistrys Willow, has been pronounced cured of the virus by Healers. The effects of the virus on her health remain." She hesitated, but Saille already had learned a great deal from just those sentences. His heart thumped hard. Ailim, at least, must have addressed his Mother-Dam as GreatMistrys Willow. She wouldn't have liked that, but would she think he would succumb to her will as before?

"T'Heather and Lark Holly are proceeding with a full examination of your MotherDam at Primary HealingHall," said Ailim.

He'd earned a little breathing time, then. "Time" again. He groaned inwardly. He was obsessed with Dufleur and time. "Dufleur?"

"She is very weary. The official papyrus lifting the ban on the experimentation of time has already been processed."

"I'm glad."

"Yes. It's never a good idea to legislate against human nature, and using a Flair talent is one of our most basic characteristics." She smiled, then her gaze sobered. "But I wanted to inform you of several matters that occurred when your predecessor was revived. First, her health is not good, though she didn't seem to accept that. I'm sure you will be able to speak with T'Heather when he escorts her there to T'Willow Residence. He stated before me and other witnesses that he believes the responsibility of running a FirstFamily Household would be too strenuous for her."

Ailim glanced down as if she'd kept notes. Knowing his MotherDam, she'd caused a scene if someone had crossed her.

"Dufleur Thyme, who has been awarded the title of D'Thyme by the way, offered her opinion that you and the previous D'Willow could make appointments with T'Ash to utilize his Testing Stones to prove who is the strongest in Flair."

Relief swept through him. He hadn't thought of that. The FirstFamilies were arrogant in their belief that the best determination of a good Head of Household was the power of their Flair. That would be so easy. "I'll set up an appointment right away."

A small cough brought his attention back to Ailim. She said, "It was noted that GreatMistrys Willow demonstrated little Flair, both prior to her entry into the cryogenics tube and upon awakening." Ailim's stare was penetrating.

"Oh," was all Saille replied, trying to keep his emotions perfectly low-key and innocent under her telempathic scrutiny.

Ailim smiled, and it was more sharp than pleasant. "I stated that I knew GreatMistrys Willow might be subject to a legal action based on abuse of Flair. Additional charges may be pending."

Saille blinked. "You did?"

Rolling her eyes, Ailim said, "She made a great many dramatic commands and demands, Saille. None of which should be pursued."

"Such as?"

"Filing suit against *Nuada's Sword* for draining her Flair."

"Interesting notion."

"But not correct."

"I would imagine not." Friend or not, he wasn't going to tell a SupremeJudge that his MotherDam had practiced her craft without the Flair that would give her insight.

"Saille, she is a nasty old woman, but her time as a Great-Lady has passed. Please handle her within the Family."

Could the battle between them involve a struggle of power

between the old and the younger members of the FirstFamilies? Perhaps. But the current Captain of the FirstFamilies Council, T'Hawthorn, and the aspiring T'Holly were canny men and of the generation between T'Blackthorn and Saille's MotherDam. She'd outlived most of her contemporaries, and still hadn't been satisfied with the length of her life.

Who could she call to ally with her against them? He still didn't know the extent of her allies, but he thought his own allies could overwhelm them, SupremeJudge Ailim Elder, Ship's Captain Ruis Elder. T'Blackthorn, T'Ash, Holm and Tinne Holly. Those of the strong, younger generation.

Of her allies Agave was dead, and T'Yew was displeased with her lying promises.

But Ailim Elder was still awaiting his answer. "I will do my best."

"That is all any of us can do," she replied. "Merry part."

"And merry meet again," Saille ended.

Ailim smiled, then the screen went dark and the panel slid back over it.

His mother opened the door and gestured his relatives in. One of his aunts carried the ceremonial sword, another the blazer in its holster.

"Your robes, Saille," his mother said, handing them to him, bright scarlet shirt, trous, and long open robe with equally long sleeve pockets, all of heavy velvet.

The rest of his relatives clumped together in small groups.

He cleared his throat. "I know we discussed the possibility of the previous D'Willow being cured of the virus and revived. That has happened. She is undergoing a physical at Primary HealingHall and will be escorted here by T'Heather."

A grumbling murmur filled the room.

He lifted a hand, and they fell silent. "I don't intend to relinquish the title or my position as the head of this household."

Tense bodies relaxed.

Saille's smile was wry. "We all know how difficult a person the previous D'Willow can be, so prepare yourselves." He drew himself up to his full height. "I am requesting that we all participate in another loyalty ceremony."

"Of course, Saille," said his mother. Everyone else's agreement followed quickly. It was if they didn't even need to consider the matter. Saille found his hands clenched around the clothes and eased his grip. "Thank you. That helps me more than I can say. I expect the previous D'Willow to swear loyalty to me also, or suffer the consequences of being disinherited from the Family."

There were gasps, but no protests, again lightening the burden of his responsibility. "The glider carrying the former D'Willow and T'Heather should be arriving soon. I have been told that her health is not good."

"Will only make her nastier," someone muttered.

Neither Saille nor anyone else disagreed.

"I'll dress in the conservatory. The ceremony will take place in the great room where there's more space." He didn't want his MotherDam in this room he'd made his own. Didn't want to be reminded that the chamber had once been hers and she'd been the most powerful person in his world.

He turned toward the conservatory and saw his mother place the small box with the gold ring her HeartMate had brought for her, which the HouseHeart had given him, on the desk. "What is that?" he asked sharply.

She flinched. Her fingers twisted. "I don't know. I found it with your clothes." She gestured to the leaf on his chest. "I thought it was another ancient symbol of the house we didn't know about."

He went over to her and kissed her cheek. He hadn't figured out a way to discuss the ring with her. She'd need to be prepared. "I'm sorry I snapped at you. I didn't mean to. We'll talk about it soon."

The Residence said, "I have been informed that the glider from Primary HealingHall carrying D'Willow and T'Heather is on its way."

"I'll go dress." He entered the conservatory and once again the earthy scents wrapped around him, reminding him of all he had to lose if he mishandled his MotherDam—his Family's respect, the Residence, his title, his own craft. The tension was painful.

Saille fumbled with the buttons and tabs of his clothes. Finally he would meet his MotherDam as equals, squarely face the woman who'd scoffed at and scorned and belittled him all of his life.

The woman who'd had power over him and hadn't hesitate to use it. The woman who hated him just because he was a mal and her successor.

Fury with her, at all the wrongs she'd done his mother an his Family bubbled through him. He'd have to keep his tempe under control, watch his Flair, too.

He went to the open square of brick in the middle of the con servatory, which had been filled with potted plants, and which he'd had cleared so he and Dufleur could dance there. He sa until he was calm enough to lead his Family.

*T*he glider emblazoned with the arms of *FirstLevel Heale*, GrandLord T'Heather drew up in front of the Willow Resi dence. Everyone was as curious as he, Saille thought. The crowded around the front windows to watch. He'd done his bes to prepare his Family, and the general mood was nervous antic ipation.

His own mood was dark, though he kept a slight smile on hi face. His HeartMate hadn't believed in him or his love. Though he stood among Family members who loved him, he felt alone and cold and more than a little empty.

A Willow footman lifted the glider door.

"Who are you? We don't have men working in the house hold," snapped Saille's MotherDam as she was helped out.

"I'm Salix, and there are several male Family members o staff, now. T'Willow values us."

"Stup." She snorted. "That will certainly change." But she leaned heavily on Salix and on T'Heather, who flanked her. She didn't look good. Narrowing his eyes, Saille noted that her aur flickered in unnatural colors—a result of her time in the cryon ics tube? She wore a simple patient's robe.

His mother stood just inside the door of the great room, he hands fisting and relaxing again and again. "Mother." He me her gaze. "Do you want me to accompany you to the door' Would you like others to stand with you? Or would you like to stay here?"

She shuddered out a breath. Her aura, too, flickered wildly Spots of color showed on her cheeks. "I'd forgotten how much dislike her. How difficult it is to wear a mask of politeness fo her."

He crossed to her and took her cold hands. "Don't. You don't need to do anything you don't wish to." He glanced around at the others. "That goes for all of you."

"Saille, go sit in the head of household thron—chair," his mother ordered. She raised her chin. "I am the T'Willow Housekeeper, I will meet T'Heather and bring . . . GreatMistrys Willow . . . here." Spine straight, she left.

Saille went to the large carved chair and sat on the new plush scarlet cushion, adjusting the ceremonial sword and blazer, setting his expression into mild interest.

As was customary before a loyalty ritual, everyone else stood.

He listened to his mother open the door to T'Heather and his MotherDam. He unlocked his jaw, eased his shoulders, regulated his breathing. He was ready.

"I demand to be taken to my suite, the GreatLady Suite. I'm hungry, send me up some food at once. Furrabeast steak as I prefer, tatoes with gravy. I don't know why I have to ask, all should have been ready for my arrival." His MotherDam's voice was as shrill and demanding as ever.

His Mother's response was too low to hear.

"You stupid girl, where are we going? Have you completely wrecked the household schedule? I'm not a bit surprised. You were never any good without close direction. Let go of me. Let, go, I say."

"Calm down," interjected T'Heather. "You may have a cup of clucker broth for dinner. And lean on me and the footman. If the lady says you must attend T'Willow in the great room, that's where we will go."

"You know nothing of my Family affairs, Heather."

"On the contrary, I am very aware how a FirstFamilies household should be run." The Healer's voice was steel. "Do not test my patience too far, Willow." He grunted. "I already regret acceding to your wishes in not bringing a glide chair or cot for you."

Everyone in the great room was silent. The women had stiffened with anxiety again.

Salix, T'Heather, and his MotherDam had taken no more than a pace into the great room when she dug in her heels and her tones got even louder and more obnoxious. "What is going on here?"

"Greetyou, MotherDam." Saille used a touch of Flair to have his voice carry over hers. "What is going on is a Loyalty Ceremony. The rest of the Family has graciously agreed to renew their vows. We only wait for you. You shall be first."

While she gasped and gobbled, Saille turned his attention to T'Heather. "Welcome to T'Willow Residence, GrandLord T'Heather. I thank you for all your good care of my MotherDam, please make yourself at home. Can I offer you food or drink?" Saille gestured for the other footman to take T'Heather's place in supporting his MotherDam, then indicated the large sideboard set with meat, pastries, and ale, the standard food for a Willow Loyalty Ceremony.

"Thank you, T'Willow, I am fine." T'Heather took a seat in a fat armchair near the door, then wiped his perspiring forehead with a softleaf. He settled in as if he were about to watch a show.

"MotherDam?" Saille gestured her to stand in front of him.

They locked gazes and there was a pause of several seconds, then Saille whispered a couplet under his breath and summoned a steady wind with his Flair to push her toward him. She and the footman looked startled.

Before she was halfway across the room, she let out a wail, then, "I can't. I can't. This is too much to ask of a poor, old woman." She began to wheeze, but even behind the tears of exertion in her eyes, Saille could see the calculation.

Saille lifted his hand. All the Family except his MotherDam came to him and arranged themselves around his chair.

T'Heather's brows wiggled up. "Impressive."

Inclining his head to his MotherDam, he said, "You may rest, then, but be aware that this matter is only postponed. You will be expected to pledge your loyalty to me the next time you leave your rooms. I have assigned you the rose guest suite. You will not be served any food or drink in your rooms. The Willow footmen, Salix and Coville, will attend you. Mother, will you lead the way for the three of them?"

His mother ducked her head in overdone obedience. "Yes, T'Willow."

Everyone waited quietly while his mother moved with dignified grace toward the door, then his MotherDam puffed after her, steadied by the footmen. Just like his MotherDam to sum up the situation in a brief scan and play the invalid so she could put off the moment of reckoning until she'd planned better.

"Thank you all," Saille said. "Please put the food and drink away for now, and I'd appreciate it if you all remained ready for the Loyalty Ceremony."

There were murmurs of agreement.

Saille rose and went to T'Heather and bowed. "Can we talk in my ResidenceDen?"

"I think we'd better." T'Heather stood.

Thirty-three

❧

$\mathcal{A}$s soon as they entered the ResidenceDen and the doo closed behind T'Heather, he said abruptly, "I'm sorry she's her to disrupt the household, T'Willow."

Saille had gone directly to the bar to pour them each whiskey. T'Heather took his and swallowed it down in a lon gulp.

"Fact is," T'Heather continued. "I told her a year ago to pre pare for her transition to the Wheel of Stars from the virus." H grunted. Saille took the cup from his hand and poured anothe measure. "I told her a decade ago to retire. She never listened t me, so I doubt if she will now."

Saille sipped his own liquor, shook his head. "She won' listen to me."

"A difficult, willful woman. Her health has been bad for long time. The virus made it worse. Now through the miracle o Dufleur Thyme, the virus is gone, but the deterioration in he bodily systems is still substantial." He went over and slouche onto the large leather couch.

Saille stared. In the dimness under the couch, yellow eye blinked. Myx was there, and now Saille could feel the touch o his Fam, radiating support. It helped. *Thank you.*

I love you, said Myx. *Healer good man. Listen to him.* H shifted subtly on his pad.

I love you, too, Saille said, then dragged his mind back to th harsh topic. "In your considered opinion, how much time doe she have to live?"

T'Heather snorted. "To make trouble for you all as Great Mistrys Willow? Six months." He studied the amber liquid i his glass. "If she gave up the ructions and allowed herself to b pampered, followed a good diet, exercised some . . ." T'Heathe swirled the drink, then took another swallow. "Two years. A the most." He met Saille's eyes. "We both know she won't d that."

He fell into silence, and Saille didn't interrupt, preoccupied with how his MotherDam would try to circumvent his orders—issue counterorders and spew filth at the person if they weren't followed. She'd ruled this household. Perhaps he could have a Family meeting and rearrange duties. Younger, stronger members of the Family, whose loyalty was always to Saille, men relatives who'd come to the household from outlying estates to live in the city, could interact with his MotherDam. Older members who'd lived under her thumb could take a well-earned rest or holiday or try some other duties.

Frowning into his glass, T'Heather said quietly, "Why would someone go to such lengths to live a few more months?"

Trying to keep his voice perfectly even, Saille replied, "She always knew she'd be D'Willow, was always given her own way. Enjoyed her life and her title and her great power. I don't think she's accepted death."

T'Heather grunted again. "What's to accept? It's the natural cycle of things." Now his violet eyes raised to Saille's. "A person's soul is drawn into a human form, they live, the soul learns, the body dies, and the soul progresses." His gesture was an open sweep of the hand. He rolled his big shoulders. "Though from what I observed as how she conducted this life of hers, I don't envy her the next. Lessons to learn." He placed his glass on a sidetable and rose. "We Healers have mended what can be mended in her. I will, of course, continue to be her personal physician. Call on me any time." His smile quirked. "My fees are extortionate." He went to the door.

"I do have a question," Saille said.

T'Heather paused, hand on the door latch.

"If I were to send her to the country—"

But T'Heather was shaking his head. "Sorry, but not this winter. Not in this cold. Even a short journey would be hazardous."

Saille pried his teeth apart to ask the final question he wanted to hear for himself. "In your considered medical opinion, could she carry out the duties demanded of a FirstFamily GreatLady?" Duties she hadn't shouldered for some years due to her lack of Flair.

"In my considered medical opinion she could."

Saille stiffened.

"For about a month. Then her health would fail. She will, of course, try." He sighed. "You will, of course, oppose her. Try to be gentle. She is not an estimable person, but she is a human being. And you are right, she is afraid of death. She must be panicked at the thought of it to go to such lengths to live. Not something I understand. I pity her."

With his best bow, Saille said good-bye to T'Heather and let his mother show the GreatLord out.

*D*ufleur didn't know how she was going to correct her terrible mistake—not of helping his MotherDam, that was bad but not the worst. The worst was that she hadn't believed in his love. Because she hadn't believed in herself. Because most people she'd come in contact with, especially her parents, had belittled her. And she'd never matured enough to know that their vision of her was false.

She was a valuable person. She was honorable—she fought for her father's good name. She was a survivor—she'd managed to put the murderous attack on her behind her. She knew her craft—she could kill a fatal virus through the manipulation of time. She was learning not to be cowardly.

And it wasn't the recent events of exonerating her father and proving her own research abilities and strong Flair that had made her see who she was and accept her own flaws and strengths.

It was Saille. He'd taught her to believe in herself. Just by believing in her.

Now she had to show him that she'd learned her lesson. Would he think she was apologizing for reviving his Mother-Dam if she came to him as his HeartMate? She didn't want him to believe there was any other reason for her to accept her lovely fate than Saille himself.

There would be work to be done in the Willow Household, since GreatMistrys Willow would try to return to her old ways, usurp Saille's position. Dufleur could stand with Saille, against his whole Family if need be. Help him deal with the tyrant and his Family. Give him strength and comfort in this test of himself and his will.

And she would.

How to show him that she loved him, that she would never

oubt him again? She lay back on the bed and opened her mind. airyfoot tromped up to her stomach and settled there.

Dufleur sensed the quiet wind of time. There were more molecules of time here than other places, and a little more concentration would remain when she left. The secret room, however, now seemed more a ritual place, as it had originally been, ather than a laboratory, a brief episode in T'Winterberry Residence's life.

Her mind caressed the stone containing the essence of 'Thyme Residence. Hers. She was probably now D'Thyme, nd a little warmth came to her at that thought, but what once had een her destiny and her major ambition was not as vital.

She followed the flow of time around the room, noticed the wirl around the no-time safe.

Saille's HeartGift!

She'd never returned it to him.

She'd never formally accepted it, either.

Until now.

Surely he'd know when she opened the pouch and saw what e'd given her. Know she'd accepted him and his HeartGift.

Know she loved him and would always do so, that she no onger had shields around her heart and she'd accept the Heart-Bond. More, she'd *initiate* the HeartBond in their next bout of oving.

Where was her HeartGift?

She'd made one. Stowed it back in the corner of the closet. pellshielded and bespelled for her to forget about it.

Until now.

Not only would she open their bond wide and accept Saille's HeartGift, but she would take her own to him. Fully vulnerable, f he cared to reject her.

A lump jammed her throat shut at that thought, but it was ight. Giving Saille the chance to love her or not, accept her ack into his life.

She was not a coward anymore.

Still her palms dampened and her pulse sped as she rose rom her bed and went to the safe. It was still transparent, only he could see the pulsing red aura inside.

She inhaled deeply. With an even voice she recited the couplet to unlock the safe, with steady fingers she drew the door pen.

Lust washed over her, and she welcomed it. The essence of her lover, her HeartMate drew her. She wanted Saille, yearned for his body, needed his spirit close to her. Heat suffused her passion settling in her nerves, welling in her core. Greed for the man, his arms around her, his body damp atop hers, entering her, filling her, possessing her.

Her fingers trembled as she reached for the red silkeen pouch that she'd made herself. Her fingers slid over it, so sensitive that she felt the tiniest stitch. She whimpered in delight, feeling the Flair and essence of herself merged together with the Flair emanating from his HeartGift, as right as anything in life or time. Her fingertips tangled in the strings, and she was panting when she had it firmly in her hand.

Anticipation skidded down her spine, thrilled her every cell as she opened the pouch. She frowned when she saw a small brass and wood box that showed a corner of scarlet silkeen fabric caught between the edges. A wave of passion—as if Saille had come close behind her, brushing her body with his nude one.

She staggered to the bed.

Fairyfoot opened one eye, grinned. *You have it. The Heart Gift. Good.*

"Yes." She could barely get the word from between her teeth. Her body was hot, clothes constricting, binding her in places so she could hardly stand it, harsh against her skin which only wanted the slide of Saille against it.

She fell on the bed and moaned in rising desire.

Fairyfoot hopped aside and stalked away.

With fumbling fingers, she drew out the box, and her hand clamped over it, impressing the pattern of the metal on her palm.

But it wasn't enough. She had to see what he'd made her. She had to claim what was hers. Her vision dimmed, and she thought she saw him in the shadows of the room. *Come to me,* she sent to him but knew he wouldn't. It was her turn to come to him, heart, mind, body open for him, offering all. One by one she forced her fingers from the box, stuck her thumbnail in the crack, opened it. The box tilted in her hands, the fabric and swathed object rolled out and lit on the bed, gleamed pretty white and green and gold. A thimble, glazed white and painted with tiny thyme sprigs.

Perfect. She touched it, and it slipped onto her middle finger.

Perfect. Her release rolled through her, as if he'd stroked her to climax.

Taking off his robe, Saille laid it over the round arm of the couch and smoothed it. Myx came out from under the couch, stretched, trotted over to Saille's robe, and sniffed at it. Sneezed. *Strong smell.*

"Incense."

The cat wrinkled his nose, sat and cleaned his whiskers with paw. *Cats have nine lives.*

"I've heard that."

It is true. But We go into the shadowlands a little between each life. So We know of this transition death. It is nothing to be frightened of. A path to the next place. Like your Wheel of Stars.

"Good of you to tell me." Saille had always thought of death as a door.

Myx cocked his head. *You still not happy.*

Saille lifted a shoulder. Waiting on the conflict wore on him. *You need nice fat rat.*

"Uh—" He'd accepted Myx's gifts with profuse praise. But before he could say anything else Myx was through the cat door and into the cold. *Good hunting*, Saille sent.

Yes. I need to hunt. Too much inside makes a Cat slow.

I've never seen a faster cat, Saille said.

I am faster than old Zanth.

Saille was still smiling, his mind and emotions and links wide open, when Dufleur's mental fingers stroked his body, settled on his cock, and lust took him to his knees. She had his HeartGift. *Not again.*

Yes. Again.

Come to me, she called.

He couldn't. He wouldn't. He couldn't let her wound his heart and throw it out into the cold as she'd done the HeartGift itself.

She'd opened the pouch and took out the box and fit the thimble on her finger. She'd accepted it.

His last coherent thoughts were that this was not a good time to be ambushed by lust for a HeartMate who'd hurt him deeply.

Did Dufleur think that if she accepted the HeartGift everythin
was mended between them?

Desire and despair filled him as her orgasm triggered his.

*D*ufleur *lay physically satisfied and emotionally wrenche*
Saille had participated in the mental loving, as usual, but it ha
been less loving and more sex. She'd completely opened he
body, mind, soul, but he'd kept their link narrow.

She'd sensed his hurt, tried to send love, contrition, comfor
but he'd refused it. She'd fumbled with the HeartBond, too, bu
she thought they could only HeartBond when they were physi
cally making love. She still didn't know as much as she shoul
about HeartMates and HeartBonds and everything.

Stopping to research it, even to ask Winterberry Residence
Library, would be cowardly. She rewrapped the thimble in th
silkeen, in the box, in the pouch. Then she rose from the be
and went to cleanse herself under the waterfall, aching insid
because she knew Saille was far ahead of her in recoverin
from the bout of lust and had already washed and had hi
clothes cleaned and dressed again. He was refusing to accep
that their mental mating was anything more than a bout of lust
sex. As she had once refused.

Now she understood how much and how often she'd hur
him, and her tears mixed with the clean flow of the waterfal
She ached. He ached. And it was all her fault. She'd been cow
ardly and clumsy, as clumsy as she'd always sensed she woul
be. Self-fulfilling prophecy.

She'd no doubt be clumsy in the future.

But she wouldn't be cowardly. She set a spell to dry her a
she chose her clothes. Her very best daywear. A gold damas
tunic she'd embroidered herself with the bright blue stylize
cloud-like symbols that meant "time" to the Thymes around th
long sleeves and the hem and side slits. She dressed in very fu
blue trous embroidered in gold that gathered at the ankles an
the waist. The latest, expensive fashion. Saille deserved th
best. She slid the red pouch containing his HeartGift into th
long pocket of her left sleeve.

She, too, had made a HeartGift during her third Passage—
the fugues that freed Flair—three and a half months ago. She'
wrapped it, put it in a drawstring bag and spellshielded it.

She had accepted his HeartGift. Would he accept hers?

Going over to the closet, she found the corner where she'd placed her HeartGift and drew out the soft rectangular package. His thimble HeartGift had been the perfect fit. She didn't know how that happened, but she figured that what she'd made would fit him, too.

"Fairyfoot?" she called.

The FamCat trotted in. *I am here, to accompany you to Our new home.*

"Only if he accepts us."

How could he not want Me? Fairyfoot actually winked at Dufleur, and she laughed some of her nerves away. She put on her formal cloak and fastened the silver clasp, again a stylized cloud, whispered a small weathershield. She was teleporting, but she was also acceding to Saille's wishes in being prepared for winter otherwise.

After checking to make sure the T'Willow Residence teleportation pad was empty, she visualized the corner of the sitting room—Saille's mother's—Arbusca's—favorite public sitting room. Dufleur was surprised how easily the image came to her, as if she would always know how the light would slant on a winter afternoon.

She scooped up Fairyfoot. "Ready?"

Ready.

A slight *whoosh* later, and they were in the soft and pretty rose chintz room. Arbusca put a hand to her bosom, looking startled.

Dufleur clutched Fairyfoot. Saille's mother. Courage. "I am Saille's HeartMate," she said baldly.

Arbusca's round motherly face relaxed into a smile. "I know, dear."

"Of course you do." Dufleur put Fairyfoot down gently onto her paws, taking the time to suck in a good breath, straightened, and met Arbusca's gaze. "I've made a wretched mess of this whole HeartMate business."

Saille's mother looked sympathetic. "HeartMate courting is more often difficult than not."

"Arbusca, I want you. These footmen are clumsy. We won't keep them here in the Residence. Come transnow." The former D'Willow sent the clipped order echoing through the Residence, using the house's Flair.

"She's here, that horrible woman is back!" Saille's mothe
snarled.

Dufleur stared. She'd judged Arbusca to be calm, gentle
easygoing.

"I suppose you think I shouldn't say that about my mother."
Arbusca straightened.

"She *is* horrible," Dufleur agreed.

Cruel and nasty and horrible," Fairyfoot said.

Arbusca let out a breath, squeezed her eyes shut, opened
them, and rubbed her temples. "Nothing but complaints and de
mands, but that's not the worst. And she *radiates* malice.
swear she *whips* you with negativity as well as her sarcasm. She
abused my son to me, and I listened." Arbusca shook her head
"I don't know how I lived with her for all these years. And I be
came accustomed to the energy and happiness in the Residence
without her. I don't know how I can possibly live with he
again. It's like trying to wear garments you've outgrown. She
sorely tries my temper." Her hands fisted.

Impulsively, Dufleur reached out and took Arbusca's fists
"You must know I was the one to revive her. You must hate m
for it."

"Of course not."

"I know Saille can handle her. You don't doubt him, d
you?"

"Of course not!" That was said with more fervor.

Dufleur searched her face. "Tell me what I can do. Some
thing I can do to make this easier on all of you. My ally, Supre
meJudge Elder, is considering legal options, but those can tak
time. Is there anything I can do here?"

Arbusca began to shake her head, then a considering look
came to her eyes. "We know she kept memorysphere journals
But we haven't been able to find them. She would have gloated
over her misdeeds in them."

We can do this, Fairyfoot said.

Thinking that the old woman might also have put down oth
ers' misdeeds, like T'Yew's, Dufleur was determined to help. ".
can find them, fix it so she won't have power over any of you
again." Dufleur shifted, met Arbusca's gaze steadily. "But later
Right now I want to see Saille and . . . tell him I love him," she
ended in a whisper.

"He's in the front great room." Arbusca shook her head. "He's learned a great deal of patience, my son."

"I know. It can be irritating."

Arbusca smiled briefly, then sobered. "He gave my mother n ultimatum and is waiting for her to come and pledge her loy-lty." Her fingers twisted in her long tunic. "He might have to vait more than one day."

"Then he will. He won't be intimidated by her. Won't let our Family suffer under her anymore. He can handle her."

"Yes." Arbusca huffed out a breath. "Yes, he can. Now if nly the rest of us learn how to do so."

"I won't let him intimidate me, either," Dufleur said.

"But love must come first," Arbusca said. "Thank you for oming to him."

"I have made a mistake, now I have to fix it," Dufleur re-eated and crossed to the door, opening it.

Fairyfoot purred loudly. *He loves Us.* She twitched her whis-:ers at Arbusca. *All of Us.*

"Yes, I know," Arbusca said.

Dufleur waited until Fairyfoot joined her in the hallway, then :losed the door behind them. Each step she walked down the orridor increased her anxiety. Saille knew she was here, yet lid not communicate with her, didn't widen their link.

Each Willow she met smiled at her, and she felt the weight of heir expectations. She rolled her shoulders. Better get used to he responsibility. If she succeeded in her mission.

By the time she reached the great room, she was panting un-teadily and had to mutter a spell to keep her perspiration from taining her clothes. She hesitated at the door, then decided nocking and waiting for an answer from him would be more :owardly than discourteous, so she opened the door and walked n, closing it after Fairyfoot. The FamCat immediately went to a :hair and sat, watching with big eyes and purring—in support, Dufleur hoped.

Thirty-four

❤

*S*aille was in full FirstFamily GreatLord regalia, and her
knees weakened. He stood before a chair that looked like
throne, and at his side was a table holding a fancy antique swor
and blazer and gold box. FirstFamily symbols. What was sh
doing, thinking to claim him?

He looked stern, forbidding, as if she was a mistake he'd pu
behind him. "Dufleur," he said coolly.

"You were right. I was wrong."

"About?"

"About courage. About cowardice. About valuing the opin
ions of others instead of believing in myself. About the whol
HeartMate thing."

"A long list."

"Yes." Despite her earlier resolutions, she stuck her finger
in her hair, tugged at it. "I hurt you."

"Yes."

She closed her eyes. This was horrible. She was handling
all wrong. But she'd persevere. "I've been too much trouble fo
you. Like I've always been to everyone." She sniffed, opened he
eyes. "But I'm going to continue to be trouble for you. To mak
mistakes with you. To hurt you and myself and be inept. Becaus
I love you, and I'm not letting you go." She reached in her sleev
and pulled out the beautiful red silkeen bag containing hi
HeartGift. "I was going to give this back to you. So you coul
reject me, but I've decided against that." She was rambling, fum
bling for words as always, but he would have to learn to live wit
that, too. "I hurt you, and that's the worst sin of all." Tear
started leaking from her eyes, and she dashed them away. Sh
walked straight up to him, toe-to-toe. "No one is ever going t
love you as much as I love you, Saille."

He blinked, and their bond widened just enough for her t
sense his softening. She grabbed a softleaf from her sleeve, too
blew her nose, threw the tissue away. "I brought my HeartGif
to you." She withdrew the spellshielded package from he

leeve and put it on the desk that held the Willow Family pos-
essions.

She opened her arms wide. "I am yours, Saille. I always have
een, but have let my own fears and others' opinions and actions
eep me from you."

Saille saw her swallow. Her eyes wider than he'd ever seen,
er hands more nervous. It was good she was apprehensive, it
neant she cared. More than just sex and affection and gratitude
nd whatever other bonds he'd created between them.

She stepped up to him, put her hands on each side of his
ace, as he'd so often done with her. "I love you, Saille. I want
> HeartBond with you."

The door swung open, and his MotherDam stumped in, fol-
owed by his mother and several of his other relatives.

Nasty old woman is here, Fairyfoot projected loudly enough
or everyone to hear.

"An animal. In my Residence. Unacceptable."

"She's a FamCat, sentient, as you heard," Saille said. "I have
ne myself."

"I will allow no flea-bitten animal in my house."

Fairyfoot growled and leapt down, heading for D'Willow.
leas were a sore topic with her. "Fairyfoot, please me and Du-
leur. Don't upset the former D'Willow." He showed his teeth in
. smile. "We prefer to handle her ourselves."

Contenting herself to stalk around D'Willow with a thrash-
ng tail, Fairyfoot said, *I am a good and loving Fam. Woman is
: mean old hag. No one likes her.*

"I want that cat out, now."

"No," Dufleur said.

Old D'Willow looked at her with disdain, then switched the
ame gaze to him. "I won't be taking any Loyalty Oath to you."

Dufleur said, "You will take the oath, or I will prosecute you
.s an accessory to the murder of my father. I'm sure given the
tate of your health, we can keep it only to SupremeJudge Elder
nd a committee of the FirstFamilies Council."

"You can't." She seemed to sway, but stuck out her chin and
noved forward until she leaned on the throne-chair. Saille eyed
he seat. The arms didn't look wide enough to accommodate his
MotherDam's mass. He realized he was amused. Surely that was
he ultimate indication that he'd overcome any fear he'd had of
his woman, that he was now amused by her?

"No one will believe you. Your father was mad and dishonoable."

Dufleur snorted. "That old tune. He couldn't have been smad, since we worked together and I had the skill and knowedge to revive *you*."

"You broke the laws of experimenting with time in Druida

Dufleur shook her head at old D'Willow. "Wrong. My actions in reviving you were perfectly legal, sanctioned beforehand by the Healers, who were there when you awoke, if ycrecall. You've lost several months of time, D'Willow."

"The FirstFamilies Council will stand with *me*!"

Dufleur cocked her head, now *she* appeared amused. They'both grown, then. Separately and together. "Truly? How marof your alliances hold? How much goodwill do you have witthe members of the Council? I can't think that it would bmuch. You are not a pleasant person." She smiled, a genuine radiant smile to Saille. "And Saille T'Willow has a great deal cgoodwill. He's consulted with many, has proven himself stronin Flair and common sense, and has been a great deal more accommodating than you." She ended softly. "You can't wianywhere—not in the Courts, you are an accessory to murdeYou can't win with the FirstFamilies Council, you have no alliewho will fight with or for you. You can't win in a pure trial cstrength, because your Flair has been gone for a long time, anthe Ship and T'Ash can testify to that. I won't let you win. I lovSaille, and he loves his Family, and *we* won't let you win."

"You can't win in the Family," Saille said.

Anger twisted his MotherDam's expression. "You arwrong. I will always rule this Family." Her lip curled. "Evethough it's obvious you've been poking and prying into my afairs."

Arbusca's chin trembled, but she squared her shoulders. Shturned to Saille and held out both her hands. He took them automatically.

"I pledge to you on my most solemn Vow of Honor, that will follow you, Saille T'Willow, as Head of the Willow household. I do this of my own free will and because I know you arthe best person to serve the Family and the estate."

A tide of pure love came from his mother to him, and thbond between them doubled and redoubled.

He cleared his throat, struggled to get the words from h

throat. "I promise that I will set the welfare of my Family before my own, that I will protect and nurture each member of the Willow Family and seek to better this GreatHouse in every way."

"No!" shouted his MotherDam.

The others were lining up behind his mother.

"Hasn't it ever occurred to you why you caught the rare milain virus?" Dufleur said quietly. "The effect of so many broken Loyalty Oaths to your Family. We've all seen how the Hollys suffered. Now you are a good example, too."

"Lies!" she shrieked. "You told her, boy, didn't you, to get her on your side."

"What?"

"Poking and prying and using what you learned against me! That gold box there of your mother's. So he found it and gave it to you, Arbusca, just to alienate you from me."

Arbusca stared. "What?" she said faintly.

"That gold ring, the one your HeartMate gave me for you. Your low-class, rude HeartMate who couldn't appreciate you. Your son told you about it, how I kept it from you. Now you're in a snit and paying me back."

Arbusca's aura flashed, Flair spiraling out of control along with her temper. Saille had the oddest vision of her self-control disintegrating.

"What! My *HeartMate* gave you something for me, and you never told me!"

His MotherDam had a temper. He did, too. But he'd thought that had passed his mother. Apparently not.

Face red with fury, eyes wild with pain, Arbusca snatched the ceremonial blazer from the table and shot D'Willow.

Gasps started from throats, abrupt movements—D'Willow twisting, Saille jumping, hands to cover mouths or try to help—froze as Dufleur stopped time.

They were all aware of it. She whirled to D'Willow. "Your choice. I can release time and let events take their course."

With obvious effort, the woman rolled her eyes toward her torso. The blazer beam would hit near her heart.

"But this action costs us. All of us." Pain knotted her nerves, biting, snapping. Sweat coated her body.

No, D'Willow projected. Dufleur didn't know if she was the only one to hear the old woman. A band tightened around

Dufleur's temples, throbbing. She couldn't hold time for very long, even augmenting her Flair with others', with Saille's. Soon her vision would fade, then she would collapse.

Moving through the thick fields of so many people was difficult. Dufleur calculated her best action. D'Willow was closest.

Dufleur lifted one foot, placed it a few centimeters away. Lifted another. Near enough to D'Willow to set hands against her.

Push. Push. Push.

Could she succeed?

Her breath labored, her field of vision narrowed.

One. Last. *Push.*

D'Willow fell slowly, then faster, and when she was a few centimeters from the thick rugs, Dufleur released time and folded to the floor herself.

Gasps. Arbusca's finger releasing the trigger of the blazer, dropping the weapon. Saille continuing on his plunge across the room.

Then screams. Sobbing from Arbusca. Comforting words.

The feel of Saille lifting her into strong arms. His set face.

"She's convulsing!" someone said.

With effort, Dufleur watched as old D'Willow's body shook.

"Her heart," Saille said.

No one rushed to the woman. Perhaps no one had the strength—physically or the will, Dufleur had used their Flair and energy, too.

Froth and a gurgle escaped from D'Willow, then came the scent of death.

"It's over," Saille said. "Mother, come with me to put Dufleur to bed."

Dufleur let darkness snatch her away.

*W*hen she woke in Saille's bed, that massive generational bed, she blinked in surprise that everyone who had been downstairs in the entry room was gathered around.

A small smile curved Saille's lips. "A meeting."

Clearing her throat, Dufleur said, "I must say something first." She looked at Arbusca Willow. "I did it for you. Not for her. You are the heart of this Family."

Tears still trickling down streaks on her face, Arbusca nodded. Dufleur figured she hadn't been unconscious for long. Less than she would have expected for such an effort. She groaned. Fat, soft pillows propped her up.

One of the ladies bustled forward, with a tall porcelain cup with steam rising. A sweet smell teased Dufleur's nostrils.

"Drink this." The woman held out the mug.

Dufleur's fingers twitched, but she couldn't raise her hand.

Saille took the mug and put it against her lips. The herbal tea was just hot enough to soothe her throat but not burn it. When he felt better, she turned her head away.

"Drink it all," Saille said.

"No," she whispered.

"I think—"

"Let the girl be, so we can talk this over." The one who'd brought the mug retrieved it from Saille. She sent Dufleur a steady look. "You did the right thing. We all agree. You were right in what you did."

Dufleur only saw nodding faces around her, not a trace of doubt. Maybe that would come later.

"You saved us," Saille said simply. "You prevented a tragedy that would hurt this Family for generations."

"Especially if what happened ever became common knowledge," someone said.

Saille's expression hardened into steel. "I will want everyone's solemn Vow of Honor, on pain of banishment to the country, that you will not speak of the events that took place here. Ever."

Shaky assents came from the women.

"You must report me to the guards," Arbusca said.

"No. That will never happen. Dufleur's right. You're the heart of this Family. I don't know how we'll do without you when your HeartMate claims you." He kissed her hand, the one that wore her HeartMate's gold ring.

"I can't be rewarded for—"

"You made a mistake. A mistake that would not reflect well on the Family. Therefore it will remain a Family secret." His mouth pulled down. "We have plenty of secrets, and all of the recent ones because of my predecessor."

Exchanges of curious looks.

"You will have to live with your secret, and the knowledg of what you did and what you are guilty of, and that the Fami knows. That is your punishment."

Arbusca lowered her head, face flushed. "Yes, Saille."

All Families have secrets. Especially FirstFamilies. I kno many. And I know All About Time, Fairyfoot said smugly, mo ing from where she'd stretched along Dufleur's side to her la Her purr revved.

But Dufleur had tensed.

Saille frowned. "Dufleur has her own secrets. I hope sh shares them with me, and together we will decide how much t tell the rest of you. But again, there will be Vows of Honor in volved, and breaking those will have an ill effect on you health."

"I don't think I'd care to know," someone murmured. Ther was some agreement.

"Very well. These will be secrets between the GreatLord an GreatLady of the House of Willow." He picked up Dufleur hand and pressed a kiss to her palm, sending her strength an energy.

The Residence said, "FirstLevel Healer GrandLor T'Heather is here to examine the body."

At that, the women whisked away to their duties, leavin Dufleur and Saille alone. He sat on the bed next to her, put hi arm around her. "You are such a fascinating woman, Dufleu and Flair such as yours should have been incorporated into th FirstFamilies long since."

"I'm not sure how much I want to tell the FirstFamilies."

He kissed her lips, a gentle brush. "That is your decision."

"One I'll make with you. I can share everything with you." / great weight drained from her. She wasn't the sole person re sponsible for decisions about time.

"Thank you," Saille said wryly. He played with her fingers "I've ordered a large meal for you."

There was a knock on the door. Saille rose. "All your fa vorite food. And that's your dinner." One side of his mout lifted in an unamused smile. "Now I go deal with T'Heather."

"Her heart did give out," Dufleur said. "I can reverse tim and stop the disease, but not all the side effects."

Saille sighed. "Then there will be no trouble from T'Heather."

"I shouldn't think so." Dufleur pushed the covers back.

"Don't get up. You should rest. Perhaps I should have him look at you—"

"No. I know the effects of my usage of Flair far better than you, T'Willow. I am D'Thyme."

He smiled, opened the door, and the scent of the food that made her mouth water also made Dufleur reconsider.

Dinner in bed. When had she ever had dinner in bed?

I will give you everything. I will cherish you. I will pamper you.

She almost snorted, but her eyes stung, and she liked the sentiment, at least.

*W*hen she'd finished the tray and felt much better, she remembered her vow to find the *late* D'Willow's memoryspheres. She slipped from Saille's rooms to the suite next door.

She entered the room and wrinkled her nose at the scent— too much stale perfume. The sitting room was cluttered with furniture, knick-knacks, objects of all sorts. All the walls except for the one that held floor-length windows were covered in bookcases. No wonder even a large and efficient staff failed to find a few memoryspheres, though it was obvious a search had been made. There must be hundreds of hiding places.

I will look in the bedroom that attaches to FamMan's sitting room, Fairyfoot said, trotting off. Dufleur smiled faintly, sure the FamCat would be looking for an old connecting FamDoor, or scouting a place to put a new door. She'd wanted these rooms after all.

Shutting the hall door, Dufleur went to a small clear space in the middle of the room and centered herself and her Flair. She had a HeartMate connection with Saille, not a HeartBond, not yet, but the next time they loved . . . She had a faint connection with all of the Willows through Saille. Including his Mother-Dam.

More. Dufleur had laid hands on old D'Willow, knew the cells in her body that had carried the disease. Had manipulated the disease in those cells, killed it. Yes, she had a link to D'Willow.

And determination.

And perhaps just enough emotional distance from the old woman to find what the Willows couldn't.

She was stronger in her Flair now and knew more about working with time. She gathered all the molecules of the Time Wind floating in the room to her. She stretched her senses searching for something hidden, something secret.

Show me, she prayed. She shoved the Time Wind violently away from her. *Go to something hidden, something secret something not seen for five months, two eightdays.* She saw a red flash wash against a fist-sized area of white wall, a small stretch between books. Walking toward the bookcase, she saw the bookend on the left against a row of volumes of *History of Celta*. It was a bronze hawk in flight, a symbol of the Willows Then came the small space, nearly out of her reach, and another bookend, this one glass formed as two maidens, one in the horns of a waxing moon, one in a waning moon. The books to the right of that holder were thin volumes of ritual templates by the order of priestesses, the Maidens of Saille.

Dufleur touched the wall, felt a little shock. A spellshield over a no-time. She grinned and rubbed her fingers. There wasn't a no-time on Celta she couldn't open. She didn't touch the wall, but let her fingertips hover a millimeter from it. With her Flair she sent the Time Wind in the room through the wall to touch the Time Wind in the no-time safe and *pulled.*

Pop! Though it was a small sound, the concussion hurt her ears. Fairyfoot yowled from the bedroom. The noise echoed through the Residence.

Dufleur! Saille's mental voice was concerned.

The safe crumbled to dust and three memoryspheres fell into her palm. She sent the image to Saille.

Rolling the memoryspheres in her palm, Dufleur smiled. *I am here to support you. Always.*

Come.

We are coming, said Fairyfoot. *This old woman's old room needs Famdoors.*

Thirty-five

❤

Dufleur held the hall door open for Fairyfoot, glanced round the rooms, sighed. She supposed these would be her rooms now. A lot of decorating would need to be done.

The members of the household were following their usual pattern. The advent of old D'Willow had been a disruption—perhaps as much as a century of disruption—to the general tenor of the Willow Family. She'd been an exception to the Family characteristics, not the rule. And her domination of the Family had been harsh. Harsh enough to act as a warning for generations to come. Another tyrant might not find it so easy to subject the Family.

Especially if they had Thyme blood. Her belly quivered at the thought. She wanted children with Saille. She was floating in lovely visions, when a voice demanded, "Where is my daughter?"

Her pretty dreams shattered. Her mother.

Not a huge problem, like D'Willow, but sometimes a continual, irritating problem was worse.

"Welcome, GrandMistrys Thyme," Saille's smooth voice said. "You know T'Heather."

"My daughter's not hurt!" Dringal screeched.

Dufleur's heart twinged at the anxiety she heard in her mother's voice. She was being too hard on her mother. She would enjoy being part of a GreatHouse Family. And she certainly wasn't as dreadful as old D'Willow. The Willows would absorb her and perhaps, like a clam around an irritant, create a pearl. Dufleur chuckled at her own whimsy and moved toward the entryway.

"Your daughter is fine. Consulting with me on how her MistrysSuite rooms should be decorated. I'm sorry to say that my MotherDam died."

Dringal snorted. "Should have died months ago like a decent person would have. All this bother. Though it did clear my husband's reputation."

The women made her welcome over dinner, and to Dufleur
surprise, her mother decided to stay in the new house, at lea
until D'Winterberry passed on.

After dinner, her mother left for her new home, and the re
of the household vanished.

Saille sighed. "One more duty, and we will be free the rest
the evening to please ourselves."

Myx sniffed, turned to Fairyfoot, *Mice in the stridebeast sta
bles.*

Fun. Fairyfoot cocked an ear at Dufleur and Saille. *Human
need to be alone together.*

"Yessss," both cats said and nodded at the same time. Fo
now, any competition was set aside—or would be confined t
hunting.

We go. Fairyfoot rubbed against Dufleur, smacked her ta
against Saille's legs. *I knew We all would be well.*

"The confidence of cats," Saille murmured as they watche
the Fams bolt through the ResidenceDen Famdoor.

"What next?"

Saille grimaced. "Business." He pulled out one of D'Wil
low's memorysphere journals she'd found. He accessed certai
portions by saying the names: Tinne Holly, T'Yew, and the re
of the list of mismatches his MotherDam had made.

Here she'd kept detailed notes, her fury when matches wer
wrong due to her lack of Flair—but which she blamed on any
thing else but herself.

"Sickening, isn't it?"

Dufleur hugged him tight. "Yes, but it's over."

They listened only as long as it took to understand wher
Saille and the Family stood, then Dufleur stopped the recita
tion.

"I think we'll have to listen to these in increments."

"Yes, but let me take care of the Yew matter, first." H
smiled crookedly. "I'm going to invoke your name and al
liances, trust me?"

"Always."

He closed his eyes, let a long breath out. When he raised hi
lashes his blue eyes were brilliant and full of love. She didn'
think she'd ever get enough of that look.

"I can, and will, share everything with you, Dufleur." H
took her hand, linked their fingers. "You're really here."

"I will always be here."

"Then nothing in my life is too bad to face. We'll work through this together."

"Yes."

Saille nodded, then donned his stern face again, a FirstFamily GreatLord. He tapped the scrybowl on the desk and left a long scry in T'Yew's message cache. "We found my predecessor's private records. As you may imagine, we would prefer to keep her ethical slips in the Family. However, I, as head of the Willow household, will not be following the path she took. The Willows are agreed that should it be necessary in the future, the contents of the memoryspheres will be revealed to the proper authorities. Since my HeartMate, D'Thyme, is allied with the Elders, that would be SupremeJudge Ailim Elder. I trust you will cease any plans you have for my threatened 'ruin.' A sworn—by Vows of Honor—and sealed papyrus roll has already been forwarded to the SupremeJudge in case of any sort of accident." Saille paused, let *his* voice hold threat this time. "We are aware of the various bargains you made with the Burdocks and my MotherDam regarding your wife. We know that when your wife comes of age she can renounce her marriage to you. We will be observing that event with interest. T'Willow and D'Thyme. End."

Then he leaned back in his comfortchair, once again closing his eyes, and she slid into his lap, and they stayed there, together, and it was so sweet Dufleur didn't calculate the minutes.

After a while, he set her on her feet, patted her bottom, rose himself, and tucked her arm in his as they walked upstairs to his suite. The very domesticity of his gestures made her throat clog.

He murmured a Word, and soft light illuminated the sitting room where they'd first made love.

"We are finally alone. And you know what I want?"

She swayed into his arms, wrapped hers around his neck, rubbed her body against his. Just the feel of his chest against her breasts, his rigid arousal against her abdomen, sent tingles of pleasure through her, readied her body for loving.

Loving this man for the rest of her life.

Nothing could be better.

She set her teeth gently in his earlobe. He jerked, gave a small laughing groan.

"What do you want?" she whispered.

"My HeartGift."

She blinked, pulled back. "I haven't given it to you! Oh Dear."

"So get it."

Sending her Flair questing, she found the packet she'd brought from T'Winterberry Residence so long ago—this morning—still on the desk in the Entry Hall.

With a swoop of her hand, she 'ported it up, handed to him, then took a few steps back and forth. Not really pacing.

Not really nervous.

He was her HeartMate, after all.

They'd solved their problems. This time.

He slowly opened the drawstring of the bag, pulled out a wrapped package.

Dufleur cleared her throat. "If you dismiss the spellshield we'll be overcome by lust."

He raised and lowered his eyebrows, grinning. "I know." The outer cloth covering disappeared.

"Slippers," he said. They were scarlet with bright blue embroidered interlocking hearts. He put them on, sent her a look, and she *felt* the lust as it bubbled up from his feet.

Then her clothes were gone with a Word, and so were his. He tossed her onto the bed, and she opened her arms and legs to him, letting hot, flashing passion drench her, spin her away into total sensation.

She arched, moaning as need spiraled tight. Grabbed at him, welcomed him.

They moved together, and he was there in her and with her, and she never wanted another millisecond of her life without him.

He groaned, and it reverberated through her. How he needed her, wanted her. Enjoyed her.

Orgasm caught her, and him, and her whole body tightened and released, and she sent him the sparkling golden HeartBond.

He took it and it wrapped around him tight, as tightly as it bound her, bound them together.

The night was quiet and white and cold.

Saille slipped from the bed and said a tiny weathershield spell. She'd given that ability to him.

He grinned and padded across the thick carpet to place the slippers in a display case next to her thimble, now understanding what the glass cabinet was for. His MotherDam had kept several sets of matchmaking divining tools—cards, sticks, runes—in there, but she hadn't been a HeartMate. Her mother, the previous D'Willow, had been, though, and plenty of other heads of households. The glass box had been ladened with love and pride from the emanations of many generations of Heart-Gifts.

Then he turned back to the heavily framed bedsponge, where Dufleur opened sleepy eyes and smiled at him.

The smile that touched every cell inside him.

He went to the bed, lifted her, took her to the hot waterfall, and made love to her again. When she was leaning weakly against the wall, he grinned and banished the water. "Soft dry," he ordered, and a gentle wind flowed around them. Taking her hand, he led her to the bedroom and handed her a looserobe he'd had Dandelion Silk make for her from the special fabric he'd had imported.

She studied the gown. "It's fabulous."

It was without any decoration. "I thought you could embroider it as you pleased. If you pleased."

Her smile bloomed once more, and she stroked the sleeve. "It's a cherished gift already, and will hold a lifetime of stitches." She shared an image with him of the robe covered with patterns and images celebrating great events and small.

"Wonderful," he rasped, dressed quickly in a new, casual evening suit as she stared. "Come."

"What?"

"Something I've planned for our first night together as HeartMates."

Curiosity ran down their bond, and he took her hand and led her from the room, through the sleeping house to the conservatory. "Fairy lights," he said, and they winked on, cunningly arranged to spotlight living blossoms. Dufleur sighed.

She turned to him to stop him, pressed her body against his, and kissed him, sending him all her love, all her joy at the life they would share.

He disentangled her arms from around his neck and stepped back, flushed streaks on his cheekbones. Clearing his throat, he said, "No loving. Yet."

With an elegant, formal gesture, he tucked her hand in the crook of his arm, and they strolled to the center of the garden where the square of bricks showed empty. Her heart picked up beat, and she smiled, then laughed as she put her left hand on his shoulder and gave her right hand to him.

"D'Holly's HeartMate Waltz, please," he said, and the wonderful music, the notes echoing with Passiflora's Flair and gathering Flair from them both, swept around them in music that they'd forever feel.

He took her in his arms and whirled her into a waltz. As usual, she couldn't keep from melding against him. Melding her life into his until they were inextricable. She let the music filling the conservatory suffuse her, let all the bonds of restraint vanish.

Her Flair soared, and they dipped into the Time Wind, so easy to do that now, and they whirled into the Future. They danced in a spring meadow, a country estate. Saille did not falter, but squeezed her hand, a smile curving his lips. They danced in a clearing, the ground prepared for the building of the new Thyme Residence. A new HouseHeart containing the Thyme HeartStones was already hidden deep underground and protected. The stones seemed to hum with the music.

Saille's eyes sparkled, and he quickened his steps. She matched him effortlessly.

Further ahead in time. The conservatory was gone—no, not gone, but expanded—trees and plants surrounding a rectangular floor of polished black stone with gold streaks, an arching framework of—something—supporting an incredible weathershield that let snowflakes drift around them but kept thc air warm.

Startled faces of oddly dressed people watched them. Dufleur thought she saw resemblances to those she knew—surely that man had T'Ash's eyebrows, and that woman looked like a blond, female version of Vinni T'Vine. She smiled and nodded.

Saille grasped her tighter still and spun them along with the fast beat, laughing. Dufleur laughed, too. "I love to dance," she said, and let the Time Wind blow them home.

They were back in the small, square flagstoned floor in the middle of the conservatory. Saille stopped. They both breathed hard. His head lowered, his lips a breath away from hers, he said, "I love you."

She met his steady eyes, reveled in the solidity of his body.

He'd be with her, supportive, all the days of her life. "I love you. So much." Her voice caught, but she didn't need words as they kissed. As they loved. She only needed to feel and to give, and receive.

The wind of time was nothing compared to the ocean of love they drifted in together.

Turn the page for a preview of

Heart Fate

by Robin D. Owens

Coming September 2008 from Berkley Sensation!

*L*ahsin slid through the shadows of T'Yew Residence, escaping. Her husband. His Family. Her life. She was as unobtrusive and light-footed as a mouse. But she was used to being mouselike in this place since the very beginning of her marriage to the master, FirstFamily GrandLord T'Yew, at fourteen.

He hadn't ordered her to his bed tonight. She didn't know why, only blessed the fact. She couldn't expect him to miss another night of rutting this week, and she was sure her Passage—the fever dreams that would free her Flair, her psi powers—would come soon. Passage would debilitate her.

She'd heard that second Passage came like a fickle storm—first a strong wind and a spattering of rain, then dying down, finally hitting with awesome force. Now, at seventeen, the first dizzying eddy marking the start of her second Passage had swept over her just yesterday. She thought. She hoped.

Because with the first indication of second Passage, a Celtan was legally an adult. She could legally go, now; didn't have to endure an underage marriage.

She *would* go. Despite vows, despite the physical connection made during sex, she wasn't completely bound to T'Yew. Because she'd been wed at fourteen she could escape. She prayed that the laws had not somehow been changed between the time the old book she'd found was published.

Most noble children didn't leave their homes when they were seventeen, more like twenty or twenty-two, if ever. Usually there was plenty of room for them in a great house.

But she wasn't a child, and this huge echoing castle constricted her, stealing her air, every minute. She could do *nothing* right in their eyes, T'Yew's and his daughter Taxa's. They often told her she was incompetent, helpless, *useless*. So she'd decided. To. Just. Leave.

Her fingers barely touching the cold marble of the wide banister, she trailed them down, keeping track of her progress, counting the sweeping steps.

She should check on T'Yew. Her Flair was erratic and fluctuated in strength, but he and she were bound by sex and other links. She sent a spurt down the mental tie she kept as thready as possible.

He snored in his bed, that huge, horrible Master's bed in the huge, horrible MasterSuite. Some woman was with him—the new servant from a distant branch of the Yews, here to work in the Family Residence.

Good luck to her, because she was good luck to Lahsin. If her luck held, she'd be away from Druida City and north to Alfriston before the Yews and her own Family, the Burdocks, realized she'd run away. They wouldn't look north. There was no reason for her to go in that direction. No Family holdings, and everyone knew she was sensitive to cold. Once they searched Druida, they'd continue southward, to Gael City.

Alfriston was a long two days' walk away. She'd make it, she hoped. She *had* to be there, find shelter and work before her full Passage started and she'd be vulnerable for days. So far there had only been a half septhour of torment, enough to accelerate her plans to escape. She'd been useful to T'Yew as she was, after only one Passage, but if her Flair bloomed strongly, as both Families anticipated, they'd never let her go.

If they caught her, life would become worse. They'd keep her in nauseating depressFlair bracelets all the time except when they wanted to use her. It wouldn't just be a punishment. Like the septhours in the dark dungeon. Like her husband's sweaty body straining and forcing into her.

Don't think of that, of him! If she did, terror would eat her alive. Panic would paralyze her. If she considered what they might do to her, she might simply shudder to death in horror.

Who knew what they'd say publicly when they discovered she was missing? That she was mentally deficient? That she needed a loving home, loving arms to support her during her Passage? She had to clamp a hand over her mouth to stifle the bitter laugh, hold still a few breaths. And that cost her.

So close to escape, her blood pounding in her veins at anticipation, at fear of discovery, she knew by the soft quarter chiming of the antique clock that she was behind schedule. She'd planned on being through the entry hall and to the side door by now. Instead she was at the bottom of the stairs, facing the front door. She blinked, trying to make out the shapes of the few elegant pieces of furniture, the doorway to the right that would lead to the correct corridor.

Do you leave, then, D'Yew?

She flinched, froze in her tracks. It was the voice of the house itself, the great Residence, speaking in her mind. Of course she should have expected it to feel her movements, but she thought she was beneath its notice.

I leave. My second Passage comes. A thought occurred, giddiness swirled through her. A witness! The fliggering Residence was a witness! *You are my first witness,* she spoke to the house in her mind as well as in low, hissing words. "I, Lahsin Burdock, repudiate this marriage to Ioho Yew, GrandLord T'Yew. I, Lahsin Burdock, repudiate this marriage to Ioho Yew, GrandLord T'Yew. I, Lahsin Burdock, repudiate this marriage to Ioho Yew, GrandLord T'Yew." As she said the words, several tiny spiderweb threads linking her to him shriveled.

I hear you, the Residence replied coldly. *I no longer recognize you as D'Yew. You are no longer mistress of this house.*

She snorted at that. She'd *never* been mistress of this Residence. Lahsin panted, her rabbiting heart might burst from her chest. Would the Residence rouse T'Yew? Taxa? Anyone else in the household? No one would help, all the servants were Yews, all would stop her. All knew Ioho liked her under his thumb.

But I do not let you leave. You are a wretched thing, but T'Yew wants you.

A whimper caught in her throat, rippled from her. She wouldn't give up. She grabbed her bundle and stumbled toward the door. The Residence didn't send even a tiny glow to the lamps to light her way.

She tested the door. Locked. A small chuckle came in her brain, the Residence itself, playing with her, having too much fun to call T'Yew or Taxa. She muttered the password couplet and the physical locks and bolts snicked open. The door—all the doors and windows—were heavily spell-shielded, as was common to First families.

No choice. She'd always had a little Flair for spellshields, now she'd have to gather what she could, along with her courage, and test it. She *would* leave, even if she tempted death by trying to teleport, something she hadn't mastered. Again her mind scrabbled: spellshields or teleportation?

I do not let you leave, the Residence taunted. *I do not let you leave or steal from the Family.*

Flinching, words stuttered from her. "I don't have much. Only some clothes, old clothes; nothing jeweled. My, uh, the skycrystal necklace T'Yew gave me for my wedding. Before we married. He gave it to me, when I was Lahsin Burdock. It's mine." She wet her lips. "Some food. Bread and cheese and furrabeast travel sticks from the no-time. I, uh, missed several meals lately. This food would have been given to me when I was, uh, D'Yew."

You have gilt.

"Only a few coins. You know the NobleCouncil sends me a little monthly allowance. My Family gave me a dowry." Just a token and less than the bribe T'Yew had given them, not much, but something. Did she forfeit that to T'Yew? She didn't know. One thing she hadn't researched. She nearly moaned.

You have the Family marriage bands. Cowardly runaway thief.

She'd nearly forgotten them. Gathering all her wispy Flair, she said the Unbinding Words she'd secretly learned and memorized. The armbands fell off and clanged on the marble threshold. Lahsin started.

I am no longer D'Yew. I have nothing D'Yew would have. Let me go!

No.

The timer chimed again. Too late, too late, dawn was coming.

Worse had come to worst. She set her sack down, placed both hands against the door, leaned against it.

What do you do little no-Yew? Another snide chuckle.

She couldn't let the house distract her. Was that a creak of a floorboard overhead? She had to get out.

Screwing her eyes shut, she *willed* her Flair to come. It *had* to come. She sent all her desperation into the calling of it.

It hit her like a sizzling wildfire. She saw, heard, touched, *tasted* the spellshield in the door, knew the weaving of its fabric. Yanked it apart.

OUT! She didn't know if she screamed aloud or not. Couldn't tell because the Residence itself was screaming.

POP! She stumbled back at the force. All the shields were down. Every single one. Gone from all windows, all doors.

In fact, all the windows and doors were gone. The double front door fell outside before her in a slow motion.

Lahsin felt the Residence shudder, implement emergency procedures to protect the Family and itself, raise a weathershield. Draw on all its stored energy.

Too busy to hinder her now.

Appalled at what she'd done, unsteady on her feet, she snatched up her bag and stumbled into the night graying into day, circling around the door. The front door, the major door to the estate. She'd leave as she'd come. That felt good, right.

Outside, she saw a glittering scarf of stars with one of the waxing moons caught in its shining swath, Cymru moon. Oh, she was nearly gone!

She ran.

Ran down the gravel path of the glider drive. Ran around the curving road, still in sight of the house because the trees were bare from winter. Ran and ran and ran to the front greeniron gate which she struggled to shove open only enough for her and her bundle to squeeze through. No spellshield here either.

The whole estate? She'd blown the spellshields for *the whole estate*? Blinking and shaking her head, she decided she didn't know how she did it, but it was done. Now she was running and leaving those behind defenseless.

No, Iolio and Taxa and the Residence and all the rest of her tormentors would *never* be defenseless. Never vulnerable. Never beaten.

Her nervous laugh began ugly, then picked up a note of exhilaration.

She was out! Out of the estate by herself for the first time in three months!

And she was no longer D'Yew.

Almost.

She had to repeat her repudiation of the marriage to three neutral parties, three entities with no interest in her—not her Family or friends or lover or HeartMate—before she was free. She felt the mental bonds to T'Yew she'd always kept narrow, loosen.

Clouds swept away from the second moon, Eire. She saw the road and knew where to go.

But she was too close to the estate. She breathed deeply. And ran some more, ever faster, ever freer! Soon she *would* be free,

free of all hideous Family obligations. She'd never go back. Never, ever. Not to her Family—she only trusted her older brother—not to the Yews.

She thought she'd die before she'd be forced back. T'Yew would punish her if she fell under his hand again, the new punishments. There'd be blows. There'd be horrible thrusting of him into her.

The Burdocks and the Yews, both warped Families. She would never be part of that again.

She ran down the wide road past FirstFamily estates. All FirstFamiles were warped. Her blood sang with excitement, with freedom.

Until she ran into a large, solid man who grabbed her as she rocked on her heels. He wore guard livery.

She hadn't even made it out of Noble Country.

Enter the rich world of historical romance with Berkley Books.

Lynn Kurland

Patricia Potter

Betina Krahn

Jodi Thomas

Anne Gracie

Love is timeless.

penguin.com